DEAD OF WINTER

Lee Weeks was born in Devon. She left school at seventeen and, armed with a notebook and very little cash, spent seven years working her way around Europe and South East Asia. She returned to settle in London, marry and raise two children. She has worked as an English teacher and personal fitness trainer. Her books have been *Sunday Times* bestsellers. She now lives in Devon.

DEAD OF WINTER

LEE WEEKS

**SIMON &
SCHUSTER**

London · New York · Sydney · Toronto · New Delhi

A CBS COMPANY

First published in Great Britain by Simon & Schuster UK Ltd, 2012
A CBS Company

3 5 7 9 10 8 6 4 2

Simon & Schuster UK Ltd
1st Floor
222 Gray's Inn Road
London WC1X 8HB

www.simonandschuster.co.uk

Simon & Schuster Australia, Sydney

Simon & Schuster India, New Delhi

A CIP catalogue record for this book is available from the British Library

Paperback ISBN 978-1-84983-857-3
Ebook ISBN 978-1-84983-858-0

Typeset by Hewer Text UK Ltd, Edinburgh
Printed and bound in Great Britain by CPI Group (UK) Ltd, Croydon CR0 4YY

For my sisters Sue and Clare and their unedited love

Chapter 1

Totteridge Village, London Outskirts, 7 December

Peter felt his back wheel slide on the ice and compacted snow as he turned off the gritted main road and onto the lane. The weather was getting worse.

Shit . . . he swore to himself . . . *This is definitely the last call of the day.* It was nearly dark at just three o'clock in the afternoon. He was looking forward to getting back to his woodburner and his supper.

As he crawled up the narrow lane the headlights on the old Jeep bounced back from the fast-falling snow and black hedges loomed up on either side of him. He rose another half a mile, out of the freezing fog, and saw the house on the right-hand side. *Blackdown Barn* was etched on a plaque fixed to a stone pillar on the right. He pulled over and leant forward on the steering wheel to get a better view. It was the first time he'd seen the house properly – usually the trees obscured it from sight. It was the first time he'd been this way since the leaves fell and the snow came.

No cars on the driveway, no lights . . .

He thought about driving off. He was cold and hungry. He'd been dropping leaflets all day. But he hadn't worked for three weeks and today the weather looked like it was improving. He had to get some money in for Christmas; his kids had lists a mile long. He spotted a mailbox on the opposite pillar to the plaque. Leaving the engine running and headlights on, he got out of the car and opened the box but shut it fast as soon as junk mail started spewing out. He looked up towards the house and sighed to himself – he'd come this far, he may as well drop a leaflet through the door.

Reaching into the car, he switched off the ignition and took out the keys then gave the door an extra shove with his hip to make sure it stayed shut. He'd have to change the car early in the New Year. The old Jeep was due for its MOT in February; it would definitely fail it this time round.

He paused before opening the gate, rattled the latch, and counted to ten. In his wild teenage years he'd stolen a car. Just as he was pulling away and wondering who would be silly enough to leave the keys in the ignition, he'd heard a low growl from the back seat and what he'd presumed to be a dark rug covering a large bag on the back seat turned out to be a sleeping Rottweiler that was waking up fast. Peter sustained bite wounds to his head and arms before crashing the car into a bus. Now he had a real fear of anything with fur, four legs and teeth. Ten came and went – no dog. Walking up the driveway he made a mental list of jobs to recommend to the owner . . . *they'll need the tops lopping off those trees . . . and that hedge needs cutting back* . . . The security lights didn't come on . . . *maintenance as well . . . ideal.* At the front door he knocked and waited and then slipped a leaflet underneath as he turned to leave. Halfway back to the gate a scream pierced the freezing air. His boots dug into the gravel and he turned to listen.

'Hello . . .?'

His breath came out in a frozen cloud. It hung in silence.

Walking past the front door he followed the path around to the side of the house and unlocked the side gate. He inched forward, keeping close to the wall. Beneath his boots the soft path turned to hard concrete slab. His fingertips touched smooth glass and then nothing as the space opened up before him. He stopped. Something was moving in front of him in the darkness. Something had stopped to listen to him; was breathing when he did and was waiting for him.

'Anyone there?'

He waited, listening, his heart thumping in his ears. A twig snapped to his right. He swung round. Two eyes glared up at him from the ground. Peter screamed, stumbled backwards and landed *bang* on hard stone. A flash of fur and the eyes were gone.

He sat there for a moment shaking his head. *Cheeky bloody fox . . .* He smiled, embarrassed and relieved. *Why hadn't it run away earlier? It should have been off at the first sign of intruders.* He lifted himself onto his knees and placed his hand down for support. It covered another's. A bony hand reached for him from the ground.

Chapter 2

DC Ebony Willis knelt beneath the security lights that now shone down from the gables of Blackdown Barn. It was ten-thirty p.m. The snow had stopped falling; the night had brought a biting wind. She stopped what she was doing to listen to the sound of a car approaching; someone was over-revving, sliding on the ice as they crawled up the lane. She heard the engine cut and the slam of a door. Next she heard her new boss's voice as Detective Sergeant Dan Carter stopped to talk to the officer guarding the gate.

'Sorry, Ebb . . . it took me for frigging ever . . . I'm not usually late, honest.' He began walking up the driveway towards her. He was rustling a packet of nicotine chewing gum in his fingers, trying to force a piece out. 'There was a pile-up on the way. Cars were sliding all over the frigging place. I thought the big freeze had finished?'

Ebony stood and tucked her phone back into her jacket pocket. The jacket was zipped up to the neck: fitted, padded, small neat collar. She wore thick tights beneath her work trousers, thermals under that. Her breath was white from the cold.

Dan put the gum in his mouth, pulled up the collar of his coat and stuffed his hands in his pockets. 'It's arctic out here. What we got, Ebb?'

'A gardener found a body at the back of the house, Sarge. They've been digging for a while now. Doctor Harding's here.' She stood and turned her face from the wind.

'Did you get the gardener's statement?'

'Yes, Sarge.' She dug in her pocket and opened her notebook. 'Peter Gallway, lives in the area. He came here looking for work. He went round the back when he thought he heard a scream, he thought someone might be in trouble. Turned out be a fox.'

'Do you think he was casing the place?'

Ebony shook her head. 'He has form; but it's not for burglary; he told me about it as soon as I asked. He was done for joy-riding when he was a teenager. I checked it. Looks like it was a one-off. I think he's straight.'

'You alright? You look freezing.'

Carter hadn't quite worked out the new addition to the Murder Squad. She had one of those faces that was hard to read: angry, sad or just concentrating?

'I'm fine, Sarge.' Ebony wiped her nose surreptitiously with the edge of her forefinger. It felt wet. She dived into her pocket for a tissue.

On the rare occasion Ebony wore make-up it was to tone down her features, not exaggerate them. She had an over-large mouth, eyes too big set in a narrow face. Altogether it made for an interesting rather than pretty face.

He looked towards where she'd been scraping the gravel when he arrived. 'Find something?'

'I was looking at this.' She knelt back down and shone her torch into the scooped-out hollows where tyres had been resting. 'Must have been a big vehicle . . . heavy.'

Carter squatted down beside her and looked along the driveway to a second set of indentations, now softly coated by a layer of white. 'Yeah, about twelve feet long: big van, small lorry – too big for a domestic vehicle.'

Ebony scraped away the fine layer of snow. 'There are leaves in the bottom here. The last leaves fell about two weeks ago.'

Carter straightened up. 'Good work, Ebb.' He tried to push his hands further in his pockets; they didn't quite fit. 'We'll get a mould taken of those tyres.' Carter swivelled; compressed snow squeaked beneath the sole of his expensive boots. 'Nice place this.' He nodded appreciatively. 'Kind of place I was thinking of retiring to . . .' He looked back to wink at her. 'Course, have to get better on the take . . .'

'Not my cup of tea, Sarge,' she replied, no smile. 'Too remote.'

'Yeah you're right, Ebb. Never get a Chinese delivered out here.' He turned three-sixty degrees. 'It looks like it could do with some TLC. Looks neglected. A camera flashed at an upstairs window. 'Did SOCOs say when they'd be finished?'

'Yes . . . It'll be another couple of hours before we can go inside.'

Carter tried pulling his collar up further. 'Lucky bastard.' He looked up at the white-suited figure standing at the bedroom window twirling a brush in the bottom corner of the windowpane.

'Sir?' An officer appeared beside them and handed them a packet each with protective suits and over-boots inside. 'Doctor Harding says she's ready for you.'

For once Carter was glad to put the suit on; usually it made him sweat. He finished pulling up the hood as they followed the officer around the side of the house and through the open garden gate.

'Is this the route the gardener said he took, Ebb?' Carter shone his torch into the undergrowth to his right. It was too thick to see anything.

'Yes, Sarge.'

'I wouldn't have come round here in the dark.'

She shone her torch along the conservatory window and traced the smear of human contact across the grime. 'He said he felt his way round against the glass.'

'Bloody eerie sound a fox makes.' Said Carter. 'Must have been starving what with the snow. All the foxes I see round my place seem to prefer "à la carte". Bold as brass. Big buggers. Swagger up to your back door and give you their order. Fries on the side.'

A blonde-haired woman in a forensic suit looked up from beneath the tent as they approached.

'Sergeant?'

'How's it going, Doc?' Carter walked over to her as she knelt by the side of the grave next to an open body bag. 'What have we got?'

'It's a woman,' said Harding. 'The body's been dismembered. We're about to start digging it out now. I wanted you to see it first. This is what the fox had a go at. This was above ground.' Harding picked up the woman's arm from the body bag. The bones of the forearm were exposed. Skeletal fingers were chewed into a bony claw.

Ebony walked around to the far side of the hole and knelt down to get a better look. Inside the grave the woman's legs were laid out side by side. Her shoulders and head rested close to the top of her legs.

'Is it all there?' asked Carter as he peered into the hole. 'Her head looks like it's where her torso should be.'

'It's normal for the thorax area to decompose first,' answered Harding. 'Especially if she was opened up, which it looks like she was.' Harding pointed to the beginning of a slit at the base of the woman's neck.

As Harding talked, Ebony knelt and reached inside the grave. She rubbed her fingers lightly across the flesh on the woman's shoulder then examined the residue on her fingertip.

'What is it, Ebb?' asked Carter.

'Grave wax, Sarge. She's been in here some time.'

'Clay soil . . .' said Harding. 'Retains moisture. Enough of it turns them into soap . . . eventually.'

Carter looked at Ebony curiously. He hadn't heard a squeak out of her since she arrived at the Murder Squad two weeks earlier. But tonight, if someone could come alive around the dead, she just had.

'Plus there's decomposition of the head, hands and feet,' Harding added. 'That coupled with the depth she was buried means she's been in here at least three, probably six months.' Harding leant back and called to the photographer to stand where she was and take another shot of the grave. 'I'll let you know after soil analysis.' Harding nodded to an officer standing by and waiting to start excavating the body.

Carter stood and walked across the paving slab towards the rest of the garden, a neglected orchard which began where the patio ended. Harding joined him. 'You'd think . . .' said Carter as he took off his glove to find a way under his forensic suit and into his pocket, '. . . they'd have buried the body in the garden, not the patio.'

'Too many roots. Too many trees, I suppose,' answered Harding. 'You put her in a shallow grave and animals would scatter her bones all over the neighbours' gardens; not what you want when you've got friends coming around for a barbecue. Plus you'd have to put up with the smell of rotting flesh in the height of summer, which is when I guess she was buried. No, they put her in here because they didn't want her ever to surface again. It was unlucky – the small retaining wall that held the patio in place collapsed and exposed the foundations. The fox must have had access through there . . .' She heard Carter fiddling with the plastic wrapper from the nicotine gum. Harding was dying for a cigarette. She'd been at the house since seven p.m. She'd arrived just after Ebony. Now she needed a hit of nicotine and a triple espresso. She would have asked Carter for a piece of gum but she couldn't bring herself to; there was no way she was prepared to own up to a base weakness like nicotine addiction. Harding prided herself on never letting her guard down, except when she was blind drunk and that didn't count. 'All the drains will need digging up under the house,' she said.

'Yes. We're going to be here for weeks.' Carter blew a silent whistle out of the side of his mouth. 'It'll cost.'

Back in the tent, Ebony watched the excavation. The grave had been dug out a metre extra at the feet of the woman's body. The hole was three feet deep and now six feet long. Only one officer was allowed into the grave to carefully manage the excavation as he stood at the end of it and painstakingly scraped the soil away from around the body. Ebony watched his white back arch awkwardly from the grave as he wiggled, maggot-like, struggling to move in the tight space. Tracing the outline with his trowel, he scraped gently around the edges of the body. He removed the woman's legs one at a time and handed them up to Ebony to place inside the body bag, then he stood and stretched to relieve his aching back.

'Can you dig there for me?' Ebony looked past him at an object that had been hidden by the legs. Her eyes focused on the rounded end of a hipbone and a dark shape the size of a melon nearby.

The officer crouched low, bent double to scrape away the frozen clay soil. She watched him as he picked his way around the object. It was beginning to loosen at the edges. He switched to working with a dental pick, delicately chipping at the stubborn soil until it lifted in small chunks. Ebony saw the object move slightly, then give way to the last of his efforts as he prised it from the clay and she saw it slide into his hands. It was muddied but perfectly formed and coated in white. He passed it up for her to take it from him. Ebony stood and carried it outside the tent. Carter and Harding had their backs to her.

'Sarge?'

Carter turned round to see her holding the corpse of a baby in her hands.

Chapter 3

The lambs bleated in the cold. The wind and snow came driving off the Yorkshire Dales onto the small farm. It was a risky business lambing now. The Dorset Horn was a breed that could produce lambs all year long but they required more looking after if they were to thrive in this harsh environment.

Callum Carmichael ran his hand over the belly of the sheep ... she was overdue. She flinched at his touch. Jumper was an expert mother. She was one of a hundred ewes in the old barn.

Jumper had been with Carmichael for six years now. He had hand-reared her. In the field, she came when he called her name. In the summer months the sheep were allowed outside but now, in lambing season, they had to come into the pens: six feet by four. Foxes had claimed lambs before, as had badgers and buzzards. Everything was hungry now in the worst winter for a long time.

Carmichael looked into the stall next to Jumper where a newborn lamb was suckling on his mother, its tail wagging furiously. Carmichael looked back at Jumper and decided he was probably being over-cautious and to let nature take its course, but to check on her again in half an hour. He called Rosie the sheepdog to follow him out of the barn. On his way down to the house he made a last check on his horse. Inside the stable, he slipped his hand between Tor's back and his fleecy rug and was reassured that he was warm enough. He should be: it had taken Carmichael an hour that morning to bank the straw up high against the walls of the stable.

Stepping back out into the yard, Carmichael locked up and turned his face from the blizzard as he whistled for Rosie. Taking a last look around, he unlatched the back door of the house that had been his home for the last thirteen years since his wife died.

As he walked through the kitchen he pulled the pot of stew from the top of the Aga and left it to one side. He knew he should eat but he hadn't the appetite. Instead, he walked through to the sitting room and took his Steyr Scout rifle from the gun cupboard, opened it and inserted a magazine. Then he locked it and left it leaning against the doorframe.

Logs were burning in the Inglenook fireplace. It must have burned the same way for three hundred years.

Carmichael went to the dresser, picked up the bottle of Scotch and carried it across to his desk and then he opened his laptop, waiting for it to fire up before he clicked on his music library. It had been a long time since he had listened to any music. Too many memories; too many feelings. Green Day blasted out. It made him smile. He could see his wife Louise's face now as she'd pretended to hate it. She'd left him in the lounge with his music and his glass of red and she'd come back with Sophie; both of them wearing earmuffs. He smiled at the memory. He hadn't allowed himself even the good memories for a long time . . . he didn't know why they were coming back tonight. Something in the weather or the world was overpowering him. It was going to be a long night. He poured himself a few fingers of single malt. It melted in his throat and burned as it slid downwards. Standing on the broad hearth he nudged a half-burnt log with his foot, sending up a spray of sparks. His face was bright from the fire, his dark hair wet from the snow. He picked up the photo of Louise smiling at him, Sophie in her arms, and took it over to sit in front of the fire and sip his Scotch. The bridge of his nose burned as his eyes filled. He ran a finger across the photo and held it to his chest as he sat back and listened to the crackle of the fire, felt its warmth through to his bones. He heard his Jack Russell terrier Rusty sigh from his basket as it watched him. Carmichael didn't even realize he was crying.

'Enough,' he said out loud, stood, drank the whisky down, and called for Rosie as he pulled on his overcoat.

The bitter wind sliced his face as he opened the back door and walked back up to the barn. He switched on the light. The barn was musty with the smell of lambing. He couldn't see Jumper. He walked through the barn slowly, as if walking in tar. In the orange hue the sheep's eyes stared at him as he passed. The lambs stopped suckling to watch his slow progress. Carmichael kept walking; kept moving one heavy foot in front of the other. Walking in a dream, in a memory. His mind was spiralling back thirteen years, to the day he had walked towards the open door of a small holiday cottage where his wife and child were staying for the weekend. His breathing quickened until it wheezed in his chest as he stepped inside a world that should have been filled with the sound of laughter and chatter and heard only the droning of flies. He turned his head to look at the ewes but instead he saw his wife Louise looking at him, her face splattered with blood. She reached out a bloody hand to him. A cry caught in his throat; the ewes heard it; they turned their heads to listen. The noise jolted him back to the barn and Louise was gone. Jumper was on the floor of her pen. He could smell the stench of the lamb. Its body half out, stuck, breach position. It had died inside her womb and turned toxic and now she could not be rid of it. He ran back to the house and pulled out the box of medical supplies from the tack-room cupboard . . . he cursed as he searched for the antibiotics he needed and found just a small amount. She needed a big dose to save her. He had barely any. The vet hadn't had any on him the last visit and then the snow had come. He picked up the supplies and carried them back to the barn then he knelt beside the ewe and injected what he had into the muscle in her leg before starting to cut out the lamb. For three hours Carmichael worked with the stench of the lamb in his nose . . . By the time he finished the task Jumper was dead.

Chapter 4

'You alright, Ebb?'

She nodded but her eyes stayed focused on the house. They were sitting in his car at the edge of the driveway, still waiting for permission from the SOCOs to go inside. The first lot of furniture had been loaded into a van and was headed back to the lab. Ebony hadn't said much since the discovery of the baby. Carter looked at her profile. 'Not nice,' he added. She shook her head but didn't speak. 'Those tyre prints, Ebb? Someone must have noticed a big vehicle sat on the driveway. Must have been at least the size of a pick-up truck. Surely the neighbours saw what cars were parked here. Did they know who lived here?'

'They keep themselves to themselves, Sarge. I went round to speak to them after the gardener left. They never saw anyone move in or out. They had no idea who lived here.'

'So much for people being friendlier in the country. If this was in the East End the neighbours would know everything.'

Ebony watched curiously as Carter squished the old piece of nicotine gum back into the empty space in the packet and popped a fresh one in his mouth.

'Does that stuff help?'

'I hope so. Tried cold turkey but couldn't hack it. Trying to give up . . . you know . . .' He glanced across at her. 'For the baby . . . My girlfriend's pregnant.'

'I heard. Congratulations. Is she feeling alright?' Ebony had never met Cabrina. It felt strange asking after someone she hadn't met but Jeanie the Family Liaison Officer had told her all about it and Ebony had listened politely. Jeanie sat opposite her in the office. Jeanie and Carter used to be an item.

Carter sighed. 'She's okay . . . I suppose . . . She's back living at home with her parents.' Ebony glanced across to see if she had heard right. Carter leant back against the headrest and stared out of the windscreen at the sky. The night was losing its grip and making way for dawn. A tinge of purple was creeping into the sky. Carter had a boxer's nose. It had been broken so many times that the cartilage had been removed to allow him to breathe. Now it was straighter but flatter than it was designed to be. He cared more about his hair than he ever let on; it was thick and black, a heritage from his Italian mother, cut in a Tintin quiff at the front. 'I used to think she was bad enough once a month. Once a month I could cope with: knew what she needed . . . knew how to make her happy. Now I have no frigging idea what she wants. Whatever it is, it's not me at the moment. It's all talk of her and the baby *managing*.'

'Sorry.' Ebony didn't know what to say. 'I'm sure she'll come back soon. Pregnancy does funny things to women.'

'Yeah, so I heard . . . back there?' He gestured towards the house. 'You know a lot about forensics?'

'I did some at uni . . . it interests me, that's all.'

'You need to get out more, Ebb.' He smiled. 'You glad to be working in the Murder Squad?'

She nodded. 'It's what I wanted. I requested it.'

Carter shifted a little in his seat so that he could turn and face her.

'Why? What was it about it that appealed?' Ebony shrugged. She buried her chin further into her scarf. The car was beginning to feel too small. Carter knew she was getting uncomfortable. It only made him push her a little more. 'You know, Ebb, we're going to spend a lot of time sat in this car together. It's going to get very boring if you don't start opening up.' She turned to see if he was teasing; he was only half smiling. He was watching her intently; seeing how far he could push her before he was in danger of making her mistrust him. 'Good detectives need to allow themselves to feel things: emotions, raw stuff. I bet you most detectives in the squad would rather watch a good rom-com than a film where people blast the shit out of each other. They are sensitive souls – too much, sometimes.'

'I know how things feel.' She looked at Carter; something about his manner reassured her. She realized he reminded her of a boy she once knew; a boy who'd befriended her in one of the homes she'd stayed in.

'I'm not having a go at you, Ebb, believe me. I'm just saying, you bring a lot to the table. You're bright, eager. I can see you know your stuff. You can make it really work for you as a detective. You'll get further than I will, that's for sure. You okay?'

'Fine.'

'Okay . . . What were your initial thoughts when you saw the baby?'

She sat up: alert. He smiled to himself. If there was one way to get close to Ebony it was through dead bodies. 'Just delivered. Cord still intact. Grave wax the same as on the mother's body, buried the same time. Someone's dirty secret maybe? Perhaps he got rid of his wife and baby to make room for someone else.'

'He's got money.'

'Yes, Sarge, and he's young enough to attract women.'

'Fit enough to bury them under the patio.'

'Over thirty-five, under fifty-five then, Sarge.'

'But why did he choose to kill them here? In this way? If I had money I would go abroad on a holiday and have an accident happen to my wife.'

Ebony looked towards the house as the front door opened to Blackdown Barn.

'Someone's on the move, Sarge.'

They watched a tall frame emerge into the light at the front of the house and start to walk down the drive towards them and the empty car parked behind.

'It's Trevor Bishop from Forensics. That means SOCOs must have finished the initial search. We can go in, Ebb . . . rock and roll . . . let's go.' Carter got out of the car.

Bishop was loading bags into his boot.

'You off, Trev?'

Bishop nodded: 'Getting back to load these prints into the system.' He lifted his case in. 'I'll see you at the meeting at eight. We're going to be back-and-forth here: still need to pick up the rest of the furniture; it has to be done in stages.' He handed them some more suits from the boot of his car. 'Change your suits before you go inside.'

'Will do.'

Inside the entrance Sandford, the Crime Scene Manager, head of the SOCOs, was dismantling the door to a room on the left.

'How's it looking, Sandford?' Carter asked. Sandford didn't answer and stepped past him into the lounge. 'This place even *feels* dead.' Carter stepped in with him and stood in the middle of the room looking around. 'Exposed brickwork and low beams. Nightmare to clean. Full of spiders.'

Sandford didn't stop what he was doing. He was thinking to himself . . . '*Rustic charm lost on him . . .*' He picked up a power tool and applied his weight to the hinges of the door. Sandford wasn't keen on Carter. There was something about him that irritated him. Maybe it was the rattle of his heavy gold signet bracelet or the immaculate hair. Maybe it was that Sandford was pretty sure Carter had never been to a rugby match in his life; preferred to watch the footie down the pub with his mates probably. Whatever it was . . . it riled him.

Sandford kept working as he replied: 'No one left here in a hurry. We'll be lucky to get much.' He glanced Ebony's way as she stood in the entrance. She was new to him.

'Just saw Bishop leave . . . seemed happy.' Carter stepped back into the hall. 'We allowed all over the house?'

'Are those new suits?' Sandford turned and looked them over. 'Any cross-contamination from the garden and we'll be crucified.'

'Yep . . . suited and booted.'

'Okay, carry on . . . but keep contact down to a minimum. Enter anything you find in the log . . .'

Carter glanced Ebony's way and flicked his eyes towards the stairs. 'We'll start at the top.'

Ebony followed him up the broad sweeping staircase, a heavy white painted banister to one side and a large expanse of smooth plastered wall to the other. They came out on a broad landing. The layout mirrored the downstairs. On the left, above the lounge, was the master bedroom. To the right the corridor ran the length of the house and bedrooms came off it left and right. 'I'll start in here, Ebb.' Carter turned left. 'You go the other way. Tell me what you find: first impressions count, keep talking to me.'

Ebony pushed open the first door. The room smelt musty; the walls looked clean. She worked her way down the corridor.

'How many bedrooms you found?' Carter called out to her after a few minutes.

'Four up this end, Sarge, two en suite. All been slept in. They have a "lived-in" smell but someone's gone to lengths to wash the walls.'

'They got beds?'

'Yes. The beds are still here. They look very clean. No mattress covers.'

'This one hasn't. Come and take a look.' Ebony made her way back to where she'd left him. She crossed to stand next to him at the window overlooking the front of the house.

'This is the biggest of the rooms, Sarge.'

'Must be the master bedroom, Ebb. But why is there no bed in here and no curtains either?' She followed his gaze down over the tops of the trees at the edge of the property: still dark silhouettes. The small digger had arrived and two officers were clearing a path to get it round to the back of the house. The dawn had just managed to take hold of the sky but it had a greenish hue; it was full of snow. In the distance was the glow of London.

He looked down at the floor. 'Why is there lino in this room? And if you were going to have lino in a bedroom why would you choose blue? It's like a dentist's.'

'It isn't typical bathroom lino, it's thicker, more expensive.' Ebony paused. It was one of those times that she realised she knew something without knowing why. Because it meant something. It had meant something to her when the social worker gave her mother some money to furnish their council flat. That day they had walked around every cheap flooring place they could find and all she remembered was her mother's growing disappointment. 'We can't afford that Ebony – not that lino anyway: it's too expensive.' She remembered the feeling of building anxiety: always watching her mother; always trying to keep her happy. Keep her under control.

'There's been a bed on here ... you can see its imprint. A single bed – funny imprint it's made. It's been dragged maybe.' He stood back to gauge the size. 'Why in the biggest room do you put a single bed? Could be a kid's room, Ebb?' He looked around him. 'But it would have to be a very tidy kid not to scuff the skirting, let alone put their hand marks on the wall.'

'The walls have been washed, Sarge. You can still see the cloth marks. And this room doesn't smell like the others. It doesn't smell slept in.'

'The smell of people gets in the carpets, in the walls. I know what you mean, Ebb. This room smells like new plastic.'

Ebony went into the en suite bathroom.

'What's it like in there?' Carter called out. He knelt on the floor to measure the indentations where the bed had been.

'It doesn't feel like a woman's bathroom, Sarge,' she answered, standing in the white-tiled room. 'It's not pretty, just white: ultra clean.' Ebony's voice echoed. 'And it doesn't smell so much of perfume, more of mothballs, old-fashioned. The same smell as the bedroom.' She stood looking around at the glass shelves on the walls. 'Someone had a lot of things they needed to keep in here, off the floor – keep clean.'

Carter came to stand in the doorway. 'Yeah . . . too clean . . . too sterile. What was that bloke's name? The one who didn't like germs?'

'Howard Hughes?'

'That's it . . . maybe someone's a Howard Hughes type. Everything has to be bleached and kept up away from contamination. I'm going to end up like him if I don't watch it . . . already see the signs of it. Cabrina says it's like living in a show home.' He winked at

Ebony. He could see by her face she didn't know how to take him. He wondered if she ever opened up to anyone. 'Let's go and see if the SOCOs have finished downstairs.'

At the bottom of the stairs Sandford was packing his drill away. He glanced at them as they came level.

'I'll finish up here and get my initial report to you in a few hours,' he said to Carter with a nod towards Ebony. 'Don't want to be long from here. There's a lot of work still to be done.'

'Good man,' Carter answered.

Ebony noticed that Carter talked differently to people with posh accents. She wasn't quite sure whether he was taking the piss or just feeling awkward. 'We won't be long either. We'll finish looking around here and then we need to get back for the autopsies. Forensics might have got something by then.'

Sandford slammed his toolbox shut. 'Maybe.'

They left Sandford to it and walked down the corridor that ran almost the length of the house. On one side was a formal dining room and a study, on the other a snug room and a second lounge. At the end of the corridor a large kitchen opened out and led to a conservatory on the left. A utility room was at the back and to the right of the kitchen, a Dutch airer hung empty from the ceiling above them, and a washing machine sat with its door open and a plastic basket on top, a strange reminder that there was normal life in Blackdown Barn. Through the utility room a cellar door was open.

Carter flicked on a switch that illuminated the stone stairs and they made their way down. The smell of damp hit Ebony as she descended. The cold chilled to the bone. Carter stopped at the bottom, a large bare space, pitch black in its corners beneath low rafters and in hidden alcoves. He gave a small two-footed jump. 'New, solid floor. I can smell sweat, rubber in the air. Maybe they had a gym down here, Ebb.'

'Could be, Sarge.'

'That's what happens when you quit smoking, Ebb. You start smelling everything. I can smell a bacon sandwich being cooked half a mile away. I've already put on a few pounds . . . muscle, of course . . .' He turned to wink at her but she wasn't looking or listening to him: she'd walked on down to where the cellar narrowed. A door opened to her right. Inside was a room just big enough for a single bed and a chair. It reminded her of a place she had stayed with her mother once, reminded her of so many places. It had the same smell of damp. The corners of the rooms where mould collected. It was colourless. It was bare. She had spent a lot of her childhood sitting on a bed like that, trying hard to do her homework, her world constantly shifting beneath her feet, moving on, getting better.

'Sarge?'

'What is it, Ebb?' Carter appeared beside her in the room. 'Fuck . . . this is definitely the economy accommodation.' He looked at the bed. 'Forensics will be taking all this as soon as the transport gets here. Christ . . . how many people lived in this house, Ebb?' Ebony didn't answer – she was busy putting on latex gloves. 'What are you doing?' Carter watched her.

She knelt on the floor and stretched her right arm underneath the bed until her shoulder was wedged against the frame; she ran her hand along the bottom of the springs.

'This bed wouldn't take the weight of a pregnant woman.' She moved her arm down the bed, sweeping the underside as she went. Ebony had spent so much of her childhood in bedsits and emergency housing that she tried to leave something for the next child wherever she went. Sometimes it was a smiley face sticker, stuck to the leg of the bed. Other times it was a cheap toy, the kind you get free in cereal packets. Other kids left her things.

When she drew her hand back, she was holding a piece of red cloth.

'What is it, a piece of clothing?' It uncurled in her hand. In its corner was a fleck of white and the beginnings of a golden embroidered circle.

'Not sure. It was tied on to the springs.'

They heard the sound of the SOCOs making their way down with the exhibit removal team. Ebony dropped it into a plastic bag and put it in her pocket.

'Let's go, Ebb. We'll leave them to it.'

On the way back to Carter's car, still wearing her gloves, she took out the piece of cloth from her pocket and looked at it again. As she pulled it flat she saw the beginning of spokes inside the golden circle.

'What football team do you support, Sarge?'

'Tottenham, why?'

'Who's your biggest rival?' He looked across at her. She stretched the cloth tight and held it up to show him. At the edge of it was the start of a golden gun barrel. 'I think someone was an Arsenal supporter.'

Chapter 5

They arrived back at Fletcher House with twenty minutes to spare before the meeting at eight. Fletcher House was just behind Archway Tube station. An innocuous-looking building from the outside; it appeared to be like any other office block except that there was no reception area and visitors had to make it past the bombproof security and the SOCOs vans in the car park. Across London there were two other buildings like Fletcher House; together they split London into three large policing districts to cope with major incidents and served the whole of the Metropolitan Police District. Each of the buildings was home to four Major Incident Teams, MITs. Ebony and Carter were part of the Murder Squad in MIT 17. The rest of the MIT called the Murder Squad 'The Dark Side'. They both worked in the largest room, the Enquiry Team Office (ETO). It was where the bulk of the work was done by the team: six long desks with officers sitting opposite one another.

'I hear you had a busy night?'

Ebony's station was diagonally opposite Jeanie the Family Liaison Officer. She was rated as the best FLO there was on any of the murder squads. She was good at making families talk, gaining their confidence; at the same time she got the best for them. She had gone through a lot of training to specialize but it was clear to all that she had found her niche. Jeanie was on the phone when Ebony sat down. She was 'on hold'.

Ebony nodded. 'Get the feeling it won't be the last busy one. It's a big area to search.'

'Yeah, I saw the boys getting excited about all the equipment they had to order. Boys' toys: diggers, thermal imaging, the works.' Ebony smiled. 'I hear you were partnered with Dan Carter. How was it?'

'It was good.'

Jeanie lowered her voice, held her hand over the mouthpiece of the phone. 'Great guy, fantastic detective, nightmare as a boyfriend. Believe me: seriously high maintenance. I take my hat off to Cabrina for making him move up the ladder of commitment. A kid is something I could never in a million years imagine Dan having ... Sticky fingers all over the silk sheets? No way.'

Ebony looked across at Carter. It occurred to Ebony that Jeanie didn't know that Cabrina had gone back to live with her parents. Carter looked her way and winked. She smiled back. He went back to focusing on the paperwork on his desk. Ebony's eyes settled on the wall behind him where there was one of several white boards around the walls of the ETO. The one behind Carter was divided into columns with the name of the investigation, the team, the date it commenced. Unsolved and current murder enquiries stayed on the board. Blackdown Barn was already up there. At the very top of the list was a case nobody in

MIT17 had been allowed to forget. It was the Carmichael case; the time when a policeman's family was murdered.

The ETO was filling up with officers all coming in for the initial meeting about Blackdown Barn. Ebony leant forward to see the corridor outside. Doctor Harding was easy to recognize – short, thin and blonde. Unmistakeable, the way she stood with her legs apart, stretching the limits of her size six pencil skirt. Harding had the reputation for being a ball-buster. She was a difficult one to fathom. There was something about her that Ebony liked, her toughness maybe, her enthusiasm for her work. She worked hard and played hard. But she was known to be ruthless in her professional and private life. She collected other people's husbands like pairs of shoes. Someone else was there. By the way Harding was looking up as she talked, Ebony guessed it was Superintendent Davidson, the six foot four head of their department.

The door opened and Harding came in. She went to the far side of the room and sat down ready to be called on as one of the experts. She crossed her slim legs, the top one twitching as she stared straight ahead, apparently lost in her own thoughts.

Carter got to his feet and walked over to Ebony's desk.

'You ready to address the meeting, Ebb?' She looked at him blankly. 'Only joking. I wouldn't be that mean, would I, Jeanie?'

Jeanie nodded and mouthed, 'Oh yes.' She was listening to the woman on the other end of the phone explain why she couldn't help. 'Thanks for nothing.'

She put the phone down. 'Just ignore him.' She made a face at Carter and shook her head, pretending to be cross.

Carter grinned. 'She loves me really.'

He turned to watch Davidson close the door behind him and stand waiting for the last rumble of conversation to evaporate. Carter went back to his desk. Davidson's voice boomed over the heads of the officers.

'Last night, at a house near Totteridge a gardener uncovered a grave that contained a woman and her infant child. DC Ebony Willis and Sergeant Dan Carter were the first detectives at the scene. Sergeant?' He handed over to Carter. Carter had remained standing. He pinned a map up on the notice board behind him.

'They were buried under a patio at a house in Totteridge, about eight miles northwest of here. For those of you who don't know the area, it's a picturesque village with farmland around it. This house is down a country lane off the main A5109 road which runs east to west. As its name would suggest, Blackdown Barn is an old barn conversion. So far we know little about who was supposed to be living there. The house appears to be empty, recently vacated. It looks likely they left two weeks ago. We know there is someone named Mr Chichester from letters in the mailbox. We'll find out all we can today when we get hold of the deeds to the house and trace the owner. We started house-to-house in the area this morning, hoping to catch people before they headed off to work. So far most people have told us that this is a rented property and that the owner lives in the Channel Islands.'

Carter clicked on the 'play' button on his laptop and a virtual tour of Blackdown Barn came on screen.

'The house itself has five bedrooms upstairs and a further one in the basement. We'll know more when we get hold of the owner of the house and find out what furniture is his. This house could potentially house many more, but if we're just going by the number of beds, must be five people at least.'

The master bedroom came onto the screen and Carter paused the video. 'Whoever was living there didn't leave in a hurry. They cleaned up thoroughly before they left. Most fixtures and fittings are still there and the beds have been taken away for DNA analysis. This room, the master bedroom overlooking the front of the house, is the exception. This room is different to the others. It has no carpet or curtains, the bed's gone but there's evidence of a single one having been in there.' The video continued through the house and down into the cellar. He paused it when it came to the small room off the wine cellar.

'There was an extra bedroom down here.' He allowed the film to run on before pausing it again with the view of the interior of the room. 'There's a camp bed down there which we don't think would take the weight of the pregnant woman but we'll wait for the DNA results. It's certainly not a place someone would choose to sleep. It's cold and damp. Under the bed we found a scrap of red material that we believe to be a piece of an Arsenal football shirt, attached to the springs.'

The video switched to an outside view.

'There is evidence of a large van having been sat on the driveway and it was there for some time. We're having a mould taken of the imprint. Maybe they used that to transport things from the house. As we follow the film around to the back of the property we find the gravesite.'

Carter passed over to Harding: 'Doctor Harding certified the remains and carried out post-mortems on the two victims.'

Harding stood and opened her notes. She took over the video control from Carter.

'If you want to open the email I sent you you'll get the photos from the burial site and the autopsy.'

Ebony was already looking at the dismembered remains on her screen. She flipped back to the burial site and the woman's body in the grave.

'A woman, Caucasian. Until we can identify her I've given her the name Silvia. Silvia was approximately five foot four, in her mid-twenties. She was buried a metre and a half below the surface of the patio. Buried face up. The manner in which she was laid out was not a haphazard act: she was placed rather than thrown. The body has been dismembered at the major joints using a power tool, probably a small hand-held circular saw. The edges are uniform; bone splintering is minimal. It's a neat job. Very tidy. Initial soil analysis surrounding the body shows that this was probably done *in situ*. Small fragments of bone were found in the surrounding soil. We will have an accurate date for burial after larvae tests are carried out but I estimate she's been in the ground five months.

She was buried in summer. We found traces of bramble pollen.'

Harding moved to the next image in which the body had been washed and laid out on the mortuary slab.

'Strong athletic build: well nourished. No previous fractures. She has a large contusion over the left eye which looks like it maybe have also been a friction burn. I have sent the skin from the area away for analysis.' A photo of the torso came on screen. 'Silvia has been extensively mutilated internally. She was opened up down the centre of the torso from sternum to pubic bone. Decomposition of the torso prevents us from recovering her organs or stomach contents.'

A slideshow of the autopsy shots came on screen.

'Apart from the facial injury she doesn't appear to have any other obvious wounds, was well fed and would have most probably been able to carry her baby to full term. She was killed shortly after giving birth by Caesarean section.' Harding paused the slideshow at the photo of the baby. 'Her baby is female, approximately thirty-six weeks. I have named her Fi. She was delivered but her airways were not cleared. Fi never took a breath. In all other ways the baby appeared to be perfectly healthy although a few weeks early. Fi wasn't Silvia's first child.'

Harding sat back down. Davidson elevated his voice a notch and fixed his eyes on each member of the team in turn.

'Our lines of enquiry will follow these paths: get the deeds and trace the owner. Find out who Chichester is. We estimate that he has been out of the house for two weeks. Not a lot was happening in those two weeks. The snow brought the whole of the UK to a standstill. Where did he go? Get out into the village of Totteridge and ask questions about who lived in the house. Post a manned mobile unit at the end of the lane where it meets the main road and talk to passers-by. We need to find out if there was a phone line in and see what that throws up. Trace the utility bills, council tax, TV licence, everything. The postman, the local canvassing politician. Anyone that might have visited this property. Someone must have knocked on the door for some reason. Right now we have a lot of groundwork to do. Missing Persons. Is there a record of a pregnant woman attending the local hospital? Does she have another child somewhere? If we find out *who* the victims were then we can find out *why* they were killed and by *whom*. We will be bringing cadaver dogs and thermal-imaging equipment in.' Davidson wrapped things up. 'Carter, can I have you in my office please?'

Trevor Bishop checked his watch again; he knew he was late for the meeting but he was still working on the prints he'd found. He loaded the last print from the master bedroom at Blackdown Barn onto his PC for scanning and cross-matching. It was a thumb, forefinger and partial palm print that he'd lifted from the bottom of the windowpane. Someone had tried to open the sash window. It had been newly painted at the time and must have been hard to shift. Someone had tried really hard. It was a great print to find. It was the best one of the night.

He sat back in his chair and took off his glasses; they sprang off his face and clattered on the desktop: *unbreakable,* the optician said. He couldn't help giving them a little test every day. He could leave the computer to do its job now. One print collided with another and separated. The program scrolled through its data. Ninety ridges, bifurcations and relative locations: ninety points of similarity and the match would be made. Of course the skill would come in evaluating any calluses, dirt, cracks or scars, but first he had to let the computer do its work. He checked his watch again: *bugger*. He hated being late. He sat back and looked at his screensaver of Stonehenge. Somewhere inside, a zillion cross-matches were being verified: the database was being checked in cyberland and it would take as long as it would take.

Five more minutes and Trevor was about to leave it and go. He hovered the mouse over Stonehenge, ready to click the 'shut down' button, and then he saw it . . . the computer told him there was a positive result.

He drew his chair back to the monitor and watched the match take place. On the left of the screen was the print from Blackdown Barn; on the right was the one matching, its fingers splayed, the forefinger and palm the clearest. The one on the right printed in blood. He shook his head as he sat back in his chair and rocked to and fro. In front of him the match confirmed. He remembered it well. Had it really been thirteen years ago?

Rose Cottage: Lydd Road, Camber Sands 17 May 1998.

The first officer on the scene had walked into a house of blood and butchery: one woman in the lounge, her naked body split open from her chest downwards; in the kitchen another woman . . . the same. Upstairs, a little girl's arterial blood dripped from the ceiling in the bedroom, her throat cut. The first officer at the scene was Callum Carmichael. The woman in the kitchen was his wife Louise; the little girl upstairs was his daughter Sophie.

Chapter 6

Carter followed Harding into Davidson's office. Harding sat in a chair by the window, beneath the framed portrait of Davidson meeting a retired Prime Minister. Davidson turned to see Bishop walking in behind them.

'Trevor? You didn't make the meeting?'

'Sorry, got delayed. But it was worth it.' He closed the door behind him. Davidson sat down behind his desk. Bishop put two A4 printouts on Davidson's desk next to one another. 'Let me show you. I ran a check on a print I found last night in Blackdown Barn. See the points highlighted in yellow? It's a perfect match to one from a cold case.'

Davidson smiled. 'Great result, Trevor. What was the cold case?'

'This one—' Bishop tapped his finger on the print to Davidson's left, 'was found at Blackdown Barn. And this one?' He looked up at Davidson. 'Found next to the body of four-year-old Sophie Carmichael thirteen years ago.'

Carter was struggling with the name for a few seconds before the realization crossed his face and he turned to Trevor. 'Sophie Carmichael? As in Inspector Callum Carmichael?'

Trevor nodded. Harding said nothing. She was watching Davidson's reaction as he bent over the prints and his hands gripped the edge of the desk. Carter looked around at the others. His eyes rested on Harding. She was still watching Davidson. He could see that she needed no reminding about the case. But then, he knew she had been there. She'd been the pathologist then. Davidson looked up after what seemed ages. He had composed himself a little.

'Do you have a name for me, Trevor?'

'No, sir. But there is no doubt.'

'There was someone in the frame for it at the time, wasn't there, sir?' Carter looked at Trevor and then Davidson. There seemed to be an awkward silence. Davidson didn't answer; he looked deep in thought. The room had become charged, poised. Trevor answered.

'Maria Newton. She was the mother of the other woman murdered in the cottage along with Carmichael's wife Louise. Her name was Chrissie Newton. She was there with her baby son Adam who survived the attack. Maria Newton died before we could take her prints, two weeks after her daughter was murdered.'

'Shall we allocate officers from the team to reopen the case, sir?' Carter asked. Davidson still didn't answer. He continued studying each photo in turn as if hoping to find a discrepancy in the match; but he couldn't. He glanced Harding's way. She stared back at Davidson but gave nothing away. She knew, more than anyone else in the room, what this news meant to him: not a great opportunity to clear up a cold case, especially one that he had failed to crack first time round. It meant his failings would be under scrutiny again.

'No. Not at this present time. Not until we have something more to go on. We don't have a name. We only have a match. We can't spread our resources too thin. We don't have the money to chase up a cold case at the moment. We are stretched to the limit already.'

'Sir?' Carter waited. Bishop wasn't hurrying to put the prints away. Everyone was waiting. 'This is a hell of an opportunity, sir.'

'Maybe . . . maybe.'

'Sir?' Carter looked confused. Harding and Bishop said nothing.

'I will not be rushed into a decision. I need time to consider the implications of this. Before I am ready to reopen the Carmichael case I want to know what we are letting ourselves in for.' He looked around the room. No one was moving, everyone waiting for him to say more. He sat back in his chair. 'You forget I was the SIO then too. We took on the case because we felt we owed it to a fellow MET officer to handle the case within the MET. I thought I was taking on a fellow officer's case and we would come out of it getting justice for him, but we didn't. We came out of it with two women and a child brutally murdered and seemingly the only person who could have done it was him. We came out of that case with more questions than we went in with.'

Davidson stared down at the prints on his desk.

Bishop spoke; 'It was difficult. Louise and Sophie weren't meant to be there that evening. Carmichael was supposed to pick them up but he didn't show. He was the first on the scene the next morning. He said he arrived at about eleven. On that Saturday evening someone went to Rose Cottage and they brutally murdered everyone in the house except for the baby, who they left sedated, perhaps they had plans for him and ran out of time.' He shook his head. 'This wasn't a quick process. These women were butchered, tortured over many hours. Louise was raped.'

'Yes,' Davidson agreed as he looked down at the prints on his desk. 'And the only DNA apart from a handprint, *this* handprint—' he pointed to the partial palm, finger and thumb print on his right, 'was Carmichael's. *That* was everywhere in abundance. He was covered in his daughter's blood. He said he moved her. But why would a trained police officer do such a thing?'

'Different when it's your family, I suppose,' said Carter.

Davidson shook his head, a worried man. 'The more we looked into it the worse it looked for Carmichael. Things began to be uncovered about him. It turned out he was going through a bad time. He'd been behaving strangely, out of character, before it happened. He was diagnosed with massive mood swings. He was ex-military. He had Post-Traumatic Stress Disorder.' Davidson sighed. 'Carmichael was our chief suspect for the murders at Rose Cottage. But we didn't have enough evidence to charge him. He was in no state to tell us what happened. So, we protected our own that day. We closed ranks. It left questions but no answers.'

'Could he have done it?' Carter asked.

'Easily.' Davidson nodded his head slowly. 'Would have been very easy for a man trained like he was. He was in the Special Boat Service. He'd been held captive at one time.'

'Did he ever show signs of cracking beforehand' sir?'

Davidson looked across to Harding for an answer.

'No,' she said. 'But we know a lot more about Post-Traumatic Stress now than we did then. It could have come out at any time.'

'And,' said Davidson, 'the women would have trusted him. Carmichael could have walked in, killed his daughter Sophie without anyone knowing and then come back downstairs and killed the women. He could have been there all night. He had no witnesses to back up his alibi that he arrived the next morning. He could have been there all night.'

Carter shook his head. 'What's the motive, sir?

'He inherited a lot of money when his wife died. Maybe that was it, or maybe he was not himself that night. Maybe he went in there with one of his military buddies, off his head with drink, drugs, PTSD. It took a madman to do what someone did at Rose Cottage and Carmichael fitted the bill.'

'What about Chrissie Newton's mother? What made her a suspect?' asked Carter.

'She had known mental problems,' said Bishop. 'She was on medication and was volatile. She and Chrissie had fallen out in the weeks before Chrissie's death. The scene looked like a maniac had done it. People, the press, made assumptions that she had killed herself out of remorse for her actions and set her own house on fire.' Davidson looked up at Harding and then around the room at the others. 'We let that presumption ride. Maria Newton died before we could verify that it was her print next to Sophie.'

Davidson gathered the prints together and pushed them across the desk to Bishop. 'You can go, Trevor. I'll let you know what we're going to do about it in due course. And Trevor? This whole conversation stays within this room, understood?' Davidson looked at each person in the room and waited to get their individual agreement. Bishop nodded, picked up the prints and left. Harding remained. She sat watching from the sidelines. Her top leg twitching. Davidson looked at Carter. 'I want you to find out everything you can about Carmichael now. Go and see him. He lives on a remote farm in Yorkshire. Find out what he's been doing for the last thirteen years. He didn't explain some things at the time. Find out why he moved his daughter at the scene. He was a trained police officer – why would he move one of the bodies? I want to know what the state of his marriage was. If he was screwing someone I want to know . . . ask around. Ask Robbo in Intelligence. He worked with Carmichael. Now, after all this time, people might be willing to open up. If there is anything about Carmichael we didn't know thirteen years ago I want it out now, do you understand, Carter?' Davidson waited. Carter nodded.

'I would like to send DC Willis down to Rose Cottage, sir. We need to get the whole picture.'

'Okay, but DC Willis is to be made aware that the only leads we are looking for are ones that will help to solve the Blackdown Barn case. I repeat, I am not reopening the Carmichael case at this stage. Understood?'

'Yes, sir.'

'Concentrate on the bodies we have now.'

'I'll go with her to Rose Cottage,' said Harding.

Davidson looked over at Harding and Carter could see his mind working.

'Do you think that's necessary? Our priority is here.'

'Any help I can give might be useful at this stage. I went there the first time round. It's surely better to have her go with someone who worked on the case last time.'

Davidson nodded but he didn't look pleased about it.

Carter left Davidson's office and walked back down the corridor to the second largest office on the floor, the Major Incident room. It was the room where all the initial calls came in and the information was loaded onto HOLMES, the central program which sifted and collated Major Incident data. The room had four long desks and housed eight staff in all, at the moment there were just two: Robbo and Pam the civilian employee who answered the phone and logged the calls.

Robbo had worked in nearly all the departments within the 'Dark Side' of MIT17.

'Did you hear about the print Bishop found?' Carter sat down next to him and helped himself to the bag of Haribo sweets next to Robbo's PC.

'Yes. It's a turn-up for the books.'

'Any thoughts about it?'

'Plenty.' He pushed the plunger on his cafetière down and indicated that Carter could grab himself a mug. Robbo looked across to Pam to ask if she wanted coffee. Pam was the woman Robbo's wife had been convinced he'd been having an affair with at the last social. Robbo was flattered his wife thought he could still muster up some interest from the opposite sex but Pam was happily married and Robbo had never been remotely tempted to stray in his twenty-three year marriage to Arlene.

'We're trying to put together a whole picture of Carmichael. You served with him, didn't you? What kind of bloke was he?'

'Yes, I served with him. There's a few of us here that were around then: Davidson, Harding, Bishop, Sandford and me.'

Robbo had joined the Force at the same time as Davidson. They had worked together often along the way but while Davidson had flown up the ranks, Robbo had clipped his own wings. He loved what he did and he knew he did it well but he would stay a DC because he couldn't take the stress of being in command. He never sat the exams to take him any higher.

'I didn't socialize with him. He wasn't one for going off to the pub after work. He was fanatical about the job: you got the feeling Tactical Firearms Inspector was the role he's been made for. Plus he had a huge knowledge about Intel work. I wish I had him working in here now. He was allowed access to stuff in the

SBS, spyware that we can only dream of. There was nothing Carmichael couldn't hack into.'

'I've been asked to look into the Carmichael case by Davidson.' Robbo stopped pouring out the coffee and looked at Carter with an inquisitive expression. 'Discreetly,' clarified Carter. 'So I need you to dig it all up for me; all the stuff they didn't want to talk about at the time; all the things they *really* don't want dug up now.'

'That discreet, huh?'

'Yeah . . . If they didn't want me to they shouldn't have given me the job. The first thing I want to do is look into who else was in the frame for it.'

'There was Chrissie Newton's mother Maria, who died in a fire.'

'I need the report into that.'

Robbo wheeled his chair across to his PC. 'Okay, I'll get it for you now. I remember it at the time. She died two weeks after her daughter was murdered. I remember people trying to interview her about it. She was barking. She had collected ten years' worth of newspapers in her house, piled up in the rooms. The place went up like a matchbox. Okay . . . here it is . . .' He printed off the report. 'Inconclusive, basically.'

Carter took the sheet from him and skim-read it. 'Not obviously arson as in petrol through the letterbox. It was blamed on faulty electrics. She had antiquated wiring in her house. It wouldn't have taken much. The whole house was gutted and most of it fell down. It made for an impossible job forensically.'

'Chrissie Newton's father, James Martingale, was he in the frame?'

'No. He wasn't here; he was working in one of his hospitals abroad.'

'Is he still working as a surgeon?'

'Very much so. He operates on the rich and famous. He's become a big name in these last thirteen years. He's the brains behind that chain of private hospitals – the Mansfield Clinics. They're big money, with hospitals all over Europe and South Africa. They specialize mainly in cosmetic procedures.'

'There must be stuff to dig up on him.'

'I'll give it a go but I know he's Mr Charity. He gives away a massive chunk of the hospitals' profit mainly to children's charities. He set up a charity in his daughter's name after she was killed: the Chrissie Newton Foundation. At the time he put up a million-pound reward for information leading to the arrest of the murderers. Still didn't get us anything – in fact it slowed things down as we had half of our officers out on wild goose chases as so many of the calls that came in were false.' He shook his head sadly. 'I remember the whole thing was a mess; nothing went right. Forensic exhibits were not stored properly. We didn't have a drying cupboard for the blood-stained clothing then. Louise Carmichael's was hung up next to her husband's and Christine Newton's clothes to dry – bound to be cross-contamination. There were no leads that didn't keep doubling back to Carmichael. In the end it was damage limitation rather than justice. Maria Newton was killed in the fire and the press pointed the finger at her and we just let it stay pointed. Carmichael went to live like a hermit – he doesn't keep in contact with anyone so far as I know – and the case just gradually faded away and slipped down the list of things to deal with. Tell you what, Carter. It feels good to see it back at the top of the agenda.'

'It's not there yet. Davidson won't reopen the case until he has a reason to. He says if we solve Blackdown Barn, we'll go a long way to solving the Carmichael case.'

Carter went to find Ebony.

'We need to talk. Let's grab a coffee.'

The canteen was busy. Ebony's housemate, Tina, worked behind the counter. She was on the cooked food section today. Her eyes lit up when she saw Carter, and Ebony groaned inwardly when she spotted Tina had fresh lippy on. *Christ,* she thought, *she's been waiting for him* . . .

Carter winked at Tina and she giggled.

Ebony put her tray forward. 'All-day breakfast please, Teen.' Tina loaded up Ebony's plate. She hovered with a spoon dripping beans over Ebony's tray.

'More beans, Ebb?' she said in a sickly sweet voice, her eyes on Carter.

'No, thanks . . . me and the tray have got enough.'

Carter counted out his change for his coffee and cake and Tina placed it neatly on his tray.

They went to sit on the far side of the canteen. Carter shook his head in disbelief as he watched Ebony tuck into the plate of food.

'Christ, where do you put it all? You must have hollow legs.'

Ebony reached over for more ketchup while Carter took out the Carmichael file he'd got from Robbo.

'We have a lead on this case but it's not the easiest. Have you heard of Callum Carmichael?'

She froze, mid-mouthful. 'The policeman whose wife and child were murdered in a holiday cottage?'

'That's the one. Trevor Bishop found a print in the master bedroom at Blackdown Barn that matches one at Rose Cottage where the Carmichael murders happened.'

'I only vaguely remember the case; I was a teenager at the time. I was surprised to see it still on the board when I started here.'

'It will stay on the board until it's solved.'

'I looked it up after I saw it there. The press coverage was mixed. There was talk of there being a cover-up. There was very little to go on.'

'The handprint was it. That was the sum total of evidence. I've been talking to Robbo. He was serving at the time. He says it was a mess-up. Just now, in his office, Davidson glossed over certain facts but it's well known that there was cross-contamination of forensic samples: some DNA samples were lost, others corrupted. They didn't have the dedicated equipment we have now. Things weren't as slick.'

'What's going to happen now, Sarge?'

'For whatever reason, Davidson's not prepared to reopen the case at the moment. He wants us to do some groundwork first. He's asked me to find out everything I can about Carmichael. He wants an update on Carmichael's life. He wants to know what he's been doing for thirteen years and he wants to know if there's any dirt that people didn't feel they should dish up at the time but will now.' Ebony stopped eating, her eyes widened. 'Yeah . . . I know,' said Carter. He pushed the file across to her. She began looking at the handwritten notes of the first officer to respond to Carmichael's call:

17 May 1998
Arrived at Rose Cottage 11.35 a.m., responding to call from Inspector Callum Carmichael. Inspector Carmichael is present at scene. He appears to be in a confused state and is saying very little. He is showing signs of having handled the bodies. He has blood on his clothing. Three bodies: two women and a female child. There is a male infant alive upstairs, who appears to be sedated.

The first body is that of Christine Newton. She has been cut open down the length of her torso.

Ebony looked at the photos: Chrissie Newton's naked body was on the floor in the lounge. She was lying on her back, her arms loose at her sides. Her head turned to one side. The whole of her torso was opened up like a butchered pig.

Carter reached over and closed the file as someone walked past their table.

'Read it later. Davidson wants us to go to Yorkshire and talk to Carmichael. We'll catch a train up there tomorrow and get a car left for us at the station. He lives in the middle of the Yorkshire Dales; it will take us too long to drive the whole way. In the meantime talk to everyone you can about him.'

'Did Davidson say how he thinks Carmichael could have carried it out, Sarge?'

'It was a toss-up between money he stood to gain and PTSD. Carmichael had served in the SBS. He had seen action in Iraq. He had been part of Special Forces. Davidson says he was diagnosed with mood swings. He said he could have gone into military mode and gone berserk.'

'PTSD isn't a bad mood.'

'Exactly – it's a mental disorder where people can kill and not remember. Or they choose to see it another way. This is all according to Davidson and Harding, who was the pathologist at that time. Basically, this is the last thing Davidson wants six months away from retirement. He wants us to go and see Carmichael, talk to him, tell him just enough to see if he has anything useful for us and ask him if he wants to add anything to his original statement; he must have thought things over in all these years. But the main thing is, Davidson wants him contained. If he plays nice we'll keep him informed; throw him the odd stick to retrieve and pat his head when he does. Go with Harding this morning to Rose Cottage where the Carmichael murders happened. Ask her to fill you in on the background. She did the autopsies that day. According to Robbo she was over-friendly with Davidson at one time.' Carter smiled. 'It's going to kill Davidson if he has to reopen the case. Bet he never thought he'd see this resurface. But you know what they say, Ebb. Shit sticks and bodies float.'

Davidson went to the bathroom next to his office and looked at his reflection in the mirror. Today he had on a deep blue shirt and a darker blue jacket. Grey trousers with a permanent crease. His wife Barbara bought his clothes, but he never thanked her for doing it. Their marriage had lost any ember of excitement. He had long since stopped trying to make her feel treasured or even wanted. Divorce was out of the question. He'd be damned if he'd hand over half of everything. Not at this stage in his life. Barbara could carry on enjoying her benefits as she'd always done. She'd always been happy to take a back seat. He'd worked hard to court business acquaintances outside the Force. Davidson promised himself a life again when he retired. He had a few interesting offers: big corporations that wanted him on their board. He would be travelling a lot, he would be flying first class, staying in top hotels, Barbara wouldn't want to come. If things had worked out well in the Carmichael case then Davidson wouldn't have had to work at all after the Police Force. He'd be Commissioner by now and retire on a massive pension. As it was, if things went badly again he would be lucky to get a job delivering groceries after he retired. The thought made him sweat. He splashed cold water onto his face then stood looking at himself in the mirror. Small beads of water still dripped from his sallow skin. Okay ... he'd made mistakes. Just six months until he could retire, for Christ's sake. But why now did he have to find himself back in the nightmare with Callum Carmichael?

Harding came into the bathroom. She came to stand next to him. The fact they had once slept together gave them a familiarity with each other.

'Barbara still buying your shirts?'

He turned away, pulled down a paper towel and wiped his face, small precise dabs then went back into his office; she followed. He felt a flash of anger. Once more she had overstepped the mark. Once more he felt the urge to see her naked.

'Aren't you supposed to be on your way to Rose Cottage this morning?' He sat down behind his desk.

'Yes. The owners are sending over a key. Apparently the place has hardly been touched in all these years.'

He stared at her. She knew he wasn't really listening to her. He was white with rage. She didn't flinch.

'You can't ignore it, John. You can't stick your head in the sand . . .'

'Thank you for your support in the meeting this morning.' He was petulant.

They listened to the sound of doors banging: people in the corridor outside his office. The Murder Squad in full work frenzy. It was what they lived for. It was what they did. But Davidson had had enough. He was six months from retiring and every part of his body and soul wanted out now, wanted a new life; he deserved it.

'It's no shame to admit the procedures let us down at the time. Everything's in the open these days,' Harding said as she sat down across from him. Davidson pursed his lips, leant forward, elbows, forearms on the desk, and pressed his fingertips together. He didn't answer. He looked at her coldly. She glared back. 'We did our best with what we had at the time.' Davidson sighed, annoyed, exasperated; Harding stayed cool: 'Reopen the Carmichael case, John.'

He flashed her a defiant look. 'No.'

She persevered. 'These are different times; transparency is the new gospel of the day.'

'No . . . not transparency, people just want to know every sordid fact, even if they don't understand it. They won't care about technical reasons why we didn't get a conviction in this case. Why should they? The buck will stop with me . . . I have everything to lose now. I made the mistake last time of thinking I would come out of it with a bright future ahead. I thought I would take on the case and reap the glory – after all, Carmichael was a war hero and a well respected officer. Carmichael wasn't even capable of an alibi. It didn't take long into the investigation for me to realize I had backed the wrong bloody horse.'

Chapter 7

Carmichael hauled Jumper's body out into the snow and stood over it. The wind and snow swirled around him, as if he stood inside a Christmas paperweight that someone had shaken. Sophie had had one in her stocking. It was plastic with a reindeer inside. She had been so excited about Christmas. She came into their bed that last Christmas morning and hugged his neck and he had breathed in her sleepy smell and knowing there would never be a more perfect love. Like the first day he'd held her in his arms, wet from the womb, and he'd vowed to protect her forever.

'Come on then.' He had picked her up in his arms and carried her to the window and held her tightly as he opened the curtain very gradually. Sophie had held her breath for a few seconds as she pressed her palms to the cold glass and then gasped. Outside the snow was falling.

Now the sky and the ground merged as the blizzard swirled around him and the dead sheep. He knelt beside Jumper and picked up handfuls of snow, his bloody hand leaving red prints on the white ground. He took out the knife from his belt and began skinning her.

Chapter 8

Sandford looked down from the window in the master bedroom at Blackdown Barn and watched the young policeman on duty at the gate. It was starting to snow again. The officer outside had been there since seven. It was mid-morning now. Inside the house it had fallen quiet. His SOCO team of four were spread out throughout the house, conducting grid searches in each room. He tapped on the window and the young officer turned around. Sandford made a T-sign with his fingers and the officer grinned and nodded. Just as Sandford turned back from the window his eye was drawn up to the corner of the room and something sparkling there. He stood on the stepladder to reach into the corner of the ceiling cornice. A staple was punctured into the plaster. He picked out the mini pliers from his tool belt and gently wiggled it free. With the staple came a tiny fragment of plastic sheeting. He looked at it on the edge of the pliers. He held it in his hand and phoned Robbo.

'What's the thickness?' Robbo asked.

'I would say one mil. PVC.' Sandford looked along the ceiling. 'Puncture marks every metre.'

'Okay,' answered Robbo. 'Rolls of plastic sheeting, one mil by a metre. I'll find the manufacturers and get samples. How's it looking out there? You dismantled the whole house yet?'

'Yeah, funny . . . nearly. We're going to start digging up the basement today. Needed to get some results back from the gym equipment enquiry first.'

'Yeah, I followed it up. There was a runner, a multi-gym, and an exercise bike down there. What's the flooring?'

'It's felt. I'll get it bagged up and sent your way before we start digging. Did the gym company say they'd cleaned it yet?'

'Yes. It's been sent out again so no chance of DNA from it. Do you think there's a chance there's a body under the basement?'

'Could be. We're still looking for the kid in the Arsenal shirt. We've put cameras down the drains, no extra vermin activity. No lumpy stuff that could be flesh. Pitch pipes too; they're old – at least fifty years – and they're blistered so if there were any chunks of flesh larger than a couple of inches square they would have got snagged.'

'Is it freezing out there?' Robbo reached over for the cafetière as he smiled to himself. The cafetière was wrapped in a leopard-print body warmer: a present from his wife: tongue in cheek, homage to his feminine side. He found it really useful; it kept his coffee hot for an hour.

'We've got heaters in the mobile unit out the front. We can make tea. But yes . . . it's bloody freezing. I'm sure I'll be used to it by the time I finish here – either that or it'll be spring. It's a massive house.'

'You can ask for a bigger team if you need to pace it up.'

'No. I need to keep control of who's dismantling what. There are four of us – that's enough. If you're interested you could come and take a look and lend a hand, though?'

'Wouldn't want to get in your way.'

'Very considerate.'

Robbo never left Fletcher House except to get in his car and drive home. In all the years Sandford had known Robbo he'd watched his agoraphobia grow. Without his realizing it Robbo was no longer able to work away from his desk.

Sandford hung up and looked at the piece of plastic again; a fine blond hair was caught between it and the staple. He went across to the collection of samples he had on the floor and picked out one of the small brown bags with a see-though square section in its front; on it he wrote: *piece of plastic from ceiling cornice, bedroom 1.*

He opened the crime scene log and drew a diagram of the master bedroom and where he'd found the scrap of plastic. He rang his wife.

'No, definitely won't be home tonight, love. I'll try and make it tomorrow for a few hours. Sorry ... happy birthday, love ... yes ... I'll be thinking of you. Kiss the kids for me and you too of course. Love you.'

Chapter 9

Ebony sat beside Harding as she threw the Audi sports car around the unfamiliar roads on the drive out of London towards the Sussex countryside. The snow grew sparser on the roads as they neared the coast. Some of the fields had a hint of patchy green.

'Thank you for coming, Doctor.'

'It's not a problem. We'll run through the case notes and crime scene diagrams when we get there. I'll be interested to see any similarities with Blackdown Barn that come to mind. Did you speak to the owners of Rose Cottage when you got the key?'

'Yes. I met Mr Dalson, the owner, at the Tube station. He was on his way to work. He told me they inherited the cottage from an aunt. When they inherited it, it came with a list of people who regularly hired it for set times in the year. Chrissie Newton had come the year before for the first time. She was lucky, one of the regulars dropped out and she took their May 15th to the 21st slot.'

'What's happened to it now?'

'No one's booked it since. He told me that they had only visited the cottage a handful of times since it happened. They just haven't decided what to do with it. They've thought about selling it but want to keep it in the family. I think he was hoping if they waited long enough they wouldn't remember what happened there. Did you come to the cottage at the time, Doctor?'

'Yes.'

Ebony watched the town quickly disappear and the countryside take over. They were headed on the Hastings Road towards Camber. Camber was a broad sandy beach popular with people coming from the city. Ebony had been there once before on an outing from one of the children's homes she stayed in. Two and a half hours crowded into a hot minibus and then let loose for a fabulous day of sand and sea and freedom. She and Micky had spent the day jumping the waves and building sand castles. She would always remember the smell of the sea as they got nearer to it and the excitement she felt. She could smell it now.

'Did you know Carmichael, Doctor?'

'Not well.'

'Did you like him?'

Harding lifted her hands from the steering wheel in a shrug gesture: 'I had no thoughts either way.'

'What about his wife?'

'I met Louise once, that's all. Carmichael was lucky to get her. She was beautiful, bright. She was an heiress from some major margarine company. Although the money didn't come till she was thirty. She wasn't born with a silver spoon. But she could have picked anyone.'

'You think she made a mistake?'

'I think she had her work cut out. Carmichael wasn't a man without a past.'

They drove down the secluded lane off Lydd Road, close to the long stretch of sandy beach. The cottage was the last one on the left. A man was working in the garden. He stopped what he was doing, pinning a rose back against the stone front of the house and waited as Harding parked up outside. Ebony got out of the car and took out her warrant card to show him.

'We won't disturb you – we just want to take a look inside.'

'No problem.' He smiled. 'I just look after the outside. You have keys?' Ebony nodded.

He was a posh gardener type with wild unruly hair and a cheeky smile. Harding went back to the car for her bag.

'Have you been looking after this garden for a long time?'

'About thirteen years. I look after the gardens of all the holiday cottages on this lane.'

'So you know the history of this place? Were you around when the incident happened here?'

He nodded. 'Sort of . . . I had just started working but I was actually on holiday that week. I came back to it.'

'What's happened to the property since then?'

He shook his head. 'Nothing really. After it happened I rebuilt this wall to the left of the gate. It got knocked by one of the vehicles. Apart from that, nothing's changed. Except no one comes here now.'

Ebony opened up the file she was carrying and turned the pages. 'Doesn't mention the wall being knocked down in the report.'

He shrugged, shook his head. 'Someone knocked down the corner of the gatepost. I presumed it was when they were reversing, trying get round – it's a tight spot.'

'So you rebuilt this section?' Ebony pointed to the pillar and the edge of the stone wall.

'Tidied it up more than rebuilt.'

She bent down to get a better look. 'Where was it knocked down, the middle?'

'No . . . at the top.'

'Can I have a number for you, in case I need to ask you any questions?'

'Sure . . .' He smiled. He went to his Land Rover, which was parked up the lane at another house, and brought her back a card.

'Sorry it's a bit muddy.' He grinned as he tried to wipe the thumbprint from the surface with the cuff of his jacket. 'I did tell someone at the time about the wall . . . but they didn't seem that interested.'

'Thanks . . .' Ebony took the card. She looked up from reading his card: Marty Readman, landscape gardener, to see him staring at her. She looked away fast as she felt the heat come to her face. She wished she didn't find it difficult to talk to good-looking men. Harding was waiting for her. As Ebony unlocked the door and opened it the low winter sun flooded inside and set the dust spinning. They stood in the doorway. Ahead of them were the stairs to the upstairs floor. To the right were the living rooms.

'When you came here that morning, Doctor, what was it like?'

'I was on my way back from Brighton when I got a call asking if I could cover for a colleague who was on duty but sick. It was a sunny day. It had been a glorious weekend. It was on my way home so I agreed. When I got here the officers who answered the 999 call from Carmichael were gone; two from the Brighton murder squad were already here.'

'Why did they hand it over to the MET to deal with? Why didn't it stay with the Brighton squad?'

'Because he was a serving MET officer, I suppose. Davidson made the decision he wanted to do the best he could for Carmichael. That turned out to be an impossible task. I didn't question it at the time. Of course . . .' She turned to look at Ebony in the gloomy hallway. 'That was the first mistake.'

Ebony opened her file. 'Here in this hallway there were bloody smears on the wall and Louise's hand-prints all the way down it. It says in the report that the blood on the wall was Sophie's. She must have seen her daughter killed, at least wounded, before she was dragged down these stairs.'

They walked into the first room on the right.

'Chrissie Newton was in here.' Harding pulled away the rug that covered the stone floor in the lounge. 'This is the spot.' A fat brown spider scuttled away towards the hearth.

Ebony held the picture of Christine Newton in her hand.

'Was the woman from Blackdown Barn, Silvia . . . was she opened up like that?'

'Yes.'

Ebony walked across to the window and pulled back the curtain. The gardener had gone 'They found an open bottle of wine, half a glass poured out. It was left over here beside this window; there was a small table here at the time. Maybe she was watching someone arrive when she drank it, never finished it.'

Ebony followed Harding as she walked along the hallway and down two steps to the stone-floored kitchen. 'And Louise Carmichael was in here. Over there by the back door. Sophie was laid out beside her.'

Ebony stood in the kitchen by a small table. 'Sophie had collected pebbles. They were found a bucket in here on the kitchen floor. They must have spent the day on the beach. Then come back here, given Sophie and Adam their tea: they found the washed-up plates, kids' knives and forks on the draining board.'

They walked back past the lounge and Ebony led the way up the stairs. Shadows of the dead ivy outside the landing window flitted across the old plaster walls.

'All the bodies were on the ground floor. I never came up here. I had no need,' said Harding.

At the top of the stairwell they came to a small bathroom with an old enamel bath.

'It says in the report that the water was left in the bath, just six inches. There were toys in there. So Louise must have been bathing Sophie when it started.'

'Louise?'

'Coming, Chrissie,' Louise called down from the bathroom. *'Just giving Sophie a bath.'*

Chrissie stood at the bottom of the stairs:

'I've started on the wine . . .' she giggled. 'Do you want me to bring you a glass up there?'

Louise leaned her head back towards the door. She was on her knees beside the bath, her hands in the water. 'You did well to hang on . . .' She smiled as she filled up one plastic beaker with water and tipped it into another; Sophie was concentrating so hard not to spill the water that her tongue stuck out the way her dad's did sometimes, when he didn't realize he was doing it. 'You carry on . . . I'll wait, thanks. I'll read to Sophie and get her settled and then I'll be right down. Are you sure you don't mind us staying for another night? Callum must have got held up at work. I am sorry.'

Louise swished the water back and forth through her fingers. She listened and heard Chrissie sigh. She smiled at Sophie.

'I know that Callum and I have been through a lot. I know that sometimes it all gets too much for him.'

Louise made the face that always made Sophie laugh. It was a gorgeous laugh that tilted Sophie's head backwards and came from the middle of her body: pure joy.

'What are you going to say to him if he does turn up?' Chrissie called up from the foot of the stairs.

'I don't know.'

'He cheated on you, Louise. You can't just ignore it.'

'I'm not ignoring it . . . I've thought about it for so many nights since I found out. I've tried so hard to make sense of it.'

'What is there to make sense of . . .? He's a lying, cheating bastard. He slept with another woman.

You're more forgiving than I could ever be, Louise. I like Callum but I know I could never forgive him. I'd leave him if I was you.'

'I can't. Whatever he's done . . . I know that he loves me and he loves Sophie. And I know that he's sorry.'

'Anyway, it's your business and don't be silly, it's no problem to put you up for another night; I'm glad of the company. Someone's arrived.'

Chrissie turned at the sound of a vehicle turning in outside. The cottage was at the end of a lane. No one needed to come down that far unless they were coming specifically to the cottage.

'Maybe that's Callum now.'

She carried her glass of wine into the lounge and drew back the curtain to look outside.

Ebony walked into the first bedroom on the left. The rooms were dark, the walls bare. Harding came to stand beside her. Ebony looked at the crime scene plan of the upstairs.

'This is the room where baby Adam was found alive.'

'He'd been taken to hospital by the time I arrived.'

They went into the next room. The bed had gone. Only faded paintings of country gardens and bluebells in the spring remained on the walls.

'Louise and Sophie slept in here. Louise may have had time to put her to bed, but she didn't have time to go back into the bathroom and empty the bath, tidy it up.'

'There was no trace of anaesthetics in Sophie's

bloods,' said Harding. 'All the others were anaesthetised before being killed.'

'She would never have got her to sleep naturally if she was frightened.' Ebony shivered; the cottage was colder inside than it was outside. 'If she knew there was trouble coming Louise must have hidden it well.' Ebony looked upwards. 'It says in the report that Sophie's blood was across the ceiling. It was a quick death then, an execution. Maybe to shut her up.' She glanced across at Harding at the same time as she flicked through the notes from the scene.

'So Louise witnessed her daughter's death, or at least the start of it, and then she was dragged downstairs and raped.'

'Yes,' said Harding. 'Louise's body was naked when it was found downstairs. Her knickers and shorts were found in the lounge. The rest of her clothes were missing. She had multiple bruises on her arms and legs, groin area, consistent with rape.'

Ebony stood on the landing and looked down the stairs. 'She was dragged downstairs and then she saw her friend being horrifically and slowly murdered and waited three hours to be killed in the same way herself.'

Harding joined her at the top of the stairs. 'Pressure marks and nylon fibre imbedded in the wrists and ankles of both women. They were rendered inactive, also given large amounts of sedation, which could have been used to keep them quiet while being tortured. Someone spent hours on these women.'

'You knew Carmichael. Do you reckon he could have done that?' asked Ebony.

'Yes,' answered Harding. 'He could have. He was trained to murder when he was with the SBS. He could have done it in his sleep. Carmichael had secrets, Ebony. Things emerged about him after the murders.'

Ebony stopped on the first step of the stairs and turned back to Harding.

'It turned out he'd had an affair six months before the murders.'

'Who with?'

'A civilian woman who worked in MIT 11.'

'Where is she now?'

'Emigrated shortly after it happened. She hasn't been back. I checked that out earlier on today. She had a cast iron alibi at the time; she was at the bedside of her mother who was dying of cancer.'

'Did it shock you to find out he had an affair, Doctor?'

'No.' She shook her head. 'Why would it? You know how it is. The teams spend days locked together in the same place. They don't get home even to sleep. They have a hard time holding down relationships outside the Force. He was an attractive-looking guy. He wasn't my type – typical army type: quiet, brooding but he was the kind that if you saw him often enough, worked with him, then maybe he could get under your skin.'

Harding passed Ebony and started to walk back down the stairs. Ebony went to follow but stopped at the landing window two steps down from the bathroom. It overlooked the garden and then in the distance the sea stretched glittering on the horizon.

She told herself Carmichael would have stopped at the same point and seen the same horizon. He would have stood here with the blood of his family on his hands. His daughter's body in his arms. And she knew . . . if he didn't kill them then he would have stood here, his heart breaking, and sworn vengeance.

'But why?' she asked Harding. 'What would he have wanted or gained?'

'Money? Who knows. Madness doesn't need a reason or a profit.'

'Do you think this case was handled differently because Carmichael was a policeman, Doctor?'

'Of course . . . You have the emotional attachment that so many people felt to him. Carmichael was a serving officer. *Of course* the police handled it differently.'

'How differently?'

'We had to weigh up the effect of it; we had every journalist camping outside the police station wanting blood, wanting it to be Carmichael who'd done it. We were trying to catch a murderer. We had to keep things quiet while the investigation was ongoing.'

'And from Carmichael himself?'

'Yes . . . Details were spared from him. Plus he was a suspect. He didn't help himself. He went into meltdown. I remember it well. Things were very difficult at the time . . . decisions were made that maybe now seem strange. But, at the time, we did what we thought was best, Chief Superintendent Davidson included. We all tried to help him. Carmichael was his own worst enemy.' Harding glanced over at Ebony.

'Do you think the Super will reopen this case?' They walked towards the front door.

'Davidson will do the right thing. I'll organize a SOCO team to go through the place again,' said Harding. 'Plaster walls like this can hold DNA samples for many years.'

She looked at Ebony as they stepped out onto the path. 'You're a good choice to look into things, Ebb. I have confidence in you. You need my help? Just ask. We're all on the same side.'

'Thanks, Doctor Harding.' She followed her out. 'There *are* a couple of things I wanted to ask you about the autopsies. I was expecting to see a toxicology report, liver biopsy . . . I couldn't find either.'

Harding looked momentarily flustered but recovered fast.

'Come to my office when we get back and I'll give you the original autopsy reports with my notes.'

'What was the actual cause of death, Doctor?' They walked to the gate and stood looking back at the cottage.

'Sophie died from a single cut to the throat severing the carotid artery. Louise died when they cut out her heart. Chrissie the same.'

'What did you think had happened here when you came here that day thirteen years ago?'

'I thought some mad man, or men, had come into this cottage and had subjected the women to something unimaginable, killed Sophie in front of her mother, and slowly and mercilessly cut the women to death before removing and eating their organs.'

Chapter 10

Ebony got a call from Carter just as Harding dropped her back outside Fletcher House.

'How was it, Ebb?'

'Just on my way up, Sarge.'

'Don't bother coming up, I need you to head down to the Tube. Talk to me on the way. How did it go at Rose Cottage?'

Ebony turned and walked back along Macdonald Road towards Archway Station.

'As far as I can see the whole crime scene was ill managed thirteen years ago. No one took the gardener's statement, for instance. He said he rebuilt a section of the wall that was knocked down by a high-sided vehicle. Plus, half of the autopsy reports are missing.'

'What did Harding have to say about that?'

'She didn't. She said she'd give me the full report plus her notes later on today.'

'How did you get on with her?'

'Okay. She's a bit frosty, defensive even. Sticking up for Davidson. She said she thought at the time they could be dealing with a cannibal killer. No wonder they wanted it kept quiet. It sounds like the SIO panicked.'

'Yeah. He cared more about brushing it under the carpet than solving it.'

'Nothing's been really messed with in all these years. Harding agrees it would be worth bringing a SOCO team down and looking at it again.'

'Okay, we'll get Sandford onto it. I've been in touch with the owner of Blackdown Barn. The neighbours were right – he lives on Jersey. He hasn't been there in years. He leaves it to an estate agent called Simpsons. It's just on the high street in Barnet, two minutes from High Barnet tube. Go straight there for me, Ebb. The owner – manager – Mr Simpson is expecting you. I'll see you back here afterwards.'

'Okay, Sarge.'

Ebony came out of High Barnet tube station, walked into Simpsons and showed her badge to the first woman on a row of desks. She was shown through to the manager's office. He had the file already waiting for her. He handed it to her as he looked at his watch.

She took it from him and pulled up a chair.

'Thank you, Mr Simpson but I would appreciate it if we run through this together? It's just in case I need to query anything in it; it will save time.'

'Uh . . . now?' He scratched his forehead. His hair had taken on a Friar Tuck look – two long thin brown islands either side of his head, parted by a sea of baldness. Ebony nodded. 'I have an important meeting in ten minutes.' He looked at his watch to emphasize the point.

'I suggest you postpone it for an hour.'

He nodded his reluctant agreement.

He went back behind his desk. 'What can you tell me about the tenant at Blackdown Barn?'

'His name was Chichester.'

'Did Chichester say he was going to live there with anyone?'

'Occasional guests.'

'What did he look like?'

'I never actually got to meet him – we conducted all our business over the internet. Chichester saw photos and I videoed the house so he could have a virtual tour.'

'Have you still got that video, please?'

'No . . . we can't keep every bit of correspondence, but I have the photos.' He handed her a packet of prints. Ebony took them out to look at. They were photos of each room with dimensions written on the back.

'Then what – after you emailed him these photos and he saw the video?'

'He took the tenancy on for a year, paid upfront. He'd been there since January.'

'So he left early.'

'Yes.'

'Did he inform you of that?'

'No.'

'Did you think that was odd?'

'Well I do now.'

'But you weren't unduly concerned?' he shook his head. Irritation was creeping into his demeanour as he fiddled with his cuffs and looked everywhere in the room except at Ebony. 'What about the utilities?' asked Ebony. 'There must be money owing?'

'He insisted on having meters installed in Blackdown Barn. I had to see to that before he moved in.'

They studied the photos. Ebony looked at the one of the master bedroom. 'The carpet was replaced with lino in this room. Why was that?'

'Chichester had very exact requirements. Replacing the carpet with linoleum was one of them.'

'Did he tell you why he wanted the works done?' Simpson shook his head. 'And you didn't think it was odd to want to put lino in a bedroom?' He shrugged. His face was turning red. 'You must have had to agree the work with the owners?'

'Well, it wasn't always necessary to bother the owners. I have handled their properties for many years. Chichester covered the whole of the costs. I didn't feel I needed to . . .'

'Can I please have a full list with all the receipts from that refurbishment.'

'I no longer have them – I'm sorry. As I said, I can't keep everything.'

'Can I see Chichester's original emails to you?'

'Again I'm sorry. It's eighteen months since I first received them from him. They are no longer on my computer.'

'You seem really sure about that. What about in your Sent Items or Trash folder? Do you need me to wait whilst you check?'

'I can assure you there's no need to check. They are definitely not on my computer.'

'Do you remember anything about the way he worded them that might help us find out what kind of a person he was? What about his spelling?'

'Good.'

'What about the way he wrote things, could he have been foreign?'

'I have no idea.'

Ebony looked at the photos again. 'Did you oversee these works yourself? Did you have this lino floor laid?'

'Yes.'

'Did you make a private financial arrangement with him?'

His face reddened some more. 'I had a lot of extra work.'

'Is that normal practice to make a private financial arrangement with clients without informing the owner of the house?'

'I wouldn't say it was an arrangement. There were costs incurred. The family are more than happy with the rent they received from Mr Chichester. I don't see why I should have to answer any more of your questions.'

'I suppose the thing is, Mr Simpson, at the moment you are the nearest thing we have to a friend of Mr Chichester. You got the house ready for him and a woman and her baby were murdered there. You don't seem overly eager to help me with this. It's an offence to withhold information and this is a murder investigation. We can talk here or I can take you in with me now and you can make a formal statement. I can also ask for these premises to be closed down while we conduct a search for the missing invoices. It's up to you.'

He paled. 'Of course. I will be happy to answer any questions.'

'Let's take another look at these photos and you can run through each one with me and tell me what he said he wanted to keep and what he didn't.'

Ebony stopped off to see Harding afterwards. She looked up as Ebony came in; she was studying the diagrams from the original crime scene at Rose Cottage. She closed the file, opened a drawer, and pulled out three autopsy reports from the victims at Rose Cottage before handing them over to Ebony.

'On no account share this information with anyone. I trust you to be discreet. Now is not the time to make things worse. We all did the best we could; that includes me.'

Ebony looked at Harding's face as she handed over the reports and thought she looked almost vulnerable: brittle under the hard shell. But Ebony knew very well that Harding had got to where she was in life by destroying marriages and people and if she was attempting to show Ebony her vulnerable side there was probably a plan.

'Of course, Doctor.'

'Are you going to see Carmichael tomorrow?'

'Yes.'

'Come and see me when you get back.' Harding turned back to studying the file on her desk.

Ebony headed home on the number seventy-three. Four stops from home she managed to get a seat. She looked out of the window and watched the snow coming down. When it had first hit it was fun – now it was a pain in the arse. The bus smelt like a wet dog basket. Outside, Christmas lights fought hard to colour up the sleet and snow.

She heard her housemate Tina's heavy metal music as soon as she put the key in the door.

Tina's voice came from the kitchen. 'Ebb?'

'Yeah, it's me . . .' Ebony put her coat over the banister, took off her shoes and put them by the front door.

Tina emerged stuffing toast into her mouth and wearing the maroon dressing gown that her nan had given her for last Christmas. Everyone in the house walked around in duvets and dressing gowns. It was impossible to keep warm. The house was old and draughty and the radiators were too small and decrepit to cope. But the rent was cheap so no one dared complain to the landlord.

'Any news?'

Ebony shook her head. 'It's not going to happen, Tina. I told you he has Cabrina. He's practically married. Cabrina's pregnant.'

'Bollocks . . .' Tina screwed up her face. 'Oh well.' She turned up the stairs and went up to her room. 'Back to the dating sites.'

Ebony walked through to the kitchen, made herself some tea and poured out a bowl of cereal then she went upstairs. Her room was on the top floor. It had everything she needed: a bed and a desk. If she wanted to watch telly she made herself be sociable and sit in the lounge. It didn't come easily for her; she wasn't used to it. That was why she'd chosen to live in a house with three others. She wanted to get used to it.

It was a lovely room that made her smile when she went into it. It overlooked the street below and had a London plane tree right outside her window. In the spring the birds came to sit in it and sing in the morning. It had been like a Christmas card when the snow covered its branches. But the downside of the room was that it was furthest from the bathroom, two floors up and last to get the heat into the ancient radiators.

She set the tea and cereal bowl on the desk and took out the file. Ever since Carter had told her about the handprint match she had been talking to people who remembered the case. She phoned Carter.

'Sarge? I found out as much about Carmichael as I can. I talked to several people this afternoon: people who knew Callum Carmichael at that time. But I can't find anyone who counted him as a mate.'

'He wasn't that type . . . loner . . . but great boss. So frigging good at his job. He was an inspector in the Tactical Firearms Unit. Not the kind of job you make mates in.'

'But as a person?'

'Can't answer that one . . . I didn't know him that well. I'd just joined when it happened . . .'

'I did get a bit of back history from Sandford,' said Ebony 'and I talked to the local police in Kirkcaldy where he grew up and got hold of his dad. Carmichael joined the Marines at eighteen and went to Devon to train. He was in trouble for minor offences when he was a teenager. Lucky not to get a sentence.'

'So he might have had a little help with signing up?'

'Yes, could have. His dad is a local publican. Well respected. Carmichael did well in the Marines. He served in the Falklands straight away. Then he was recruited into the SBS at twenty-two. He served in the Iraq War and in January 1991 he was sent to try and rescue a previous mission that had gone wrong. He was captured and subjected to violent torture which included burning and electric shock.'

'Tough bloke, Ebb.'

'Yes, but this is what I can't find out, Sarge. I can't find out where he was after he left the SBS and before he joined the Police Force for almost a year, October 1992. I can't find any mention of it. It's one of the things I'd like to ask him tomorrow. Harding seems to think he was definitely suffering with PTSD. But none of his workmates made any observations about strange behaviour or a change in his attitude around the time of the murders. He did have an affair, though.'

'Is that our motive then, Ebb? Kill the wife and kid and start again with wife's money and the new woman?'

'Except the new woman left for Australia soon after and according to her statement at the time, the affair had been over for a few months. Carmichael has never remarried. So I don't know really. I have the full autopsy reports now. I'll read them through and be ready to clarify things with Carmichael tomorrow. It will take me a few hours to go through it and then I'll bring my bag into the office, ready to leave early tomorrow morning, Sarge.'

'Stay there, get a few hours' kip.'

'Okay, Sarge . . . and Sarge, I talked to Mr Simpson, the letting agent: Chichester bought the bed in the cellar himself. That means the Arsenal shirt is down to him and nothing to do with the previous tenant. We were right about the room with linoleum – he had the carpet removed before he got there and had the linoleum put down, and more shelves put up in the bathroom.'

'What about the curtains in that room, Ebb? He left them in every other room, why not there?'

'I asked Simpson about those – he said Chichester told him he'd be bringing his own.'

'Sandford's found what looks like the remnants of a plastic curtain up at that bedroom window. We need to find out what that room was intended for: don't think it's a bedroom. Maybe it was a place to store something that needed to be kept germ-free.'

'I'll talk to Simpson again. He needs leaning on; he made money out of Chichester that he doesn't want to talk about. He also deleted emails that went between him and Chichester.'

'Did you manage to find out what Harding really thinks about Davidson and the situation? Davidson still doesn't want to reopen the case.'

'I think she's keen to get it right this time – she gave me the full autopsy reports – but at the same time she supports Davidson.'

'Covering her arse then . . .'

'Looks like it, Sarge. I'll talk to her again when I get back tomorrow. She wants me to let her know how he is.'

'Pass by me first. There's only one person Harding cares about. And only one back she's watching, and that's her own.'

'But she does care about doing her job, Sarge. She doesn't like getting things wrong.'

'No, well, good luck with getting to know Harding. It would take a braver man than me.'

'What time are we leaving tomorrow, Sarge?'

'Not me, Ebb . . . just you. You are a fresh pair of eyes, no preconceptions. You can see it as it is. Anyway, I'll be more use here. You alright to go on your own? You were trained as a FLO.'

'Yeah, but it was decided I wasn't really cut out for it.' She paused, turned towards the window. She was thinking. She caught her reflection in the glass. She looked like a frightened rabbit: all eyes. She looked away quickly. 'Okay, no problem.'

'Take an overnight bag. There'll be plenty of motels to stay in nearby. You'll be fine. Ring me.'

Ebony put down the phone and got into bed, pulling her duvet around her as she snuggled down for a few hours work. Tina knocked in the door.

'You free?'

'Sorry, Teen. Give me an hour or two and I'll take a break then. You okay?'

'Just need a girly goss and a catch-up that's all. I want to show you some of the other guys I've been looking at on the dating sites. Some really gorgeous ones – be great for you.'

'Okay, give me a while. I'll come and find you when I'm done.' Three hours later she heard Tina moving around in the bedroom below, getting ready for bed. Ebony felt a pang of guilt. She thought about getting up and going to say goodnight and spending ten minutes trawling through Tina's choice of men on the internet – men who were always flashy and fancied themselves much more than they did Tina. But Ebony knew it wouldn't be just ten minutes and she still had a lot of work to do. She'd gone through Carmichael's file a hundred times and still she hadn't found the answers she was looking for. Why would someone kill them in that way and why did they leave the little baby alive? She spread out the pictures of Louise and Chrissie and looked at them again. Her eyes went from one to another. Something was bothering her. Blood. Where was the blood? The women should have been lying in pools of it; it should have been everywhere. But it wasn't. She looked at the list of forensic samples that had been deemed to be cross-contaminated. In death the women had touched one another. Their backs had touched somehow. Ebony began re-writing her findings. What if the samples were not corrupted? It was getting light when she finally slept where she sat on the bed, surrounded by pictures of the dead.

Chapter 11

Carter came off the phone to Ebony and walked into the Major Incident Room. Robbo was sitting at his desk with his cafetière. When he saw Carter coming he slid his chair from one end of his desk, picked up a sheet of paper, and slid back.

'Here's how far I've got.' He read from the sheet in his hand: 'The vehicle in the driveway at Blackdown Barn: a man . . . Mr Arnold Williams . . . delivers the bi-monthly parish paper to Blackdown Barn. He remembers seeing a van in the driveway on several occasions. It was a large Transit type, almost like a Tourer, but regular-shaped, not fancy: no windows; it was white.'

'Number plate?'

'No . . . he says the back doors of the van were always covered.'

'We know its length. Find me a make and model. Use the moulds from the tyre tracks to see what tyres it took.'

Robbo pointed to the screen. Carter came round to have a look.

'I fed in the information from the tyre prints and it came up with a basic model of van; most of the major manufactures made a Transit-type vehicle like this. It's a working van rather than a run-around. The tyres indicate that it's less than three years old. Meant to carry a lot of weight.'

'Ebony says that when she went back to Rose Cottage she met a gardener there who says he repaired the gatepost after that night. It took out the whole upper section in a clean chunk. Could it be this van type?'

'There was no mention of that in the case file. I never saw a statement from him.'

'Yeah, I know. We need to get the exhibits from the Carmichael case back over here from the warehouse and see for ourselves.'

'So how's it going working with Ebony Willis?'

'Yeah . . . I'm sending her up on her own to interview Carmichael tomorrow; she's swatting up on the case tonight.'

Robbo gave him that look that said: *interesting but risky.*

'She'll be alright.' Carter sucked his finger where the cuticle was bleeding.

'Hopefully . . . She's a bright kid.'

'Funny how you see her as a kid.'

'Everyone's a kid to me. I'm not long after Davidson when it comes to retirement. Of course I don't have any choice, being a DC. He could stay on. You help solve this one, Dan, they should seriously consider you for promotion.'

'Maybe. I won't hold my breath. Just passing my exams doesn't seem to be enough. Ebony will probably get there before me.'

'Ebony's going to have to battle against prejudice. She's going to have to prove herself every step of the way if she hopes people will forget what happened to her. If she hadn't already joined the Force when it happened she would never have been allowed in.'

'That would have been a tragedy,' said Carter. 'I can see how much she loves it. She wants this career so badly. She'll make it, despite what she's been through – or maybe because of it.'

'Yeah,' said Robbo. 'She's a sponge when it comes to info, techno stuff. She's been asking me about the latest in this and that. Even though it's not her department.'

'You should have seen her around the bodies . . .' Carter smiled. 'She practically climbed in beside them to interview them.'

Robbo sat back in his chair, shook his head. 'You'd think seeing your mum stab someone forty-seven times would put you off bodies for life.'

Chapter 12

The sky was steely grey and the further north Ebony drove the thicker the snow fell. She wasn't a confident driver. She'd only taken her test when she wanted to join the Force and she didn't own a car. The hire car was new: a poppy red Renault Clio. It smelt much too clean and chemical-y and the unfamiliarity did little to reassure her that she was capable of driving in conditions that no amount of driving lessons could have prepared her for. It was already nearly dark at only two in the afternoon. Ebony looked at the sat nav for encouragement. It hadn't talked to her for ages, not since it sent her on several turnoffs and then abandoned her on what looked like a road that no one had used for a hundred years. The hedges rose to block her view of anything but the winding lane in front.

She needed a pee. She slowed right down at the entrance to a field then she got out and waded through the snow, knee deep in places. Crouching behind the hedge, she dropped her trousers and peed into the snow. The icy wind started her teeth chattering. She wasn't happy. She was a London girl, not meant to go more country than Kew Gardens. This was proper countryside. She cursed Carter. He had known it would be like this, miles from anywhere and anyone. She pulled up her pants and walked back to the car.

Just as she put the car into gear and began pulling away, a woman appeared at her window. She had eyebrow and nose piercings. She wore layers on layers, and wellington boots. Her henna-red hair fell in snow-flecked plaits from beneath a bobble hat.

'Hi . . .' Ebony wound down her window. 'I'm looking for a farm owned by a man called Callum Carmichael?'

The woman stared at Ebony for a few seconds, checking her out, before walking around the front of the car and opening the passenger door. She got in as if she had been waiting for a taxi, and Ebony was it.

'Go straight . . .' She took out a packet of tobacco and started rolling a cigarette. 'You a friend?'

'Of Carmichael's? Not really, just need to see him about something. You? Sorry . . . you can't smoke in here . . .'

'I'm not going to. I help him sometimes.' Ebony looked sideways at the woman. She was a 'once wild' teenager. She was pretty but neglected. She smelt of patchouli oil and bonfires. She was beginning to defrost, her plaits were now steaming. 'I help him with the lambing.'

'Is it lambing time now? It's the winter.'

'Carmichael produces lambs early. Saves buying foreign. People like to eat lamb for Easter. Got to be fattened in time. Not me. I never eat 'em. I know 'em all by name. Be like eating one of my own family.'

'What about him, Carmichael? Does he know them all by name?'

'He does but he pretends not to; it's easier to kill them that way.'

Carmichael stopped chopping wood to listen. Rusty, his Jack Russell terrier, had begun the low growl that signalled the approach of visitors. Carmichael put down his axe and came out of the log store. He wiped his brow on his shirtsleeve as he watched the car lights coming up the lane from half a mile away. He held his hand up for Rusty to be quiet. He glanced across at his rifle resting on the inside of the woodshed door.

Ebony turned the car into the yard, narrowly missing the wheelbarrow full of steaming horse manure, and came to a stop outside the stables. Rusty ran over, barking excitedly. Carmichael watched Bridget, his farm hand, and a young woman get out of the car; he made no attempt to call Rusty away. Ebony wasn't fazed. She lived in an area where pitbulls came out at night. She reached down to pet him. His barking turned into excited whines, his tail wagged. Bridget walked across the yard, head down, and merely glanced Carmichael's way as she said:

'Police . . . found her taking a piss in the lower field.'

'Inspector Callum Carmichael?' Ebony pretended she hadn't heard.

Carmichael didn't answer. He picked up the handles of the wheelbarrow and wheeled it across to the far end of the courtyard so that he could tip out its contents on to the dung heap.

'I need a few words please, sir.'

He put down the wheelbarrow and looked at her. 'ID?'

Ebony pulled out her warrant card and held it up for him to see. He appeared to look at her face rather than the card yet her name still seemed to register.

'DC Ebony Willis?'

'Yes . . .' Ebony replied.

He finished filling hay nets and tied them inside the horse's stall then he picked up his rifle from the wood-shed and walked past her.

'Follow me.'

Ebony had her eye on the gun. It was very like the rifles they used in the Police Force, with a shorter barrel and only a metre in length. But it was definitely made for hunting: it had a powerful looking scope attached. Judging by his eyesight and the way he'd read her warrant card, Ebony thought that he could probably hit her running at a mile away with or without a scope.

She followed him into the house. The farmhouse was Spartan, austere. It was certainly never going to make it onto the top of a biscuit tin.

'I won't take up much of your time, Mr Carmichael, and then I'll be on my way.' They walked through the tack room, up a step and into a stone-floored scullery. Carmichael propped the rifle next to him as he sat on a stool and pulled off his boots. He said nothing as he washed his hands in the sink.

He looked at her as he dried them on a towel above the sink.

'Relax . . . If I wanted to kill you I'd have done it by now.' She watched him with the same intense look she always had, but he didn't know her. He took it to be anxiety. 'Besides . . .' He hung the towel on a hook to the right of the sink. 'There's no way you'll be going anywhere tonight. The lane is almost impassable already; surprised you made it. In half an hour it will be sheet ice. In that car – you'll be lucky to get ten metres.' He wiped the mud and debris from the gun barrel with an oiled cloth. 'It will be more trouble to drag you out of a ditch than it will be to put you up for a night.'

He unclipped his hunting knife and placed it on the shelf. Walking up the few steps and into the kitchen he indicated that she should follow.

'You hungry?' He went across to the Aga and pulled the pot of stew from the hotplate. 'Sit down. Make yourself useful . . .' He set the loaf of bread and a knife in front of her on the scrubbed table top.

Ebony sat down and took the opportunity to look around the kitchen while Carmichael was busy. It looked like no one had decorated for a hundred years. It was clean and functional. It hadn't made it to the rustic chic pages of a magazine: no hanging copper pans or bunches of dried herbs. No unread recipe books. Carmichael walked past her carrying the logs he'd been chopping. She heard him stacking them beyond the kitchen. When he returned he took two bowls from an oak dresser and spooned in some stew. He opened two bottles of beer and placed one in front of her. Then he sat down opposite.

He didn't hide his scrutiny. Ebony wished she had a napkin, kitchen roll, anything; she'd splashed her chin and had wiped it lots of times but her hand still felt wet.

'You're very young.' He paused while breaking his bread open. 'How long have you been a detective?'

'Four years. I've been in the Force six altogether.' She looked at Carmichael's face just a few feet away across the table from her. She was re-reading his file in her head: the keenest marksman in the Metropolitan Police Force. His photo taken with the rest of the fire-arms team. His smile proud, his gaze steadfast. Thirteen years looked like twenty. He was weather-worn, bearded, sunburnt from the wind and the rain. Special Forces before the police: SBS. He had once taken out four members of the top Iraqi military. He had sat in one spot for a week and waited to kill one man.

'You've done well to get into the Murder Squad so quickly.'

'I have a degree in Criminal Justice and Law. I think that helped.' Ebony was feeling like the inexperienced copper she was. Carter must have known it would be like this. Why had he sent her on her own?

'There are lots of people with degrees but not every-one knows how to make them count in police work – or in everyday life.' He finished eating his stew before her and he sat back in his chair and watched her eat. She never left food. Carmichael continued to scrutinize her. 'So you could have chosen to go into a career in Crime Analysis instead or in Profiling? You could have gone into the law side of things?'

'I could have.'

'But you chose to go for less pay and longer hours and join the force?' For a minute he thought she wasn't going to answer; he could see her mind mulling things over. You could never accuse her of being loose-tongued. That was an admirable quality in Carmichael's books. He hated pointless chatter. He lived most of his life in silence out of choice. It seemed to him that he was the one asking the questions. She looked at him, her expression unchanged:

'I wanted a challenge.'

Carmichael smiled. 'Fair enough. What about your family? You're mixed race, aren't you?' She nodded as she dipped her bread into the stew. 'I know the name . . . Willis . . . you're the officer whose mother was convicted of murder? I read about it.'

She looked up and saw his eyes drilling into her.

'Yes.'

'Finished?' He stood and took her plate from her and stacked the dishes in the sink. She stared at his back. She wondered what he would ask her about it and what she would say when he did. But, when he turned back she could see he'd finished with the subject.

'Great stew,' she thanked him.

'One of my lambs.' Ebony wondered if it had had a name. 'This way . . .' He picked up a basket of logs and led the way into the sitting room. Apart from a sofa and an armchair, the only other piece of furniture was a desk in the corner. The fireplace dominated the room, ancient, imposing. A massive oak beam framed it. Carmichael stacked the logs either side of it. To the left of the fireplace was the doorway to the upstairs, to the right was a dresser. On it were several books about farming, lambing, looking after sheep. There was one about the Yorkshire Dales. There was another about medical procedures in the field. *The History of War*. The *Times Atlas* had a shelf all to itself. There were travel books about South America, Argentina. Above all the books she saw a photo of his wife and child. She recognized it from the case file.

He knew that she was looking at it. 'What do you want to ask me?' He began cracking small twigs for kindling.

'In the last twenty-four hours there's been a murder on the outskirts of London. We found a print that matches one at the cottage where your wife and child were killed.'

There was a pause of several seconds. Carmichael began constructing the fire: stacking the kindling against paper rolls.

'Do you have a name?' He reached to his right and pulled a long spill from a holder.

'No . . . We just have a match.'

'Where?' He picked a lighter from the dresser and lit the spill.

'Northwest London.'

'I said where?' He paused and half turned towards her but did not look at her.

'A converted barn near Totteridge.'

He lit the tight wads of newspaper beneath the kindling and fanned the flame, then he picked up two large logs from the side of the massive grate and propped them against the kindling. He rested an elbow on one knee as he watched the growing flame. The light from the fire cast harsh shadows in his lined face. For a big man his body moved gracefully. His hands were precise and quick as they moved to catch the flame and fan the fire. Ebony noticed that kind of thing. She was the opposite: always clumsy. She always felt awkward. Her bones were big, gangly. Her hands and feet were large. Her broad shoulders were too wide for summer dresses and petite pretty clothes. She should have been a runner. She should have been a basketball player; her dad was athletic. Her mum was academic. But her mum hadn't been clever when it came to choosing men and her dad hadn't run away fast enough.

'How many bodies?'

'Two . . . a woman and her baby.'

He moved the smouldering sticks into the flame. She had read his file: there was nothing Carmichael hadn't seen in the world; there was no nasty experience he hadn't been through. He was a methodical killer, a man who could kill to order. He could go into a frame of mind where he felt nothing for anyone. She saw the scars on his arms. There were white raised lines made by something she'd read about when she'd researched him. What did the term 'violent torture' mean? Amongst other things, it meant 'the scalpel'. Its knife-like electrode that cut, burnt and cauterized. She knew he would have suffered more from wounds that couldn't be seen on the surface. Ebony watched his movements and it struck her how gentle he was.

Carmichael sat back to give the fire a chance to take hold. He turned to look at her.

'Tell me about the victims.'

'The mother was mid-twenties, Caucasian, healthy, and had been pregnant before. The baby was about thirty-six weeks. The umbilical cord was cut. But it never took a breath.'

'No "missing persons" answering?'

She shook her head. 'Chief Superintendent Davidson is concentrating resources on finding that out.' She watched him prickle at the mention of Davidson's name.

Sparks sprayed out like fireworks and a burning scrap of wood landed on the rug in front of the hearth. He squashed it between finger and thumb.

'How was she killed?'

'We don't know yet.'

'I want to see the forensics report.'

Ebony didn't answer. She knew he wouldn't be allowed to.

'The man who we believe carried out the murders went under the name of Chichester. Does that mean anything to you?' Carmichael shook his head. 'Can you tell me what you remember about that day at Rose Cottage?'

He shook his head again. 'I try and remember as little as possible.' He looked away for a few minutes. The silence resounded round the room. He looked back. He searched her face. 'What does Davidson expect from me? He mishandled it from day one. He followed the wrong lines of enquiry. Whoever did it was long gone by the time he got his head out of his arse.' Carmichael raised his voice but then it softened just as quickly. 'Has he reopened my case?'

She shook her head. 'Not yet, but we are pushing for it. There is a lot of respect and loyalty for you in the department. People will do everything they can to get a result this time.'

He prodded the logs with the poker. 'I won't help Davidson just so that he can get a lucrative fucking retirement deal after he leaves the Force. Come back to me when the case is reopened.'

Ebony sat on the sofa, hugging her legs in close to keep warm. Bridget came in and stood in the doorway:

'I've finished feeding the animals. Does tha want me to stay?'

'We'll manage, thanks. How are you getting home?'

'I'm staying with my dad tonight; haven't been able to get to him for three weeks; I'll drive tractor across the fields.' Her eyes went back to Ebony . . . 'I'll be back tomorrow, in the morning . . . early . . .'

'Okay.'

Carmichael thanked her and then turned his attention on the catching fire. Bridget took a last look at Ebony and was gone. A draft of arctic air came around the room as the door swung behind her. Ebony shivered. Carmichael stood and went to a box chest at the far side of the room, opened it and pulled out a shawl. 'Here, put this round yourself.'

'Thanks.' She took it and wrapped it around her shoulders. 'It's beautiful.' It was hand crocheted. The intricate weave looked like thick lace.

'It's a nursing shawl. It was my wife's.'

Carmichael picked up the whisky bottle from the dresser. He poured out two shots and handed one to Ebony. He drank his whisky as he leant against the oak beam above the fireplace.

A few minutes passed as Ebony stared at the fire and Carmichael stared into his glass.

'Can I ask you some things about your past?'

'You can ask.'

'You were tortured in the Iraq war?'

'Yes.'

'Are you allowed to talk about it?'

'Allowed, yes, some of it anyway. But I don't choose to.'

'Can I ask you about what you did after you left the Special Boat Service? Where did you go?'

Carmichael moved the logs around on the fire. He pushed the small sticks into the flames. His fingers were hardened to the pain.

'I went travelling.'

'Where did you go? I've never been abroad.'

'Never?' She shook her head. 'Then I envy you. You have a world waiting for you out there.'

She smiled. 'Maybe one day.'

'I didn't go anywhere specific. I searched for answers. I never found them.' She looked at him with an expression that told him that wasn't going to be enough of an answer. 'South America, Africa, Europe. I told you I was searching.'

'Searching for answers to do with Louise and Sophie?'

'Yes. Mostly.'

'Did you find anything?' He shook his head.

She wrapped the shawl around herself and sipped the whisky. It wasn't a drink she liked and she wasn't much of a drinker, but the Scotch warmed her. She looked at him.

'You resigned. Why didn't you fight it? You have a lot of support from serving officers in the MET.'

He threw another log on the fire. Rusty jumped up onto the sofa next to Ebony. She was grateful for the heat of his small body as he lay across her lap. Carmichael shook his head, stared into the fire.

'My mind went into meltdown.' The fire crackled. 'I trusted those in charge to think for me . . . big mistake.'

'Did you ever come up with a motive for the murders?'

He shook his head. 'I delved into Louise's life before she met me . . . nothing. Nothing she hadn't told me.'

'What about Chrissie?'

'She studied medicine at Edinburgh. She went off travelling for a year. She got pregnant – by accident or by design, I don't know.'

'Did you meet her father?'

'Yes . . . at the funeral. James Martingale is an arrogant fuck but you can't argue with the amount of money he puts back into charities. Chrissie had an older half sister; I never met her.'

'Were they here in the UK when the murders happened?'

'No. Did you see his statement?'

'Yes. I read it last night. I just wanted to hear things from you.'

He looked at her and almost smiled; deep creases were indented either side of his face. Ebony saw a glimpse of the handsome man of thirteen years earlier. 'So . . . at least I'm not the chief suspect in your mind, otherwise you wouldn't have come here alone. Thanks. It's a solid gesture . . . it's been noted.'

Ebony stroked Rusty's velvety ears. He sighed. The room felt warmer.

'Why didn't you go there, that night, to pick them up like you were supposed to?'

'I got drunk. Blind, steaming drunk.' He spoke softly as he stared into the fire.

'On your own?'

'Yes. No one walks away from war and isn't affected by it. You wouldn't be human. You eat, sleep and pray to stay alive and see your family again but, when you do, you don't know which is the reality any more. You live in constant alert mode and fear and nothing is real any more. Louise understood me when no one else did ... and Sophie gave me a purpose to my life ... but ... sometimes I needed to be alone. Sometimes my memories are too much for me. I thought they needed a break from me too ... I know how difficult it was sometimes.'

'Was your marriage okay?'

He looked at her, surprised. 'You mean about my affair?

She nodded. 'Just seems an odd thing seeing that you were a family man.'

'What you mean is: was it so out of character that it means if I could do that, I could do anything?'

'No, not really. I just would like to understand what made you do it.'

He prodded the fire with a poker as he talked: 'I'd like to say I really understood it, but I don't. I had a brief affair with a woman I worked with. I let my guard down. I knew we were attracted to one another, had been for a long time and I kept well away from her until I had no choice but to see her every day, all day, all night. We ended up working together, staying late, we ended up in bed. She wanted it to happen, badly, and I was going through a phase of feeling unworthy, self-destructive. You destroy what you treasure most because you don't think it can be real, it can't last. I was guilty of believing I didn't deserve Louise or Sophie. I regretted it as soon as I did it. It was one night, that was all. I told Louise. I couldn't have kept it from her. Maybe I should have.'

'How did Louise react?'

'She considered leaving me, I know. She knew I was sorry. I wasn't sure whether things would ever be the same between us or that she could ever forgive me.'

'When you arrived that day at Rose Cottage and you saw what had happened. When you looked at the bodies . . .'

He bowed his head. 'Jesus . . .'

'I'm sorry . . .'

'Don't be.' He looked up and smiled sadly. 'You have a job to do.'

'Can I ask you why you moved the bodies?'

'I moved Sophie . . .'

'You didn't move the others at all?'

He shook his head as he swallowed the last of his whisky and wiped his burning mouth. He stared into the fire as he talked. 'I got to the cottage and knew something was wrong even before I had parked the car. The curtains in the lounge were closed. The door was open. I saw Chrissie first. I walked into the kitchen and found Louise: butchered.' He looked into the fire and coughed to clear his throat and his head before going on. 'I looked around and I called Sophie's name. Then I ran upstairs and found the baby, Adam, first;

he was asleep, doped, but alive, and I had a few seconds' hope that I would find my daughter . . .' He swallowed, shook his head. 'They cut her throat.' He stared at the fire. His voice dropped until it was barely audible over the hiss and crackle of the burning wood. 'I know I shouldn't have touched the crime scene but this wasn't a crime scene; this was everything in the world I cared about and it had gone. These were my angels. I carried her down to lie next to her mother.' He turned to look at Ebony and shook his head to clear it. 'I don't know why they did it but no matter what anyone says, if you ask me, it was premeditated, it was planned. There was a reason why my family died. Now we know that's true because they're back and killing again.' The firelight reflected in his eyes. 'I've waited a long time for this day to come.'

As he stared at Ebony she saw the eyes of a troubled mind that was never going to find peace. She'd seen it all her life. It was the look of someone not destined ever to live a normal life and be happy. The eyes were full of demons and nightmares. Ebony had seen eyes like that before, in the tortured souls that looked at her when she went to visit her mother. Broadmoor was full of them. Her mother was one. Rusty barked; Ebony jumped. He stood alert on the sofa and tilted his head to listen to some noise from outside. Carmichael held up his hand to silence him. '*Stay.*'

'What is it?' Ebony whispered.

Rusty jumped down from the sofa. Carmichael put his foot out to stop him but Rusty jumped over it. 'Rusty . . . COME!' Carmichael picked up his rifle as he ran after the dog, but Rusty was already out of the door.

Ebony threw her coat on and ran towards the barn and the dreadful sound: the lambs like babies with their high-pitched cries and the deeper distressed bleating of their mothers trying to protect them.

The barn door was open. Inside the sheep were stampeding round their pens and the bodies of the killed lambs were littered in the straw. She stopped in the doorway. Carmichael's face was murderous as he turned towards her, rifle in his hand. He swung away from her at the sound of snarling and yelping coming from the rear of the barn. He started running towards the sound, calling Rusty's name as the sound of a dog's growling turned to squeals of pain. The squealing stopped and an eerie silence fell in the barn as Carmichael searched the pens. The sheep scattered. He found what he was looking for. Rusty's body looked as if someone had tried to skin it. Carmichael placed his hands beneath him and lifted Rusty out of the blood-covered straw. He carried him into the house.

The dog fox stopped on the brow of the hill and looked back down at the farmhouse. He saw the big man carrying the dying dog. The dog's warm blood was on his mouth. Its flesh was in his teeth. He saw the pheasant that Carmichael had set to trap him, still hanging there, swinging now. Above him his mate stood guard, in her mouth the body of a newborn lamb.

Chapter 13

Carmichael laid Rusty on the kitchen table.

'Look after him while I fetch the medical kit.'

He came back with an armful of neatly folded towels, old but clean, and a medical chest.

'What can I do?' Ebony asked.

Carmichael took out his knife and cut into the material so he could tear them into pressure bandages. 'Lie him on the towels. I'll be back in a minute.'

Carmichael disappeared. Ebony lifted up Rusty's limp body, wet with blood, his flesh exposed, ripped over his flank and back. The fox had tried to tear him apart. Carmichael returned with a bowl of warm salted water and for the next two hours they worked together to sew Rusty up.

Carmichael pushed his hair back from his tired eyes. 'He will survive or not.' He picked Rusty up and lay him in his basket. He was just about alive. 'There's nothing more we can do: I don't have any antibiotics to give him. I need to go out. Leave him here and go to bed. Upstairs, first door on the right. Bathroom's the second one. It's primitive but it's clean.' Carmichael was rubbing soot into his face. He smelt like he'd rolled in a dead animal and then slept on a dung heap. Ebony heard him linger in the tack room. Then he was gone.

In the lounge the fire was dying down. Ebony put another few logs on it and covered Rusty with a clean towel. He didn't stir.

She went across to the dresser and picked up the photo of Louise and Sophie and wondered how many times Carmichael had held this photo in the lonely evenings he spent there on his own. Apart from the shelves with their few books, his writing desk was the only other personal addition to the room: neat, plain and functional, like the rest of the house. Sitting on the top of it was an old silver tankard used as a penholder and, the most incongruous thing in the room, his laptop, the newest and the best piece of kit. She went to open it and then stopped herself. Whatever she found on there it would have been left there on purpose, just for her to find. Then he would lose his trust for her. Already she understood that much about him. She looked around: the desk had one long thin drawer under its top. Ebony gave it a little rattle to see if it would open. But it was locked. After a last check on Rusty Ebony opened the door to the upstairs. At the top of the landing there was the guest room on her right and then the bathroom. The bathroom was warm because it was above the Aga in the kitchen. Ebony brushed her teeth and opened cupboards. What little there was, was laid out in military order: toothbrush, paste, floss, antiseptic cream. Every surface was wiped and spotless on the old shelves that looked like they had been put up by someone a hundred years before. Carmichael had never put his stamp on the house: he was just a visitor. When Ebony emerged from the bathroom she opened the door opposite it, across the landing. The room smelt of saddle soap and liniment and a whiff of sheep. The bed was made with military creases. In the corner there was a cloth wardrobe that looked like it had been a temporary measure but never replaced. Now it was on its last legs. He hadn't spent money on any of it, thought Ebony. If Carmichael had inherited all his wife's large fortune then he hadn't spent it on himself. Inside the wardrobe was a shelf stacked with small piles of perfectly folded T-shirts and sweaters. On the top of the wardrobe was a rifle bag.

She closed the door quietly and went back to the guest bedroom at the top of the stairs. Inside the room it looked like Carmichael had gathered anything feminine from all over the house and put it in there. There were old flowered curtains and peeling rose wallpaper. There was an old fifties dressing table, white, with a cracked, mottled mirror and a matching freestanding wardrobe that must have been someone's idea of chic at one time. She turned the small brass handle on the wardrobe door and cringed as it squeaked on its hinges. She paused, no sound from anywhere in the house. She was pretty sure Carmichael would hear her if he was back inside. Inside the wardrobe were a few padded hangers hanging empty from the brass rail and on the floor were boxes covered by a tartan blanket. Ebony peeled the blanket aside and carefully prized open one of the two boxes. Inside it was packed neatly with mementos, knick-knacks. She lifted out a photo album that was resting on the top and turned the pages of Carmichael's former life. It started with Christmas and Sophie standing by a snowman. It was spring by the end of the album. Sophie was running towards the camera; Louise was running after her laughing. The next one, Louise must have taken. It was a strange sight to look at Carmichael laughing in the photo. In the spring photos Louise and Sophie were wearing the same clothes as in the photo downstairs. Must have been his last recorded happy day with them. It must have been some of the last photos they ever took as a family. After she'd made up the bed from a neatly folded pile of bedding left on top of it, she phoned Carter.

'Don't seem to be any motels round here, Sarge.'

'Yeah . . . knew you'd be alright, Ebb. What is he like then? What do you think of him?'

'You'd like him: he's straight out of a Call of Duty game.'

'Is he going to be useful to us?'

She paused; her eyes settled on the photo of Louise and Sophie.

'*Useful* probably isn't the right way to put it. He's living in limbo. His whole past is locked away in boxes. He lives very frugally, as if he's about to move on any minute. He's a man in no-man's land.'

'So he couldn't add anything to his original statement?'

'He didn't exactly refuse. He started to tell me what happened when he went into Rose cottage and found them but then his dog got savaged and he's gone out to try and kill the thing that did it.'

'Shit . . . told you, Ebb, it's dog-eat-dog out there in the country. Do you think he knows stuff we don't?'

'I don't know. He lives like a hermit. He doesn't have anything in his sitting room except some books on faraway places and sheep-farming. His laptop is his only expensive piece of kit. But it's the best: the newest on the market. He has no telly, no entertainment except that. All he has is his photo of his wife and child and the internet.'

'We need to know everything he does. I need you to get him on our side, Ebb. You can bet your life when you leave him tomorrow he is going to be working on this twenty-four seven. I need you to gain his trust. Whatever he finds out we want to know.'

'I'm not sure I was the best person to come up here. Why did you think he would trust me? '

'Because he doesn't trust easily and neither do you; and both of you have good reason.'

When Ebony came off the phone to Carter her mobile rang. She looked at the number on the screen and closed her eyes, took a breath.

'Hello, Mum.'

'You didn't come. I waited for two hours, just sat there, waiting . . .'

'I told you I wouldn't be able to come for a couple of weeks, Mum. I'm sorry. We have a lot going on at work. Did you get the parcel? Did you have a good birthday?'

'No . . . they wouldn't give it to me. They accused me of stuff again. I didn't do it.' Her voice rose an octave or two as she went into child mode. 'How can

I have a good birthday? My life isn't worth living. I'd rather be dead. No one loves me. No one cares.'

Ebony squeezed her eyes shut and her fingers dug into the side of her face without her realizing.

'Don't worry, Mum. I'll find out what happened to it. Don't worry about anything. I'll sort it and I'll come and see you as soon as I get another visiting order. I love you, Mum.' The phone went dead.

Chapter 14

Carmichael climbed over the five-bar gate that led into the top field. He jumped silently down the other side, crouched and waited, watching for movement. The last shower of snow lay untouched on the ground. It gave off a light all of its own. Like walking on the surface of a full moon. He was glad to leave the house. He could only think alone. Ebony's presence in the house disturbed him. Working together to patch up Rusty had felt too close, too intimate for Carmichael. Out of nowhere Ebony had entered his world, bringing with her the past. She smelt of the police station. She had the look that he remembered. She had the hunger to make a difference that he'd felt once.

He kept to the shelter of the hedge as he made his way up the side of the field. The tracks were clear in the snow; two foxes had come this way. He crouched low and looked towards where they had stopped to assess the situation. And there Carmichael turned and looked back down to his farm. Ebony's red hire car was a new addition to the familiar scene. He saw the outline of the pheasant hanging there. He knew the foxes would have seen the same. They would have waited and considered their strategy there but not stopped for long – fresh tracks were leading away from the hedge and across the field; here they separated. They had left the pheasant hanging in pursuit of richer pickings. Carmichael kept on his route around the edge of the field, keeping his profile low. He moved cautiously, with a measured pace. He came to the top corner of the field and looked across. Now, beneath him, he saw the dog fox's silhouette; its moon shadow in the snow.

He stood still and watched as the fox began to move and loop around and down the opposite side of the field, making its way back down to its lair. Carmichael stayed very still. He would position himself and wait until it came back into his line of fire. He knew the fox wouldn't be able to smell him. He was camouflaged with its own scent, excrement from an old den. But the fox would hear him. He had to be ready for one perfect shot. He lifted the rifle to his shoulder. He looked through his night scope and saw the animal's sinewy shoulders moving athletically, stealthily as it walked sure-footed across the snow and down. Then it stopped. It turned his way. Its eyes flashed in the dark at the same time as the bullet flashed through the air.

Chapter 15

Harding took the foetus from its drawer in the mortuary, held it in her hands and placed it in the scales. Three pounds two ounces. Fi was a good weight at thirty-six weeks; the last couple of weeks would have seen her put on a few more pounds. Things didn't usually affect Harding; she hadn't a maternal bone in her body, but the waste of life before it had ever had a chance was symbolically terrible somehow. No one ever intended this baby to take its first breath. Jo Harding turned from studying the X-rays and watched Mathew the diener as he delicately laid out the tools for the next autopsy. She loved his hands: they were expert, long-fingered, big but subtle in their touch.

He looked across at her. 'I had a call to say that some of the forensic results for Fi are back, Doctor Harding. They've been emailed to you.' Mathew didn't mind working late. He was softly spoken, soft-mannered. Mathew had had many women in his life. They trusted him. He was their friend and he was quietly confident and knew when to wait and when to listen. Someone like Harding made a welcome change for him. He knew if they continued working late into the night they would have many more nights together.

Harding had more energy and enthusiasm than any woman Mathew had ever slept with. She was physical with him. She was angry inside. He would learn a lot from her. He knew he had to enjoy it while it lasted. When she tired of him there would be a new posting for him and a new diener for her.

She walked back to her desk and checked her emails. She printed the results and snatched them up in one hand, car keys in the other. She turned to Mathew:

'You don't have to stay.'

'That's okay. I'll hang around.'

'Please yourself.'

Harding went out to the consultants' car park and pressed the key fob on her red Audi TT. She drove the short distance over to Fletcher House to take the news to Davidson.

As Carter passed Harding on her way out of Davidson's office she had a smile on her face that was a mixture of smug and satisfied. He wondered whether he'd find Davidson with his pants round his ankles or hanging from the ceiling . . . he wondered which scenario would do it for Harding. Carter definitely did nothing for her. She either liked boys wet behind the ears and half her age like Mathew her diener or she liked men with power and position: men with a lot to lose, like Davidson. Carter was grateful he was neither. He had enough troubles in his private life. He'd been faithful to Cabrina . . . not an easy thing for him. The thought of moving on, starting again, wasn't easy either.

He knocked and Davidson called for him to come in. Davidson looked fired up. He was almost smiling. He motioned for them to take a seat and then he handed Carter a file across the desk. Clipped to the front page was a mug shot of a man with designer stubble over a less than handsome face.

'This is the father of our dead baby . . . His name is Sonny Ferguson. Father was an old East End villain, name of Dexter.'

'Yeah . . . I recognize him. His dad was still around up until a few years ago.'

'Yes. Dexter ruled Soho for twenty years. When Dexter got killed Sonny took over but he isn't the man his father was, thank God. He hasn't the brains. Bit by bit he's lost Dexter's hold on the drug empire. Now he concentrates on people-trafficking.'

Davidson waited a few minutes for Carter to finish reading the front page of the file then he pushed another photo across to him. It was a shot of Sonny talking to a slighter, older man outside a club.

'His DNA is on file because he was accused of raping a seventeen-year-old at the beginning of his career. It went to trial but the girl dropped the charges at the last minute. This photo was taken in the last year. It was a surveillance operation by MIT 10 into the use of trafficked women in clip joints in Soho. This is outside Digger Cain's club on Brewer Street. Digger has a warren of clip joints going in Soho. As soon as we shut one down another three spring up. He was caught on camera then. The Crown Prosecution Service decided there was insufficient evidence to bring a conviction. Digger tidied up his act, on the surface. We know Sonny was providing Digger with trafficked girls as escorts and we believe he still is. Word is Sonny and Digger together provide the UK clip joints with their girls from the Eastern bloc.'

'It would fit for Silvia if she was trafficked, raped,' said Carter. 'But Sonny's twenty-eight; he's too young to have been around when the Carmichael murders happened. Plus . . . he doesn't fit the type we are looking for – Chichester.'

'He may not be Chichester.' replied Davidson.'But he has questions to answer, not least how the mother of his child came to be buried under the patio.'

'Yes, sir.'

'In the last year Sonny has been narrowing down his enterprise; mainly because he's being squeezed hard by the new gangs. Some of them have taken over the clubs north of London. We know he still has business with Digger though; he goes in there most evenings.

'Is the surveillance cell still in operation? Do we have an undercover officer available, sir?'

'No. But maybe we can still use the building opposite. Find out.' Davidson reclaimed the photos on his desk, placed them together. 'And find Sonny.'

Chapter 16

Carmichael watched Ebony drive away down the lane. He watched the red dot of her car follow the undulations of the land until it disappeared from sight. Then he took out his phone and looked at the screen as he waited for it to respond.

Ebony pulled over to reset her sat nav to get back to the station. As she did so her phone lit up in her bag. Carmichael looked at his screen. It was asking him for an instruction. Did he want to test the program? *Yes he did.* Did he want to turn on the microphone? *Yes he did.* He put the phone to his ear and listened. He heard Ebony talk to herself as she read out the instructions for getting to the airport and keyed them into the sat nav.

Carmichael pressed 'finish' on the screen and he turned away from watching the lane. He took a deep breath of the cold fresh air and briefly closed his eyes to the low winter sun. Then he headed up over the gate to the paddock and walked up towards the top of the hill, from where he could see for miles. Rosie followed him up there. He sat on the trunk of a fallen tree that he planned to clear away in the spring and Rosie jumped up beside him. This was his favourite place on the farm. From here he could see across the magnificent Dales. Here he could lift his face to the sky and know that there was nothing between him and the clouds above. On the starry summer nights, when the heat and the memories would not let him sleep, he'd sat out there alone on his hilltop many times. Thirteen summers, thirteen springs, and now, on this winter's day, he knew what it had all been for. He knew where he belonged. He said farewell to his farm.

He walked back inside his house, through to the sitting room and his gun cupboard. He took out his Steyr Scout rifle, laid everything on the kitchen table and took out his cleaning kit. Spreading the lubricating oil on a cloth, he worked it into the metal. He cleaned the barrel with rod and cloth. Afterwards he went upstairs to his bedroom and pulled down the gun bag from the top of his wardrobe. Inside it was a fleecy moisture-proof lining. He brought it back down to the kitchen and packed the rifle inside along with his hunting knife and some basic medical supplies. When he'd finished he went into the sitting room and sat at his writing desk, took out the key from its hiding place in the false bottom on the tankard and unlocked the drawer. Inside was a journal: a woman's diary. 'Louise Carmichael' was written on the front. He didn't open it. He knew what was written in it. He kept is as a reminder that he had betrayed her. It was still splattered with her blood.

Chapter 17

By three in the afternoon Ebony was back at her desk in Fletcher House, with Jeanie working across from her. Carter had swapped his desk and now he sat back to back with her in the ETO. He swivelled his chair around to talk to her.

'Did you know that Carmichael speaks Spanish, Ebb?' Ebony didn't even ask what had prompted his question. She had become used to the way Carter's brain worked by now. He liked to think and talk at the same time, throw the ideas out in the air and see what they sounded like; his thoughts didn't always follow one another. 'Why did he move his daughter – do you know?'

'He said he didn't see it as a crime scene, more personal. He admits he lost control: broke down. But he didn't move the other women. He also admits the affair, a short-lived thing, and puts it down to being self-destructive.'

Robbo came into the ETO and walked across. 'You survived a night in the wild then, Ebb?' He pulled up a chair between Ebony and Carter. 'Why didn't he show up that night, Ebb? What did he say?'

'He got drunk . . . alone.'

'Well . . .' Robbo chipped in. 'The killers can't have known he wouldn't turn up . . . so Louise and Sophie were never meant to be the target: they were never meant to be there. Chrissie was. She rented the cottage. She chose her guests. What did he say about Chrissie?'

'He said he didn't know her well. She was his wife's friend. She was a very private person, nervous around men. They were never in a position where she would think of opening up.'

'He said that, did he? That's not what I heard,' said Robbo. 'I heard Louise and Chrissie became friends via Carmichael. Chrissie was someone he met when he was in the SBS. She was called out to an emergency and they met then, kept in touch. Maybe her father James Martingale will know. Although I doubt it. I don't think Chrissie Newton got on with her dad.'

Ebony was thinking things through; she had that horrible feeling that she'd been lied to.

Robbo enlarged a photo on the PC screen.

'How would you like to look like that at sixty-eight? This is James Martingale.'

'Very Pierce Brosnan,' said Carter.

Robbo scrolled down the screen:

'I've been finding out about him. He donates huge amounts to research facilities in universities around the UK. He's a very wealthy man. I've found pages and pages on Google; none of which says anything personal. I haven't come across any angry clients or court cases but, I did see an interesting guest list for the last annual dinner party for the top brass of Martingale's Mansfield Group. Guess who was on the top table?'

Carter shook his head.

Robbo's eyes opened wide behind his wire-rimmed glasses. He mouthed, 'Davidson.'

'Shit. You're joking.'

Robbo shook his head, grinning. 'I would say he's been offered a very lucrative deal to sit on the board when he retires. Any trouble, he's going to be able to sort it with his old pals he's made over the years in the Force. When it comes to licensing or planning permission, for instance. If you're an ex-chief super-intendent in the MET people are going to listen to you.'

'No shit . . .'

'He's not the only one that Martingale is courting. Harding has received quite a bit over the years from Martingale and the Chrissie Newton Foundation.' Robbo brought up a Google search. *Top surgeon donates new dialysis machine to NHS hospital.* 'He gives a lot of laboratory equipment to Doctor Harding and her Pathology unit.'

'No wonder Davidson's not so keen on reopening the case . . . embarrassing to haul your prospective boss over the coals,' said Carter. 'But what's happen-ing about the surveillance on Digger's club . . . any news about Sonny?'

'We're hoping to move cameras into the flat oppo-site: it'll take two days to get permission and set up. We should have a good chance of finding Sonny. I've managed to get quite a lot of info on him from vari-ous UCs working on drugs seizures in the last two years. He has a big coke habit. Sonny's a party animal. He does the circuit of all the clubs almost every night.

Sometimes see him with a woman ... different one every time.'

'What about in his organization?'

Robbo shook his head. 'He works alone at this end but he relies on a network of agents and couriers and sub-lieutenants around here and Eastern Europe. He finds a safe house to bring the girls in, stays in it for a few months, then finds somewhere else.' Robbo handed round photos of Sonny taken from surveillance cameras and CCTV footage. His black leather jacket and broad shoulders were recognizable in most of the photos. 'He's a big fish in a small pond: a creature of habit. Sonny goes to see Digger most evenings as he makes his rounds of the dealers and the lap dancing clubs. Over the years he's built up a close relationship with Digger. Plus Digger was a great pal of Sonny's father.'

'Maybe there's a father-son relationship going on there?' said Jeanie.

'Maybe, but I doubt either of them goes so far as to actually feel affection. Both of them have been linked to violent crimes in the past. Here's a picture of Digger.'

Robbo gave them a photo of a slim, dark-haired man in his sixties coming out of Cain's.

'Smart-looking guy.' said Carter, 'he's got the same look as Martingale.'

'Yeah, definitely. In his early days Digger could have given Tony Curtis a run for his money in the looks department – now he's more of an ageing Dirk Bogarde. An immaculate dresser. His suits are made in Savile Row; his shoes handmade in Italy. Digger has pretensions of being a tumble-down-toff but it had never been proven. His mother was a colourful figure in Soho. She ran one of the first high-class call girl rings. She supplied London's rich and famous with girls. She made enough money to send Digger to private school and he went on to Oxford to study English, but he came back to his roots in the end.'

'What's his sexuality?' asked Jeanie.

'Digger likes slim nubile boys.' He placed another photo on the desk. It was one of Sonny and Digger together walking towards Sonny's car on Brewer Street.

'Digger keeps Sonny in business. Digger says he doesn't take trafficked girls any more but he's lying. He doesn't put them on show any more, but he has escort agencies and brothels that spring up all over the place. Sources say that Sonny just gets the girls then unloads them and gets another lot. Digger does the rest. He puts them to work.'

'And,' said Carter, 'Sonny's also been responsible for breaking the girls when they get here: it's a good explanation why Silvia was carrying his child. Do you have an address for him, Robbo?'

'Yes . . . Lives with his mum in Southwark. At least, he gives that address.'

'Is Martingale here in the UK?' Carter pressed for a print out of the photo of Martingale. '

'Yes, he is at the moment. He's working out of his hospital, the Mansfield, in Hammersmith.'

'Well, while we wait for the surveillance on Sonny to be organized, we'll pay Martingale a visit – see if he can tell us any more about his daughter.'

'Will we need to get permission from Davidson, Sarge?' asked Ebony.

'If you ask . . . you won't get,' said Robbo.

'Better not to ask then,' Carter grinned. 'Let's go. Rock 'n' Roll, Ebb.'

Chapter 18

It was five p.m. when Carter and Ebony drove into a broad well-maintained car park. The snow had been cleared and piled into the corners. Perfectly even-sized pine trees bordered the car park. They looked as if they'd been ordered from a catalogue and arrived fully grown. There were a few cars in the staff and consultants' section, half a dozen more in the patients' ample parking area.

'Not like your NHS car parks. What did Robbo say this place specializes in, Ebb?'

'It's a general private hospital, Sarge. You can come here if you need a facelift or bypass surgery, but the Mansfield Group is best known for private cosmetic work.'

They walked across to the entrance, up the steps and through two sets of glass doors. The lady on the reception desk had *Ivy Morell* on her name badge.

'Ivy. Beautiful name.' Carter smiled at her and showed his warrant card. She blushed like a schoolgirl. 'You mind telling Mr Martingale we're here to see him please, Ivy?'

She showed them through to a waiting area where Nikki, Martingale's PA, greeted them. She was perfectly groomed, her hair swept back into a sleek chignon. Carter was captivated. She was not interested. Ebony watched amused as she realized that Carter had a thing for ice maidens.

'Mr Martingale will see you now.'

Ebony watched her as she hovered in the doorway. She didn't take her eyes from her boss. There was only one man she cared about. Carter would be disappointed.

'Thank you for seeing us, sir.'

Martingale's office was dark walnut and heavy leather. His desk was in front of a wall of windows with integral louvred blinds, adjusted to allow the right amount of sunlight into the room. A single orchid was just beginning to flower pale pink. He sat back in his Italian leather chair and swivelled it slightly back and forth as he watched them enter. He had a handsome, lightly tanned face which was creased with deep laughter lines, and thick salt and pepper hair. His cuffs were rolled up and he wore a platinum sports Rolex on his wrist, its blue face bright against the silver hairs on his arm. He had the look of a man between rounds of golf.

'I am happy to help. Please sit down. I must apologize, though . . .' Martingale smiled. 'I have a full list today in theatre and a patient being prepped at the moment so I can give you ten minutes. What is it about?'

'I appreciate that . . . we won't keep you long . . . we just thought we should update you on recent events that have relevance to your daughter's case.'

Martingale pressed a button: 'Hold all my calls and stall theatre for me please.' He turned back to Carter.

'Please do go on. I've waited a long time for news about my daughter's case. Did you find fresh evidence?'

'We have a connection to it. The body of a woman and an infant have been found murdered at a house north of London.'

'Is the woman connected to Chrissie in some way?'

'We don't know yet: we haven't been able to identify her. We are not sure whether she's from the UK. She could possibly be a trafficked victim brought over here to work in the clubs.'

'So what is it that connects her to my daughter's murder?'

'We found a fingerprint that matches one from Rose Cottage. It's early days but it means that whoever killed your daughter is here in London.'

'And still killing.'

'Yes.'

Martingale sat deep in thought.

'I appreciate it's a shock, sir; a reminder of what happened; but it's also a chance for us to catch them this time.'

'I hope so. What do you want me to do?'

'We just need to ask you some questions. We want to take a fresh look at events thirteen years ago. Reading the notes isn't the same as getting it from the horse's mouth . . . as it were . . .'

'Is the case being reopened? Did Chief Superintendent Davidson send you?'

'No, sir. Chief Superintendent Davidson didn't send us. I am in charge of re-examining the facts surrounding the case but we are not re-opening it at this time. He believes we will get the best results from solving the current case. I just wanted to make sure you were kept informed from the beginning.'

'Okay . . . well . . . thank you. Tell Davidson I will be only too pleased to help.'

'That's very kind. I just want to go over a few things with you. Did you then or in the last thirteen years ever think that you might have stumbled on a reason why Chrissie was murdered?'

'No. I will never understand it. She was a young woman beginning a career that she'd studied hard for. She had a new baby; she'd just started on life's journey. I could not and I cannot think of a reason why someone would kill her.'

'What about her baby son Adam – he survived Rose Cottage and the attack. Do you ever see your grandson?'

'Unfortunately not. I would have loved to have him live with me but my daughter and I were not on the best of terms at the time of her death.'

'Where is Adam now?'

While Carter asked the questions Ebony looked out of the window. She watched a taxi turn into the car park and head round to the back of the hospital out of view.

'I can't help you there, I'm sorry. I don't know.'

'But you must have some contact of some kind.'

'I am sent an update every year and I pay into a fund for his schooling and his welfare. He will always be well provided for. I hope that one day he will ask to see me and get to know me.'

'How did that happen?' Ebony asked, speaking for the first time. 'Did Christine make a will saying he wasn't to live with you?'

'Not quite.' Martingale allowed a little frost to creep into his voice. 'She named Louise Carmichael as her first choice of guardian in the event of her death. Failing that, Adam was to be put up for adoption.' Martingale eased his strained expression slightly. 'I cannot tell you how much it has troubled me that my daughter and I did not have the best of relations when she died. I thought we would have time to make up for all those lost years. I left it too late. I threw myself into my work after her mother left and, as she made it so difficult for me to see Chrissie, I gave up too easily. Her mother Maria was a troubled soul. She kept my daughter from me all those years.'

'What was Chrissie like?' asked Ebony.

'She was a steady girl. She wasn't beautiful like Maria. But Maria's looks never brought her happiness. Looks are overrated.' His eyes stayed on Ebony.

'When you attended Louise and Sophie Carmichael's funeral, Mr Martingale, did you meet Callum Carmichael then?' asked Carter.

'I think so. The police officer? Yes . . . I did, briefly: tall, military type. I went there to pay my respects. I didn't stay long. I felt for him . . . such a tragedy. I remember he stood silent. No emotions. No feelings. In shock, I suppose.'

'Must have been a very difficult time for you all,' said Carter.

'The most stressful time in my life . . . terrible.'

'Mr Martingale, did you ever think that with all your success you might have made enemies?' Carter asked. Ebony had gone quiet.

'It would be impossible for me to say categorically no. But I can't see why I would have . . . but people sometimes don't understand what you're trying to do, trying to achieve.'

'You've built an empire, haven't you? Hospitals all over the world?'

Martingale smiled, embarrassed. 'I feel proud of what my team and I have achieved but I wouldn't go so far as to call it an empire.'

'Do you have any other businesses apart from the Mansfield group?'

'All my other business enterprises are connected with the hospitals.'

'Would that be research, that kind of thing?'

Martingale was half watching Ebony as Carter asked the questions. He could see her eyes taking in every detail of the room.

'Research? Yes.' Martingale answered. 'That is exactly the kind of thing.' He smiled at Carter. 'Sometimes it's easier to set up a company and manage supplies and sourcing machinery, transporting goods et cetera oneself. Sometimes it's necessary to run the whole show from start to finish to get the job done properly, wouldn't you agree, Sergeant?'

Ebony switched her attention back to Martingale. 'Totally.' Carter nodded enthusiastically. 'Is it possible to have a list of those companies you're involved in then, sir?' Martingale looked a little surprised at the request. 'It's just that we have to consider the possibility that these murderers have followed you here. We want to keep you safe.'

'Of course. I'll get my accountant, Justin, to prepare that for you. It will take a few days.'

'Just a profile, an overall picture . . . if you wouldn't mind.'

His PA knocked and entered as Carter asked:

'One last thing, sir; I appreciate you're a very busy man. Have you ever heard of a person going by the name of Chichester?'

Martingale shook his head. 'Sorry.'

'What about Digger Cain or Sonny Ferguson?'

'No, I'm sorry. I've never heard of those names.'

'Mr Martingale . . . I'm sorry to interrupt. The patient is deteriorating. He's quite poorly.'

'Okay. I'm coming. Please excuse me.' Martingale turned to them with a professional smile. 'It's an emergency. One of my staff's children is in need of an appendectomy.' He opened a box on the desktop and took out a business card. 'Here is my private number.' He gave the card to Carter. 'Please feel free to ring or call in here at any time and please keep me informed. My PA will see you out.'

Carter thanked him and they followed Nikki back past reception. 'Sorry, Miss? I didn't catch your surname? You worked for Mr Martingale long?' he asked.

'Nikki de Lange. Yes . . . I have, a long time.'

'You have a slight South African accent, don't you?' said Ebony.

'Ah . . . can you hear it?'

'It's only faint.' Ebony tried not to stare but she wondered why anyone who looked as beautiful as Nikki de Lange ever messed up their face with surgery as she obviously had. The thing was, it had become too perfect. It was expressionless. It could have been sixteen or sixty. 'Did you travel with him from South Africa?' she asked, trying to stop staring.

'Yes, I am his personal assistant. I travel with him wherever he goes.'

'Must be like being married to the job.' Carter looked back and smiled. Nikki de Lange had come to a halt by the hospital doors.

'My husband doesn't mind. He comes too. He's Justin de Lange, Mr Martingale's accountant.'

'It's a family affair,' smiled Carter as he thanked her and shook her hand.

They walked back across the car park.

'What did you think of Martingale?' he asked Ebony.

'He's very self-absorbed; loves himself. Thinks he's God.'

'Controlling?'

'Yes, but I guess you have to be a bossy type if you're a surgeon.' She glanced across at Carter as they walked. 'He'll tell Davidson we came to see him.'

'I know. But what can Davidson say, Ebb? This was just a friendly visit, wasn't it? Only polite to keep him informed. Did you see his watch . . . big money, Ebb. He's slick.'

'Definitely.'

'Expensive threads. Smooth finish. Bit of a Don Juan, don't you think?'

She looked across at Carter. 'Who?'

Carter looked back surprised for a few seconds. Then laughed. 'Don't you know your classics? Casanova: sophisticated. Ladies' man.'

'Yeah ... probably. He doesn't look like a man who ever does things spontaneously. Never flustered, always calm.'

'That's the key to him maybe. We'll push him for that list later on today and we'll get Robbo onto it. Martingale's got to have an Achilles heel, everyone does. It might be money or women ... yeah ... he looks like a man who could be driven by pleasure – what do you think, Ebb?'

'His PA definitely loves him. I get the feeling she was hovering outside the door waiting to rescue him from us.'

'From our questions? Something she didn't want him to talk about?'

'Not so much the questions as the intrusion into his world. Memories maybe about his daughter dying. It's got to be hard for him to hear it gone over again. Whatever it was, she couldn't wait to get rid of us.'

'Not *us*, Ebb.' Carter looked across at her and winked. 'Couldn't keep her eyes off me.'

Ebony rolled her eyes skyward and exhaled loudly. 'Yeah right.'

'See, Ebb ... have to have a backup plan in case Cabrina ditches me for good. I reckon we would make a lovely couple.'

'She's too old for you, Sarge.'

'What? Ebb, are we talking about the same woman? She's about thirty-five *and* she's definitely interested in me.'

'She's had so much work done on her face: Botox, fillers. She couldn't look interested if she tried.'

Carter stopped walking and looked across at Ebony's poker face and laughed. 'You might be right, Ebb. Let's head back to Blackdown Barn, and see if it can tell us anything new.' They got settled in the car, Carter at the wheel. 'Have you got the gardener's number? I want him to be available when Sandford goes down there.'

Carter drove out of the car park while Ebony found Marty Reedman's card in a side pocket of her bag and phoned him. She could hear the sound of cars passing as he answered.

'Sorry . . . caught you at a bad moment?' she asked. 'It's Detective Willis here, we met at Rose Cottage.'

'Of course I remember you – I don't get to meet many detectives. I can talk . . . just working on a garden in town, sorry if it's noisy.'

'I wanted to ask you more about the section of gate-post you rebuilt.'

'Go on.'

'When did you come to the cottage? How soon after the murders happened?'

'I came back from holiday, as I said. I was working on one of the gardens nearby. I saw the police there and told them who I was. I offered to help. They asked me if there was anything different in the garden: anything there that shouldn't be, or not there that should. I said "no" but when the officer went back inside the house I realized the gatepost wasn't right. When I took a closer look at the damage I saw a small square of material, blood-soaked. When the officer came back I told him what I'd found and showed it to him.'

'What happened then? Did you get asked to make a statement?'

'No. That was the last I heard about it. I was told by the owners that the police had finished; I could go back and would I do something about the gatepost? So I did. I rebuilt it as close to the original as I could.'

'Did you use the exact same stone again to rebuild it?'

'Most of it, yes, and what I didn't use I kept. You'll find it to the right of the front door at the cottage. I thought I might reuse it somewhere else. But I haven't done so yet.'

'Thanks, that's really helpful. I'll find out what happened to it. I'll be in touch.'

'Glad to help . . . I was going to ask . . . if you need any more help . . . if you need to ask me anything else . . . we could talk over coffee or a drink?'

'Um . . . yes. Thanks. It's possible. Shall I call you if I need more help?'

He laughed. 'If that's what you want then that's good. I appreciate you're busy at the moment but can I use this number to text you now – in a few days – and see when you're free?'

'Of course . . . good idea . . . bye for now.' Ebony glanced across at Carter who was looking back and forth from her to the road and grinning.

'What was that?'

She shook her head. 'Just the gardener, Sarge.' She gathered her thoughts quickly. 'He says the original stone is still there, what he didn't use to rebuild the gatepost he left by the side of the front door. He also says that he told the officer at the scene about a piece of evidence he found by the gatepost: a piece of blood-stained material. I've looked through the list of evidence, Sarge, and I didn't find it listed.'

'Okay. Ring Robbo and get him to make sure all the exhibits from the Carmichael case are brought back from the warehouse. Also, ask him if there were any vehicles reported damaged by officers attending the scene that day. And tell him to chase up the ambulance driver who picked up baby Adam. Someone would have had to report damage to their vehicle.'

Chapter 19

Carmichael opened his laptop and connected his phone then waited for the instructions on the screen.

Did he want to download files from host?

Yes, he did.

He downloaded the photo of Sonny outside Digger's club and saved it to his phone. Then he rang an old friend.

'Long time no speak, Carmichael. It's good to hear from you. How you keeping? I heard you became a sheep farmer?'

'Hello, Micky. Yeah . . . I'm heading back into the real world now. I need some help. The people who murdered my wife and kid are back in the UK.'

'Ask away.'

'I need you to do some intelligence work for me? Find out all you can about some people past and present. I'll cover expenses for you.'

'Sure; I need a rest anyway, put my feet up.'

'Yeah. Saw you'd been rowing the Atlantic with your mates. You should try and challenge yourself a bit more.'

Micky laughed. 'I'm working on it. You keep in contact with any of the others from our regiment?'

'I have some numbers but I'm not sure who's still around. I need to update some software. Have you got someone who can help?'

'Sure. You tell me what you need and I'll get it for you. What do you need from me?'

'To start with I need you to find out all you can about a man named Digger Cain. He owns clip joints in Soho and a legit club called Cain's. I want to know what else he makes money from: legit or otherwise.'

'What do you already know about him? What are you looking for specifically?'

'He's the top man in a chain of club owners who pass trafficked women around the clubs and brothels here in the UK. He distributes and sells the girls on. One of the women ended up under a patio in Northwest London. I want to know if Digger could have put her there and if he could have anything to do with killing my wife and child. I'm looking for a connection to *specific* people. I'll email you it in more detail. I also need your help in creating a new persona for myself. I will have to be able to gain entry into Digger's world. I'm going to base it around the time we spent in Mexico in '91 – most of the guys we were looking at then are dead.'

'You want to go backwards and rewrite history? Tricky.'

'Yes, but it just needs to gain me access and then I'll be in and out before anyone realizes it doesn't add up. I don't have to set myself up as a major player in the Tijuana Cartel. I just need to be an "also-ran".'

'Sounds like it would be fun to weave yourself into the search engines and distort the truth a little. I'll enjoy helping you with that. But Carmichael . . . you don't need to pay me. I owe you from way back.'

'No . . . all debts are paid. Can't think of a better use for my money than watching you break another record.'

Micky shifted in his seat and lifted one stump at a time to rest on a stool in front of him. He began unhitching his artificial legs as he talked to Carmichael. Micky's eyes went up to the photo on his wall next to the medal he'd received after he stepped on a mine and lost both his legs from the knee down. Carmichael had carried him to help and then returned for one of the bloodiest revenge attacks that their platoon had ever witnessed. It wouldn't go down in history as one of the most ethical operations but it had done the job.

'What you going to do when you find the people responsible?'

'I'm going to kill every one of them . . . slowly.'

Carmichael worked all night as he watched the information come in from Micky. He sat at his desk, kept the fire burning and focused like he hadn't done for many years. He set a trail of retrospective events in place. Micky instant-messaged him all through the night. They went back and forth with ideas.

'Airforce do?' Micky wrote.

'Yes.'

'You had a girlfriend who disappeared. How does that sound?'

'Captured by little known rivals to the Tijuana Cartel? Sounds perfect, Micky.'

Together they threaded Carmichael's name in where there was a gap and only the dead knew the truth. Now he was Mr Hart: money-, arms-, drugs- and people-trafficker. He was as well connected to the great but dead names as you could get.

Carmichael had almost finished packing when Bridget arrived at ten the next morning. He saw her pass by the window on her way to the barn.

He went over to the shelf and took down the photo of Louise and Sophie and put it in the bag. He shut down the laptop and closed it up before packing it away in the holdall, then zipped it up ready. He walked out through the kitchen and tack room. The skinned dog fox swung from the end of a hook fixed to the edge of the stable block outside. Half of its face was missing where the bullet had passed through. Carmichael crossed the yard, opened the stable door, and led Tor out of his stable and tied him to a post in the yard.

Tor gave a sigh and then he snorted white dragon breath into the air through his flared nostrils as he shifted his weight from one leg to the other, pawing the ground with his unshod hoof gently scraping at the hardstanding.

'Alright, Tor . . . stand still.'

He stripped off the horse's rugs and hung them over the open stable door. Then he picked up the brush and brushed long hard sweeps down over the animal's flanks. Tor turned to bite him. Carmichael swore at him and the horse moved one ear at a time as it listened, then it shook its mane and carried on transferring weight from one leg to another.

Bridget passed him on her way down from the barn. She came to press the flat of her hand against Tor's soft velvet muzzle. He began licking her palm.

'I am going away for a while, Bridget. Look after things here for me till I get back. The sheep will need extra care now otherwise we'll get no more lambs from them.'

She looked at him over Tor's neck. 'How long for?'

'I don't know.' She looked away. 'I'll leave enough money and I'll leave instructions with the bank so that you can get what you need.' She nodded. 'You stay here at the house and look after the animals. I don't know whether Rusty will make it but I trust you to do the best you can for him.'

She picked up the fork, went to get the wheelbarrow and started mucking out Tor's stable. Twenty minutes later she heard the motorbike start up. She stopped working and listened to the sound of him leaving.

Carmichael stopped off at the bank to sign papers. He got a shave, a haircut. Four hours of riding, allowing for a stop-off at an out-of-town shopping outlet to buy some clothes, tools and get some cards printed up. He made sure they were sleek and top-quality, black and gold with just his name and his mobile number, then he drove through London and pulled his Triumph Tiger motorbike into the space in front of the old club in a run-down side street of Shoreditch. The estate agent stopped talking on his phone as he saw Carmichael get off his bike and walk across. He shook Carmichael's hand with his hot one.

'Great premises. Fab property. You certainly know a good deal when you see it. The owners are keen to get the property let.' Either side of the club were empty properties. 'This is *the* area in London. You're guaranteed a great business once this is up and running.'

'Why is it empty?' Carmichael asked, but he already knew the answer. He followed the young Indian, heavily weighed down with muscles and jewellery, as he opened an envelope with keys inside and began unlocking the doors. There were locks top and bottom of the door and a padlock in the centre. Carmichael looked up to where the CCTV camera had been. Someone had ripped off the bracket but the plate was still drilled into the brickwork; that would save him some time.

'They had some sort of trouble with the last tenants. Nothing to do with the landlords or this area. It was a personal matter.' The estate agent smiled nervously and unlocked the large doors into the dark. 'The press exaggerated things the way they always do.'

'Yeah . . . I'm sure.' Carmichael smiled to himself.

'There are offices behind here.' They stood in the club, a cashier's office to the left. The estate agent closed the doors behind them. 'I'll show you those in a minute.' Stepping further inside he switched on the lights. 'The landlords have kept the electricity running here so that we can show you round properly. Here to the right are stairs up to the cloakrooms and a further office and storage space. 'Straight ahead is the main section of the club. If you'd like to follow me . . .' Inside, it still had the smell of years of smokers and spilt drinks embedded in its nicotine-filmed walls and spongy floor. A long bar stretched away to the right, the dance floor was down a few steps to the left. It was long and rectangular, a raised area to the left: dancing poles at either end of the floor; above it two cages were on a raised plinth, the hook and chains that held them in place still there. 'Just to let you know, Mr Hart, the owners would accept a slightly lower offer than stated. And we can settle it all today. If all is agreed I have been instructed to give you the keys. You'll have to apply for a licence but it shouldn't be a problem.'

'Got the contract for me to sign?'

When the estate agent left, Carmichael locked the main doors and went back around the club. He unlocked the door next to the cashier's booth and walked into the first of two back rooms; one was storage, the other, an office which would be his bedroom. All that was left in the room was an old safe, a set of plastic chairs and a filthy mattress. He would have time to buy himself a camp bed. He'd do it tomorrow. He wouldn't be sleeping there most nights, but he'd need somewhere safe to rest and, by the time he finished making it that way, the club would be a fortress.

Back at the bar, he sat on a stool opposite the empty optics and the dusty fittings that had once shone on a nightly basis; but not brightly. This was never a pukka club; this was a shabby nightclub in a once shabby part of town. It had been a notorious place for trafficked girls and gangsters. That was why Carmichael had chosen it. He opened his laptop on the counter. He had already decided on a name for the club: the Velvet Lagoon. He'd apply for the licence to reopen it in the morning. He wouldn't get it, but that didn't matter. By that time it would all be over. The place echoed to the sound of his fingers on the keyboard. Occasionally he heard the scuttle of a rat as it came up to investigate the new arrival. Carmichael opened up a ham sandwich he'd bought when he stopped on his way down and threw a corner of the crust over towards the sound of scuttling.

He turned his attention back to the screen as Ebony logged on. She was writing her notes up about her visit to Rose Cottage: Carmichael watched as Ebony typed in the password. The spyware recorded every key stroke she made and typed it directly onto his screen.

Forensic evidence missing: contaminated. She was raped. Semen on/inside the body of Louise Carmichael ... find these samples ... re-draw scene-of-crime plans. Go back to Doc Harding and talk through autopsy notes, missing sections ... enough blood? What was Carmichael's relationship with Chrissie Newton ... did he lie to me?

Carmichael picked up his holdall and placed it on the bar top then he unzipped it and took out his rifle in its slimline fleece bag. He hopped over the bar and knelt down amongst the debris that had been left by the quick departure of the club's owners. Someone had ripped out the glass-washing machine. Carmichael reached a hand in and felt the space that was left beside it. It was dry. He slid the rifle into the gap and hopped back over the bar.

He took out the new clothes he'd bought on the way and tore off the labels then he repacked them into his expensive new bag. He'd already booked a room in the Lansdown, a boutique hotel off Oxford Street. He had never allowed himself to spend his wife's money before: the thought of touching it had been abhorrent to him. But he'd been waiting for this time.

He went around the club and re-drilled every lock and changed it. He put up web cams and aligned them over the entrance to the club and around the building. He made sure every point of entry was secure. Nothing was going to get into the club uninvited and, once inside, nothing was going to leave without his permission.

Chapter 20

'Doctor Harding?' Ebony found Harding working at her PC. 'Thanks for making time to go through the autopsy results with me.'

Harding swivelled round on her chair, took off her glasses.

'How was it with Carmichael?'

Ebony nodded. 'Yeah. It was interesting.'

'What's his life like now?'

'I don't think he's ever moved on from what happened.'

'How did he react to the fresh evidence?'

'I don't know. I feel a bit like I've opened Pandora's box. Maybe that's exactly what I was meant to do?'

'Did you ask him about the affair?'

Ebony nodded.

'What did he say?'

'He said he was feeling self-destructive at the time.'

Harding frowned and then turned back to her desk.

'Pull up Mathew's chair – he's gone to chase up some results. What do you want to ask me? You have my attention for twenty minutes.'

'I wanted to go through some of the facts with you and make sure I understand them.' Ebony opened up her folder and spread out the crime scene diagrams on the floor.

'These are the original crime scene drawings from the time,' said Harding. 'They place Chrissie Newton here in the lounge as we saw when we went there and as I found her when I certified her death.'

Ebony laid a photo of the body on top of the room plan. 'Her injuries were vast. We know her killer used anaesthetic. The bleed would have been massive.' She looked at the photos of Chrissie Newton's body. 'It doesn't look as if there was enough blood considering their injuries. I mean . . . wouldn't you expect the blood to be everywhere? What did you think at the time?'

'I thought that if she had been laid on something as she was killed that it would be about right. A towel or absorbent sheet. Not too difficult: minimal bleed. When the heart stops so does the bleeding.'

'But that would have taken some organizing: coming fully equipped. Not a last-minute thing. This is the photo of how you found Louise.' Ebony pointed to the group of photos from the crime scene.

'Correct.'

'Does it look like she was placed there to you?'

'Carmichael moved the bodies.'

'He moved Sophie, not Louise.'

'He definitely touched her. They died face up and they were found that way but there was movement in between. The blood had shifted a little and then rolled back to settle down the back, buttocks and calves.'

'But Carmichael arrived long after they were dead. Lividity settles after six to eight hours, doesn't it?'

'We only have Carmichael's word that he wasn't there before.'

'What about the cross-contamination between the women? It says in the report that the women had each other's DNA on their bodies: skin cells, blood, hair on their backs? How can you explain that?'

'Natural if they'd been sharing the house. They could have lain on the same blanket. Look . . . procedures let us down that day. We cannot be sure it wasn't a basic mistake made at the crime scene or when the samples were taken from the bodies.'

'You took the samples, didn't you, Doctor?'

'I did but I wasn't responsible for ensuring that the bodies arrived to me in the condition they should have been. It's possible they were contaminated at the scene. And Carmichael cannot be trusted to recall what he did accurately.'

'And Carmichael's DNA?'

'That was there in abundance. His handprints, his sweat, his saliva on his wife's hands, his kid's face.'

'But semen. If he raped her? How long can semen last?'

'In a dead body? Two weeks.'

'And in a live body?'

'They are swimming about alive, motile, for four to six hours, then they begin to lose bits of themselves: first the tails drop off, then the heads. You can still find heads and tails in the vagina for up to seven days, in the rectum two or three days and in the mouth less than twenty-four hours.'

'Did you find motile sperm from Carmichael?'

'No. His were fragmented sperm.'

'So Carmichael had sex with his wife a few days before she was murdered.'

'Probably within the week but not within that forty-eight-hour period. Nothing can be exact. Except he could have used a condom when he raped her. We found tissue tearing around her mouth which indicates that she was forced to perform fellatio, but all traces of spermatozoa in her mouth had been destroyed.'

'Was his DNA on Chrissie Newton?'

'Yes, it was. Under the palm of her hand there was his sweat.'

'But she wasn't raped?'

'No.'

'I can't see him as a rapist, Doctor.'

'Rape is a common tool of warfare, remember. He might have done it before, might have been ordered to. What if he wasn't even in a state to recognize his wife and child? PTSD could have done that to him. You say he told you he was feeling self-destructive, that's why he had the affair. How much more self-destructive can you get than killing the people you love and that love you?'

'So if we say it was Carmichael . . . just say . . . he raped his own wife and killed his child. But he didn't rape the woman he cared least about? Do you think he could have cared for her?

'It's possible.'

'If Chrissie was targeted then it could have something to do with her father. Do you know James Martingale personally?'

'I have met him a few times.' Harding studied Ebony's face. Ebony felt her bristling. 'I've done the odd bit of private work but it's not me . . . sucking fat out of one end to inject in the other. My ex, Simon, works for him. Have you been to see Mr Martingale?'

'Yes. Carter and I went to the hospital to see him.'

'What did you think of him?'

'Nothing like a mad professor type, is he? He's suave, sophisticated, sort of aloof.'

'He's a megalomaniac, but then you have to be to achieve what he has. He is God in his field and he's managed to make millions out of it. You have to admire that. He gives a lot away to charity, as I'm sure you know. I wouldn't have a lot of this expensive equipment if it wasn't for his generosity. But as a father he failed spectacularly.'

'I re-read Martingale's statement . . . He wasn't in the country at the time of the murders: he was working in his hospital in Poland.'

'James Martingale was never here for Chrissie, dead or alive. As I say, I think he failed her spectacularly; he just didn't exist for her. He left her in the hands of a woman with extreme mental illness . . . who needed to take vast quantities of medication to get through a day without killing herself or someone else; he left her to fend for herself. Thank God he also left her with enough money that she could board for the whole of her school life; then go far away to a university in Scotland. But as you know, you can't keep on about it; it was a shit childhood . . . get over it . . . move on . . . Christ knows you did, didn't you?'

As Ebony walked back to Fletcher House she mulled it over. Ebony shouldn't mind Harding being blunt. She was blunt herself. Harding seemed to be offering a friendly hand, albeit in her usual awkward way. Ebony had to accept that her life was out there for the world to Google, but she didn't have to like it. Everyone knew about the case of the serving officer whose mad mother had killed her partner; stabbed him how many times exactly? Everyone knew that her own daughter had arrested her.

Chapter 21

The Lansdown had a suite waiting for Carmichael. He'd left his bike back at the Velvet Lagoon in Shoreditch and bought a brand-new silver Jaguar XKR on the way. He had it valet parked at the Lansdown and then carried his own bag up to his suite.

As he slipped his card in the lock and opened the door it brought back memories of his life with Louise before Sophie came along. He had wooed her with weekends away. He had been romantic. He'd almost forgotten that. Yes . . . he'd pre-ordered the specific room, the meal. He'd done everything to win her love. So many regrets: he wished he'd never met her. He wished for her sake that he'd never come into her life.

Carmichael showered and hung his new suit in the steamy bathroom to get rid of the creases. Once he was ready he looked at himself in the mirror. He stood tall and stared at himself as if he were looking at a stranger. He hadn't worn a suit since the day of the funeral. It was a long time since he'd looked at himself, in a suit or otherwise. He only ever saw his face when he bothered to shave. The years working on the farm had turned his body into a lean and muscled machine.

There was no fat left on his body or his face. He looked at his expression and hardly recognized the darkness he saw there.

The music from the piano bar drifted across to him as Carmichael walked through the lobby. He walked across to the bar and ordered a Scotch then checked his phone. He had a missed call from Ebony. He knew what she wanted to ask him. She wanted to ask what his relationship with Chrissie Newton had been. He had watched her type up her thoughts. He knew that she'd been to see Harding. Ebony was his eyes and ears. He saw by the GPS signal that she was on her way back to Fletcher House. He flicked his phone back to regular settings and a weather report flashed across the top of the screen. His phone was still giving him a weather report for the farm.

Carmichael swallowed his drink, signed the bill, and left. Outside, the snow was steadily falling. He jumped in a cab and got it to drop him at the end of Brewer Street. Then he walked along the narrow street, listening to the Christmas music and the sound of people: a mix of shoppers and party revellers in the build-up to the Christmas holidays. The streets were decked out with Christmas lights and lanterns. He kept his head down as he approached Cain's night-club and ducked inside the door.

Cain's club was open from nine in the evening until four-thirty in the morning. It was a gentlemen's club that had gone a little bit shabby. The door was opened for Carmichael by two doormen while two hostesses in bras and suspenders hovered in the warmth of the inner entrance hall. They escorted Carmichael down a short hallway, past a flight of stairs leading to VIP lounges and private rooms, and into the main bar area. It was a mix of old exposed brickwork and swathes of red velvet curtain. Its leather couches and exposed brick pillars divided the club into intimate areas where small groups of men could enjoy a private dance while sitting around drinking.

Carmichael took a seat at the bar. 'Good evening, sir.' The barman came across to him. 'My name is Ray. What can I get you to drink?'

'Evening, Ray. I'll have a large measure of good Scotch and have a drink yourself. Tell Mr Cain that Mr Hart is here, please. He's expecting me.'

'Of course, Mr Hart, and thank you.'

Carmichael then went to sit in one of the booths. A woman in a black lace corset was dancing on the podium stage where three poles were set in a triangle. She wrapped her thighs around the centre pole and whipped her sleek ponytail through the air in circles. Carmichael was only half concentrating on her, the other half mentally working its way around the club, matching the layout Micky had emailed to him with what he saw in 'real time'. He knew that at the far end of the bar was the door to the cashier's office and a link to the clip joint, Crystal Blue, next door. He knew that somewhere past the three poles was the door that led to the upper two floors, the back entrance to the next floor of the club, and Digger Cain's private apartment. He knew what Digger Cain looked like. It had been many years since he saw him in the flesh. Not since he had attended a firearms situation when he first joined the Force. A man had threatened a customer in the building opposite Cain's nightclub. He'd talked to Digger briefly then. He saw him now emerging from the door at the far end of the bar.

When the dancer finished her set she came over to Carmichael. He watched her walk across. She sat next to him, her body turned towards him.

'What's your name?' asked Carmichael.

'Tanya.'

When Ray brought Carmichael's Scotch she ordered a glass of champagne.

'Where are you from?'

'Just outside Kiev.' She had beautiful strong features and her body was as lean and muscled as a racehorse.

Beneath the heavy makeup it was clear she had been pretty once but her skin had suffered from the lifestyle. Her eyes were dead.

'You're a long way from the Ukraine. What brings you here?'

'I came to study English.'

'You find this is a good place to learn English?'

She studied Carmichael. 'Not bad. You meet nice people. Nice men like you. Men who might want to see me dance and pay twenty pounds.' She smiled.

'Very good. Not quite perfect. You need to work on your intonation. But here.' He took out two twenties and gave them to her. 'Maybe later.'

She smiled. 'Thank you. Are you a tourist?'

'Sort of. Tell me . . . Is this what you came to the UK for?' He flicked his head towards the podium.

'No, I didn't come here to be a dancer. I came to work with children. I joined an agency to work as a nanny for children but . . . I had to pay the agency back for my flights, accommodation.' She looked around and stopped talking, smiled nervously as Ray watched. 'The agency was not truthful.' She kept smiling.

'Let me guess . . . you're still paying?'

'Of course.' She looked at Carmichael, deep and long. She kept a smile on her mouth. 'Please. I hope I can entertain you some time.'

Carmichael caught a glimpse of the inside of her left arm; it was bruised. She shook her head when she saw him looking at her arm. 'I'm not a junkie.' She stopped as she saw Carmichael's eyes flash and focus on a man walking their way. Digger Cain was heading towards Carmichael's table. Tanya got up to leave. Digger sat down and called Ray over to bring him a drink. Ray arrived with a bottle of Scotch and two glasses.

Digger scrutinized Carmichael. 'Have we not met before . . . Mr Hart?'

'I don't think so.'

Digger had already added up the worth of the man sitting opposite him: a grand for the watch, nearly that for the suit. Five hundred for the shoes. The man had bought the best and he wore it well. His body was muscled and lean. His height gave him power. His face was tanned and rugged. His hair black, neat, short, understated. He could have been an older Armani model.

Carmichael looked across at the bar. Ray the barman was talking to a man sitting on a bar stool who was rhythmically swilling the contents of his brandy glass as he turned his head and watched Carmichael and Digger in conversation.

Digger sat back in the seat. He stretched out an arm on the back of the alcove as he sipped his Scotch.

'You come highly recommended, Mr Hart. I hear you're interested in recruiting dancers? You want to join our network?'

'Yes. That's right.'

'Have you got the premises?' Carmichael sat back. Digger continued: 'I looked at your club. You had trouble in the past; you lost your licence?'

'Not me. It belonged to others. They got careless. They irritated the wrong people and weren't respectful to the right ones. I've made sure it won't happen again. This is a fresh start, a brand-new venture, and I don't foresee any problems with licensing restrictions or visas. The local police and I have come to an arrangement. I am paying into their pension plan.'

Digger gave a gesture of approval. 'And . . . the last owners? What happened to them?' He fixed Carmichael with a look that said he already knew the answer but wanted to see if Carmichael would lie to him.

'They flew back to Sarajevo, in the hold.'

'What if I said they were friends of mine?' Digger eyeballed him.

Carmichael leaned forward and picked up his Scotch. 'No offence . . .' he held up his drink in a small salute. 'Then you'd know they deserved it.'

Digger coughed, rattling phlegm in his chest.

'Yes. They were a thorn in my side. They gave people like myself a bad name.' He grinned at

Carmichael. 'I prefer dealing with the English. I would be happy to offer you girls.'

He looked around the booths; the club had yet to fill – it was early, not quite ten. He nodded his head towards the man at the bar and he disappeared for a few minutes. When he reappeared he had a young girl with him. Her bony frame was skinny and tall; she had on a silver bikini. Her legs wobbled in five-inch heels. The man dragged her forward towards the last of the three poles and tried to make her dance.

Digger kept his eyes on Carmichael as he inclined his head towards the podium: 'As you can see . . . we have the merchandise . . . for the right money. Alright, Mr Hart . . . let's talk business."

The girl hung onto the pole as if it were a rope dangling over a river of crocs.

'We have someone who gets us girls. He has good agents over in the Eastern bloc. They groom the families, neighbours, work mates, anyone who wants to make money from selling to us. There's never any shortage of girls because there's always a shortage of money.' He looked back at the girl.

'This girl? What's her story?'

'Her name is Anna. She went to help a neighbour in the market. Anna is an orphan. There is no one to come looking for her. He sold her as well as his potatoes. Enterprising, these people. This is Anna's second day.' She hung off the man's hands like a crying rag doll as he hammered his hips against hers and simulated sex. Her mouth opened to cry but no sound came out.

'Every day there's a new lesson,' Digger explained.

Carmichael watched as Tanya came out and draped her arm around the man's neck and tried to kiss him. It was only a temporary distraction; he pushed her off and continued tormenting the young girl.

'In a few days' time she'll learn to use her mouth for something more ... useful.' Digger's laugh cracked. He coughed phlegm into his mouth and spat into a cloth handkerchief. He looked at its contents, folded it and put it back in his pocket. The man pushed Tanya away.

'How does it work?'

'They start their working life here in London. After we acclimatize them we provide them with various job opportunities. Some of them come into the UK legitimately and have no problems working, others need a little discretion. We have something for each of them besides finding work in clubs. We have: live sex chat, web rooms, escort agencies and massage parlours. We move them around the clubs in our network every couple of months ... we move them on to other cities: Leeds, Manchester, Bristol. We get a new shipment in about once every few months. Would you like to try Anna or Tanya?'

Carmichael shook his head. 'I never touch the merchandise.'

Digger nodded and flicked his head towards the man with Anna. 'Neither do I. I leave that to Sonny over there.'

Chapter 22

Carmichael went back to the Velvet Lagoon that evening. He sat at the bar in the darkness staring at his laptop; his face lit by the flickering screen. He heard the rustle of the rat getting braver now as he threw it another piece of bread. It was not alone. He watched them run at the edge of his vision. Micky wanted to talk to him.

Carmichael phoned him.

'Digger has money hidden all over the place. I've found out that he owns several properties in Central London. He has been seen with celebrities. He was quite a catch in his youth; had a former Miss World as a girlfriend. Nowadays he tends to hold court in Cain's rather than venture far. He lost a lot of money on the stock markets. Digger hasn't got the money he used to have but he has plenty tied up in property. If Digger had something to do with your wife and child's murders it must have been for a profit. Digger has become nastier and more hermit-like as he's got older. Even his clubs seem to have declined and they are no longer the favoured haunts of the celebrity circuit.'

'Yeah. He's gone down the seedy route; ripping tourists off in clip joints.'

'There's no doubt Digger could do it. I've been looking into Martingale. Whatever Martingale does he does for a price and for fame. He sponsors so many good causes. He has funds going for research into just about every known disease. But Martingale doesn't do anything if no one's watching. He's devoted his life to writing papers.'

'But his personal life?'

'You guessed it . . . something had to give and that was it. He's had two failed marriages; both times lasted months rather than years. He still has no shortage of women . . . he's been linked to quite a few, but he never takes it to the next level with them. He's in love with his work and maybe himself. Most of his decisions in life have been driven by financial gain. He was offered permanent teaching positions in most of the leading hospitals; he turned them down. He keeps his hand in with the NHS, maybe doing one or two high-profile operations a year, but most of the time he's delegating and not doing.'

'What about his whereabouts? What's his address for most of the year?'

'He is seasonal. He likes his springs here. He likes to show orchids and there are shows all over the country. The biggest, most prestigious happen in March. He has to come here from Christmas to get them ready. When he's here he lives in his mother's old home in Hampstead. It wasn't where he grew up. He spent most of his life living abroad when his father was in the army.'

'You asked if Digger knew Martingale? The answer is yes, they were seen around in the Sixties although they didn't really move in the same circles for long. Martingale would have probably gone into Cain's. It wasn't quite as seedy then.'

Carmichael thanked Micky and hung up. He went into the office and dragged out the old abandoned mattress and pulled it down to the far wall of the club. He propped it up and pinned five pieces of paper on it: one in each corner and one in the centre. He drew a circle on each then went behind the bar, pulled out his rifle and switched on the night vision. He took a shot at each target in turn, working his way round the four corners, and finally he took a shot at the centre circle. Then he walked over to see how he'd scored. He was dead centre on four out of five. The bottom left was a millimetre off. For the four he'd hit he drew smaller circles an inch away from the first ones. For the fifth he'd have to wait till he got it right. Carmichael walked back to the bar and looked back at the laptop.

He went back to see what Ebony had been writing:

The more I listen to people talk about Carmichael, the more confused I am. I have to stay with my own impressions. I believe he is someone who served his country, served his family to the best of his ability. If he failed in either it would have eaten him up. If he failed he wouldn't want to live with himself. But mental illness turns some people into monsters ... could my mum have killed if she hadn't been really sick? Not herself? She says she can't remember doing it ... can she? I saw her that day. I saw the monster she became. She says she doesn't remember. A moment of madness is one thing. But watching someone bleed to death on the kitchen floor while you calmly make tea? And Mum lies. I have heard her make up stories all my life. She's an expert liar. Carmichael lied to me . . . has he lied to himself? Is he like my mother? Is he a monster?

By the end of the night the mattress was peppered with holes.

Chapter 23

The next morning Carter walked into the Intel office. 'Is the surveillance on Cain's in place, Robbo?'

'No . . . not yet . . . I'm waiting to hear. The problem is the property was put up for sale and is under offer and the buyers aren't going to let us in there.'

'Fuck . . . is there anywhere else we can use? We can't afford to wait any longer. If Sonny gets wind of things he'll be gone. Soon Blackdown Barn will be all over the news and Chichester will know that his treasure didn't stay buried. Realistically, Robbo . . . how long . . . any hope?'

'Realistically? Too long.'

'Right . . . decision made . . . we'll do the heavy-handed approach instead.' He phoned Ebony. She was in the warehouse looking at the rest of the Carmichael exhibits and organizing for them to be shipped back to Fletcher House.

'Meet me in Soho.'

Carter parked the car in the underground car park. He emerged up on ground level, pulled up the collar on his coat and waited by the paying kiosk for Ebony. He sent a text to Cabrina.

'Can't bear the thought of Christmas without you.'

Ebony found Carter scrolling through his messages. He put his phone away when he realized she was there. They walked along the water-logged pavement where the melting snow had turned into dirty slush. They stopped at the Crystal Blue: the clip joint next to Cain's that Digger also owned but didn't admit to. It was part of the same building, connected by an entrance behind the bar at Cain's.

An ageing Thai woman dressed in an elf's costume stood in the doorway. She huddled by an electric heater in the entrance before stepping back out onto the street and trying to coax someone in.

'You wanna see me dance? Five pounds.' Her teeth chattered with the cold.

'Is Santa in?' Carter asked.

Two men appeared behind him. One did the talking. The other stared.

'Two hundred for two drinks. Two hundred more to see her dance.'

'A lovely girl like that . . . too cheap. Do you take plastic?' Carter opened his wallet and took out his warrant card. 'Is Digger here?'

The man spoke in Russian to his silent friend and then left to deliver the message. He returned a few moments later.

'Come with me . . .'

They followed him next door into Cain's. Three women were practising their Xmas-themed strip on the podium when Carter and Ebony were led to Digger's table. He was sitting on the edge of the dance floor at one of the tables framed by velvet curtains. Ebony had a quick glance around the club. She'd heard of it, of course, but never been inside. She was surprised to see how jaded it looked. The women carried on dancing to 'Santa Baby'.

Digger watched them walk across towards him. He kept his eyes on Carter. He was trying to get the measure of him by his walk, his demeanour. He could see the glint of gold on his fingers. Carter looked down at Digger and smiled:

'Mr Cain?'

Digger returned his smile. 'Detective?'

'I'm Sergeant Carter and this is DC Willis.'

Digger leant back to get a better view of Ebony. He smiled at her. She didn't smile back.

'Know him?' Carter showed him the photo of Sonny taken outside Cain's.

Digger took the photo.

'No, sorry.'

Ebony walked across to a woman washing glasses behind the bar. Digger nodded across to Ray the barman to stay with her.

'Do you know this man?' She showed her a photo of Sonny. The woman looked across at Ray. Then she shook her head. Her face was grey: waxy, sweaty. 'ID?' Her bones stuck out of her narrow shoulders. 'I need to see your ID,' Ebony repeated.

Ray came to stand very close. 'I look after it for her.'

Ebony turned to face him. 'And what about you . . . some ID?'

Ray smiled. 'Sure . . . Miss . . . it's in the office. Don't keep it on me, you understand; I'm as British as you are, of course.'

The woman returned to washing glasses, head down. Ebony glanced towards the table and Carter. He was still talking to Digger. Digger's attention was elsewhere.

'Get it now.'

Ray went through the door at the end of the bar. Ebony waited a few moments and then she followed. Ahead of her was an old part of the building, the paint on the walls peeling from the damp. She tried the handle of the first door on her left. Inside, a woman was changing. She froze when she saw Ebony. Ebony stepped inside the room and let the door close silently behind her.

'Your name?'

'Tanya.'

'This man, Tanya?' She held up the photo of Sonny. 'You know him?'

For a few seconds Tanya hesitated then she gave a small nod.

'Here?'

'Yes. He was here last night. He's here most nights.'

There was the sound of a door closing further down the corridor and then approaching footsteps. Ebony stepped back out into the corridor.

Ray looked past her into the dressing room.

'You need a warrant to search.'

'Just looking for the toilet, got lost . . . Got the ID?' She took it off him and looked at his first and then the woman's and gave it back. 'Thanks . . .' She followed him back out into the club. Carter was ready to leave. He was wrapping up:

'We know you know him, Digger. Shall I tell you why? Because he is one of the biggest traffickers of women in the UK – one of the last of the Brits to still be running a racket with the Albanians and the Romanians.'

Digger swept his arm around towards the stage and the three women.

'As you can see, my dancers are locals.'

Carter looked at the dancers. 'Keep it that way. We'll be here tomorrow and every day after that, Digger, until you start remembering who and where Sonny is. We'll be putting a squad car outside your club twenty-four seven just to reassure your punters that the police care. Here's my card. You phone when you have a sudden urge to save your business.'

Back on the street they passed the porno elf, who was shovelling noodles into her mouth from a take-away box. She scowled at them.

'I found one of the girls backstage who recognized Sonny,' Ebony said as they walked back to the car. 'She said he was here last night.'

'By now he'll know we're after him. Digger will have seen to that. Digger won't like us going in there. He won't like the extra police activity affecting business. These are lean times. He may be keen to distance himself from Sonny. He certainly won't want him in his club. Sonny will do one of two things – go underground or brazen it out.'

Chapter 24

At eight that evening Carmichael parked his Jag behind a red Ferrari outside the small cocktail bar off Islington Green. This bar was new to him but Islington Green was the same as it had always been. Across the road from where he parked, there was the same fruit and veg shop that he and Louise had made special trips to. He was amazed at how whole areas of London had changed since he'd been away, while other places hadn't even changed shopkeepers.

It was a tiny bar, like sitting in someone's front room. There were a few friends at one of the tables and a couple at another. The mood was dark and intimate. As he walked in he saw Sonny, his broad thighs perched on the edge of a bar stool.

'What you having?' Sonny asked.

'A single malt. Thanks for agreeing to show me round . . . appreciated.'

Sonny grunted. He wasn't happy. Since the police visit earlier, Digger had ordered him to hang fire on bringing any more girls in for a few weeks and told him to stay out of Cain's. Digger was hoping the new man Hart would discreetly take a few of the girls off his hands.

When the drinks arrived they moved to one of the tables and sat across from one another.

'So . . . where did you come from, Hart? Did some checking. You seem to have arrived here out of thin air. You got some high-up friends – but most of them are dead.' He made a sound like laughter and his eyes narrowed like a cat's as he studied Carmichael. When Sonny blinked his eyes shut a little too long it was as if they became stuck for a fraction of a second. 'You spent some time in South America? What was your business out there?'

Carmichael smiled into his whisky. 'Staying alive. What does anyone do out there? Same business the world over . . . make money.'

Sonny sat back and studied Carmichael. 'You buy a brand-new car like that?' He gestured towards the Jag outside. 'You must have made a lot of money. There's a lot about you which looks good on paper but doesn't really add up – like the fact you walk like a Para . . . you got Sandhurst on your CV?'

Carmichael smiled. 'It's a good guess but it's not right . . . airforce, not Marines.' Carmichael was about to see how Micky's story would stand up to scrutiny. 'You want to know how? I'm going to level with you, Sonny, because I think maybe we can do business better that way. I was in the airforce straight from school; got my pilot's licence there, learned to fly a helicopter and just about anything in the air. But by the time I was thirty I was sick of it; realized there was more to life than serving queen and country and I could earn a lot more doing commercial work. For a time I worked in the Pacific, tracking tuna, then I went off travelling, went to join an old girlfriend in South America. Then she disappeared on me. I went looking and found out that she'd been acquired by some local cartel. I joined forces with the men I needed to get her back. I found my skills were sought after. Started making a name for myself transporting people in and out of trouble; I'm a good shot, I can handle myself. I'm discreet, hard-working.'

Sonny couldn't hide the admiration on his face:

'Did you get her back?'

'Yes. But, you know what? Love's a fickle thing and I have to say it didn't feel the same. Shortly after that she disappeared for good.' He watched Sonny's reaction. Sonny laughed.

'It's a good story, Hart. Let's hope it's true, for your sake. You want to see what Digger was talking about? Let's go.'

So far so good; well done, Micky, thought Carmichael.

They drove down towards Finsbury Park in Sonny's red Ferrari and stopped on a street with once-elegant Victorian semi-detached and terraced houses. Now the big houses had been subdivided so many times they had become warrens for prostitutes and pushers. After they parked up, Sonny called three lads over and paid them twenty quid to both look after the car and leave it alone.

Sonny led the way across the street and in through a wrought-iron gate to a house second from the end. They had to step over a pile of rubbish at the foot of the steps leading to the front door. As they walked up the steps a dog went ballistic in the basement flat trying to get out to rip them to shreds. Sonny rang the bell to the ground-floor flat.

They heard the sound of keys in the door. A sickly-looking mixed-race lad answered the door. He had big ears, bad skin and his head was too small to be shaved the way it was.

'You wanna clean up outside, Tyrone; we'll be attracting vermin,' Sonny said to the boy. He shuffled nervously in front of them; his clothes were baggy, the crotch of his jeans between his knees, as he led the way inside.

'Yes, boss. Sorry, boss . . . it's the foxes. They got clever, worked out how to open the rubbish box.' Tyrone looked at Carmichael.

'Yeah, well clean it up before the neighbours complain and you get a visit from the filth.'

'It's all good, boss.' He punctuated his speech with sniffs from his cocaine-wrecked nose.

Sonny slapped him on the back. 'Course, Tyrone.' Snot erupted bubbling out of both nostrils and was retrieved by a sleeve. 'Of course it is . . . This is Mr Hart. He's come to look at the merchandise. Tyrone here is the manager. I bring the girls in and Tyrone looks after them for Digger. Plus he earns a bit on the side for his friends, which he thinks I don't know about.'

Tyrone turned and raised the free arm as a greeting – the other one still wiping away snot. He did his best to look happy to see them. He didn't look quite so happy with the news that Sonny knew he let his friends have a special deal with the girls.

'Show us then,' Sonny ordered.

Inside the windowless rooms girls stared out at them. Four to a room they waited in their underwear to be chosen. Carmichael thought they looked at him the way his sheep did when they were waiting for slaughter. He recognized the young country girl Anna from Digger's club. Her eyes lingered on his. He thought about Sophie.

'Do you want to choose some girls, boss?' Tyrone asked. Sonny looked at Carmichael. He shook his head in answer.

Sonny led the way back towards the front of the flat and into a room on the left. A screen showing porn was on in the corner of the room. The room had an aroma of sickly sweet perfume and sex. There was a Florida-style cocktail bar in the corner. There were two sofas, and a coffee table between them.

Sonny went across to the bar and poured Carmichael a large whisky and handed it to him. The porno moaning in the background rose and fell.

'You interested in these girls?' Sonny asked.

Carmichael shrugged. 'Maybe. I was looking for top quality. Not sure these fit the bill.'

Sonny looked momentarily put out but recovered fast. 'You tell me what you need and I'll get it special order.'

'Sounds promising. You're an ambitious man, Sonny . . . You purely about supply? You're not interested in having your own club?'

He shook his head. 'I like what I do. I want to hang onto my head. Don't want to have it kicked in. I know what I'm good at. At the moment . . . If I could I would take over some of the routes from the fucking Turks and Albanians.'

'. . . it's just Digger you supply? And Digger makes arrangements to sell the girls on?'

'Yeah . . . like I said . . . I'm up against it with the fucking Turks and Albanians. I have to keep my hand around their throats otherwise they'd have me.'

'So what? You just waiting for that day?'

'No. But it's a hard business to trust in. I want to take over a couple of the big routes. Most of the contacts from the old days have gone. At the moment I don't step on too many toes. I get left alone.'

'So you need to stamp on some heads, not toes.' The room had become charged. Sonny was beginning to get excited.

'If I had the backing . . .'

'I might consider investing in your business.'

Sonny crashed his glass against Carmichael's and beamed. Carmichael stood and downed his drink, ready to leave.

'Show me some of the competition. I want to take a look at some of the other clubs.'

Sonny looked momentarily reluctant. Digger had told him to stay out of sight.

'What the hell.' He picked up his keys.

On the way out Carmichael shook hands with Tyrone. Tyrone felt a crackle of folded paper in his palm. He waited until he'd shut the door and double-locked it on the two men then he went into the kitchen and told the girl making toast to get out. He pulled out the piece of paper and looked at it.

On it was written a phone number and attached was a credit note for £10,000.

Ring me tomorrow at 11.30 if you want to cash it.

Carmichael and Sonny drove to a club in Islington. While Sonny went to the bathroom to cut himself a line of coke, Carmichael tipped crushed horse tranquillizer that he'd brought from the farm into Sonny's drink. Sonny came back from the bathroom wiping the cocaine from his nose.

'Drink up!' Carmichael handed Sonny his glass and knocked back his own. Sonny obliged by doing the same. Carmichael got up to leave. 'I've seen enough here – let's go somewhere else.' Out on the street Carmichael went round to the driver's seat. 'I'll drive. You'll get nicked.' He held up his hand for Sonny to throw him the keys.

Sonny shrugged. 'Okay . . .' He threw them across and opened the passenger door. 'Give me the chance to chop another line.' He dropped into the passenger seat and opened the glove compartment. Carmichael saw the butt of a revolver. Sonny rooted round and then took out the packet of coke he found. Carmichael braked just as he unfolded it. 'Fuck . . .' it showered like fine talc over his lap. 'I'll get some more . . . no problem.' He squinted at the road ahead. The car twisted and turned down back roads. 'You know where you're going?'

'Yeah. Staying off the main roads, don't want to get pulled over. Not when you're wearing a lap full of Columbian snow.' Carmichael looked across at Sonny, whose head was nodding as he grinned. 'Hey, Sonny . . .'

'Yeah?'

'Just curious . . . You ever get a thing for one of the women?'

Sonny looked across at Carmichael. He grinned sleepily.

'No such thing as a *thing* for a woman like that. Treat them like animals . . . it's a business.'

'You must have fathered a child or few?'

Sonny snorted. 'Sure . . . it happens . . . get rid of it.'

'You must get some strange requests: freaks, specialities?'

'Digger orders something special sometimes.'

'To work in the club?'

'Shit, no. I mean special, weird – he passes it on to someone else.'

'Weird? As in?'

'Had to send her for tests – blood, that kind of thing.'

'Anyone ever order a pregnant girl from you?'

'Yeah, Digger wanted a pregnant one once. Now the police are asking about her.'

'When was that?'

'About a year ago now I got her for him. She was one of my girls.'

'Do you know what he did with her?'

'Nothing to do with me.'

'What about Digger?'

'Or him. She was for his friend. I brought her in. Digger passed her on.'

'Who to?'

'I never met him. What's with the questions?'

Carmichael changed gear, the car slipped along the waterlogged streets of melting slush.

'Just that I had a kid once.'

Sonny closed his eyes. 'Yeah . . . nice.'

'A kid can rip your heart out and stamp all over it, more than any woman. You make a promise to a kid, you have to keep it. They trust you. There are consequences if you let them down, if you fail them. You ever think about consequences, Sonny?'

Sonny didn't answer. He had fallen asleep.

Carmichael pulled onto the slipway. The Thames was inky black. The water was running fast, pulling the mass of black back out to sea. A Christmas boat party was in progress. The sound of laughter and drum and bass drifted across the water. Carmichael sat for a moment watching the lights on the water before he turned and punched his fist hard into the side of Sonny's head. He reached into the glove box and took out Sonny's revolver before releasing the handbrake and stepping out of the car.

Chapter 25

Carter had gone to lie down in the exhibits room where they'd put up a camp bed. He left instructions to wake him in three hours. They were taking it in turns to grab a few hours' kip through the nightshift. In the ETO, Ebony looked across at Jeanie. She looked very pale.

She was on the phone to her husband Noel.

'I'm not going to make it back, love . . . give her a kiss from me . . . I expressed milk; it's in the fridge.' Jeanie closed her eyes as she listened to her partner's silence – not hostility, just concern. But they had no choice. Noel was going to be another couple of years studying for his teaching qualifications and one of them had to pay the mortgage. *Damn* . . . Jeanie felt the tingling in her breasts as she heard Christa cry in the background. Jeanie snapped her eyes open and put a smile on her face as she answered: 'No, not coming back at all tonight, I'm sorry. Looks like we'll all be working nonstop until this case ends . . . love you.'

Her hand lingered on the phone as she finished her call and looked up from her thoughts to see Ebony pointing discreetly at a damp patch on Jeanie's chest.

'Oh shit.' Jeanie brought her arm across to hide it. She stood and pushed her chair away. 'I've had enough. I'll be back in a couple of hours. I need to get home and feed my baby. If Davidson asks, tell him it's milking time back at the zoo.' She smiled at Ebony. 'Won't be long. I'll see you in a couple of hours – four max. I'll take my nap at home.' She picked up her bag and left.

There were only four of them in the ETO now. Ebony went to talk to Robbo, sitting on his own in the Intel room. He was on the phone to Sandford, who was at Blackdown Barn.

'Yeah . . . I'll ask her now.' He held the phone away from his mouth and looked up at Ebony as she walked in.

'Sandford wants to know whether you want to go back to Rose Cottage with him and Bishop?'

'When's he going?'

'Tomorrow sometime. He'll let you know. Yes or no?'

'Yes. If I can.'

'He wants you to get hold of the gardener anyway.'

'Okay. I have his number.'

Robbo got back on the phone to Sandford. 'She'll come with you, if she can . . . but she'll contact the gardener either way and speak to you tomorrow . . . By the way . . . I've contacted several manufacturers for plastic curtains. I've got the samples for you. Yeah, yeah . . . I'm alright here thanks. It's nice and warm here in the office.'

Robbo hung up and checked his watch. 'Although probably no good to call your gardener now at three-thirty in the morning. Right . . .' He clapped his hands together in front of his face and snapped his eyes open wide. 'Coffee and then back to work. You heard from Carmichael since you went to see him on the farm?'

'No. I have a funny feeling he's not there.'

'Yeah . . . that was always on the cards,' Robbo shouted over grinding coffee beans. 'You couldn't expect him to take it lying down. You tell him the people who killed his wife and child are back in town and you send him an open invitation to hunt for them himself. He's got nothing left to lose. You better go back there and see if you can find out where he's gone.'

'If he did come looking . . . how would he do it?'

'If I was him? Either I would get to someone in this department – call in an old favour, ask *me* for instance – or I would dig up any contacts in the underworld I could beg, steal or borrow from and go undercover.'

'Has he?'

'What – asked me? No. I checked with Sandford and Bishop – none of us have had a call or any contact with him. He doesn't need us then. He must have another way in.'

'Would you have helped him?'

'Probably. We all feel like we let him down. We let his wife and child down. Nobody came out of it with justice. It was in the days before we had a designated murder squad. A team would have been assembled when it happened. Davidson was in charge. It was up to him to choose his team – doesn't mean they were the best for the job. Davidson would also have been

responsible for all the clever stuff, working out logis-
tics, analysing; all the things he doesn't have to do
now . . . we have crime analysts to do it.' Ebony took
a cup of coffee from Robbo and looked around for
the sugar. He gestured over to the shelf with the coffee
beans. 'What was he like when you went to see him?
What is his life like out there? I haven't seen him since
it happened.'

'He lives in the middle of the Yorkshire Dales. The
nearest town is twenty miles away. He lives like a
hermit really. He works really hard. I don't know
what else to tell you. I felt he was just working; it
wasn't a home. Maybe that's the kind of man he
always was. What was he like thirteen years ago?'

'He was dedicated to his job, to his family. That
was his world. He hardly ever came out with the
lads. It wasn't surprising he lost it after the murders.
Someone pulled his world from under his feet. He
had nothing left worth living or staying together
for.'

'Really? He fell apart?'

'Oh yes. He had what would have been called a
nervous breakdown, except no one wanted to call it
that.'

'Could he have had mental problems before the
murders? He had an affair. Did that surprise you?'

'Yes. It did. I'll be honest – I find that completely
out of character.'

'Do you think he could have killed his wife and
child, Robbo?'

'I think he could have done it if he had already gone
stark raving.'

'Certain parts of Rose Cottage look like that's what happened. There's a madness out there but also a containment. You know what I mean? Yes, the women were horrifically mutilated, parts of their bodies removed, but at the same time, where is the blood? If someone ran through rampaging and killing, how come they anaesthetised them first?'

'You cut someone open they usually die. You cut them open under anaesthetic you have a while to play.'

'It must have been planned. The way Blackdown Barn was planned. If it's the same man: Chichester?'

'Has to be the same killer. The monster's still out there.'

Chapter 26

Carmichael slipped Sonny's key into the main door of the old apartment block on Shaftesbury Avenue. It was four in the morning and Soho was quiet. It was nearing kicking-out time for clubs like Cain's.

Keeping his head down he walked up the stone stairwell. The echo of a homeward-bound drunk filtered up the stairs. Somewhere on the upper floors a cat meowed to be allowed inside one of the other flats. Carmichael walked to the end of the first landing. He unclipped his hunting knife from its sheath on the inside of his calf and concealed it in his left hand as he slipped the key into the lock and turned it. Silently he opened the door a few inches and listened. There was just the hum of a fridge, the dripping of a tap. He felt to his left on the wall: no alarm box. He opened the door wider and slipped inside. The flat was in darkness; just the orange glow of a streetlamp filtered in through a gap in the curtains. The door clicked shut behind him. It was then he heard a voice.

'Where have you been? I've been waiting ages. I'm in here . . .'

Carmichael walked along the corridor and nudged the bedroom door with his foot. A woman was in bed.

She froze when she saw Carmichael standing in the doorway. Carmichael looked around the room.

'You alone?'

She nodded.

'Get dressed.'

Carmichael went to check in the other rooms. When he got back into the bedroom she was fastening her bra.

'You expecting anyone besides Sonny?'

She shook her head. 'Is that his name?' She glanced up from pulling down her T-shirt. 'Is he coming back?'

'No.'

She stared at Carmichael for a few seconds, not sure whether she was relieved or whether she'd found herself a worse problem.

'How do you know Sonny?'

'I don't really. I came here last night. He went out and left me to wait for him.' She was pulling on her jeans and turned to Carmichael as she searched for her shoes. 'I fell asleep.'

He looked around the bedroom. It was a man's décor: black, red and grey. 'You a prostitute?'

'Escort,' she snapped back as she searched around for her bag. 'Haven't been doing it long. My ex-husband fucked off and left me with debts. My first client robbed me and now this one has run off.' As she talked she kept one eye on Carmichael and one on her escape route.

'Time for a change of career, maybe?'

She picked up her bag. 'Yeah, seems a good plan.'

'You been here to this flat before?' She shook her head. She pulled her hair back into a ponytail and Carmichael could see her face for the first time.

'What's your name?'

'Pamela.'

'*Real* name?'

She smiled. 'Linda.'

'How did you find Sonny?'

'I'm registered with an escort website. He got in touch through that.' She was looking towards the door. 'Look . . . I have to be getting home; the cat will need feeding . . . you know how it is?' She looked up to see him staring at her.

'You don't look like an escort.'

'Thanks.' She smiled. 'Girl-next-door kind of thing. He specifically asked me to turn up in jeans and a T-shirt. Shit, I should have made him pay me before he left.'

Carmichael reached inside his coat pocket and took out a card and three hundred pounds.

'Hope that helps. If you remember anything else or anyone gets in touch about Sonny, let me know.'

'Thanks, I will.' She stopped in the doorway, looked back and smiled.

Outside, she pulled up her hood against the cold and hailed a taxi at the end of the road. She sat in the back and pulled out the black and gold business card Carmichael had given her.

Michael Hart.

His mobile number and nothing else.

She took out her phone and made a call.

'It's Nikki de Lange. Sonny's dead. We have trouble on our hands and his name is Hart. Meet me in five hours, usual place.'

Chapter 27

Cain's finally kicked the last punter out and closed its doors. Tanya sat at the dressing-room mirror in her T-shirt and knickers and looked across at Anna hiding in the corner. Tanya put down the cotton wool pad caked in makeup and smiled at her as she waved her over. Anna stared back, unsure, until a second wave saw her get to her feet and walk cautiously across. Tanya turned the chair next to her round and Anna sat down.

'Close your eyes,' Tanya said and mimed the action when Anna didn't understand.

Anna felt the cool cream spread over her skin as Tanya wiped her face in sections. She cupped Anna's face in her hands when she was done. Anna's eyes opened slowly: reluctantly she emerged from a memory stored in her senses where a mother she had once known had cared for her just like that; had touched her just like that. Tanya smiled at her, looked deep into her eyes and then hugged her. Anna lay limp in her arms and started to cry.

Digger didn't knock before he entered the dressing room. The dancers were used to it. Anna sat back in her chair. Tanya turned back to the mirror and picked up a fresh cotton pad.

'Tanya, I have a client for you. Get dressed and hurry. A taxi is coming in ten minutes.'

Tanya nodded her agreement but her face clouded over as she reapplied foundation to hide her bad skin and scraped her hair back. She drew kohl into the rims of her eyes and applied mascara again. She stood and pulled on her floor-length military-style coat and stopped as she saw Anna still watching her. She went across to her and rested a cold hand against Anna's baby face. Anna reminded her of her four-year-old son Jakub who she'd left behind for her mother to look after. Tanya smiled and leant in.

'Close your eyes.' Anna did as she was told. Tanya kissed each eyelid in turn. That was the last thing she'd done when she said goodbye to Jakub. She'd kissed his eyelids and said: 'Remember me when you close your eyes, I will be with you.'

Outside, the taxi was waiting, Tanya stepped inside and closed the door and it pulled away. Inside the taxi someone was waiting for her. She smiled. She remembered him from somewhere. At first she thought it was a punter. Was it a man she'd been sent to meet in a hotel room? He was good-looking anyway. As he moved across towards her on the back seat of the cab, she looked down at the bruising on the inside of her elbow and then she remembered that this was the man who had wanted her tested.

Carter heard the buzz of his phone as his alarm went. He'd set it because he knew Ebony would give him a few minutes longer than he'd asked for. He washed his face in the bathroom, spent five minutes re-gelling his hair. Then he sprayed deodorant inside his shirt and sniffed his armpits to make sure he was passable before emerging to locate Ebony, who wasn't at her desk. He found her with Robbo.

'Greetings . . .' Robbo looked up as Carter entered.

'Any coffee?' He looked around and saw the half full cafetière then helped himself.

'Ebb, you better get a few hours' kip now.'

'I feel fine, Sarge.'

'Yeah, but you've got a long day ahead. I need you to head back to Carmichael's farm today and check on him. Things have gone a little quiet.'

Tanya felt the cold air whoosh around her as she moved through the air horizontally. Trolley wheels rumbled, vibrating below her body, and then everything echoed around her as she entered into a building and the wheels found a smoother surface. When her eyes managed to stay open for a few seconds they saw a high ceiling with pipes running across it.

She was lifted from the trolley, guided onto a bed, hands held her weight. She opened her eyes briefly and looked around the unfamiliar room. It wasn't a hotel room. It was a hospital.

Tanya's eyes were struggling to stay open. 'What are you doing?' She saw a nurse walk around the bed and then start undressing her. She felt the cool air in the room flow over her body as the nurse drew back the covers and began to wash her. She took her time – long, slow, warm strokes that soon turned cold on Tanya's skin. But Tanya didn't mind as the warm flannel stroked her tired limbs. Her mind wandered back to being in a bath with Jakub; the first time he had laughed. Then she thought she could hear his breathing as he lay beside her sleeping. Feeling heavy now. Her arm was being pulled out straight. In her dream it was her son Jakub pulling it. What did he want? *Mama? Mama?* Tanya felt a sting in her hand but still she could hear the rhythmical breathing of someone asleep. She felt another's body next to hers.

'Jakub?'

She struggled to open her eyes and turn her head to see her son. A woman's face was inches from her own, watching her.

Chapter 28

That morning Carmichael watched Tyrone shuffle his way between the tables over to where he sat with a double espresso in the busy café. He grated a chair out opposite Carmichael and sat down. 'Got your message. Have to be honest wid you, I don't really understand what you want from me . . . as much as I appreciate the offer of ten G, I ain't figured out how I earned it.'

'You will.' Carmichael pushed an envelope across the table to him. 'Sonny is dead. I am taking over.'

Tyrone looked momentarily shocked until the feel of the wad inside the envelope calmed him. He stuffed it inside the pocket of his jacket and looked pleased with himself.

'You'll get a lot more money if you co-operate. I want a list of all Sonny's contacts. I want to know everyone he deals with. You know Digger Cain?' Tyrone nodded. 'Digger gets no more women. None of these women leave your care. I expect you to look after the women till I say I'm ready. You tell them I'm the man to deal with. No one – I repeat, no one – takes any of those women out of that house . . . understood?'

Carmichael waited as Tyrone shuffled in his chair, dug his hands in his pocket and then settled down again. He looked across at Carmichael.

'No can do.' He shook his head, wiped his mouth. 'There's outstanding deals. Sonny set them up. They got to be honoured.' Tyrone was chewing the inside of his cheek.

'What deals?'

'Digger wants most of these girls I got: six, two young ones.'

'Stall him for a few days. I'll cover it by then. What else?'

'Sonny told me to find a special girl.' Tyrone looked nervously at Carmichael. He was looking squeezed. 'It happened a while ago, the same thing . . . I have to test the girl. If it comes up with what they're looking for then they pay. Just the one pays the same as ten girls—'

'What's the test?'

'Starts with blood.' He shrugged. 'If she's got the right blood she has more tests.'

'What for?'

'I don't know what for; I never asked.'

'When was the last time you found the right girl?'

'A few hours ago. They made a match. Girl named Tanya, dances in Cain's. Digger said someone paid a lot of money.'

'Have you been asked to test again for another match?'

'No. Might not happen again, who knows?'

Carmichael looked away angrily. 'Where did he take her . . . do you know?'

'No.' Tyrone shook his head nervously. He pulled up the hood of his parka. 'Listen . . . I ain't looking for trouble. He already paid for the girl. He took her. I couldn't do nothing 'bout it. How do I know Sonny is dead?'

'Look out for it on the news. Then spread the word with all Sonny's agents. I will pay big money to whoever comes on board with me now. I have contacts all around the world. I will shut down anyone else.'

After he watched Tyrone shuffle away Carmichael dug out the 'pay as you go' mobile phone that he'd picked up on his way down from Yorkshire. Then he sent a text voice recording to the local police in Whitechapel, telling them what to look for. He kept it simple . . .

Dead man in red Ferrari down slipway on Isle of Dogs.

Chapter 29

Ebony didn't bother to switch on the sat nav this time. She left the train station in the hire car and kept her eyes peeled for the junctions. The snow was starting to melt from the fields now, glossy and bright like wet icing on a wedding cake.

As she neared Carmichael's farm the sun was bouncing bright off the top of the buildings. The cockerel weather vane glinted as it tilted and caught the sun. Bridget heard the car approach and stopped to listen. She knew it would be Ebony; Carmichael had told her to expect another visit. Bridget stood at the entrance to the stable and watched Ebony drive in and park. Rosie went over to say hello. Bridget locked the stable and wheeled the barrow across to the dung heap past the farmhouse. Tor came to stand with his head over the stable door and watch the proceedings.

'Hello, Bridget. Is Callum in?' Ebony screwed up her eyes against the low winter sun as she got out of the car.

'No.' Bridget tipped out the contents of the barrow and wheeled it back to stand against the woodshed wall.

'Where's he gone, do you know?'

Bridget shook her head.

'How long will he be away?'

'T'aint my business.'

Ebony looked about her. 'Are you looking after things here for him?'

'Aye.' Bridget shut the barn door and walked across to the house. She scrutinized Ebony as she passed. 'What do you want?'

Ebony followed her into the tack room. 'He must have said how long he thought you would be looking after it?' Bridget didn't answer. 'Can I scrounge a cup of tea? It's a long way back. I promise I won't stay long.'

Bridget looked Ebony over, weighing up in her mind what Carmichael would want her to do and what she could be bothered with.

'Was stopping anyway.' She prised off her wellingtons in the tack room and washed her hands in the scullery sink, then walked through to the kitchen.

Ebony followed her and saw Rusty tucked up in Rosie's basket in the corner of the kitchen, a lamb in beside him. She knelt to stroke Rusty. Bridget slid the kettle onto the top of the Aga.

'How's he doing?'

Bridget nodded, softened. 'Good.'

'Who's his new friend?'

'We've had a lot of twins this year. This mother's not the best at looking after her young.'

Ebony sat at the kitchen table where she'd sat opposite Carmichael just a couple of days before.

'I'm hand-rearing this one and Rusty's helping keep him warm.'

'Can I use the bathroom?'

'Upstairs . . .'

'Thanks . . . be back in a minute.'

Ebony finished in the bathroom and she quietly turned the handle of Carmichael's room. His bedding was neatly folded and placed on top of his bed. His wardrobe was empty.

Back in the kitchen, she asked, 'Has he been gone long, Bridget?'

'Not long.'

She handed Ebony a cup of tea.

'Hours?

'A day or so.'

'Carmichael's lucky to have you here, not many people would be able to look after things for him.'

Bridget stood with her back to Ebony as she put sugar in her tea.

'Tis what I always do. Nothing queer in it. I got my dad to come down and help. We'll manage the lambing.'

'Do you know where he's gone, Bridget?'

As Bridget put her own tea on the kitchen table and her eyes settled on Ebony's face. Her eyes were the same colour as the dusky blue hat she was wearing. The lashes around them were thick and fair.

'He must really trust you then to leave you in charge of the farm. You're very fond of him, aren't you?'

Bridget looked away for a few seconds then back at Ebony. 'He took me in when I had nowhere else to go; taught me about rearing sheep, taught me how to look after things . . . and myself. He never wanted nothing from me.' She glanced up at Ebony. Ebony gave her a smile that said I know what it's like to love someone and not get it back. 'I owe him a lot. If he's in trouble I want to help.'

'You can help him, Bridget. Tell me where he's gone and I'll do my best for him. I promise.'

She could see Bridget thinking it over, her hands tight round the mug of tea.

'I told you, he's not one to trust; but he liked you.'

Ebony smiled 'He's facing a tough time.'

'Will you bring him back here to the farm, to me?'

'I promise to try.' Ebony passed her over a card with her mobile number. 'If he turns up or contacts you, let me know, Bridget. I am on his side.'

Bridget took the card. She turned it over in her hands. Ebony could see she wanted to talk.

'If he phones I'll tell him to call you.'

'Where do you think he's gone, Bridget?'

'All I can tell you is that he's taken their photo and he's taken his gun.' Her eyes flitted over Ebony's face. 'Never seen him so troubled. I think he's gone searching for the people who murdered his wife and child. Don't think he'll ever be coming back here, save in a box, to be buried up there on the hilltop.'

Chapter 30

Robbo walked down a floor to the exhibits room in Fletcher House. He keyed in his code on the door. Each murder squad in the building had their own designated exhibits room. Inside were shelves floor to ceiling with the various sizes of scene-of-crime bags, plastic containers of all sizes and packets of forensic suits. To the left was a small partitioned area where two DCs could sit.

He unlocked the door to the caged area where the exhibits were housed waiting to be taken to court or sent to the forensic laboratory. On a high shelf he found the Carmichael case exhibits, newly arrived back from the warehouse. Robbo lifted the exhibits box down and began going through the bags inside. After an hour of searching he phoned Ebony. She was on her way back to Fletcher House from the station.

'Yeah, I found it, have it in my hand right now.' He looked at the small brown packet. 'It's a piece of fabric, ten-centimetre square.' Robbo looked at it through the plastic window at the front. He moved it round. 'It's heavily bloodstained.'

'Does it say whose blood it is?'

'Yes. It's got a note attached. *Louise Carmichael's blood, found on path outside gate.* It's not fabric; it's hospital gauze. And I've checked all the police records for that day; there was no report of a police vehicle sustaining any damage on that visit. The hospital confirmed that their ambulance was not the one that knocked over the gatepost.'

Ebony left the Tube and walked past the few shops on her way back to Fletcher House. She was nearly back at the office when she saw a man walking towards her. His eyes were fixed on her from twenty metres away. He took long strides, walked straight. Others stepped out of his path. It was his eyes she recognized, the rest of him was nothing like the farmer she'd seen a few days before. Carmichael stopped in front of her. 'You want to talk?'

The café wasn't busy upstairs. It used to be the 'smoking' section and people just forgot about it now that smoking was banned. Carmichael took off his thick cashmere overcoat and put it on the seat beside him.

'I went back to the farm to talk to you. I saw Bridget.'

'She told me.' Carmichael's eyes roamed the room as he answered, checking out a man coming upstairs to use the bathroom.

Ebony looked away, fiddled with her cup.

'Why didn't you stay on the farm? Thought you understood we would keep you informed?'

'Thought I could inform myself much better. You must have known I wouldn't stay where I was. Did you honestly think I would take the information you gave me and do nothing? You chose to involve me. You came to see me . . . remember?'

'I was sent to talk to you.'

He looked at her and remembered what it felt like to be betrayed by someone in authority, someone further up the chain of command. His voice softened. 'You must have known I would do all I could to find the people who killed Louise and Sophie. I'm not the one putting your career in jeopardy. Consider the fact that they're using me and they're using you to do it.' Ebony looked into his eyes. 'We can help one another, you and I. Let me tell you what I know, then I want something back from you. You use whatever I tell you in any way you see fit. You are looking for Sonny?' She looked at him, trying hard to hide the surprise she felt. She had underestimated him, but she shouldn't have. Robbo was right: Carmichael had ways inside the system.

'Yes. We are looking for him. His DNA matches the dead baby's at Blackdown Barn.'

Carmichael didn't give anything away.

'Don't waste your time with him. Sonny is just a trafficker. He gets the girls over here and he breaks them. Sonny only supplies girls for Digger, no one else. Digger starts them on the circuit of clubs and brothels. Now your turn to talk.'

Ebony looked across at him. 'You didn't tell me you knew Chrissie well. In fact, you said the opposite. You said she was Louise's friend but actually . . . she was yours.'

Carmichael shrugged it off. 'We once thought about dating but never did. We kept in touch with a twice yearly email. After she had the baby she got back in touch with me. I was married by that time. She didn't seem to mind. She slotted in and Louise was really fond of her. From that minute on I faded into the background.'

'Why did she get in touch with you, do you think? Do you think she wanted to strike up something; after all, lots of people go back to past relationships that "might have been", especially as she found herself alone with the baby.'

'I never got that impression. But . . . as it turned out, she and Louise got on better than we ever would have. How far have you got with new evidence from Rose Cottage? Is Davidson reopening the case?'

'Not yet. He believes the key to finding out who killed your wife and child is finding out who Chichester is. I've been looking over the old autopsy reports. Did you ever see them?'

He shook his head. 'I told you – I was in no fit state to see anything for the first year. I never queried anything I was told . . . I never saw the autopsy reports. It's not something you show to the family, even if they are police. You know that.'

'There is a briefing today. We will be discussing your case. Jo Harding is going to be talking us through those autopsy results.'

'Harding has her own agenda. She hates me, always did. She was a good friend of Chrissie's. They trained together. I could see she always blamed me. Maybe she was right to . . . Harding won't like being pushed. She might be straight out of the pages of a Jackie Collins novel but she doesn't like people knowing anything about her that she hasn't told them whilst performing fellatio.'

'You might be wrong about Harding.' Ebony hid a smile behind her coffee. 'She says she barely knew Chrissie. She's fought to have the case reopened. I went with her to Rose Cottage.'

'What did you find?'

'It hasn't been touched since that day. A gardener looks after the outside, that's all. When you got there that morning did you notice a section of the gatepost was knocked down?'

'The gate was open . . . yes, there was rubble at the foot of the post.'

'Large tyre tracks were found. Something had difficulty turning. They took out the upper part of the post. A large van maybe.'

'Significant?'

'Maybe. Did you see blood outside the house?'

He shrugged. 'I don't think so.'

'Inside the house, where Louise and Chrissie were, was there a lot of blood?'

The pain on his face made him turn away, watch the street outside, see people shopping. The Christmas lights swung in the wind. Christmas music played in the café; a waft of cinnamon, clove and orange circulated. He turned back.

'Mainly smears around the walls, drips on the floor; not arterial spurts, except for Sophie. What do you think happened?'

She shook her head. 'I'm not sure. The forensics team are going back there to see if we can find out more. All I know is they might have died where you found them but I think their injuries were caused somewhere else. There's just not enough blood in the house. Whoever did it, whatever it is they wanted, they are still looking for it.'

For a few minutes they sat in silence as a waitress came up to clean the tables around them. When she'd gone back downstairs Carmichael continued: 'I know you don't have an undercover officer who can do what I can. You don't have one ready. I can be that for you.'

'It's too risky. If you need help you won't get it. No back-up.'

'I'm not prepared to wait while Davidson gets his head out of his arse. I'm not asking for help. I have nothing to lose here. I wouldn't want Davidson balls-ing it up again. I am telling you, Ebony, because I trust you and because we might need one another before this is over. Look . . . I respect you . . . You're a good cop. You do what's right for you. I'll do what's right for me and get inside Sonny's organization.'

'Davidson will have you arrested if he knows what you're doing.'

Carmichael smiled. 'Here's my number. Keep in touch. And don't worry. Davidson couldn't find me if I was sat metres from his office having coffee with you.'

Chapter 31

After the big freeze had come the big dirty melt. The Thames ran high and icy cold.

Digger kept his eyes on the pavement now turned to slush as he walked towards the escalator and the new shopping precinct. An Italian café had somehow managed to survive amongst the concessions of fast food. He liked to sit and watch the children play. He bought a cappuccino with a dusting of chocolate and sat at one of the tables on the edge of the play area. The place was busy today.

He didn't need to look to know that she had sat beside him. He felt a small flutter in his heart, the way he always did. His eyes stayed on the TV screen in the centre of the mall.

Totteridge Village bodies found.

'Morning, my dear . . .'

Nikki de Lange followed his eyes to the TV screen. 'I see you have heard the news?'

Digger nodded. His eyes were dark but a smile remained.

She looked at him anxiously, her eyes flashing towards the TV screen. She was chewing the inside of her lip like a child.

'Now, now . . .' He patted her hand. He looked at the aerial shot of the back garden, the patio and the white crime scene tent. 'Don't worry, my dear. Things will be alright. Are you feeling okay? You look pale.'

He was right. She felt nauseous; she had pains in her lower back. She followed Digger's eyes as they moved from the TV screen to watching the children playing nearby.

'I'll be better soon, as soon as it's over. I was in Sonny's apartment when a man named Hart let himself in with Sonny's keys.'

'I've met Hart.' Digger looked away from her back to the news on the screen. He pretended to watch it but she could see he was giving himself time to think. 'We need to keep a close eye on Hart.' He turned back to her. 'I think he isn't who he says he is. He walks like a Para. He smells like an ex-policeman. Oh, he covers it well enough with a backstory that reads like a Bond film but it's not sitting right. I think we should err on the side of caution and kill him. What were your impressions?'

'A man with ambition.' She couldn't hold Digger's eye contact.

Digger smirked. 'Do I detect a soft spot for the new man?'

'I just don't think we should kill him, yet. We could do with a shake-up. I'm thinking this is my time to break free with your help.'

Her hands were shaking as she lifted her cup to drink. Digger's hands were rock steady as he sipped his coffee.

'Yes, you are right, my dear.' The sound of the

children laughing in the play area filled the space between them. Digger's eyes searched hers. 'What do you want from me?'

She stared at him, unsure of his meaning and then she shook her head. 'It's all business, Digger. It has to be.'

'You want me to keep an eye on him?'

'I want you to give him what he needs to do the job we have to do and then I want out of it. I'm not going to stay with him after this trip. This trip will change everything for me.'

'Of course. I will do anything you ask me to. You know that. You are my god-daughter and I am very fond of you. Back in the days when your father and I were friends we had such marvellous times.' He looked across at her impassive face and sighed. 'I remember—' he began, but she cut him short.

'No more memories, Digger.' She smiled. She looked at her watch. 'I have to go.'

An hour later Nikki de Lange was walking along an underground corridor; she looked up at the pipes above her head. The building above her creaked and hummed with the noise of trolleys and moving beds and nurses' feet. She stopped at a room on the right and unlocked the door.

'Hello, did you miss me? Have you been a good boy?' She stopped just inside the door to cover her hands and arms with antibacterial gel and then walked across to the bed. The room had the smell of lavender. She sprayed it in a room mist. It helped him sleep. It helped him to stay asleep, just like her voice: calming, constant. It told his brain that he needn't worry; he mustn't fight it. Three weeks he had been in an induced coma. Nikki walked over to the bed and checked his chart. She flicked a switch controlling the drips into the boy's neck and wrist and pressed buttons on the monitor at the head of the bed. The boy did not stir. The noise from the ventilator: the bellows breathing was a comforting sound. She bent down to check the catheter bag hooked to the underside of the bed then she peeled back the sheet and gently washed and dried around the electrodes that were stuck to his chest. She cleaned around the entry sites into his body: the neck, the wrist, into his mouth, his nose, his groin. She massaged the muscles in his legs. She looked at his face and sighed. He no longer looked like the boy he was. The drugs had bloated his face and the corrugated ventilating tube going into his mouth had distorted it.

She walked across to the chair, picked up his Arsenal shirt and folded it neatly.

Chapter 32

'Arsenal shirt,' said Carter to Ebony as she got back to her desk. 'Large boy's. This season. They changed fabric, changed manufacturers this year. Whoever he is he loves his football enough to pay over fifty quid for a shirt.'

'Could it be Silvia's?'

'No, the DNA doesn't match.'

Carter looked at her face as she sat down. 'What is it?' She was just about to tell Carter that she'd seen Carmichael when Robbo burst through the door of the ETO.

'We got a phone call . . . anonymous tip-off about a body in the Thames. First officer at the scene said he recognized the body . . . it's Sonny.'

The water was the same colour as the sky – steely grey. In contrast the bright red Ferrari being hoisted by a crane hung like a firework in the winter sky.

Ebony had invested in a sky-blue beanie hat which she pulled down over her ears. As they turned the corner the icy fog lay like a shroud over the water. Divers were getting changed after having fished Sonny's waterlogged body out of the Thames.

'Nice motor. Pity it didn't float,' said Carter.

Harding looked up from where she knelt on a piece of plastic sheeting next to the body. She looked pale with cold. She had the hangover from hell. She and Mathew had worked late and the inevitable had happened, and when she woke up and saw his face on the pillow she had hated herself marginally more than him.

Carter squatted beside her. 'Yeah, this is definitely Sonny. This might answer why we couldn't find him.' He opened Sonny's jacket and pulled out a wallet. He passed a driving licence to Ebony. 'Run this through Robbo, Ebb, and give him the make and licence plate of car . . . see if he can come up with an address for the little mermaid here.' He turned to Harding. 'He doesn't look the suicidal type. Were his keys in the car, do we know?'

'They weren't.'

'Wasn't robbery . . . plenty of money still in his wallet.' Carter closed it up again and tucked it back into Sonny's pocket. 'How long's he been in the water, Doc?'

'About twenty-four hours max.'

'It's a dumb question, I know, but was he dead before he drowned?'

He helped her turn the body on its side then roll him onto his front as she lifted his jacket at the back and looked for signs of injury. 'No obvious bullet or stab wounds.' Carter helped her roll Sonny onto his back again and she turned his head to look at one side and the other. 'It looks like he might have had a head injury going into the water. There's bruising on the side of his head here. Could have banged his head in a panic trying to get out as the car filled up. The bruise hadn't time to spread: it's intense. It definitely occurred minutes before death and not hours. There's a line of four dark circles decreasing in size. Looks a lot like a—'

'Fist,' said Carter. 'So someone banged him unconscious with a hit to the head.' Carter pointed to the pits and scrapes of missing flesh in Sonny's face. 'How did he get these other injuries, Doc?'

'I would guess when the current dragged through the car. The windows were open. The water would have carried debris with it. The rest we can put down to the local river-life having a few meals on his face.'

The forensic photographer was done. He stood to one side viewing his work on his camera. He nodded to Harding. 'Got what we need. You can move the body now.'

'Sarge?' Ebony had finished talking to Robbo. 'Car's traced to Sonny's mother's address. They're sending someone round there now.'

Harding stood, peeled off her gloves. 'Okay. That's it for me. I'll start the autopsy as soon as I get back to the hospital.' She began walking back up towards her car.

'Doctor?' Ebony ran to catch her up. 'Could we meet up again soon? I need your help with Rose Cottage.'

'Yes. But not now and not later this evening, I have plans. Come and find me tomorrow.'

Ebony waited for Carter to catch up. He was taking his time. He called her over to take a look at the Ferrari.

'Interesting choice of slipway this, Ebb. Not many you could get down without a four by four. Not many people know about this one, not the general public anyway.' They stood watching the red Ferrari as the crane held it a few feet over the slipway; a loader turned up ready to take it. Carter walked across to the man driving the crane.

'Let's make sure she's not holding any more surprises. Set her down on the slipway for me before you load her.'

While they waited for the car to be lowered Ebony turned to Carter:

'Sarge, I saw Carmichael.'

'When?'

'A few hours ago on my way back to the office. He stopped me when I came out of the Tube. Bridget must have told him I visited the farm.'

'You should have told me straight away, Ebb. '

'I was trying to get a chance, Sarge.'

Carter turned to face her and took a step closer to make sure that in the still damp air his voice didn't carry as far as the officers around the car.

'What did he say?'

'He knows everything we do.'

'Did he know about Sonny?'

She nodded. 'He told me that he was a small part of it and not important.'

He gave a nod towards the Ferrari. 'Obviously someone agreed with him.'

'He's going undercover. He says he can infiltrate Sonny's organization.'

'Like this? Dead men's shoes, is it, Ebb? Was this Carmichael's doing?'

She shook her head. 'I don't know, Sarge.' She'd

had a sick feeling that wouldn't go away, ever since she heard of Sonny's body being found.

Carter looked away to gather his thoughts. 'You know if we tell Davidson that we have the slightest inkling this could be Carmichael's work then he'll arrest him.' She nodded. 'Did he say anything that might tell you what his plans are, where he's staying?' She shook her head. 'After all this time he can get in undercover? Shit. I take my hat off to him, Ebb. He must have had some very clever help. Or he must be taking an incredible gamble.' Carter looked across at her and smiled reassuringly. 'Okay. The main thing is he trusts you, Ebb. There's nothing to really tell Davidson. We didn't learn anything from him that's new. But we did get closer to him and that's a good start and it will do for now. But next time you tell me as soon as something happens, okay?'

She nodded.

'Start trusting, Ebb. You're not a one-man band. We're a team.'

Chapter 33

That evening Jo Harding waited for the young Irish barman from Cork to come back her way.

He'd stopped to chat with a couple of girls who were on a Friday night out. Harding tapped her new nails against the side of her glass. He glanced her way and then back at the girls, his elbow on the bar, his smile fixed. Even as he sauntered over he kept glancing back to the girls to make sure they were checking out his rear view.

Harding was irritated: *who the fuck did he think he was, keeping her waiting?* She pushed the glass towards him. 'Same again.' He smiled at her, not open-mouthed, not full like he did to the girls at the other end of the bar. He smirked almost. *Fuck him . . .* she would remember not to suck his cock the next time she took him home. She was aware of someone standing next to her. She turned to see the good-looking face of James Martingale.

'Hello, beautiful . . . as lovely as ever.' He leant in to kiss her.

'Good to see you, James.' Harding smiled. *He was still the charmer.* Seldom did she see the charm offensive aimed at her but now she felt its full impact.

Fucking men ... how come they get better-looking as they get older? Martingale definitely had, she thought. He had that confidence that says, I will be great in the bedroom; I have studied every book written about how to bring a woman to orgasm.

The barman left the girls and came over. He looked suitably impressed by Martingale, who cut a very distinguished moneyed look.

'Yes, sir?'

'A Manhattan, and put my lovely companion's on my tab.'

He turned to Harding. 'Let's move to a table.' He picked up her drink and turned to the waiter: 'Have my drink brought up.' Then he led the way upstairs to the restaurant.

After they had ordered he sat back and smiled at her. 'What's it been – three years? You look younger than ever. You had some work I don't know about? I need to know who the surgeon is if so. I need to congratulate him.'

'That's a backhanded compliment if ever I heard one but I think I should thank you. No work, and no chance I actually look as good as you're implying.'

He smiled and reached over to touch her hand. 'It's good to see you. I hope it wasn't a problem to tear yourself away tonight.'

'How could I turn down an invite from the mighty James Martingale ... I'm honoured.'

'Please ... and it's not as if we don't know one another.'

She laughed. 'Is there something I don't remember? I apologize if that's so. Obviously I wasn't that bad if you've come back for more, even if you did leave me waiting three years.'

Martingale laughed. 'No, don't worry. I am far too much of a gentleman to take advantage of a woman who has drunk too much. Plus . . . it's too boring. I like the challenge of seduction. I like to know I've earned it.'

'Is this what this is? A lesson in seduction?'

He sat back and allowed the waiter to unfold his napkin onto his lap. He smiled at the waiter, made eye contact. 'Perhaps.' He looked back at her. 'You didn't get married again? Last time I saw you were in the middle of a divorce.'

'Yes . . . a bad place to be.' She rolled her eyes.

'Happens to us all. You didn't remarry?'

'You must be joking. I've tried it twice. Both times I've managed to screw it up.'

'Never blame yourself . . . that's always my motto. Besides, some of us aren't meant to be monogamous.'

'Faithful, you mean?' She laughed.

'Call it what you will. Did you stay friends with them?'

'My last one I see sometimes for a drink. He's a criminology lecturer here in London. I don't see much of the first one, Simon, unless I see him at one of your dinners. He still works for the Mansfield Group, I take it?'

'Yes. Simon is one of our originals. He's got to be one of our highest paid surgeons. He's the house-wives' favourite. Does all breast implants now.'

'Always thought he was a tit. I should have had a better settlement.'

Martingale laughed. 'You're a funny lady. We're the same types, you and I. We are demanding of ourselves and others. It's not always easy to live with unless you're the same type . . . cheers.' They clinked freshly filled glasses. 'On the subject of work . . . you will tell me if you are in need of any more equipment in your laboratory. You know I'm always happy to write off a bit more tax for a good cause. Also . . . I wanted to ask you whether you knew anything you could tell me about the new lead in my daughter's case?' Harding now knew why the dinner invite; why the sudden interest after three years of not so much as an email. 'I had a visit from two police officers; they told me about the recent murders in Totteridge. They wouldn't tell me much more than the fact they are somehow forensically linked to my daughter's death. Is there anything more you can tell me? I don't want to get my hopes up.'

'I can tell you – it's all in the early stages. Yes, we did find a link.'

'The fingerprint? Sergeant Carter told me. It can't have been my late wife Maria then? I always thought Maria could have done it . . . she went quite mad.'

Harding was nodding; she had her most sympathetic expression on her face. She felt awkward.

'No . . . she can't have done it. Is that a relief?'

'Yes it is. It really is. It's haunted me all these years. How I might have contributed to her madness by rejecting her. How I should have tried for a better relationship with Chrissie. But . . . it leaves a massive question over the whole investigation, doesn't it? What's happening now?'

'We're looking into the case again, under a new light, new team. We're hoping we solve this new case at Totteridge and then we'll catch whoever murdered your daughter.'

'After all this time?'

'Yes. We don't know why they've come back. Sorry. It still hurts: I can see. But there is a real chance of catching them this time.'

'No need to apologize. Of course it still hurts. It will always hurt. In my darkest moments I feel somehow responsible: something I did, something I didn't do. I failed my daughter, that's for certain.'

'Since her death you've given life and hope to so many people through her foundation.'

'Yes. I hope so.' He reached over and covered her hand with his. 'I am hugely reassured that *you* are part of the new investigation. Please will you keep me informed.'

'Of course.'

'I just want to be kept up to date, discreetly; in private, without the world and his brother watching. I don't want policemen knocking on my door. I don't want the press hounding me. But I will never mind a late-night call from a beautiful pathologist to talk shop or sex or the state of the universe . . .'

He picked up his glass and drank his wine and poured them another. The bottle was nearly gone. He called the waiter over. 'Another one.'

Five minutes later the waiter returned to apologize. 'Sorry, sir, that was our last one.'

'What? For Christ's sake . . . what kind of service is that? Where's the manager?' The waiter hurried off. Martingale looked across and shook his head. 'I'm sorry. It just pisses me off. Hate incompetence.'

The waiter returned, anxious to please. 'Sorry, sir. I do apologize. We have another bottle, considered to be a superior vintage. I will bring you that one at the same charge.'

Martingale consented with a wave of his hand.

He poured the last of the bottle of wine into her glass.

'You know, Jo . . . I have a fantastic house near Cape Town, overlooking the bay. You should come out and visit me . . . I could do with the company. All expenses paid, of course; just say and I'll send you a ticket. When was the last time you had a holiday?'

She shook her head. 'Can't remember.'

'You should accept my offer of more private work too.'

'I don't mind dipping my toe in it. Can't argue about the money side of it, but I need to have the adrenalin rush, the challenge.' She looked at Martingale and thought: *smug bastard*. 'So, Mr Martingale . . . no dreams left? You have it all.'

His pale blue eyes shone in the candlelight. 'I have a dream of not dying alone.'

'Ha—' Harding just about managed to stop herself from full-on laughing in his face. *Was this a wind-up?* She searched his face for the sarcasm she expected and saw none. His eyes were shining as he picked up his glass and saluted her.

'To the most beautiful pathologist I know. Someone I'd definitely like to see more of. If she'll let me. I hope you're not feeling too tired tonight. I have a lot of skills I need to practise on you.'

'I'm all yours, Doctor; can't wait.'

Chapter 34

The next morning, on the outskirts of London the snow was melting from the hard shoulder of the M25. Two men were working their way up the verge, clearing up the rubbish and debris thrown out by passing traffic. Barry was in charge. Barry was going to be looking after Tom on his first week of work. They had been due to start last week but couldn't because of the weather. Now it had warmed up a few degrees overnight and they were back to work.

Tom was starving. They'd already been working for two hours when the motorway maintenance van stopped at the services. He bought himself a full breakfast bap, reheated in the microwave in the garage: sausage, egg and bacon, ketchup, mustard and soggy bread. He didn't care; he was so hungry.

Tom shook his head and laughed. 'Get it down you, son . . . you're gonna need all the energy you can get. It's bloody freezing out there. We got three hours till we stop again. I'm going for a piss.'

By the time he came back Tom was aiming the wrapper at the bin and wiping the ketchup from his mouth.

'Ready?'

Tom nodded. The traffic was post rush hour, lorries mainly. They headed along the hard shoulder, stopping every fifty metres to backtrack and check the verge. They split up, starting either end to meet in the middle.

Tom had his orange bag in his left hand, his metal claw pick-up device in his right. He prodded his claw into the gorse at the side of the verge to pick up the piece of black plastic that flapped in the wind every time a lorry raced past. His pincher clasped the black plastic and he pulled. A woman's grey face turned from the snowy gorse as her body rolled down onto the tarmac.

His scream was lost in the whoosh and wail of a lorry as it passed.

Barry looked up to see Tom walking backwards towards the motorway traffic. 'Watch out, mate . . .' he called and screwed up his face at the icy wind that buffeted him as the lorry thundered past.

'Oi, Tom . . . get your arse back, son,' he shouted. Tom turned and looked at him, but didn't answer. Standing in the path of an approaching lorry, he bent over, staggered backward and then a projectile vomit of full breakfast landed on the tarmac. The lorry swerved.

The woman's head turned towards the road as if she were watching the passing traffic.

Carter had hardly slept when he'd finally made it back to his flat to make sure everything was still there and to get a few hours' proper sleep and a change of clothes. Cabrina was on his mind here especially. He felt as if he were grieving. He reached out and slid his hand along the cold space in the bed next to him. Oh God ... his mind went round and round and came back to the beginning and always Cabrina was in the centre of the circle, shaking her head at him and knowing that he just didn't get it ... what had he done wrong? Now the flat could stay a mess; nothing mattered any more.

The phone rang. It was Ebony.

'There's a woman's body found on the hard shoulder at Junction twenty-three of the M25. Doctor Harding's meeting us out there.'

The M25 motorway was closed between junctions. It was causing chaos in the morning traffic.

Carter approached. 'Ebb?'

'Woman's body, sir. Thought you would want to see.' She turned to point out the van parked nearby. 'These motorway maintenance engineers found her.'

Carter stood in front of where the gorse had been cut and cleared to give better access. The woman's naked body was lying on black plastic. He could see the white-grey of her body, and in its centre, shards of white bone protruded from the black gaping hole where her insides should have been.

Carter squatted beside Doctor Harding. 'What do you think, Doc? She been here long?'

'Less than twenty-four hours.'

Harding pulled back the plastic and revealed the rest of the woman's body.

'This has all the hallmarks of the others.'

Carter stood and looked down the lines of traffic on the other side of the carriageway; their tyres noisy on the wet tarmac. 'So they left her just hidden, chucked in the bushes. She didn't die here. Someone tied enough plastic around her to transport her in the boot of a car, not to make a mess, but they must have expected her to stay on the side of the road a bit longer.'

'Animals could have started on her any time,' said Harding.

Carter turned to Barry. 'How often do you come along this strip and clean it?

'Once every two months. But our schedule's up the swanny on account of the weather. We were supposed to come along this section last week and we didn't make it.'

'So if someone knew your schedule, they'd think she wouldn't be found for two months?'

Barry nodded. Tom was sitting in the police car with a blanket round his shoulders.

'Did he move her at all?'

Barry shook his head. 'You must be joking . . . frightened the life out of the boy . . . puked every-where.' He glanced over at the puddle of bright-coloured vomit on the black tarmac.

Carter went across to wait in the car and get warm for a few minutes. He was in danger of throwing up, too.

He watched Ebony as she knelt beside the body, taking a photo with her phone. He selected a number on his mobile and hit the call button.

'Cabrina?'

'I told you, Dan, I just need to think things through.'

'You're alright though, aren't you? You'd tell me if you weren't.'

'Of course. Baby is kicking away. Keeps me awake at nights.'

Carter closed his eyes and felt for a moment as if he was about to sob.

'I want you to come back, Cabrina. I miss you. I want us to plan the baby things. Start painting the nursery, you know, get things – pram . . . and stuff . . .'

'Not the pram. It's bad luck. Anyway Mum and Dad are going to buy that . . . as a present.'

'Of course . . . how are they . . . okay?'

'So excited about the baby . . . Look, Dan, I know you're missing me and I know you're trying your hardest to be pleased about the baby. Maybe you are, in your own way, but I'm not sure if it's all enough. I need more. I need to feel secure and I don't. I never know where you are.'

'At the moment I'm sat looking at the traffic on the motorway. We've got a corpse by the side of the road.'

'I don't mean it like that . . . you know what I mean . . . you're never around.'

'I'm working. You know that.'

'Yeah, but what if there was an emergency? What if the baby was sick and I couldn't get hold of you? And I don't know whether you're ready for dirty nappies and breastfeeding and I just don't want another baby to look after, Dan. One baby will be enough. You always like things to be just *us* . . . I understand: but it will never be just us again. I'm not sure you can adapt to that.'

'You aren't giving me a chance. I want you, Cabrina, and if that means the baby comes as part of it then I'm ready.'

'You see what I mean, Dan . . . you'll have it, if you have to. It's not the same as wanting it . . . *really* wanting it.'

'I didn't mean it like that.'

'But that's the thing, Dan – you did. You *did* mean it like that. You're just not ready.'

'Sarge?' Ebony walked towards his car. Carter finished the call. He wound down the window. She leant into the car. 'I know her . . . she's one of Digger's – I saw her when I went round the back at his club. She was in one of the back rooms. She was the one I asked if she'd seen Sonny and she said *yes*. She gave her name as Tanya.'

Ebony and Carter arrived in Cain's and waited whilst the janitor went to wake Digger up. He was stony-faced as he greeted them, a fresh cup of coffee in his hands. Ray the barman was there cleaning the bar.

Digger sat down at one of the tables.

Carter placed the photographs of Tanya's frozen body out like cards, one by one on the table in front of him. 'This is one of your dancers.'

Digger looked slowly up at Carter. He placed his coffee cup down and wiped his mouth with a snow-white cloth napkin. He signalled to Ray to come over.

'Is this one of our girls?'

Ray looked at the photo. 'No, boss.'

'You sure?'

Ray nodded. A bead of sweat was beginning to form on the crease in his forehead.

'That's that then. Sorry we can't help. I warn you, Sergeant, I am going to lodge a complaint. I am being harassed.'

'Her name is Tanya,' interrupted Ebony. 'I saw her here.' Ray turned a puce colour as she spoke. 'The day we came to visit. Ray here let me look around.' She smiled. Ray went to protest his innocence. Digger held up his hand for him to be quiet.

'Okay.' Digger picked up the photo. 'Now I can see that it is Tanya. Such a shame. She was a lovely girl. She moved on, wasn't happy here. It happens. Girls come and go here. Poor Tanya; no one's safe on these streets any more. I blame the Police Force: you pay peanuts, you get monkeys. I had nothing to do with it. If you think I did . . .' Digger made a sucking noise as he cleaned his teeth with a toothpick. 'Prove it.'

'When did you see her last?' asked Ebony.

'I saw her the night before last.'

'What time did she work until?'

'Until we closed at four-thirty and then she left.'

'Did you see her leave?' asked Ebony. Digger shook his head.

Carter glanced around the club and came to rest on the web cam positioned above the bar.

'We need the CCTV footage from your cameras inside and outside Cain's for the last forty-eight hours.'

'I would love to oblige, Sergeant, but I'm afraid our cameras are under repair.' Digger smirked.

Carter rolled his eyes. 'Just lucky that we have a surveillance team across the road then, isn't it? By the way . . . have you seen anything of Sonny?' Digger's head swivelled on his neck slowly from side to side as he kept his eyes on Carter.

Carter grinned, gave a half laugh as they walked away and turned to Ebony when they got outside.

'What do you think Ebb? Does he know about Sonny?'

'Think so, Sarge.'

'Yes, so do I. But we'll keep him on his toes. Make him get careless; he has to off-load Sonny's girls now, Ebb, and he knows we're watching every move he makes. He's going to have to take a few risks. If Carmichael is undercover then we'll give him all the help we can.'

Chapter 35

Ebony watched Mathew finish laying out Tanya's remains on the steel mortuary table. He rested her head on the stand. Mathew had a bruise just under his eye. Ebony had no intention of asking him how he got it.

Carter walked in and laughed at him. 'Fuck ... that's a good one ... how did you get that shiner?'

Mathew's eyes went towards Harding. He gave a sheepish grin. 'Tripped over the other night. Had too much to drink.'

'Took an uppercut, or a jab ... bam, bam ...' said Carter, guard up as he shadow-boxed. 'Somebody shorter than you. "Fell over", my arse. You should take up boxing, Mathew. It's a great way to keep fit.' Ebony gave Carter a sideways look. He raised an eyebrow back.

Harding pulled down her visa and pulled on gloves. She came over to the table and handed Ebony a mask.

'Follow me round, Ebony. Take the photos I tell you to,' said Harding. Mathew stood ready to help turn the body, collect samples: neatly laid trays poised. Harding smiled at Ebony and handed her a camera. 'Do you know how to use it?'

'Yes. I used one in college.' She turned it over in her hands.

'Start with a view of the whole body from each side.'

Carter didn't enjoy the autopsy side of the job. He stood back with his notepad ready.

Harding spoke into the dictation machine as she walked the length of the table and got an overview of the body.

'Detective Sergeant Dan Carter and Detective Constable Ebony Willis are present to assist and record and Mathew Cummings is diener. I am about to perform an autopsy on the body of an adult female discovered earlier today on the side of the M25 ring road around London. We had to wait for the autopsy as her body was still partly frozen. The body is in one piece.' Harding walked around the table. 'The woman is well muscled, her body weighs sixty-five kilos. Her height is five foot eight. She has no obvious scars, tattoos or birthmarks. I estimate her age to be late twenties. We have identified her as a dancer named Tanya.'

Harding pulled down the light and a magnifying lens to examine the joints. She called Ebony in to take a picture.

'Bruising on her shoulders corresponding to finger marks where she appears to have been held down.'

'We'll get Bishop in here and see if we can get a print off her,' Carter said.

'An incision from pubic bone to sternum has been made already: I'm going to widen it to take it from each shoulder down to join the centre cut in a Y-shape.'

Mathew passed her a scalpel. She made a cut across from the nape of the neck to each shoulder and cut through the muscle and flesh. 'Someone has sawn through the clavicle; the ribs and the breastplate have been removed. Heart and lungs have been taken out in a block. Takes a good degree of skill to remove these so cleanly.'

She talked as she worked her scalpel beneath the flesh and skin of the neck. 'I will be removing the tongue and windpipe by working up from the skin in the upper chest.' She pulled the tongue down from under the jaw and handed it to Mathew.

'All the major organs have been removed.' She moved back down and opened up the body further. 'The stomach is still present.' Mathew handed her a large syringe and she proceeded to empty the stomach contents.

Harding moved back up the body to Tanya's skull; she opened up Tanya's eyelids one after the other.

'Unable to collect ocular fluid . . . not present.' She glanced up at Carter and Ebony. 'Corneas are missing.'

'Is that the same as Silvia?' Carter asked while Harding picked up each of Tanya's fingers and cut away the nail and the nail bed. She tapped the contents into a tray Mathew held for her.

'We don't know about her corneas; the eyes were too degraded to tell. But if you mean that she was missing her internal organs, then yes. The whole of the torso section was missing, including major organs.'

'There are incisions on the femur and sections have been sawn through and extracted.' Mathew handed her a steel ruler which she laid alongside the leg. 'Fifteen centimetre sections have been removed with a fine-bladed handsaw.' She gestured for Ebony to get as close to the femur as she could and take a look through the magnifier. 'These injuries bear a significant resemblance to the type of dissection we saw in Silvia.'

Mathew helped to turn the body over.

'There are two areas of skin grafting on the backs of her thighs and buttocks, carried out within hours prior to her death. The area is still in trauma.'

'It wasn't just organs then?' asked Carter.

'The skin is an organ.'

'I know but . . .'

'No . . . not just . . . she has had sections of bone removed from her femurs the same as Silvia.'

'Why sections of bone? What is that about?' Carter asked.

'There are stem cells in the marrow,' answered Ebony as she stared across at Harding for confirmation of her thoughts. 'Organs, corneas, skin and bone marrow?'

Harding nodded. 'Yes. She wasn't just murdered. She was harvested.'

Chapter 36

'Bloodrunners. They're gangs who sell human organs . . .'

A photo of a good-looking lad with his family came up on the screen. Robbo was in charge of the briefing; all of the murder squad were crowded into the conference room at ten the next morning.

'. . . several countries have had scandals where people have had organs stolen. Profit is always behind it. This lad went on his gap year . . . to find long-lost relatives in Poland.' The next shot was of his body wrapped in a sheet. 'His body came back to the UK minus his organs and with a full denial of wrongdoing . . . just no one knew how he died or where the organs had gone. Bloodrunners harvest organs and tissue and body parts such as hands, limbs, hearts, livers, kidneys, faces even. People wake up minus a kidney.' Photos of a hotel room and a woman's dissected body. 'In the current economic climate organ-harvesting has become a very profitable business.' Robbo talked over the images. 'Although it is not usually associated with the UK.'

'I've heard of Bloodrunners but I've never seen gangs in action,' said Carter.

Robbo continued the slideshow: the bodies of three children were being displayed; each one with a neat incision that cut the torso in half. 'Because we have a system set up which means we trust the medical experts in this country to do the best job they can with the resources available. If they say your child is too weak for an organ transplant or we don't have one suitable . . . then the child dies and that's it. In other countries where you can buy human life much more easily, doctors are more likely to say: *we can do it at a price*.'

'Can we find out what happened to Tanya's organs? Is there any way we can access lists of people waiting that would match her?'

'We can try,' answered Harding. 'But I doubt if these were sent to people waiting on the national register. More than likely her organs were sold on the black market. But it would all have to happen very quickly. Somewhere there will be patients recovering now.'

'How long does the heart last from donor to receiver?' Davidson asked Harding.

'They must be a slick operation,' said Harding. 'It takes time to harvest someone on this scale. It must have taken more than one person to get it all done at the same time and end up with usable organs. With the heart, you have a small window of use conventionally, but there are other methods available now. There are a few ways of doing it. You can inject the heart with potassium chloride: that stops the heart beating before they take it out and then they pack it in ice. It can last four to six hours depending on starting condition. Or there is also a new machine which keeps the heart beating like it would in the body and it could last a relatively long time in that state, twelve hours even. Or they can perform a "beating" heart transplant, where the donor is still alive, technically, and their organs are transplanted directly into another. All of these operations would have to be done in a hospital.'

'What about Blackdown Barn? Could they have operated in the house?' asked Ebony.

'In the master bedroom with the plastic on the floors and walls?' Carter said.

Harding thought for a few seconds.

'In theory, yes. But, the smaller the team of people around the surgeon the more equipment he will need to help him. It would have taken a lot of equipment and would have been a big task getting it all up to that floor. You'd be creating an intensive care unit in there . . . very tricky. The patient would need twenty-four-hour specialized care. Better to have made it on the ground floor, converting one of the rooms there to an operating theatre.'

'Maybe the operation was done in a hospital and the recovery period took place in the house,' said Carter. 'What about the van, Robbo?'

'If that's the kind of van we're looking at then it's tall enough to stand up in,' said Robbo. 'Yes, it's the right size and type to be an ambulance.'

'You might be able to do emergency surgery in it,' said Harding. 'You could use it to transport a patient and keep them alive. You would need it to move a recovering patient. But not a heart and lung transplant.'

'So if the operation was done in a hospital,' said Davidson, 'they could move the patient in the ambulance and put them into the sterile room in Blackdown Barn to recover.'

'To recover or to wait,' said Carter. 'And not just the patient. Patient and donor. Blackdown Barn had it all – recovery room and holding pens. That's why they picked that house. They really thought it through. Location-wise it's close to London, close to the M25 to get to airports small and big. It's a place where people don't bother to talk to neighbours and it had an owner who never came near it.'

'What was it the letting agent said Chichester wanted, Ebb?' asked Jeanie.

'He wanted semi-remote but near a major road. The manager remembered that Chichester said he'd pay a lot to be left alone. It didn't matter about the house being in poor cosmetic shape.'

'So basically he paid a lot of money for a house that wasn't worth it. He must have been a dream client.' Jeanie answered.

'So before Chichester the house had been empty for a few months?' Robbo asked.

'Nearly a year. It must have been hard to let,' said Ebony. 'Then Chichester had the work done to it; that took two months.'

'So we're not looking at a snap decision here, are we?' said Davidson. 'Chichester took a few months to find this place, another two to make it ready. This was no heat-of-the-moment thing. He planned it meticulously for a predetermined purpose. That was to harvest kidnapped victims and sell the organs to wealthy clients. So why did he leave there? Did he talk about staying on there to the estate agent?'

'Apparently there was an option on it, sir. Chichester hadn't decided. The estate agent was waiting to hear.'

'He wasn't in a hurry?'

'The agent said he knew he wouldn't be able to let it again till after Christmas. He thought Chichester would stay. That was his impression.'

'Maybe he intended to.'

'Think everything Chichester does is intentional, sir. If he left early it was because it fitted with his agenda; it was for a reason.'

'A holding pen keeping them till when? What about Silvia and her pregnancy? asked Davidson. 'Why allow her to carry the child at all if they didn't harvest it?'

'I can answer that,' said Harding. 'I had the results back for the section of skin above Silvia's left eye. It has traces of the rubber from the treadmill. She fell whilst she was running on it.'

'Why would she be running at eight months pregnant?' asked Jeanie.

'When you're pregnant the heart and lung size increases to cope with the demands of the unborn child.'Answered Harding, 'they are a muscle like others; they respond to demand. You can train them and make them even bigger. So maybe they were waiting till they were at their peak condition. The gym could have been part of preparations and perhaps the baby was "an option".'

'Option?' Davidson looked at Harding and shook his head. 'I don't follow.'

'Well, it's insurance for later, isn't it? They could harvest the mother and keep the baby as part of the family, bring her up as their own, in case other organs failed later in life. In case they needed to harvest her.' She shrugged. 'Why not? If you're that ruthless and calculating?'

'What about thirteen years ago?' asked Jeanie. 'What about Rose Cottage?'

'The piece of hospital gauze that the gardener found by the gatepost?' said Robbo. 'That must mean thirteen years ago Louise Carmichael was carried back into Rose Cottage from having been operated on somewhere else.'

'Yes . . . has to be,' said Carter. 'The bodies of Chrissie Newton and Louise Carmichael had a large amount of anaesthetic in their bodies.'

'It would answer a lot of questions,' replied Harding.

'The cross-contamination theory, for example.' said Ebony. 'Maybe there was no mistake made, after all. Chrissie and Louise were taken away to be operated on and brought back so that their bodies could be discovered at the house. That's why they had each other's DNA on their backs. They had both lain on the same place after death. That must also be why the lividity had a small discrepancy; they had been moved but then laid down again in the same position.'

'And their organs were missing.' said Jeanie.

'Not all their organs; they only removed their hearts,' Harding corrected.

'Are we sure they didn't harvest anything else?' Carter said and glanced nervously Davidson's way. 'I mean, samples got contaminated, reports had sections missing from them. I'm not being funny but how do we know?'

'I know,' said Harding, about to lose her rag. 'At the time we didn't make the full report public because we didn't want the panic that would ensue but it didn't mean to say that a full and accurate report wasn't written, because it was.'

'I meant no disrespect.' Carter held his hands up in a surrender gesture. 'Thirteen years ago the gang may have worked differently, been inexperienced, who knows?'

Harding composed herself. 'Three hours passed between first Chrissie and then Louise dying. There was definitely time to remove their hearts.'

'Then we need to find a hospital near Rose Cottage where they could have taken them.' Davidson moved to the front of the room to wrap things up.

'There are hundreds of private hospitals within range,' said Robbo. 'They could have driven to an airstrip and taken the organs a long way. We know there are illegal immigrants coming in by small aircraft on makeshift landing strips around the UK. They could easily take something like organs out on a small plane.'

'Or someone could have been waiting here for the organ,' said Ebony.

'Yeah . . . I think that's most likely,' said Harding. 'There are many hospitals within reach. I'll look into it for you. I'll find out who was working in them at that time and who was the kind of surgeon to do it.'

'I want a list of all aircraft activity after Tanya's death. If those organs were flown out of the country they would have gone minutes after her death.'

Ebony had been watching Harding for some time. It was the first time she'd ever seen her really nervous.

Chapter 37

After the meeting Harding went to Davidson's office.

'Can I have a word?'

'Of course.'

She closed the door behind her. 'I had dinner with Martingale last night.'

Davidson felt bitter betrayal well up in the pit of his stomach. He wasn't sure whether it was because he had been sidelined or whether he still wanted Harding and he knew that dinner meant dessert.

'Congratulations . . . and?'

Harding sat down. She knew he'd be irritated but she had more important things on her mind. It wasn't even as if the night had been any good. 'He seems to be perfectly at ease with the new investigation, hopeful of a better outcome this time.' Davidson looked away towards the window. He took that as a criticism. His face had become gaunt in the last few days. His eyes were dark-rimmed. 'He isn't so keen on being visited at his house. He's a very private person.'

'I know . . . I have warned Carter to be discreet; but, after all, I am doing what you suggested: handing it over to someone who I know will keep it transparent.'

'He wants me to keep him *personally* informed of the investigation.'

Davidson looked at her curiously. 'As in?'

She stared back. 'I think he was implying that he'd like me to supply him with inside information.'

'Bloody cheek.'

'Yeah. I know.' She smiled. 'Don't worry, John. I'm not that wet behind the ears. I can spot a bribe even when it's disguised inside a trip to his house in South Africa, a new CT scanner *and* enough flowers to fill a crematorium.'

'Why would he need to?'

'You know him better than me, John. You've been to more corporate dinners with him. You tell me? My guess is he's a control freak. He wants to be one step ahead: hates surprises. Hates being out of control. I think we both need to keep our distance from him, John. We don't want to be seen to be giving preferential treatment.'

'I don't intend to give him anything but what he deserves: respect and consideration. None of this can be easy for him.'

Harding looked at him incredulously, with a hint of pity as she shook her head. 'Don't, John. There'll be other opportunities . . . retirement-wise. Other boards to sit on.'

'I'm not thinking about that,' he snapped back.

'Of course you are.'

Ebony came back from the canteen and went back to her desk. She looked across at Jeanie. Jeanie wasn't looking good. She'd gone down with the pre-Christmas mini-flu that was going round the office. Her eyes were glassy, her face flushed. Ebony saw Carter disappearing in the direction of Davidson's office in the corridor outside.

'You alright, Jeanie?'

'Yeah . . . I'll survive.

'Where's Carter going?'

Jeanie raised her eyebrow in the direction of Davidson's office. 'Results from Sonny's post-mortem are back.'

Carter stood alone in Davidson's office.

'Sonny was killed by drowning but he was unconscious at the time. No sign of him struggling. There is a swelling to the side of the head which has the shape of someone's knuckles in it. There are distinctive scars on the knuckles.'

'Trevor Bishop is pretty sure we'll be able to match it to someone's fist if we get a suspect. He has ketamine and diazepam in his bloods not to mention a large amount of cocaine present in the urine in his bladder. Someone would have had to make sure he was going to sleep for a long time. His wallet was still there but no house keys.' Davidson handed Carter a slip of paper with a hint of amusement in his eyes. 'His mother had an address for him.'

Carter looked at it and read it.

'Result, sir.' Carter looked up at Davidson and grinned.

'Yes, the deeds show the flat belongs to Digger Cain.' said Davidson. 'Sandford's on his way round to the flat now.'

'Okay, sir. I'll swing by the flat on the way to see Digger, sir.'

'Has Robbo got any further tracing Tanya's last movements when she left Cain's?'

'He's looking through the CCTV film sir. The surveillance team opposite Cain's caught her coming out and getting into a cab. They're trying to get a better image of it from other cameras on the street.'

'Okay. Before you do, Carter, how far have you got with reassuring Carmichael? Has he been in touch since Ebony went up there?'

'No, sir.'

'Is he still at the farm?'

'I'm not sure, sir.'

'Find out and if he's not? We need to find him. We don't want him running loose and possibly intimidating people connected with this case. A court would throw the case out for that.'

'Yes, sir.'

'You have heeded what I said about being thorough but being discreet, haven't you, Carter?'

'Yes, sir.

'Don't go near Mr Martingale understood?'

'Yes, sir.' He pocketed the piece of paper with Sonny's address and left.

Chapter 38

Sandford was waiting for them at Sonny's flat. Ebony stood in the hallway outside the kitchen door. Sandford wasn't letting them go any further.

'Okay . . . we understand . . . we'll check in with you again later . . . but what are your first impressions? Anything interesting? Documents, clothes, PC?'

Sandford shook his head. 'Someone's been through the place before we got here. We've been through the drawers – nothing. Whoever went through Sonny's flat wasn't looking to burgle it. They left some very expensive music kit behind: a Bose sound system, antiques. They would have ransacked the place. They didn't. The person didn't break in, no sign of forced entry: they had keys or someone let them in. We might find prints but I doubt it. I tell you what I did find is this.' He held up a bag with the contents of a U-bend. 'This is from the bathroom. The hair is an identical length and shade to the hair I found at Blackdown Barn; my guess, same woman. There was also hair in the bed, same woman. There are two toothbrushes here. We should get DNA from those. I'll let you know as soon as I hear back.'

'We'll take a trip back to Blackdown Barn in the next couple of days,' said Carter. 'How's it going out there?'

'Slow. The cellar floor is proving a massive task. There are previous building works beneath it. We haven't even started on the garden yet. Cadaver dogs are due in tomorrow.'

They left Sandford to it.

Carter steered Ebony towards a café.

The café was gaudy at the best of times but now at Christmas it had been overloaded with tasteless decorations and fake snow that clung to the window and looked suspiciously real. They collected their cutlery and sat down.

'We'll keep on leaning on Digger.' Carter ordered the same as Ebony: a Full English, which was served all day even though it was past lunch time. He didn't even bother to ask them to grill the bacon. He waited for her to pass the salt. 'Sonny's death will shake him up a bit and now we have the link directly to him and Sonny,' he said as he buttered his toast. 'It's bound to make him nervous. If Sonny sold him Silvia then Digger must have sold her on to Chichester. We'll tell him about Sonny now. Maybe he's got himself involved in something he won't like.' Carter stopped and peered past the window decorations at the darkening day outside.

'Christ, I hope it isn't snowing again.'

'It's fake.'

'Thank fuck for that.' He stopped and looked across at Ebony. 'What's the matter, Ebb? You can usually talk and eat.'

'Carmichael . . . I can't get hold of him; I've been trying, every hour.'

'What's on your mind?'

'Carmichael. If he's involved, it's murder.'

'Not technically.'

Digger was eating lunch at his usual table in Cain's when they got there: eel pie and mash. He ate it with a white cloth napkin and ornate silver cutlery.

He looked up and groaned when he saw them walking towards him.

'Not again, surely?'

Carter showed Digger a close-up of Sonny on the autopsy table. 'Fished out of the Thames along with his car,' said Carter. 'Twenty-four hours in the water, the bottom feeders have been busy.'

'Good-looking chap, whoever he is.' Digger shook his head as he mopped up the gravy with French bread. 'Such a pity, a waste.'

'The car, you mean?' Carter grinned. 'Yeah, tragic. A red Ferrari deserves better.' Carter looked around, swivelled on his heels. 'You sleep here, Digger?'

'When I'm working, yes. I have an apartment upstairs. It's not palatial . . . why?' The look on Digger's face said he knew what was coming.

'You have a flat anywhere else?'

'I have a few properties in London. Why?'

'You let people like Sonny stay in them?' Carter tapped the photo.

'That's Sonny?' He leant in to get a better look at the photo. 'Sorry . . . apologies, Sergeant. I know

Sonny . . . Oh goodness, what a shame. Digger picked up the photo of Sonny's bloated, damaged face. 'Any idea who did that to him?'

'Probably that eel you're eating. The flat?'

'Occasionally I allow others to use one of my properties; it's good for business. I rented a flat to Sonny just a short walk from here. He's been renting it now for a few months.'

'Anyone else stay at that flat, Digger? Anyone been there recently as well as Sonny? Anyone else got a key?' Digger shook his head. 'Then that leaves you well and truly in the frame, doesn't it, Digger? Someone had a key and let themselves in and then promptly removed anything interesting. We've been left with Sonny's clothes and a toothbrush or two. Someone went to some trouble to clean up in there. Any ideas?'

'Sorry, Officer . . . no. Sonny paid me whether he stayed in it or not. He paid his rent on time and that is all I asked. I have no idea who stayed there with him.'

Carter sat down opposite Digger. Digger pushed his plate to one side. Ray came to take it away.

'Let's talk it through, Digger. Let me level with you. I wanted to talk to Sonny because I thought he could tell me about a case we're working on. A woman and her baby have been murdered at a house on the outskirts of Totteridge.'

Digger looked suitably surprised. 'Not the ones in the news?'

'Yeah . . . those.'

'You think Sonny had something to do with it?'

'The baby was Sonny's. Now we all know Sonny did a side-line in rape as well as trafficking. We also know that you and he were good friends, business partners. He was in here almost every night.'

'Please, Sergeant, don't waste your breath. I know nothing about any pregnant woman. All my women are happy to be here and working in my clubs.'

'The murdered woman could have been one of your girls. She could have worked here.'

'Or in any other place,' Digger said calmly.

'They cut her open, took out the baby and left both of them to die . . . nice people. You might be next on their list . . . first Sonny then you maybe? You better start talking, Digger, before it's too late. Tell me about a man named Chichester . . . he bought the dead woman either from you or from Sonny a year ago.'

'No comment.'

'What's the future for you without Sonny to supply you with girls?' Digger shook his head, went to plead his innocence again. Carter held up a hand to stop him. 'Now . . . just say you wanted more girls. Just suppose you were still in that sordid world? Who you gonna call now Sonny's gone? Anyone come forward to offer you any deals? Deals that, of course, you refused?'

Digger didn't answer straight away. He dabbed his mouth with his cloth napkin.

'I don't know what you're talking about.'

Carter smiled to himself as he turned on his heels and walked out of Cain's. The pavement slush was turning into an ice rink as the temperatures began to plummet and it re-froze. Inside the car he turned on the ignition and waited for the windscreen to clear, gave up and wiped away the condensation with his sleeve.

He turned to wink at Ebony.

'No harm in giving Carmichael a little help if he's managed to set himself up as the new Sonny, need to make it look realistic.' Carter took his phone out and read an incoming text. 'We need to head over to the Mansfield hospital. Justin de Lange has got the file I asked for on Martingale's financial interests.'

Ebony was still preoccupied with her thoughts. 'But Sarge, Carmichael said to me he knew Sonny was small fry; he may have just got rid of him to be able to take his place.'

'Yes, maybe Ebb, but this is all supposition and we don't need it right now. If we can keep up with Carmichael he may save us a lot of work. He was right, we don't have a UC agent. We need him.'

'We don't need him to be murdering the suspects.'

'Not technically murder,' he said, pulling slowly away into the gritted part of the street. 'It's probably endangering life.'

'He punched someone in the head and then left them to drown.' Ebony looked about to keep arguing the point.

'Either way, Ebb, it's over, done. We'll hear from him soon enough. I'm looking forward to meeting Justin de Lange,' he said, changing the subject.

Chapter 39

They pulled into the car park. It was four in the afternoon and already dark. Orange lights flooded the area.

'That could be Justin de Lange over there, Sarge.' Ebony looked across at the entrance as they parked up. 'He looks like he's spotted us.'

Carter looked across to the hospital entrance; a man picked up a briefcase from the back seat of his black Audi before looking their way. He was striking-looking, in jeans and a denim shirt. He had on a sheepskin coat. Expensive but casual. Ebony thought how de Lange looked like an ageing footballer with his blue eyes and blond hair falling over his collar.

'Blimey it's the lion king, Ebb.' Carter kept the engine running and sat for a minute watching him. 'Yeah . . . I agree. He's waiting for us. Should be interesting, Ebb. Wonder where wifey is.' The man smiled at them as they walked across the gritted car park to meet him.

'Justin de Lange?' He nodded. Carter made the introductions as they reached him. 'I am Detective Sergeant Dan Carter and this is Detective Constable Ebony Willis. Thanks for seeing us this afternoon.'

'How do you do? I just came out to get my brief-case. Follow me and we'll go inside to my office; it's freezing out here.'

'Absolutely . . . Lead the way.'

Ebony turned to look around the car park. She saw a car drawing in, parking in the corner; that made twelve cars in total. They walked up the ramp and through the swing doors, past reception. Carter smiled at Ivy. She beamed back. Justin led them up a flight of stairs and into his office.

'Please sit down, I'll order us coffee. How do you take it, Sergeant?' Justin sat on the edge of the desk with one leg on the floor.

'Milk and sugar please . . . Ebb?'

'Not for me, thanks.'

'Please . . . make yourselves comfortable. My wife will join us as soon as she can. She was helping Mr Martingale today.'

'You're from South Africa too?' asked Ebony.

'British.' As he said it he looked across at her and smiled politely.

'How long have you been in the UK?'

'This trip? About a month. We've been overseeing a new project in Poland.'

'This must seem almost tropical then compared to Poland?' Carter laughed.

'About the same actually.'

'You managed to keep your tan?' Justin smiled, didn't elaborate. Carter was searching Justin's face. Ebony knew what he was thinking. Justin's perfectly even tan should have disappeared by now after a month in the UK winter and Poland before that. It had to be the product of a sunbed or a bottle. 'Where were you in Poland? I went there once on a stag do. Luckily it was springtime. Although we never got out in daylight.'

'Our new flagship hospital is just outside Krakow.'

'You know what . . . I'd love to see it . . . wouldn't you, Ebb?'

'Love to. I've never been outside England.'

Carter and de Lange looked at her. 'Really?' said Carter. She nodded.

'Can you show us on your laptop?'

Justin went round to sit at his desk, opened his laptop to face him and tapped some keys.

'Sorry . . . seems to be on a "go-slow".'

'Ebb will look at it . . . won't you, Ebb?'

Ebony stepped forwards. 'Of course . . .'

'No, that's okay. Can't let anyone else onto it. You know how it is: patients' records and stuff.'

'Oh yes, of course. Understandable,' Carter said. Justin's phone buzzed for a message alert. He picked it up and read it, turned and looked out of the window, down into the car park at the front. 'Here's Nikki now. She'll be with us in a minute.' Ebony moved closer to the blind and counted the same cars in the car park as when they'd come in. The twelve hadn't changed.

'You live near here, Mr de Lange?' she asked.

'Please, call me Justin. Yes, we live here in an apartment in the hospital grounds. In the relatives' accommodation on the other side of the car park. We prefer it to staying in a hotel and we both work here in the hospital so it makes sense.'

'Ah Nikki ...' The door opened and Nikki de Lange came in. She was also in casual mode, wearing a black polo-neck and leather trousers, no makeup and her hair scraped up in a ponytail. Ebony resisted the urge to see if Carter was sweating.

'How nice to see you again, Sergeant, Constable?' She smiled at Carter and Ebony in turn and looked at Justin: 'If you're ordering coffee I'll have one please.' She threw the jacket she was carrying onto the back of the sofa and sat down, crossing her legs.

Justin buzzed down for coffee.

'Is it difficult for you working together?' Carter looked at Justin.

'No, not at all. We do different jobs, we just both work for James, that's all,' he answered. His face was difficult to read: his expression hardly changed. He gave a flick of the head as his long fringe fell into his eyes again. He was still fiddling with the laptop. The atmosphere in the room had changed since Nikki's arrival.

'He must be a very special bloke?'

'Yes he is, very special.' Justin shut the laptop irritably. 'I give up.'

'He's actually a genius, isn't he – a modern-day Louis Pasteur? If you Google him you get loads of pages: must be weird to be that famous. He's written books, papers, and theses about medical procedures.'

'He's very special,' Justin answered. Trying his best to look relaxed, crossing his arms across his chest. He hadn't gone back to his perch at the end of the desk. He looked like a man with a short fuse, thought Ebony. He was pent up. He was trying hard to show just one side of his character. He was getting irritated by Carter's style.

'Still working?' Ebony was beginning to understand what Carter was about. She could never do it. He was making himself out to be slow, a little thick but well-meaning. He was lulling them into thinking they could let their guard down. 'Is he ever going to retire do you think? He obviously doesn't need the money any more? I've looked into his empire a little. It's pretty huge.'

Nikki thanked Ivy who brought in a tray of coffee and set it down on the table in front of her. 'No, you're right. It's not about the money. It's his contribution to the world, his legacy. He's always striving for perfection, always looking to find the answers to medical conditions.'

'He's definitely carved his name in history.'

'Yes, thank you, we are very proud to be working for him.' She looked towards Justin. He nodded. It was a nod that said 'enough is enough'.

Carter turned to Justin: 'And you are in charge of just about everything else, according to our researcher? You're the nuts and bolts of this empire.'

Justin de Lange smiled. 'I wouldn't say that. I'm the spare parts man. I make sure there's enough paper in the toilets.' Nicola gave a forced, shrill laugh. 'Here . . .' He handed a smart-looking dossier over to Carter. 'I have prepared the list of companies that you requested.'

'Thanks . . . But tell me . . . you preferred the world of finance to medicine? I understand that you trained as an anaesthetist before you became an accountant?

That's a lot of years of study to then change career? What happened?'

Justin smiled. 'You did your homework. Life happened, I suppose. You get channelled into one direction when you're young and I accepted it but it never really suited me. When I was given the chance to try something new I jumped at it.'

'You don't look old enough to have done so much. I have your age down as forty-five?' Carter said. 'Surely that can't be true? You and your wife seem to have eternal youth.'

Justin de Lange smiled. Nicola's smile was a little thinner. Her eyes flicked towards Ebony. Ebony could tell that she wasn't so easily convinced by Carter's attempts to appear naïve.

'We are lucky,' de Lange answered.

Yes, thought Ebony . . . *lucky to work for a cosmetic surgeon.*

'I was wondering about the headlines in the papers yesterday about a group of what they're calling Bloodrunners?' Nikki de Lange asked Ebony.

'We are still looking into leads at the moment,' answered Ebony. 'But it's part of an ongoing investigation into the murders in Totteridge and the link with Rose Cottage.'

'I was just talking to Dad about it this morning. He's very upset by it. If there's anything we can do to help, we will.'

Carter shook his head. 'Sorry? Dad?'

'I'm Mr Martingale's daughter. There's four years between me and Chrissie, or there was. She was my half-sister. I'm the result of his first marriage. That

didn't last long either. He's not into long marriages.'
She smiled, looked at them both. 'I can see you
didn't know much about me. I'm happy to fill in any
gaps.'

'Can I ask . . .' said Ebony. 'Is your mother around?'
Nikki shook her head.

'Who knows where she is? I don't remember her.
She left me with my father to bring up. She was from
Zimbabwe. I think she's probably there now, if she's
still alive.'

'You never tried to find her? You're not curious at
all?'

'No . . . my father said she was a wild child, arty,
mysterious, and she disappeared.'

Carter smiled. 'He had a type . . . your father?'

'Type?' As Nikki looked at Carter she was turning
colder by the second. She didn't mind Ebony being
blunt but she didn't like it from Carter.

'Arty? Creative?' Carter smiled, trying to
backpedal.

'Seems so, doesn't it?' Nikki smiled with her mouth,
not her eyes. 'Glutton for punishment.'

'Did you grow up with your father?' asked Ebony.

'Yes.'

'Did you know your sister at all?' Ebony was firing
questions at Nikki de Lange, who seemed not to mind,
although Carter could see Justin getting fidgety at the
desk.

'No. I don't remember her,' answered Nikki, still
smiling.

'You must have been here at some time while she
was alive?'

'No. I wasn't always with my father when he came over.'

'You never met her?'

'I did; but I don't remember.'

'What about your nephew Adam? Have you ever met him?'

'No. I've never met him.'

'I think that's enough questions, Constable,' Justin interrupted.

'I don't mind.' Nikki turned to him and spoke the words succinctly.

'Did you attend your sister's funeral?'

'No, I was poorly at the time.'

'Right,' said Justin. 'You have the information I promised. If you don't mind, my wife and I need to get on with things now. We have lots to attend to.'

'Of course,' answered Carter. 'We'll leave you to it. Thanks.' Nikki de Lange went to escort them to the door. 'Don't worry, we know the way,' Carter smiled.

They walked back to the car.

'What do you think, Ebb?

'Lots to think about, Sarge. For a start, I don't think his laptop was playing up. He just didn't want me to look at it. Or he didn't want us to see the hospital in Krakow for some reason. For another thing . . . I can't believe she never tried to find her sister. Her *only* sister.'

'Did she seem a little false and strained to you?'

'Yes . . . they both did. There's something not relaxed about them as a couple. What a weird world she lives in. She's brought up by a man who thinks he's God and she's married his junior. What kind of a life has she had?'

'Frigging weird one if she didn't even want to meet her family.'

'Unless she doesn't want to tell us about it.'

'Out of loyalty to who?'

'To her dad maybe. She says he strives for perfection all the time. He must have done the work on her face . . . who does that? Takes a knife to his daughter's face to make her prettier? Surely your kids are supposed to be perfect as they are?'

'We don't know he did the work.'

'He's bound to have done it.'

'Do you think Martingale was secretive about her? I had no idea.'

'Hard to tell, Sarge. We didn't ask. Maybe he presumed we knew. It was no secret there was another child. Carmichael mentioned he knew there was a sister but he knew nothing else about her. We just never saw any info on her, I suppose.'

'We'll have to talk to Martingale about the Bloodrunners soon. Now that the papers have got hold of it, everyone will know, including Carmichael.'

Chapter 40

It was five o'clock and Carmichael was walking towards the Lansdown when his mobile rang.

'Hello, Hart speaking.'

'It's Linda.'

'Linda the "girl next door"? How's business been?'

'Times are hard . . . you can imagine.' Carmichael smiled to herself. 'Thought you might want to rescue me from Christmas hell. I have some information about Sonny for you.'

'Coffee or drink?'

'Drink.'

'Right answer. Meet you in an hour outside Liberty's.'

'Can we go to your place instead? I've had enough of crowds.'

'Okay. I'm staying at the Lansdown . . . Ambassador's Suite. See you shortly.'

Thirty minutes later Nikki de Lange knocked on his door.

'Hope you don't mind?' She walked into the room. 'Can we have a drink in your room here? I don't like crowds.' She took off her coat and put it across the back of the chair.

'No problem.' He opened the fridge for her to choose.

'White wine will be great.' She made herself comfortable by the coffee table.

He poured a large glass and handed it to her.

'Wonderful, thank you.' She smiled as she took it from him and took a slug. 'This is a major outing for me. Don't get out much.'

'Apart from going to strange men's houses and being paid for sex, you mean?' He poured himself a glass of wine too and said a silent cheers.

'*One* person's house.' She smiled and looked away.

'You said it was your second time.'

'I lied.'

He smiled. 'So your career as an escort hasn't had the best of starts.'

'I did get paid three hundred pounds.'

'I gave you that.' He grinned.

'Yeah . . . but it still counts.'

He laughed. 'I'm in credit, then.' She looked up enquiringly. He shook his head, grinning. 'Don't worry. It's not my style.'

'Have you ever tried it?'

'What . . . paying for sex?' He nodded. 'Yeah . . . when I was young and with the boys . . . got to admit to doing it but not sure what the outcome was – was too drunk. Woke up with the condom still on so I guess we can be sure I didn't catch anything.' She laughed. He realized it was a long time since he had heard a woman laugh. 'So you stay at home most days and do what?'

'Sell things on eBay.'

'Entrepreneurial type, then.'

'I try.'

'You make enough to earn a living?'

'On a good day.'

'Have you always been self-employed?'

'No. I was a nurse once, many years ago.' Nikki smiled. She had concocted the story late the night before and as she said it out loud for the first time it had a clichéd feel to it. But she knew that it was better to stay in the 'almost truth' zone than venture into completely unknown territory. If he wanted to know anything medical she could more than hold her own. She was taught by her father. But she hoped she didn't need to worry about that. She could see that she'd already begun to charm Mr Hart. 'I married a doctor. We couldn't have kids. I just hung around at home waiting for him to come back every day, trying to please him. In the end he left me for another doctor. Said our lives were dull. I had to agree. I didn't want anything from him. I agreed to the split. I agreed to the fact that he had earned all of the money in our marriage. Of course I didn't realize we'd been living way beyond our means and there were more debts than anything else and they were all in my name. He moved to France with his new wife and here I am. What about you, Mr Hart?'

Carmichael sat down opposite her. 'I've just arrived here in London. Been living out of a suitcase. I'll be happy to put down some roots. I'm waiting to get a licence for a new nightclub, takes a while. What did you want to tell me about Sonny?'

'I saw the news. Sonny's body being pulled out of the Thames.' Carmichael didn't comment. He drank his wine. 'Was that your business with Sonny? Was it getting girls for your club? I know that's what he does, *did*; one of the girls who got me into escorting told me she used to date him.'

'Your information?'

'I haven't really got any information. Just felt like seeing you, that's all.'

He sat back to observe her. 'Why?'

'I wanted to say thanks.'

'Thanks for what? You might have earned a lot more from Sonny.'

She shrugged and smiled. 'Maybe but it didn't suit me – escorting. I wanted to see you today because I need a job. I need a life. You're new in town. You look like you're going places. I do have a lot to offer the right man. It's just that no one sees my potential.' He smiled. 'It's not funny . . . I thought maybe I could be of use to you . . . I need a break. I need to get a job but I was never any good at cleaning floors or wiping kids' noses. I've decided escort work's not for me. I thought maybe . . . you know . . . we could see how it goes?'

'You don't know me.'

'And you don't know me. That's the fun of it. I'm sick of my life. We've all got our regrets. I want a fresh start.'

'I repeat, you don't know me.'

'You're right, but I think it's better not to delve too deeply into people's pasts. I think it's better not to ask.'

Carmichael sat back in his chair and studied her then smiled. 'I don't have time for relationships at the moment, not personal.'

Nikki laughed nervously. 'Really? Now that's a surprise. Yeah ... you're right: you don't know me from Adam.' She came over to him, leant over and kissed him: a soft kiss that closed his eyes and opened his heart valves; a feeling he hadn't had in a long time: his heart responding to the beat of another's. He slid his hands up over her hips as she stood in front of him. He was drowning in her kisses. His hands went to her waist and she undid her wrap dress for him. He pressed his face against the silk camisole beneath her dress and breathed in the scent of her warm skin. His hands slid up beneath the silk and cupped her breasts, warm, firm. It was a long time since he'd felt something so perfectly human. His fingers circled her hard nipples then he stood and pressed the small of her back to him and kissed the curve of her neck. He went to take off her silk camisole but she wouldn't let him. He got to his feet and led her to the bed, then kissed her again and touched her with a slow soft touch. His fingers barely brushing her skin. He waited until her body took control, until it needed him badly, then he rolled onto his back, pulled her to lie on top of him, facing the ceiling, and entered her. Neither spoke as she moved her body and he stayed hard inside her, touching her with feather-light fingers. 'Stay still,' he whispered in her ear. 'Don't move. I'm not going anywhere, just enjoy.' His hands held her body and his fingers applied a gentle and increasing pressure between her thighs that sent shock waves through her body. He held her tight as he closed his eyes and allowed himself to let go. He stayed inside her as he rolled them both onto their sides. He smelt the scent in her hair and closed his eyes, feeling the kind of exhaustion that he had longed for on so many nights in the last thirteen years.

She held onto his arms around her. Then she lifted his hand and placed it on her breast and held it there. He felt her heart beat beneath his hand. 'The way you made love to me . . . you knew what I needed.'

'A fluke,' he whispered into her ear.

She smiled. 'Well it was a good one. How come you're in this hotel bed with me? Can't fathom you out. You're Mr Tough guy . . . don't mess with me . . . but inside you're . . . different.'

'Don't be fooled by me. I told you I don't have time for personal. You're not exactly the straightforward kind yourself. You're obviously well educated. You're beautiful. You don't have to be shy about your body. You feel like you're lost.'

She pulled away from him and sat on the edge of the bed, her back to him. 'Yes. I feel lost.' She got up and went across to the chair where she'd put her clothes.

He lay on the bed and watched her get dressed. She picked up her coat from the chair. When she got to the door she looked back at him and lingered there with a smile.

'Lovely to see you again.'

After she'd gone Carmichael lay back on the pillows and stared at the ceiling. He felt overwhelmed by a feeling of loss. He had not made love to someone like that since Louise. Why he had felt so much for a stranger, he didn't know. He vowed to himself not to let it happen again.

As Nikki de Lange walked away from the room she felt in shock. She had hoped to get information from him that might say who he was but it hadn't seemed to work out like that. He probably knew more about her than she did him. Her body had betrayed her. Her heart had taken over. Never before had someone made love to her like that. Never before had she let go enough to really experience it. There was something about him that was so familiar.

She took the lift down to the ground floor, crossed the lobby and walked along a busy Oxford Street crammed with Christmas shoppers. She gave up trying to hail a taxi and caught the Tube to Hammersmith instead, then she walked the twenty minutes to the Mansfield hospital. She didn't pass Ivy on reception; instead she walked around to the back of the building and through the delivery bays, then left to the door to the private ward. There she punched in her code in the keypad and opened the door.

She walked to the end of the corridor and into the room at the end. Inside was a different world. It was her world. She hung her coat on the back of the door and reached for her uniform. She took off her dress. Beneath her silk camisole a scar ran all the way down the centre of her chest between her breasts. She pulled on the short-sleeved blue cotton top. Then went across to her dressing table by the bed and picked up a band to tie her hair up.

The locked-in boy lay there and listened to the noises in his room. He knew she would be coming soon. He could visualize the room. He knew where the hand basin was, where the door was, where his Arsenal shirt was on the chair. He knew that on either side of his bed there were monitors that flashed and beeped and each one had a different sound as if they were talking to one another. He recognized the door opening, the sucking sound as the air in the room passed over his body in its rush to escape the prison where he seemed to have been for ever. He tried to talk. He tried to say that he was alive. No words came out. He wanted to scream out that he existed but then came the soothing sound of her voice. She sang to him as she washed his body and he loved the feel of her gentle hands on him. She talked to him about her life. Always the same story:

When I was your age I could run fast and swim to the bottom of the pool and hold my breath for ages. I didn't have anyone to play with; I spent my days studying and at the end of each day, I would jump in the pool and swim and swim like a mermaid. But then I began to get short of breath. I got sick. I couldn't swim anymore. I couldn't run. I spent years trapped in a body that couldn't do anything. Only my mind was free. I got sicker and sicker until I wanted to die but my father wouldn't let me go. He brought me here to England and I was saved. I found a cure but it was never meant to last. So I came back here to find you. You are very special to me. You are my salvation.

Justin was agitated. He tried to steer his mind away from Nikki; it only made him feel more insecure. Right now he couldn't afford to doubt himself. Sitting behind his desk, he opened his laptop and went through his emails. He had several messages from dating sites to respond to. He scanned through the women who had responded to his advances and chose one. She had written: *Really love your profile. Thanks for emailing me your pix. I understand about the privacy thing. Anyway, you're gorgeous!!!! Love to meet.*

He typed out a reply:

You sound great fun. Let's meet tonight.

Chapter 41

Carmichael came round from his doze on the bed to hear his Skype alert buzzing. Micky was trying to get hold of him. He reached beneath the bed and pulled out his laptop. Micky's face filled a small square on the screen. Carmichael enlarged it. Micky had a newspaper in his hands.

'You seen this?' Micky turned the paper round so that Carmichael could see the headline.

Bloodrunners
ORGAN HARVESTERS
Monsters on UK streets.

It was seven p.m., Carmichael waited outside the Whittington pathology department and watched Harding emerge. He kicked his bike onto its stand. Harding looked up as she walked towards her car and saw Carmichael. She fished into her bag for her keys, then held them in her hand. Carmichael walked towards her.

'You telling me you had no idea thirteen years ago that they were Bloodrunners?' She flicked the button on her fob, the car chirruped into life. She felt a flutter of panic but did her best not to show it.

'We didn't know that then. It wasn't a world we knew about.' She looked at him. 'You stay inside the law, otherwise you risk being part of the problem instead of the answer. We are doing everything, I promise you. I give you my word. Go back to your farm and wait.' She looked quickly to her side; there was no one else around.

'I waited last time and nothing happened. I'm not sitting this one out. You made mistakes then and you could make them now.'

'There are lots of regrets. I promise you I'm going to do my very best to get justice for Louise and Sophie this time round.'

'How do I know you won't just protect your pals? You know people high up in the medical world. It takes that type of people to perform transplants.' He stepped between her and the car. 'Someone is performing these operations.' She stopped, stared up at him, shoulders back. 'A surgeon leaves his mark the way a killer does, the way he cuts – the butcher with his knife. You could take a guess at who you would get to do a heart and lung transplant, who you would choose to graft part of a healthy liver onto your pickled one, who you would choose to give you new kidneys.'

'Nobody with ethics would condone such a practice.' She tried to get past him. He stood in her way, hand on her car door.

'But they might not know where the organs were coming from.'

She shook her head, flustered. She opened the car door. He stopped it from opening more than a few inches.

'What about my wife? What did they take from her? What didn't you tell me all those years ago?'

She bowed her head. 'They took her heart. We had no idea why.'

'From Chrissie?'

'The same.'

'Is there any way of finding out who had them? Can you find out who was waiting that matched my wife's blood group?'

'No ... It has to be a match with blood, tissue, age.' She looked up at him. His face was full of anguish. She shook her head but her hands were trembling. Her eyes full of sympathy for Carmichael who stood a lonely figure. Deeply violent, dark. 'We had no leads then. Whoever they were they came and went just as fast. Look, Carmichael ... I'm sorry to say it but Louise had a common blood group. She would have been useful for transplanting organs into a wide sector of waiting recipients.'

Carmichael bowed his head, turned and walked away.

Harding got into her car and sat for a few minutes, leaning her head back on the seat as she watched him go. She had to wait for her eyes to clear.

Chapter 42

'Working nine to five!' Tina sang along with Dolly Parton as she reached in behind the shower curtain and switched the shower on full blast.

Before she got into the shower, Tina pulled the string that switched the small fan heater on in the bathroom. She knew she wasn't supposed to use it every time but tonight was a special occasion. She placed her large glass of Pinot Grigio, from the bottle Ebony had bought her for her birthday, on top of the toilet cistern and turned her music up; she'd got her music library on her phone. The quality wasn't that good but it didn't matter in the bathroom.

As she stepped in beneath the hot water she giggled to herself. She was so excited. She had finally been asked out by one of the men from the dating sites. At long last one of them had made the effort. She promised herself she would not make the mistake she'd made in the past of giving it away too soon. She'd done a lot of that after Don had left her. She'd wanted reassurance that she was desirable. She'd thought the more men she screwed the better she would feel about herself but she was wrong. She would also not make the mistake of talking about how Don had been a bastard and really hurt her. That was another thing people said she'd done and they didn't like. She'd had a year off the sites. A year of soul-searching and a year of finding friends like Ebony and feck! it was a year since she'd had sex. She was practically a virgin again. Tina giggled again as she scoured her body with the scratchy sponge. 'I deserve to be a size ten after this,' she said to herself as she hummed away to the music and rubbed her fat bits vigorously with the exfoliator.

Two hours and most of the bottle of Pinot Grigio later, Tina sneaked a look at her date as they left the cab and walked towards the hotel entrance. *Thank God I wore my Spanx pants!* Her heart hammered beneath the chunky sweater dress. *Shit . . . how lucky am I . . . friggin' gorgeous.* She couldn't help but smile to herself.

The receptionist watched them enter. It was the graveyard shift at the Brunswick Hotel. She looked at the clock in the lobby above the dried flower arrangement. The time was 3.20 a.m. All the other residents were tucked up in bed. The hotel was a small one in King's Cross. It wasn't full. It wasn't the best value or the best position for seeing the sights. It took the over-spill from the better ones.

The receptionist smiled at the couple, nodding cordially. They crossed the empty lobby, their feet silent on the carpet.

Justin caught Tina's glance and squeezed her around the waist. She was so glad he couldn't feel the spare tyre that she'd put on since the break-up. It had been hard. She had been battling with low self-esteem. It had nearly broken her. She had had to leave her home, move into shared accommodation again. She had had to start from scratch. But now this man had done wonders for her since they'd begun emailing each other. He had made her feel alive again.

They stopped and she melted as his blue eyes met hers; with his gorgeous long blond hair and masculine shoulders he looked like a god.

She felt self-conscious. What was the receptionist thinking? That he was too good for her? The receptionist was beautiful, her glossy black hair pinned back elegantly, her lipstick in place. Maybe it was true – he was every woman's dream man. They made their way up to the room. Justin slid his hand to her bottom and he squeezed. He seemed pleased with what he touched, she thought, but then again, she could tell he had also been watching the receptionist. She wasn't kidding herself; something about this date seemed too good to be true. Now that Tina was on the way up to a hotel room to have the first sex since her husband went off with the girl from his work, she was thinking maybe she wasn't ready.

Justin seemed to feel her tension, caught her looking back down the corridor as they neared the room. He gave her another squeeze.

'You look beautiful. We'll take our time, shall we? I'm looking forward to us getting to know one another.' He stopped and held her close. 'That's what I miss most since losing my wife in the car accident, just holding someone close like this. Let's just have a drink and a chat this time.'

Ahhhh. Her heart melted a little. He'd just touched on the subject of his wife's death. It was really sweet the way he trusted her. He wasn't pushing her at all but now that he put it like that she realized she'd be disappointed if nothing happened.

Once inside the room he went to the bathroom to get a couple of glasses. Then he returned and poured her a Bacardi and Coke.

He handed her the glass. Tina took the drink from him and clashed her glass against his as they said cheers.

'Thank you for just being you, Tina.'

'Ahhh. How sweet.' She moved up a little on the bed to encourage him to sit next to her.

Justin went round the room and turned down the lighting and an orange glow filled the room. He placed his phone by the side of the bed and switched on some music. Michael Bublé was singing. Tina thought it couldn't get much better.

She woke up with the mother of all hangovers. Her head was pounding. She couldn't remember a thing beyond Bublé. She lay there for a few minutes looking around the room and trying hard to make sense of the situation. The pillow beside her was empty. The bathroom door was open, light off. She seemed to be alone in the room. She felt beneath the covers; she was naked. Her clothes were neatly folded on the chair next to the bathroom. That was weird. She never folded her clothes. She lay there thinking about how her body felt. They'd definitely had a shag: she was sore. They must have done it a few times to have to make her this sore. It didn't make any sense. What had she drunk? Nearly a bottle of Pinot Grigio and two Bacardis. It was possible then, just. Jesus! She sat up in bed, resting on her elbows and looking around the room. She must have been drunker than she thought. He was definitely gone. The room was hardly touched. It looked strangely orderly: no dirty glasses, no sign of the night before. She looked across to the tea tray on the dressing table. Her mouth was drier than the Sahara. She slipped out of bed and crossed to the dressing table to make herself a cup of tea. As she waited for the kettle to boil she picked at the packets of biscuits and flinched. There was a small but deep cut at the tip of her forefinger.

Chapter 43

Carmichael sat in the darkness of the Velvet Lagoon looking at the spot of light on the dance floor. He dropped another corner from his ham sandwich for the rats.

He phoned Micky.

Micky picked up straight away. 'You okay?'

'What did you find out about Bloodrunners?'

Micky paused: 'You sure you want to hear it?' Carmichael didn't answer so Mickey continued. 'Okay. If I wanted to buy a heart and lungs in this country and pay for an operation it would set me back a hundred and twenty thousand pounds. In China or India I'd pay a tenth of that but it would be more dangerous and difficult to find a good match. Poland would be your best bet. A good match and cheap. Kidney, eight thousand. Three thousand gets me a cornea. The liver, that's a quarter section, is three thousand or a whole one for ten thousand. Foetal stem cells will set you back a thousand per twenty mil. A new pancreas is fifteen hundred. Bone marrow two thousand, heart seventy-five thousand and lungs fifty thousand.'

'You missed out the brain.'

'Used for research . . . a thousand. The total value of a human being is between three hundred and fifty and four hundred thousand pounds. That's in Europe and the USA. It would be a tenth of that in China, India.'

Carmichael put the phone down to Micky and called Digger.

Digger was sitting in the kitchens at Cain's.

'Is it my imagination, Digger, or are you attracting a lot of police attention at the moment? How are you managing to make any money with them breathing down your neck?'

Digger sighed irritably. He glanced across at Ray. The barman was sweating now, breathing in small gasps. Digger's face was red with anger but his voice stayed creepily calm.

'It is a nuisance but nothing I can't handle. Seems like your appearance has coincided with a spell of bad luck for me, Mr Hart. And not just me. Sonny was a friend of mine. Tyrone tells me that you proclaim to be his successor. You are ambitious, to say the least. Sonny built up his reputation over years. You have been here a few days and you step into Sonny's very wet shoes. You must be either extremely clever or very stupid.'

Carmichael smiled. 'Anyone could have killed Sonny; could have been an accident even; he was off his face when I saw him.'

'Yes. Perhaps. Tyrone is finding it difficult to answer me in full. He does say you have the wherewithal to do the job. He says you have girls arriving soon.'

'Yes, but I'm not happy to hand them over to you if they're going to end up on the M25 motorway. Tyrone told me you sold her on to a specific client. That person messed up. He has to pay.' Carmichael threw a crumb across to the rats. 'Seems like everyone's getting sloppy. Sonny wasn't the only one to make mistakes.' There were a few seconds of silence as Digger's face flushed with anger before he took a breath and calmed himself. He didn't enjoy being made to feel incompetent. 'I merely passed her on to someone; I had no choice: she was already bought. Hands were tied . . . you understand.' Digger looked across at Ray, who had both of his hands nailed to the table sitting in pools of blood. He was shaking violently, his face twitching in agony. 'Don't worry, people are being punished. Things are getting rather tricky here. The police are persistent. They are ruining my business and, ultimately, *all* of our businesses.' Digger listened hard; he heard nothing. He leant across and banged his fist on the top of the nail. Ray screamed. 'I don't like things to get out of hand. I will be happier when everything calms down. I don't need the aggravation. I am handing that side of the business over to you. You want Sonny's job, you got it. Sonny wasn't ambitious. He never wanted more than being a supplier. I sense that you would like a bigger stake so I am passing over part of mine to you. You bring the girls in and you manage them. I will introduce you to the other men in the chain and you can deal directly with them. You just keep supplying me and I'll be happy.'

'Okay . . . I think we can do a lot of business in the future. I look forward to meeting the club owners.'

Digger got off the phone and made another call and then he waited impatiently as he tapped his fingers on the table and watched Ray sweat. A small whimpering sound trickled continuously from Ray's mouth as he tried to control the pain.

'Here you are at long fucking last,' Digger said to the man entering the kitchens. Digger banged his hand on the table. 'Thank God for that.'

'Sorry, boss. I was on a job.' Deano stood six foot seven. He was in proportion except for his head, which was much too small for his body. One of his own hands could completely engulf it.

Deano looked at Ray as Digger talked. Since the man known on the street as DD, short for Deano the Death, had come to stand by him Ray had started crying openly. He knew there was a worse fate than having your hands nailed to a table.

'This man.' Digger showed Deano a photo of Carmichael. 'Hart. Follow him and be ready to move on him if I say.' Deano took his time studying the photo and then he nodded. He went to leave. Digger called him back and pointed at Ray. 'And take out the trash on your way.'

Chapter 44

Sandford was making a brief appearance at Fletcher House to chase up some results; he had washed down the shelves of the spice cupboard at Blackdown Barn, collected the liquid and sent it away to be analysed. Now he had to find someone who liked cooking to tell him what it meant. His back was aching from unscrewing the entire kitchen. Halfway through standing up he had felt his back seize. He leant one hand on the top of a desk as he answered his phone.

'Sir?' It was Davidson.

'Yes ... I'm back here, sir. There's still a lot to do ... I appreciate that but I want to keep the team small; save any cross-contamination. We are digging up the garden. The apple trees will take some shifting ... No ... the cellar hasn't yielded any positive results. We're down to clay soil now.' Sandford closed his phone and went over to Robbo who was back at his desk.

'Oh my God, how come they let you out?' Robbo laughed when he saw him.

'Just come back to follow up some results and to get warm.'

Robbo rolled his chair down to the other end of the desk, picked up a collection of samples and handed them to him.

'Here's the result of the plastic sheeting: three companies produce that gauge, that width. They're sending me the lists of customers.'

'Any sign of Carmichael?'

'None.' Robbo sat back in his chair and looked hard at Sandford.

'I expect he'll turn up soon enough.'

'Yeah, but in what way? We both know what he's capable of.'

'Sorry to interrupt.' Ebony came in and handed Sandford a file. 'I was told to bring you in my report on Rose Cottage.'

'Thank you, Detective. Before you go . . . do you like cooking?' She shook her head. 'What about your family? Your ethnic roots? Do you know how to cook some of the food from your culture?'

'You mean Caribbean?'

'Exactly.'

'No . . . I don't know any of my Jamaican family.'

'Okay . . . shame . . . everyone should know how to make one national dish,' replied Sandford.

'What's yours?' asked Ebony.

'Welsh cakes.'

'Ask Robbo – he cooks all the time . . .' She turned to Robbo.

'Yes, ask me. What's this about cooking?'

'About spices to be exact,' said Sandford. 'From the shelves at Blackdown Barn. What would you make if

I were to give you a mix of garam masala . . . chilli, coriander—'

'I'd make you a hot Indian curry, maybe a chilli chicken tikka masala?'

'Wait, I haven't finished the list: paprika, Mediterranean herbs, hickory essence, and pimento.'

'Oooh, interesting . . . I'd say you had a touch of the South African braai thing going on and definitely some colonial British in there. We can't go a week without a curry and anywhere in the world we colonized is the same. But the sweetness, that's the key to South African cooking: a strange mix of sweet, hot herbs and spice . . . the thought of it is making me hungry.'

'Making me starving,' said Ebony as she left.

Sandford picked up his plastic samples and left. 'Catch you lot later, back to the fridge.'

Robbo typed in the South African link. He watched HOLMES make the connections and come up with the results. He stirred sugar into his coffee and took a sip. He clapped his hands in front of his face in an attempt to wake himself up before picking up his coffee and walking into the ETO. Ebony was back to back with Carter. Jeanie sat opposite.

'Justin de Lange . . .' Robbo pulled up a chair between Ebony and Carter. 'Interpol have come up trumps. He trained as an anaesthetist but didn't go on with it; we knew that – but one of the reasons is because he was accused of rape. It wasn't the first time either. This time it was a friend of the family. Seems he'd had problems through boarding school. The school covered it up but mainly Mummy paid people off. She died while he was in med school; looks like he went travelling straight after.'

'Why would Martingale want someone like that on his team?' asked Carter.

'Yeah . . . and even more to the point, why would he allow him to marry his daughter?' said Robbo. 'The son he never had, maybe?'

'Yeah,' said Carter. 'He must have had something Martingale was looking for.'

Jeanie shook her head. 'He can't have known.'

Ebony looked at her. 'I think he must have, Jeanie. He would have made it his business to find out everything. Maybe he's using the information somehow. Maybe it works to his advantage to keep a hold over de Lange?'

'Could be,' said Jeanie. 'But where does that leave Nikki de Lange? Is their marriage a sham?'

'Carter thought so, didn't you?' Ebony answered, looking across at Carter. He nodded.

'Yeah. They *look* like they should be a perfect couple: good-looking, successful. Maybe they're too perfect. The Lion King and the Snow Queen.'

Ebony nodded in agreement. 'They seem to be the same types, both very aware of their looks, both aware of everything around them. If anything he is vainer than she is. He must have got that tan from a sunbed or a bottle. His lion mane hair is obviously his pride and joy. She seems more brittle, pasty-looking, she looks beautiful but she doesn't look healthy. I think no couple could have two people competing to be the most perfect. I would agree with Carter: something's not right. Not that

I'm an expert on what a happy couple should look like.'

Carter glanced her way, as did Jeanie. Jeanie smiled encouragement. It was the first time anyone had heard her say anything even remotely connected with her private life.

'Unless Nikki de Lange is a victim,' said Jeanie. 'She's ruled by her father and her husband . . . maybe.'

'Maybe it was part of a deal with de Lange,' said Robbo. 'You run my companies and you'll get a big slice of it in the end.'

'What about her? What does she get?'

'I don't know,' said Robbo. 'She's caught in the middle of it all, maybe. She was home-tutored by Martingale. There are no records about her exam results, her university achievements. There's not a photo of her in any newspaper clipping. It's like she's barely been allowed to exist.'

'No photos? Not even when she got married? The local press must have covered it?' asked Jeanie.

'Not even then . . .' answered Robbo. 'More than that . . . so far I haven't been able to find any proof that they are married . . . There is an entry in a midwifery hospital in Port Elizabeth for her birth. It ties in with what she said about being four years older than Chrissie Newton. Apart from that she seems to have lived her life in seclusion and maybe even isolation.'

'Daddy's girl,' said Jeanie.

'And now he's paired her off with Daddy's right-hand man,' Carter replied.

'We should try and find out more about her,' said Jeanie. 'Ask Harding . . . see if she knows any more about it than we do,' Jeanie winked. 'She likes you. Ebb.'

Carter laughed. 'Don't tell Ebony that. She'll ask for a transfer. We need to go round to Mr and Mrs de Lange and see how the happy couple co-habit.'

Robbo commandeered Carter's desk as he logged into his own PC remotely.

'Let me also show you this. You asked me to dig up any dirt I could find on Martingale. Well maybe this is not directly about him but it's about one of the companies on the list you gave me. It's a company called Remed Ltd. They are a medical research company. Bear with me.' Robbo brought up several photos on the screen. He clicked on the first one.

'This is Mr Hans Grun. And this is one of the last photos of him alive. Here he is with his devoted American wife called Patsy.'

'He looks healthy enough,' said Carter as he studied the photo of the silver-haired, fit-looking man in his early fifties.

'Hans Grun died in Soho under suspicious circumstances on one of his many visits to London on business. That was in nineteen eighty-four. They think Hans was murdered when a robbery went wrong. In his will, Hans' wife Patsy discovered that he'd left his body to science and she donated it to Remed Ltd. Sweet – you think. Very commendable that your dying wish is to donate your body to medical science? What would you expect to happen to it?'

'Used for research, I suppose?' answered Carter.

'Exactly. You're going to think the worst that can happen is some spotty-faced med school kid messes with it . . . but hey, it's in the name of science. But then Patsy decided to track down what happened to his body and here's the fun bit. Patsy discovered that her husband's bones had been melted down to make dental products for cosmetic dentistry and had also been made into a gel for plumping women's lips. Patsy wasn't happy and she sued Remed Ltd.'

'Interesting,' said Carter.

'They gave her some compensation; it wasn't illegal just a bit unethical.'

'When I looked into the shareholders in Remed Ltd I found a familiar name. Digger Cain has been there from the very beginning. He was certainly there when Hans got melted.'

'So Martingale must know Digger? He must have lied to us.'

'Not necessarily; it's Justin de Lange who set the company up and who has been running it all this time.'

Chapter 45

Ebony walked over to the Whittington Hospital where Harding worked. It was less than a two-minute walk. Carter would pick her up in thirty minutes to drive to Hammersmith and check out the de Langes' living arrangements. She took the lift down to Pathology in the basement and signed in at the reception.

'Doctor Harding, can you spare me a few minutes?'

Harding looked up from her microscope and removed the slide she was examining. It was a cross-section of one of Silvia's femurs.

'Shoot.' Harding sat back in her chair and pointed at another chair over at Mathew's empty desk. Ebony drew it over. 'How's it going?'

'I wanted to ask you about James Martingale ... you're a friend of his?

'Yes ... in a way. He's been very good to me, to this department. I told you. We wouldn't be so well equipped if it weren't for his generosity. We wouldn't have been able to carry out the investigations we have. I'm proud of that.'

'Did you know about his daughter, Nikki de Lange?'

'No. I didn't.'

'So you never met her before?'

Harding shook her head; 'I only heard about her existence the other day. I may have met her at some point.'

'Do you not think that's odd? That no one's heard anything about her before? She was Chrissie Newton's older sister. She must have been around when Chrissie died but there's no mention of her in the original report.'

'No need, I suppose. She wasn't in this country; she wasn't part of the investigation.'

'She wasn't a child then. She was twenty-seven. That's hardly a kid. She was a grown-up that no one has ever really heard about till now.'

'What's the point in this? What are you thinking?'

'That she was the child in the attic. That she was hidden away. Her dad is a bit controlling, possessive maybe?' Ebony waited for Harding to react, but she didn't. 'Do you know whether he's had many relationships?' continued Ebony.

'He had a good few. I would say he's definitely a ladies' man, but now he keeps it to sex only. He has a lot to lose, after all. The divorce settlement would make you think twice.'

It wasn't hard for Ebony to see that Harding was talking from experience. 'What about Carmichael – did you get to the bottom of his relationship with Chrissie?' asked Harding.

'He still maintains they were never lovers. But she contacted him again after all those years?'

'And she had a child by that time.'

'That's exactly what I was thinking too. She must have wondered whether he was worth a second shot, whether he was father material? But would she go so far as to break up his marriage?'

Harding shook her head, opening her hands out in a shrug.

'I don't know. I am the worst judge when it comes to looking inside people's heads. I can tell you what their last meal was but I can't tell you whether they enjoyed it. I've had more affairs than I care to mention or can pretend to feel guilty about. Some have broken marriages some haven't. Some have even done some good for marriages. But . . . the one thing I do know is that if a woman is determined to get a man she will.' She looked across at Ebony's expression. 'Yeah . . .' Harding continued: '. . . Maybe I'm not the best at dishing out pearls of relationship wisdom.'

'What about her husband, Justin de Lange? Do you know him, Doctor?'

'I know the name. I didn't know he was Mr Martingale's son-in-law. I know him as one of the trustees of the Chrissie Newton Foundation. We correspond about charity matters, that's all. I see his name whenever we get a donation to the department. I haven't met him yet. Can I help you with anything else? I need to get on with these slides.'

'Sorry, one more thing – I wanted to ask you about cosmetic surgery practices.'

'Okay, you can ask . . . not sure I can be much help. I don't work in that field.'

'I know Mr Martingale does, and some stuff's come to light about cadaver products being used?'

'Common practice. No secret.'

'Is it legitimate?'

'Yes. In this country we stay within the guidelines. Of course I could take you to twenty private clinics in Moscow where you'll be able to get foetal stem cells injected into your face.'

'What about Poland?'

'Fast becoming the place to go if you want private work done.'

'Mr Martingale has a hospital there.'

'He has hospitals everywhere. You can be sure that whatever he's doing he's staying well within the law. I have to crack on now, Ebony. Is there anything else?'

'Can I just ask you to read this when you have a minute? It's just some extra information on Justin de Lange. I'd like your take on it.' She left the file on Harding's desk.

An hour after Ebony left, Harding phoned Martingale.

He was at home; in the background she could hear music, a female opera singer, she didn't know which one.

'Thanks for the other evening,' she said. She felt apprehensive, never ceasing to feel overawed by his achievements.

'Thank you. I haven't enjoyed myself so much in a long time.'

'Really? I had you down as a man who entertains a lot.'

On a sexual level Harding hadn't enjoyed the night as much as she had expected to. Martingale was a man who made love by numbers; there was no passion. By the end she'd felt exhausted by the constant manoeuvring into positions. It was clear he'd read all the books about sex, but he'd missed the point.

'Not at all. I spend my entire life pleasing others; I forget to please myself sometimes.' Harding resisted the urge to laugh. If he was waiting for a compliment he would be a long time waiting. 'You have no idea how lonely it can be moving from place to place.'

'I bet ... so about the news ... about the investigation.'

'I saw the headlines. Is it true that these recent victims were killed by body harvesters, Bloodrunners?'

'Yes. It looks very likely.'

'And where does that leave my daughter's case?'

'We cannot be certain, James, but I think we have to accept it was the same scenario. Whoever killed Chrissie did it for her organs. Has to be a reality. Has to be considered. I'm sorry.'

'How close are you to finding out who did it?'

'The latest victim provided some clues; more than previous victims. She has fingerprint imprints on her body. She has semen in her vagina. We think someone is getting careless. You can be sure we're doing everything, James.'

'I hope so. I appreciate your help with this. I cannot stop the thought that I am at the heart of it. Someone targeted Chrissie because of me. I worry every day for my other daughter, Nikki, with these killers still around.'

'I never knew you had another daughter besides Chrissie until recently.'

'It wasn't common knowledge. I just didn't want her dragged into all this. I am a private person and so is she.'

'She grew up with you?'

'Yes. Her mother left. I brought her up. No big deal.' Harding could hear his mood switch just like in the restaurant with the wine waiter.

'Did she go to school in South Africa?'

'I home-tutored her.'

'Really? Why was that? I heard that the schools in South Africa are very good.'

She could hear him getting colder by the second. His voice became clipped, and sharp. 'I had my reasons. I wanted to keep my daughter close; I wanted control over what she was taught, and I thought I could do a better job than the schools. I was right. She turned out just as I wanted her to. She is an asset to me and my organization.'

'And your son-in-law? You must really like him; he's a big man in your empire.'

'Yes. He was a good choice.'

'He has history.'

'We all have history.'

'For rape?'

'Please!' She could imagine him rolling his eyes. 'It never went to court. A girl's hysterics, nothing more.'

'His mother paid people off.'

'Alright, okay. Maybe he got carried away. Everyone makes mistakes in their youth. Justin has surely atoned for his a thousand times over through the good work he's done for the Chrissie Newton Foundation and for the Mansfield Group. I could not have done it all without Justin. He is extremely loyal and takes away ninety-nine per cent of the stress for me; leaves me to do what I am good at: saving lives. You know what? I am a little put out by this conversation, Jo . . . I was hoping for better from you. I feel a little bit like I'm on trial here? If there's something for me to worry about please tell me. I am reliant on you to keep me informed. We have a deal.'

Harding paused. 'Deal?'

'Understanding then,' he replied. 'Is that more to your liking? The Mansfield Group has been very supportive of your department. And will continue to be so. All I ask is for a little loyalty. I think that's reasonable considering the amount of money I've invested . . .'

'Invested? There is no deal, James. I owe you nothing.'

There were a few seconds of frosty silence between them before Martingale smiled as he said, 'Of course not. I'm sorry if I got a little passionate. You owe me nothing. I guess I get a little defensive about Justin. Justin is family.'

'Are they actually married? Is there a certificate?'

'Yes. What are you implying?'

'Nothing, it's just a question . . . there's no record of it.'

'What? Is my daughter being looked into? I get extremely angry when people intrude into my privacy. What right have they? What right has anybody? I lost a daughter in this country and what justice did I get? None . . . and now the police are wasting their time investigating me, my daughter and my son-in-law? What the hell for?'

Harding took a breath. She remained calm. Harding had the knack of remaining calm when a man got angry.

'That's the way it is now, James. The internet has opened up opportunities like that. The police can check on every detail.' She heard him take control again. She heard him take a deep breath. 'You're upset. I understand.'

'No. I'm being irrational. We all want the same things. We're all singing from the same hymn sheet, after all. Please forgive my little outburst.'

'It's really not a problem.'

'When this is all over, I hope we'll be spending many more and much happier times together.'

'I hope so,' she agreed. 'Fuck you,' she added as she put the phone down.

She went over to her laptop and began to research all the hospitals in reach of Rose Cottage; and all the surgeons who worked in them. Two hours later she rang a number. It went to answer machine. She left a message:

'Simon . . . it's your ex-wife. Ring me.'

Chapter 46

Tina heard the whine of a distant police car as she walked along the waterlogged street. The snow flooded the pavements as it melted. It wasn't that the night was particularly warm. The smog trapped the light and gave the street an artificial warmth. The street echoed with the sound of her heels; she was scuffing her feet as she held the bag of shopping in each hand and trudged doggedly towards her front door. The bags were 'bags for life' that broke after one use and you couldn't be bothered to ask for another, couldn't be bothered to take the torn bag back to the supermarket and ask for your replacement 'bag for life'. *Fuck*, Tina thought, *was life just one day now?* One heavy load, one crisis point and the bag for life just broke? Life was full of false promises.

It had been a shit evening. Justin hadn't shown. He'd said sorry about the hotel; said he wanted to make it up to her. Who the feck did he think he was? Yeah, good-looking guy. She knew it was too good to be true. She was Miss Average. Ah well. She shook her head. Live and learn. What was it her friend Rachel in the canteen always said? 'You have to kiss a lot of frogs before you find your prince.' The funny

thing was that whenever she said that a mental image
of Rachel's husband came into Tina's head and the
theory wasn't worth a damn; he was pig ugly. Still . . .
whatever . . . none of it mattered because today she'd
found out she'd won a holiday. An email had come
through about what she'd won: the holiday of her
dreams . . . free cosmetic surgery. It seemed she'd been
entered in for some prize draw. She had been about to
SPAM it until she saw there was a freephone number
to ring. The woman had been so lovely on the phone
to her. Yes . . . it was true . . . she'd won it . . . what
the hell . . . she couldn't believe it. She couldn't remember entering it but she must have . . . and she'd actually won. Now she was going to celebrate with a
bottle of cheap plonk and a fish dinner.

She couldn't choose her dates. She'd had to be ready
at a moment's standby. She was going to have the lot
– lipo, breast enlargement, tummy tuck – and then
stay in a five star hotel to recover. She had been asked
a series of really weird questions: next-of-kin shit . . .
she'd put Ebony down as she didn't know who else to
put. But she had won!! She who never won anything.
If she was honest it was a little odd: the wording, the
secrecy, but then she didn't want everyone and his
brother knowing she was going for some work. She
had to call in sick. They wouldn't mind. She often had
migraines. They would think it was that. After a few
days she'd ask them to give her a week's holiday as
well. That should cover it. She'd be back in time for
Christmas. Ebony had promised they'd do nothing all
day except sit wrapped in their duvets and watch telly
and eat. Tina was going to do the cooking. She'd

already tried Ebony's food. There was no way she was going to let Ebony cook. It would be beans on toast for Christmas dinner otherwise. She was looking forward to it a lot. And now . . . she would just fly back two weeks later a new woman.

She could smell the fish and chips. Her pace quickened. Feck, the wine was heavy. She would get in the door, take off her makeup, get into her nan's dressing gown and start making a list of what she should pack.

She hoped Ebony was at home. She was just longing to tell someone.

Chapter 47

Ebony got into the detective's car next to Carter just as his phone rang.

'Yes, Robbo?' Carter answered.

'Your visit to the de Langes' will have to wait. We have a match for the Arsenal shirt. Alex Tapp, a four-teen year old, went missing four weeks ago, early November, at an Arsenal match.'

'Text me the address, Robbo; we'll go straight there.'

Carter knocked on the door. Ebony looked up the quiet street; across the road a curtain twitched. It was a long street of semi-detached houses one side, terraced the other.

A woman answered the door. She was in her mid-forties, wearing a long skirt and baggy jumper.

'Mrs Tapp? Helen?' Carter showed his warrant card.

'Have you found him?' Her eyes glued to Carter's face. She didn't look at his badge.

'Not yet . . . but can we come in please? My name is Detective Sergeant Dan Carter and this is Detective Constable Ebony Willis. Please call us Dan and Ebony. Is it all right if we call you Helen?'

She nodded as she looked hard at them for a few seconds, trying to read their expressions. A small child came to stare up at Carter and hold onto his mother's leg.

Ebony smiled at the child. He smiled back.

'Of course, sorry . . . out the way, Alfie . . .' She picked up the child and put him on her hip then stood back to allow them to pass.

'We won't keep you long; we just need to ask you some more questions and we need to get some DNA swabs from you and your husband if you don't mind.'

'I'm sorry my husband isn't here.'

They followed her into the kitchen. She put Alfie down and sat at the table. She looked exhausted. She rubbed her face with her hands. Her fingers tugged at her face, pulled down her baggy lower eyelids and revealed crimson rims. Alfie was clingy as he pulled at her skirt and tried to climb onto her lap. She picked him up and sat him facing the table. He was desperate to play. His fat dimpled hands grabbed at anything his mother didn't move away fast enough. 'DNA?' She was thinking over what it could mean.

Ebony took a test out of her bag. She cleaned her hands with an antibacterial wipe and put a pair of gloves on then opened the envelope marked 'Helen Tapp' and took out the swab. She peeled it back from the stick end.

'I just need to wipe the cotton bud end of the stick around the inside of your cheek if that's okay, Helen?' She nodded and opened her mouth ready. Alfie stared up at her. Ebony rubbed the inside of Helen Tapp's cheek for a minute.

'We found a piece of his Arsenal shirt, Helen.'

Helen Tapp fought back the tears as she shook her head, relieved.

'You haven't found his body?'

Ebony shook her head. 'No. We have not. It's a possibility that he's being held against his will. There's still hope, Helen.'

'Where did you find the shirt?'

Ebony looked at Carter for reassurance. He nodded.

'We found it at a house in Totteridge.'

'The one on the news? Where people had been murdered?'

Ebony nodded.

'Oh God. How did he end up there? Why him?'

Carter answered: 'We are working on several theories and new leads at the moment, Helen.'

'Can we please go through the details with you? I appreciate that you've talked to officers before but not to us.'

She nodded and blew her nose. Alfie had turned right round and was watching his mum anxiously. He had picked up the signs, knew the quivers in her voice, the descent into tears, knew they meant a cuddle was needed. He snuggled into her and she wrapped her arms around him.

'Alex went to see Arsenal play.'

'Does he do that often?'

She shook her head. 'No. It was his birthday. He wanted to take his friend Aaron. My husband went with them on the Underground and then he had arranged to meet them after the game and bring them home. When he got to the Tube station to wait for the boys, only Aaron showed up. He said Alex went to the toilet at half time and didn't come back to see the second half. Aaron had phoned his mobile but it was dead.'

'Had he ever gone off before?'

'No . . . never. Why would he do that? It was his birthday treat. He'd been looking forward to it for so long. My husband, Michael, went back up to the stadium with Aaron, they talked to the officials. No one had seen anything. Michael phoned the police from there.' She swallowed hard and shook her head. 'Nothing . . . it's like he's just gone . . .' Her eyes searched Carter's face for some grain of hope.

'Any problems at school, that kind of thing?'

She shook her head, weary with the same questions but trying hard to grasp at any memory that might add up to an answer for his disappearance.

'Does Alex have access to the internet?'

'Of course . . . every kid his age does.' Helen sounded defensive. 'He couldn't do his homework without it.'

'Please.' Carter kept his voice soft. 'It's not a criticism. You're right, every kid does. Just need to know if you were worried about any unusual amount of activity on it? Did you monitor it? Was he looking at it in here?'

'In here and in his room.' She thought for a moment, her eyes drifted. She smiled weakly at Alfie as he stared up at her face and grinned. 'Alex was reaching that age when he had secrets: girls, I suppose, I don't know. He's such a wonderful, caring, thoughtful lad; we've never had any trouble with him.' Helen's expression was open-ended. She looked like she wanted to say 'until' . . .

'Did he seem to be a little distant recently?' Ebony asked as she wiggled a spotty dog toy at Alfie and made him laugh.

Helen sighed. 'Yes, a little. He spent a lot of time in his room; he was a little snappy with me. I didn't think about it at the time . . . but now I think . . . yes, maybe a little changed. He was tired, irritable. He'd had his tonsils out a few months ago. He didn't seem quite himself after that. I put it down to him recovering, I suppose.'

'Can I have the address of the boy he was with please?' asked Carter

'Aaron? Yes of course.'

After they'd gone Helen Tapp counted the chimes as she pulled the cork from the wine: one, two, three, four, five chimes from the antique French clock in the hallway that she was beginning to wish they'd never had restored. It got on her nerves. It marked the passing of time in a way that she couldn't ignore.

She poured herself a large glass of red wine and gulped half of it down. Red in winter, white in summer, vodka when she didn't care what season it was and she didn't want people to see what she was drinking. Housewives all over the land did the same as her, that was a fact, she told herself.

Alfie was getting fractious. He was just beginning to do without his afternoon nap and it was now the tricky time of day, keeping him awake long enough to get past tea, bath, story and then bed. Tonight she would limit herself to one glass before he went to sleep. It didn't help her cope with him. It made it a chore. Made her snappy, made her face rubbery and ugly. Made her want to scream at the injustice she felt inside and made her miss Alex more than she could bear. She looked at her reflection in the kitchen window. Outside was darkness. All she could see was blackness and the reflection of her face, her hands holding a glass. She had never felt so lonely.

The phone rang and she slammed her glass on the table, chipping its base as she rushed to answer it. She picked it up and listened, there was the pause that meant it was a salesperson or a recorded message asking her if she'd been ripped off by the banks. Who hadn't?

'Mrs Tapp? Can we use your house as a show-home for our double glazing?'

She put the phone down and looked down the hall at Alfie, who had fallen asleep sitting up, propped against a bean bag where she'd left him playing with the Duplo. Bugger . . . he'd take ages to get to sleep that evening now. She walked over and picked him up – he was flush-faced and heavy in her arms, completely asleep. She carried him upstairs and ran a bath as she sat on the edge and swished her hand in the water. She held onto him and started to cry; noisy agonizing wrenches that came from her core and hung harsh and jagged in the air . . .

'I'll take him.' Her husband stood in the doorway looking at her with disgust and contempt on his face . . . 'Give him to me.' She didn't seem to hear him. 'Give . . . him . . . to . . . me.' He hated her when she was drunk like this. Fucking drunk at five o'clock . . . her mouth was red-stained from it, her eyes swollen, her face blotchy, ugly, drunk . . . *Christ, she looked a mess.*

'You're home early . . .' She heard the words join up and flinched. She tried a smile but then she turned her face from him as he took Alfie from her arms. She stared into the bath, swishing her hand until the water got scalding hot and she withdrew it fast.

'What the fuck are you trying to do, scald him to death? Fuck, Helen . . . you need to get a grip. Anyone could knock on the door. What if the police come back and want to talk to you? What are you going to say? I was celebrating? I felt like getting drunk? They're going to think not only has she lost one son, she looks like she doesn't know how to care for the other.'

She stood and confronted him, her eyes burning, her body trembling.

'Don't ever talk to me like that. It wasn't my fault.'

He shook his head, his eyes despising, his voice sarcastic. 'Well it sure as hell wasn't mine. And you have no idea about his life because you're always pissed by six o'clock. While I'm out working to keep this family afloat. You didn't know what he was doing on that PC; you didn't care, as long as you had enough booze to keep you going. Well I'm stopping it now. The gravy train stops here. You're nothing but a fucking housewife and no fucking good at that. This house is a mess, Alfie is asleep at five o' fucking clock and you're pissed.'

She stood and followed him out of the bathroom and down the stairs. 'Please . . . please . . . don't do this to me . . . to us . . . don't shut me out like this. We need each other now. I've only had one glass, I promise. Alfie fell asleep. You know he does it sometimes. I took my eye off him for a few minutes and he fell asleep while he was playing with his toys. Please . . . I'm doing my best. No more drink for me tonight. I'll cut right down. It's just that I'm so lonely, just me and Alfie here all day, and I miss Alex so much. I miss making dinner for him. I miss hearing him talk about his day, getting his kit ready for sports, hearing him switch the telly on in the other room and . . . I miss him so badly.'

Alfie was waking up, wiping his snotty nose in Michael's suit jacket.

'Here . . .' He gave him to her . . . 'I have to go out. I'll be working late. Someone has to keep food on the table, wine in the fucking fridge. Try not to get too pissed. Don't wait up.'

'Mike?' She called after him. 'They need you to do a DNA test. They found a bit of Alex's Arsenal shirt. Mike?'

The front door slammed shut.

Chapter 48

Back at Fletcher House Ebony and Carter joined Robbo at his desk to take a look at the CCTV footage of the surrounding streets leading to the Arsenal stadium.

'I've been looking for all sightings of Alex Tapp on CCTV in the area.'

'This is Alex leaving the stadium at half time. He's wearing his Arsenal shirt. Here he's looking around.'

'Is he looking for someone?' asked Carter. 'What's he got in his hands? Looks like a book.'

'Bigger,' said Ebony. 'A laptop, or tablet maybe.'

'Yes,' agreed Robbo. 'He's carrying it as if it's important to him, precious. Was there any mention of him having disappeared with his laptop?' He turned to ask Carter who shook his head in reply. 'Here, he crosses the road past the Tesco's on the corner, then he keeps walking. He seems to know where to go.'

'He's headed back towards the Underground station,' said Carter.

'Ah. You think so, and then he doubles back. Here.' Robbo double-clicked on another film at the bottom of the screen. 'We pick him up again walking on the pavement opposite Tesco's, as if someone has told him to double-back and throw us off the scent. Here he walks up towards Highbury Hill. Then we lose him again until ... this.' Robbo clicked on another film. 'This was taken off St Paul's Road down towards Highbury Corner, that's about a fifteen-minute walk from the stadium.' The squeeze around Robbo's PC became even tighter as everyone moved closer to get a better look at the grainy image on the screen.

'He's with a woman,' said Carter. He looked at the screen as Alex turned to look up at the woman. 'How tall is Alex, Ebb, do we know?'

'Five five, Sarge.'

'So the woman is what, five nine? She looks a good few inches taller than him.'

'She could have heels, Sarge; she could be anything from about five four.'

'Long dark hair, probably a wig,' said Carter. 'You can see how she's keeping her head down while she's talking to Alex. She knows she might be on camera. What do we think about Alex? Ebb?'

'He looks nervous, Sarge. He keeps looking over his shoulder. He's having second thoughts maybe.'

'Now her arm goes around him,' said Carter.

'Maternal,' said Robbo.

'Agreed,' said Carter. 'She's not promised him sex obviously. She's not coming on to him. She's promised him something else ... love, friendship, something he's been missing. Something he wants so badly he's prepared to walk out on his friend in the middle of his team's match on his birthday. Whatever it is she's promised it's worth the world to him.'

'There . . .' said Ebony. 'He's turning again. Looking behind.'

'But he knows he could easily run from her.' Robbo stared at the screen. He enlarged it. 'He passes a policeman there. He could easily say something but he doesn't. She leaves her arm around him and he looks up and smiles at her. He seems to be finally sure of what he's doing at this point.

'We lose him for a bit after they turn down the next street. But after a few more minutes . . . look at this.' Robbo moved onto another clip where a van door was opening and Alex was getting into the passenger seat. 'Bingo.'

'Shit . . .' Carter shook his head.

'Yeah, we have a match to the plates, but they don't belong to that vehicle. They were stolen a week before Alex's abduction. Nothing's been seen of them since that day,' said Robbo

'Who is she?' Carter enlarged the picture of the woman for a better look.

'Sandford says it's a definite result matching the hair sample from Blackdown Barn and Sonny's flat. Same woman, definitely.'

'Maybe this is her?' Carter picked up his keys and his coat and looked across at Ebony.

'Let's go, Ebb. I want to see what Sandford's found.'

Chapter 49

Carter showed his warrant card. 'Sorry, sir . . . you can't go down there.' A police officer stopped their car as Ebony and Carter turned off the main road and tried to head up the lane leading to Blackdown Barn. They were at a roadblock. 'We have heavy machinery coming back and forth; this is the only access.'

'No problem. We'll park on the main road and walk up.' Carter reversed back onto the road and parked up as close to the hedge as he could get. It was three in the afternoon.

As they walked up towards the house they heard the rumble of machinery and the muted rat-a-tat of a jackhammer breaking up concrete. An officer watched them approach. Carter recognized him. 'Alright, Jacko? How long have you been here?' Carter asked as they drew level.

'Since five this morning, Sarge. Just another couple of hours.'

'Bet you'll be glad . . . chills to the fucking bones, this cold. Anything happen today?'

'Thermal imaging and dogs, Sarge.'

'Find anything?'

'Not yet.'

'They gone?'

'Yes, Sarge.'

'Thank Christ for that; can't stand those handlers.'
He grinned. 'You want a cup of tea?'

'Please . . . two sugars.'

They found Sandford inside the house. He had a
sample bag with the contents of a drain in it. He held
up the mash of scum and hair.

'From the drain in the shower at the far end. My
guess is it is more of the same . . . the woman from
Sonny's. Her hair is everywhere.' Carter took the bag
from him and then passed it to Ebony. 'She's blonde
and losing a lot of hair.'

'How far have they got with the digging?' There
was a welcome lull in the noise of digging coming
from below them.

'They're concentrating on the house, starting on the
garden in a couple of days; then the surrounding
countryside.'

'Can we take another look around?' Carter had to
shout over the noise of the jackhammer downstairs
again.

'Be my guest.'

They walked into the kitchen. Carter started opening up the cupboards.

'Fascinating what people have in their kitchens,
don't you think, Ebb? You like cooking?'

'Not really, Sarge.' Ebony opened the fridge door
and the smell of bleach bounced off the shelves.
'Maybe it's the pregnant woman who liked to cook.'

'Trust me, pregnant women like to eat but they
don't like to cook. Cabrina gets nauseous at so many

things. She might eat a family-size pizza but she sure as hell wouldn't want to cook it. So maybe that's his first mistake, Ebb: he's left behind a little bit of his personality in this cupboard . . . If it was my cupboard it would be filled with Italian seasoning: basil, parsley, oregano. You know, Ebb, she's still not talking to me.' Ebb straightened up from peering under a wall unit and looked at him. She didn't know what to say. He didn't expect an answer. He talked as he searched through the rest of the cupboards.

'The thing is, we've been together for five years. We get on really well. Of course when she got pregnant . . . it was a shock. You know, I didn't know whether I was pleased or not . . . but I tried to be. I couldn't help thinking . . . *no more holidays, no more long lie-ins. The place will stink of nappies and Cabrina will be tired and get fat like her mum.*' He looked up to see Ebb flash him an accusing look. 'Yeah . . . yeah . . . shallow, I know. But I'm being truthful with you, Ebb; mate to mate. I wouldn't say that out loud to Cabrina.' Carter opened a large walk-in larder. He carried on talking as he disappeared from view. 'Was a shock . . . I guess. But I went along with it. We started to plan, think how it would work.' He emerged from the larder and waited to catch her eye. 'It was when she said we'd never get a buggy up the stairs to the flat and we'd have to move a bit further out to get a good school that I think I must have shown it on my face.' Carter stopped to see if the extractor above the cooker worked. It did. 'Whatever it was, I didn't handle it well. She didn't give me chance to think about it, adjust. I came back from work and she'd gone. No contact for a week. It's doing my head in. Now she's staying with her parents and they got plenty of room for the baby *and* the buggy. Now I feel like I have no idea what I can do to say: yeah . . . I'm scared but I'll give it a go. Because . . . to be honest with you, Ebb . . . people keep saying *bide your time* or *get on with your life* . . . but . . . the more I do that, the more I feel her slip away and yep . . . to be honest with you . . . it's a tough call seeing the future without Cabrina in it.'

'And the baby?'

'Yes . . . one hundred per cent, Ebb . . . and the baby. Cabrina is the baby to me . . . Whatever Cabrina wants is all that matters to me. I'm just like every other bloke. I can't decide when it's time to settle down; I need a woman to decide that for me. So . . . I surrender . . . I accept and then she's like . . . fuck you . . . too late.'

'Give her time, Sarge . . .'

Carter sighed, nodded. 'Okay, let's leave it to Sandford; he'll have this place dismantled. If there's anything left in here he'll find it. I want to have another look out the back.'

The digger was standing idle. It was a sharp and clear sky above, but no longer bright blue – it was slipping into a cold dusk. All the patio slabs were up, neatly stacked at the far side of the garden. Carter called out to one of the men drinking tea, 'Officer on the gate: two sugars.' He got a nod by way of reply. 'Ebb?' Ebony was staring at the machinery. The digger was like one she'd made from a kit once, free in a packet of cornflakes; it had

spokes on the wheels and the wheels actually turned.
'Ebb . . . you ready?'

They walked round, following the outside wall; an
original wall: each stone laid by hand when the barn
was first built two hundred years earlier. Spiders had
made funnel webs between the cracks, their webs now
frozen like fine lace.

Ebony watched Carter as he looked at his feet,
pressing the ground with his expensive boots encased
in polythene, feeling his way. She looked skyward.
The light couldn't make it through the tangled canopy
of branches. The air was trapped with the smell of
rotting leaves and past bonfires. At the end of the
garden a newer wall marked the boundary between
that property and the next and the trees gave way to
a cleared area where two composters stood, their
open ends on the flattened ground.

Ebony lifted the lid on each one in turn; both were
half full. Carter looked in and recoiled.

'Fuck . . .'

Hundreds of fat worms were stretching their ribbed
bodies over the rotting matter.

Ebony dipped her gloved hand in one of the bins
and pulled out a handful of rich brown crumbly
compost and let it sift through her fingers. Carter
stared at her as if she were mad.

'Not sure what it's supposed to look like, Sarge.'

'It should have all sorts of lumps of rotting stuff,
vegetation, kitchen waste, that sort of thing in there.'

She moved it round with her hand. 'Can't see any
vegetables or kitchen peelings in it, Sarge; it's very
fine.'

Carter looked back to the garden. 'That's a lot of compost produced from just leaves. Anything else in there?' She shook her head.

He called back down the garden and two officers arrived.

'Can you get something to slide beneath these bins? I want to empty them. I think this is shop-bought compost.'

Ten minutes later their contents were laid out on a plastic sheet and Ebony was gently scraping away the last of the rotting leaves and compost from beneath where the bins had stood.

'Sarge?' She moved the fragments of bone towards him. In the centre was a child's tooth.

Chapter 50

'Unlike the previous victims, an attempt had been made to dispose of the body by burning it.'

Davidson sat at Carter's old desk and bowed his head in thought, as if he had a heavy weight on the back of his head. Occasionally he seemed to realize what he was doing and sat upright, but slowly gravity pulled him back down.

'She was a young girl of around ten years old . . .' Harding was addressing the meeting. 'She was found by DC Willis and DS Carter in a fire pit hidden beneath a compost bin.'

Jeanie looked across and smiled at Ebony proudly. It was eight in the morning in the ETO. The room was packed to hear about the latest development.

Harding continued: 'The temperature in the pit was not high enough to have much impact on the skeleton but the flesh has gone. The bones are mainly yellowed and some splintering has occurred. We will still be able to extract mitochondrial DNA. We're waiting on results. I can't give you cause of death but it's not strangulation. The small bones at the top of her spinal column were still intact. No obvious injuries except she broke her arm in the six months prior to her death.

There is a metal pin in the humerus bone usually put in to help align it whilst healing.'

Robbo spoke: 'We think we have a match to a missing person: eleven-year-old Shannon Mannings was last seen on the Friday before the Easter weekend on March twenty-sixth 2010. She disappeared from a children's home in Wales. Hospital records show that Shannon had her arm broken on a home visit courtesy of her stepfather. We have requested mitochondrial DNA from her mother.

'Because of her home-life Shannon was sent to the children's home, which is in a rural location. We do know that she was a problem child with a history of self-destructive behaviour; sexualized young by her mother she was sexually active and undergoing counselling for it.'

Davidson stood and took over: 'We should be able to find out if she had been groomed by anyone before she disappeared. Carter . . . you and DC Willis will head up to interview the manager of the home and see if we can find out any more.'

'Jesus . . . why Shannon Mannings? There must have been lots of kids they could kill for their organs? Why didn't they find an easier target?' asked Carter.

'Because Shannon was an exact match for someone,' answered Harding.

'Pre-ordered?' Davidson looked at her. 'You're saying that they have a shopping list, these people? They don't just kill: they kill to order?' Harding nodded.

'I agree,' said Robbo. 'She was for a specific client: tissue type, blood, age type, all of it was pre-ordered. But the person she was meant for wasn't ready.

Shannon was a walking organ bank. She was kept in Blackdown Barn until they were ready for her.'

'Maybe that person also stayed at Blackdown Barn,' said Carter. 'They could have recovered there after the operation. Maybe that's why Chichester chose an expensive property. If it was just to hold the victims it wouldn't have mattered what the place looked like as long as it was secure. If it was to impress clients it would.'

'Is that possible?' Davidson looked at Harding. His face was clouded with confusion. 'Really? A bespoke organ stealing team?'

'I think it is,' said Harding.

Davidson shook his head in disbelief. 'I can't grasp it.'

'Nor me . . .' Harding agreed. 'But the facts are there for us to see.'

Davidson was still trying to take it in. He shook his head, looked around the room, his eyes settled on Harding. 'Who could live with that . . . saving someone they loved by harvesting another? Plus, logistically?'

'Logistically it would take enormous organization and insider help,' answered Harding 'You'd have to have a way into hospital records to find your matching donors. But it's not difficult. Someone working in the system now or able to hack into NHS records could do it easily. You ask me? I think it's not just feasible, it makes perfect sense: people don't care about the moral side of things any more. If your kid, husband, mother was dying, and they needed a transplant? Are you telling me you wouldn't consider buying them one? I know I would.'

Chapter 51

Carter watched as Ebony did up her seat belt.

'You okay, Ebb?'

'Yes, Sarge. I feel okay . . .'

He looked across at her as he pulled away from the parking space.

'Spit it out, Ebb. What's bugging you?'

'Just that . . . no one's heard of Shannon before today; she was a nobody who ended up murdered. There was never going to be a *Crimewatch* story about a girl like Shannon disappearing. Kids run away all the time: normal kids even from good homes, from loving two-parent families . . . Even *they* run away and are never seen again. What hope has someone like Shannon got and who cares? She's just one more troubled kid from one more kids' home.'

'I understand what you're saying, Ebb, and yeah . . . you're right . . . a hundred and fifty thousand kids go missing every year in the UK. Some of them find their way home, some end up in snuff movies. It's the society we live in; we accept it as normal but it shouldn't be. Everyone failed Shannon. She was easy prey. But if this is personal with you and you want to talk to me about stuff . . . you go ahead. I've been sounding off about Cabrina and the baby but I can listen too . . . try me.'

'I know you can . . . thank you.'

'If this is too difficult for you, Ebb . . . you say. No one will think any less of you. This is your first case on the squad. There'll be plenty more. If you've had enough, you say. I'll take someone else to the kids' home.'

'I'm fine, Sarge. It's not personal.'

They arrived at the home just before lunchtime. Mrs Warrell the manager greeted them.

'So the kids catch the school bus from here.' Carter let Ebony take over the questioning whilst he was busy looking at the place: the kids' rooms had posters on the walls; he remembered the hassle it took to be allowed to put posters up when he was a boy. He had one of Chelsea football team and another of Pamela Anderson from *Baywatch* in her red bathing suit and with a sort of floating device in her hands. No one seriously ever looked at what was in her hands. Carter had shared the room with two of his brothers, one older, one younger. No privacy to admire Pamela. He had longed for his own room. Now these kids had privacy in this home but they didn't have their family. Carter couldn't imagine a world without family, so why was it so hard to think about starting one of his own? Maybe he just wasn't ready. But would he ever be?

'Here is where they do their homework.' Mrs Warrell showed them around on each level. Ebony had gone quiet. She was looking at the locks on all the doors . . . big locks everywhere. That was the bit she never minded. She liked being locked into her room, locked into the building. She knew she was safe.

'How does any kid manage to run away from a place like this?' Carter followed Ebony's gaze to the locks.

'It was the last day of the term . . . Easter holidays. Shannon just didn't get on the bus to come back here after school ended. We cannot be with the children twenty-four seven and we try and give them as normal a life as possible.'

'Of course . . . I can see that. Did Shannon have any hobbies? Did she support any football teams? Did you ever see her wearing an Arsenal top?'

Mrs Warrell shook her head. 'I never saw her watch or play any sport really. She was a girly girl: a bit too much. We had to confiscate makeup. Her mother sexualized her way too young . . . I expect you know.'

'She had problems on the last home visit?'

'Yes, her stepfather hit her. Her mother blamed Shannon, accused her of bringing it on herself – same old story really. We stopped all home visits and we were waiting on the court case when she disappeared.'

'Did you see any problems leading up to Shannon's disappearance?'

'She hadn't been the same since her stepfather assaulted her. She became withdrawn.'

'Is there someone she confided in?' asked Carter.

She shook her head. 'She floated around at the edges of friendships but never really got close to people.'

'What about the social worker assigned to Shannon? Can we speak to them?'

'I'm sorry to say she was killed in a hit and run within days of Shannon disappearing. Someone just mowed her down near her home. The police never really came close to solving it. I guess that's the problem with being so rural. There are no cameras, no CCTV.'

'Did Shannon have access to outsiders?' asked Carter.

'What do you mean?'

'She ended up dead in a house where there was a trafficked pregnant woman. She didn't get there by accident. She was vulnerable, she was troubled.'

The care home manager was flustered and looked as though she suspected a hint of accusation in Carter's tone. She replied curtly:

'Shannon was a difficult child, Sergeant, who needed watching like a hawk – that's why she was sent to a rural location. The only contact she had with the outside world was on organised outings.'

'What kind of outings?'

'To the zoo, the museum. We even took her to Thorpe Park as a treat paid for by our sponsors, the Chrissie Newton Foundation.'

On the drive back Ebony phoned Robbo. She had two missed calls from him.

'I tried to reach you.'

'Sorry . . . there's no signal out here . . . We found out that there's a connection to Martingale here. The Chrissie Newton Foundation sponsored trips for Shannon.'

'I was just about to say that.'

'Okay . . . we'll be back in a couple of hours.'

'Okay, but if you're looking for something to do on the way back I have Martingale's home address if you want to ask him about Shannon Mannings? I checked at the hospital; he's not due in today. The receptionist Ivy says he takes Mondays off.'

'Okay, thanks . . . text it to me and I'll talk to Carter.'

She hung up and turned to Carter.

'I have Martingale's private address.'

'Ahh?' Carter looked interested.

'But is it harassment, Sarge? Davidson's keen for us to avoid upsetting Mr Martingale.'

'Is it on the way?'

Ebony looked up the postcode on her phone.

'I guess we could go back into London that way. It's North London . . . Hampstead. It *could* be on the way.'

'No problem then . . . it's only polite to keep him informed. Let's go and see what he can add to the story.'

'Do you need me to put the sat nav from my phone on loud speaker?'

'No I don't . . . Christ almighty, Ebb, you are gadget girl with that thing. Can it make us a cup of tea? You know, something I would really find useful? My dad was a cabbie. He read me the Knowledge instead of nursery rhymes. I know every road in and around London.'

'Really, Sarge?'

'No of course not bloody really.' He smiled. 'Keep it to hand, Ebb. If we get lost you can ask the oracle for directions.' Ebony sat looking at it in her hand. Carter glanced across. 'You don't need to hold it; I'll let you know if we get lost.'

'It's not that, Sarge . . . It keeps turning on by itself.' She looked across at Carter. He was alternating between looking at the road, at her face and then her phone.

'What do you mean?'

'It means someone could have put spyware on it.'

'What would someone do that for? Hack your bank account?'

'My bank texts me if any sum of money goes out of my account that's more than a hundred quid. It can't be that. Anyway, I don't have any overdraft facility and I never have any money in the bank. It must be to do with the investigation.'

'How does someone put spyware on your phone?'

She was still holding the phone in her hand and staring at it. 'It would have to be loaded on manually. It can be done in a few seconds.'

'At home then . . . who do you live with?'

'Tina from the canteen. Two other girls, one's a nurse, the other's a teaching assistant. I've never had trouble before. It doesn't seem likely they would start it now. Tina would need to go on a course to be able to do it and she wouldn't bother anyway. The others? Just can't see it.'

'Did you take that phone up to Carmichael's?'

'Yes. But I never left it anywhere for a minute. I made sure of it.'

'You sure?'

'The only time I didn't have it on me was when I was helping him sew up his dog after a fox tried to tear it apart.' She looked across at Carter. 'He wouldn't do it then?'

'Take the battery out and the SIM card. Use my phone; ring Robbo back now – he'll know what to do.'

Carmichael was still reading through the latest from Micky whilst tracking Ebony when he lost the GPS signal, but he already knew that she was in the car with DS Carter and they were driving away from the children's home where Shannon Mannings had gone missing at Easter seven months earlier.

Carmichael had known it couldn't last for ever. He'd known that at some point he was going to be shut down. He'd already downloaded all the case files and much more. But now he knew he was on his own.

Chapter 52

Ebony was still chewing things over – she had a sinking feeling about the phone.

Carter looked across at her.

'You can't do anything about the phone now, Ebb. Robbo will tell us the damage when we get back. You forget about it now and concentrate on the job in hand. James Martingale.'

Carter parked a little way up the street and they walked back to a large detached house. It took a few minutes for Martingale to answer. A cat stopped to wind around Carter's legs. Carter bent down to pet it.

'Don't touch her,' Martingale said. 'She pretends she likes you and she wants you to pet her, but if you do, she bites.'

Carter looked down at the cat, still meowing up at him and arching her back as she purred. 'Story of my life . . .' He smiled at Martingale. 'Would you mind if we talk to you for a few minutes? We tried the hospital but they said you didn't work Mondays.'

'Of course, come through, and do you mind if I carry on with what I was doing while we talk?' Martingale held gardening gloves in his hand.

'No . . . of course not . . . thought it was a bit cold for gardening?'

'Not in my garden. Follow me.'

They walked through the kitchen at the back of the house then into a room floor-to-ceiling with orchids. The room was a blaze of tropical colour and heady scent.

'Wow . . .' Carter said. He smelt the air and closed his eyes. The mist settled on his face. It reminded him of a holiday he'd had in Thailand. When they got off the plane he had felt that same humid air settle on his face. Funny . . . he hadn't thought about that holiday in a long time. It would be ages till they could go away again, especially with a baby . . . maybe not . . . maybe her mum could look after it. Or maybe Cabrina would never come back to him.

'Thank you. I think of it as my piece of heaven.'

'You've done well.' Carter pointed to a wall full of framed certificates for first place in orchid shows around the world. 'Fascinating . . . I watch those programmes on the telly sometimes – about when to cut this back, dig up that . . . don't know why . . . haven't even got a window box. But this is sophisticated stuff . . .' He knelt down to have a look at the timers on the misting system.

'Maybe you'll get a garden one day . . . then you'll be ready.' Martingale smiled and picked up his secateurs to start pruning.

'Do you mind if I take a photo to show my mum?' Carter got out his phone.

'Please . . . go ahead. I'm very proud of my orchids. I keep striving for perfection. They are wonderful survivors in nature. They don't need soil. They can grow on moss, tree fungi or on the jungle floor.'

'Are they like parasites?' Carter started taking photos.

'Not parasites. They are survivors. What is it you want to talk to me about?'

'We didn't get to chat much the other day. How is the kid, by the way? The one with the appendicitis?'

'Doing well, thank you. How can I help?'

'Can we just go through some of the events thirteen years ago? You weren't in this country at the time?'

'That's right. I was working in Europe.'

'Poland.'

'Poland . . . yes, in a hospital out there. I flew back as soon as it happened.'

'Can I ask you something about Chrissie's mother Maria?'

'What do you want to know?'

'It would be helpful to have an insight into her life. Start with how you met?'

Martingale gave a look of curious amusement.

'I met Maria when she was travelling and came to South Africa. She was a friend of a friend. We met at a dinner party; she'd already been in Africa a few months. She was an artist. I invited her to stay at my family's lodge near Kruger National Park and our romance began there.'

'The marriage only lasted a short while, didn't it?' Ebony asked.

'That's right. She was pregnant when we married and we were divorced by the time the child was born. A whirlwind romance, you might say . . .' He smiled.

'Chrissie was born in South Africa?'

'Yes . . . It was important to me to be there at the birth; to make sure everything went okay. It was just as well because the birth didn't go as planned and Maria almost died. She was very poorly afterwards. She needed to stay in hospital and I took care of things. As soon as she and the baby were well enough she left me and sadly I did not see my daughter grow up. I visited her when I came over to work. I made sure she had the best of everything but I was denied a relationship with her.'

'Seems strange that she didn't want that relationship when she was older. She followed in your footsteps, after all.'

'Yes . . . in some ways. She was more of a general practitioner than a surgeon. She followed a different, no less worthy, but different path to me.'

'And she didn't decide to come out and stay with you in South Africa? Or maybe she could have joined the family business and been part of your hospital empire,' said Carter.

Martingale smiled, flattered.

'An empire is kind of you, but it's still small in the world. I want nothing more than to do some good on this earth. I see so much suffering, especially in the poorer countries. You can't just allow these killer diseases to remain unchecked. You can't stop trying to wipe them out. I may not be any good at curing the common cold but I hope to be one step closer to curing cancer.'

'You must have made many sacrifices in your life for the sake of your career in medical science?'

'Yes, I suppose I have. I believe it is what I was meant to do. My massive regret is sacrificing my relationship with Chrissie. It was only after her death that I realized she had no one.'

'What about her mother? Were Chrissie and her mother close?' asked Ebony.

His eyes lingered on her.

'No. Anything but.' He half laughed. His teeth perfectly veneered.

'Even though she had no other children? Maria didn't marry again, did she?'

'No she didn't and yes . . . even though she only had one child Maria was an unloving mother.'

'I come from a massive family,' Carter chipped in. 'Always wanted to be an only child . . . get some attention . . . we had to fight for it. So many of us we were given numbers not names . . . you know how it is?'

Martingale smiled. 'As I told you last time . . . I have many regrets. Chrissie went from boarding school to university. She was a scholarship kid, very bright, not brilliant, but I was immensely proud of her achievements.'

'So what happened to her mother?'

'She died in a fire. Very sad. Mental illness is a great shame. It's a hard thing for any of us to understand. It's an awful thing to be afflicted with it; it's even worse to have to live with someone who has it.' He held Ebony's gaze. She looked away. 'She was dead before Chrissie's body was released. I had to bury them both. I always thought it could have been Maria who killed Chrissie. Maria got harder and harder to control and she turned psychotic.'

'Yesterday we discovered another body buried in the garden of the property in Totteridge Village. It's an eleven-year-old girl. Her name is Shannon Mannings. Does it mean anything to you?'

'No, sorry.'

'She was one of the children that the Chrissie Newton Foundation helps. She's from the Lea Vale children's home in mid-Wales.'

'Sorry. Her name doesn't mean anything to me. What a terrible shame. How did she die?'

'We don't know. Whoever did it tried to dispose of her body by burning it.' Ebony watched Carter; he had lost interest in the flowers and now was much more intrigued by the complicated timing devices for climate control. 'We identified her by the operation she'd had to put a pin in her broken arm. Don't suppose you did that for her, did you?' Carter turned back from examining the humidifying system.

Martingale shook his head again. 'No.' He turned reluctantly from Carter and smiled at Ebony.

'Okay . . . well . . . worth asking.' Carter stood up. He turned one of the pots around to get a better look and took a photo.

'Please . . .' Martingale turned it back, a flash of anger flitting across his face. Carter smiled.

'Beg your pardon.' He put his phone away.

'It's just that I have them all perfectly placed for maximum growth and light, according to their type.'

'Wow . . . that's what you call a perfectionist. Isn't it, Ebb?'

She nodded.

'I try.'

'Do you have a garden in South Africa?'

'I don't tend to it. It's more structural. It's not ornamental.'

Martingale began walking them back towards the front of the house. He was getting bored by the conversation. He was getting irritable. At the front door Carter paused.

'Sorry . . . I forgot to ask. Can I have the number of your daughter, Nikki?'

'Yes. Of course . . . wait . . . I'll get it for you.'

Martingale came back with a number written on a piece of paper. 'Can I ask you why you want it?

'It's just that she and her husband run the Chrissie Newton Foundation, don't they? I wonder if they would know the name Shannon Mannings? Apparently they've accompanied the children, including Shannon Mannings, on trips from the home paid for, very generously, by the foundation.'

'Yes, of course . . . Nikki will be very sad and shocked by this news, I'm sure. She and Justin are very active in their role as directors of the charity.'

'Well . . . thanks for your time, Mr Martingale. Thanks for your understanding. Hopefully we won't have to bother you many more times. Now I can picture you tending to your orchids . . . so beautiful. Amazing.'

'Thank you.' Martingale opened the front door for them.

'Sorry . . . Can I just ask . . . one more thing?' Carter stopped in the doorway. 'How do you manage the orchids when you go away?'

'That's what the expensive machinery's for.'

'You can check things remotely?' Martingale nodded. 'What, you just sit at your PC in Africa and check the humidity levels, set the timer, that kind of thing?'

'Exactly. Plus orchids don't flower in summer and I'm usually away then. I tend to come back in the winter. That's when they come to life.' He stepped back into the house.

'I noticed that . . . all the prizes you won in shows; they're all in the springtime.'

'Yes.'

Carter turned to wave at Martingale at the end of his garden.

'Charming bloke.' Carter winked at Ebony. 'But remember, Ebb . . . not parasites, survivors.'

'He seemed to have a touch of Obsessive Compulsive Disorder, Sarge. He definitely didn't like you messing with his plants.'

'Think we saw a little flash of temper then, don't you, Ebb? He's not a man used to compromise. He doesn't like being challenged.'

'Control freak, Sarge.'

'Yes. We know he lives in a bubble. His work and his flowers seem to be all that matters to him. Let's keep pushing, Ebb. I want to know the real Martingale.'

Ebony wasn't sure whether Carter was being mischievous or whether he was excited by the thought of peeling off Martingale's armour.

Carter took out his phone and the piece of paper

Martingale had given him and dialled the number for Nikki de Lange: 'Straight to answerphone, Ebb. It's either engaged or switched off ... what a surprise.'

Chapter 53

Back at Fletcher House Ebony went to find Robbo. He was at his desk. She gave him her phone, the battery and the SIM card.

'What's the score, Robbo?' Carter joined them. 'What kind of damage and who would do it?'

'Okay, the news isn't that good. Because it's a smartphone it stores all your emails and passwords and has access right across all your private stuff. It can download your music, your photos. It knows the location you took your photos. It can access all the other PCs you use because it knows your passwords. Have you changed all your passwords?' She nodded. 'You're going to have to get a new phone as well as a SIM card. He can just order a replacement SIM card for that phone otherwise.'

'Oh God.'

'Also . . . and this is very interesting . . . if you saw it switch on by itself that's because he was listening to everything you said. All your private conversations, all the meetings we've had in here.' Ebony groaned. Robbo continued: 'The only small scrap of good news is that it stops here with the change of passwords. The even more bad news is that, to be honest, he's already downloaded everything personal of yours anyway. He must have known he'd only get one window of opportunity and he took it. This was never meant to stay on your phone long. He knew you'd find it and by that time he had what he wanted. Carmichael can do this kind of thing in his sleep. He trained me in a lot of stuff I'm not allowed to do.'

'Oh God . . .' Ebony could see her career whistling past her ears. Now she wasn't just hurt that Carmichael had done it to her, she was angry. 'Has he been able to get into HOLMES?'

'I don't think so. The only way to hack into the machines here is if you load a dodgy attachment. HOLMES wouldn't really interest him anyway. I think he'd be more interested in the emails that fly around the office and all the stuff that you're looking at.'

'He knew about Sonny then?' Ebony was feeling sick.

Robbo nodded. 'I expect so but, Ebb . . . just get on with your job. Carmichael is one of those that you couldn't keep out if he was determined. You saved him a bit of time maybe, but you couldn't have stopped him.'

'I take full responsibility, Ebb,' said Carter. 'I sent you up there on your own. It was always risky.'

Robbo shook his head. 'Just because he hacked into your phone doesn't mean he doesn't trust you, Ebb; the opposite. He chose to see the investigation through your eyes. He trusts your interpretation of it.'

'Exactly,' said Carter. 'Try phoning him again on the way to the de Langes' apartment. He must know we know about him now. He's on his own now.'

*　　*　　*

Ebony hadn't got through by the time they parked up and Carter rang the bell for the janitor at the block of flats in the grounds of the Mansfield, opposite the hospital entrance. They didn't get any reply. Carter pressed all of the buttons and someone buzzed and let them in.

'Second floor, Sarge.'

They walked up the stairs. On the second floor a woman came out of her flat to see who it was that she'd let in.

'Hello . . . police.' Carter showed his warrant card. 'Thanks for helping us. We're rubbish at breaking and entering aren't we, Ebb?'

The woman smiled. 'I thought you might be the postman. I've been waiting for days for a parcel.'

'Been a long stay for you here, has it?'

'Yes . . .' She sighed. 'My husband is in the hospital. I'm desperate to get home but he wants me here so . . . what can I do?' She rolled her eyes and smiled. Ebony checked the address she had for Justin and Nikki de Lange. She knocked on the flat door opposite.

'There's no one in there.'

'You sure?' asked Carter.

'Very sure. I wish there was. There's no one but me in this whole place . . . '

They left the apartment block and crossed over the car park to the hospital. Ebony caught a glimpse of Justin de Lange at his office window.

'What exactly is it you need from me, detectives?' Justin asked as Ivy escorted Carter and Ebony into his office.

'A little girl, Shannon Mannings? Her body was found in the garden at Totteridge.'

'I am really sad to hear about it.'

'We thought the name might ring a bell? She was from a children's home in Wales. It's one that the Chrissie Newton Foundation help,' said Ebony.

'Well I didn't know her personally. I've never met any of the children that we help.'

'Of course, just thought I'd ask.' Carter smiled and continued: 'One of the things we have to consider is whether someone is conducting a personal vendetta against Mr Martingale or whether he is somehow linked to the killer without knowing.'

'I don't see how.'

'Chrissie Newton, Mr Martingale's daughter, was murdered, and now one of the children that her foundation helps is also murdered. Do you see what I'm getting at?' Carter asked.

'The Chrissie Newton Foundation has helped many thousands of children over the years. It would be impossible to link one little girl's death to it.'

'Mrs Warrell, who runs the home in Wales, seemed to think you accompanied them on outings sometimes,' said Ebony.

'Me? No . . . I'm afraid not. I wish I had the time. I'm sure she has seen me in my official capacity as one of the directors of the Chrissie Newton Foundation. I remember visiting the home on a few occasions over the years. But I don't get time for much else.'

'We need help really, sir.' Carter took the lead.

'Of course . . .' He smiled sweetly. 'If you think I can.'

'We now think that this group of Bloodrunners in the news at the moment were responsible for killing Chrissie

Newton all those years ago. This is a team of people –
we know there are more than one. We believe they kill
to order. We presume Chrissie Newton was a match for
someone and Louise Carmichael must have been the
same.'

Justin de Lange shook his head. 'It's just
incredible.'

'I'm sorry, sir. I know it seems far-fetched,' Carter
carried on. 'Seems like it couldn't happen. We were
the same . . . weren't we, Ebb?' He turned to her; she
nodded. 'We thought it sounded like one of those
science fiction films. Then, like so many things . . . the
more we looked into it the more we found it wasn't so
uncommon. We also found out that you once unwit-
tingly bought a product for use in one of the Mansfield
Group's cosmetic procedures that was traced back to
someone's dead husband?'

'It was a long time ago. Now I'm more careful
about where I source our products.' Justin's face had
taken on a grey hue.

'Where do you get them now?'

'They come from large medical research companies
who specialize in it.'

'We believe you're involved with a company who
specialize in cadaver products?'

'It's not looked on like that. People donate their
organs for use after death. They donate their bodies
for medical research in certain fields. Or if they are
healthy, their bodies go to help cure many horrible
conditions: diabetes, heart conditions, burns . . . inev-
itably some ends up in the beauty business but it's still
a very worthwhile medical procedure. What is

sometimes considered left over can be used for other procedures. One dead body can provide many living ones with a range of products. It's perfectly legal.'

'Give me an example. It's fascinating.'

'A lot can be achieved without using invasive surgery. Wrinkles, for instance. A filler for the upper lip, to smooth it out. It's a gel made from human skin.'

'Dead people's skin? Where do they get their bodies that they harvest?' asked Carter.

'As I said . . . we wouldn't use the term "harvest" and that's not my side of the work but I know they come from donated bodies or bodies left for research.'

'Research? So helping someone's lips to look plump is research?'

'Correct. Sold legitimately by non-profit-making companies.'

'Companies that pay their execs huge money and offset the rest? Like Remed Ltd?' Carter shook his head as if he could hardly believe what he was saying.

Justin smiled at Carter. 'Very cynical. Not us. We pay huge taxes in several different countries, as you will know if you have my finances under scrutiny.'

'Are these procedures you carry out here?' asked Ebony.

'Some of them, yes . . . all legitimate, widespread, well-tested procedures.' Justin looked momentarily riled but was met with Ebony's deadpan face.

'My understanding is that these people – Bloodrunners – offer a black market in living donor products: organs, stem cells, foetuses. Is it the same thing?'

'Of course not. These are cadaver products, legitimate.'

'You used to perform transplants?'

'I used to assist, when there was a need.'

'In the Mansfield?'

'Yes, that's right. I have done but not for a long time.'

Carter turned back from looking at the picture on the wall . . . a blow-up photo of an orchid on canvas. 'You're a very clever bloke. You must have studied very hard for two careers. Must have been hard to choose which one to go for.'

'As I told you before . . . I preferred business to medicine.'

'Back in the days when you did transplants all the time. Did you know where those organs came from?'

'Sometimes we might meet the donor – if, say, a relative was donating their kidney.'

'What about a liver? Can more than one person share a liver?'

'A liver can be split and used for more than one patient. Yes. It is grafted onto the unhealthy liver.' Justin stared at Carter. The room had become very still.

'So that has to come from a dead person?'

'Correct.'

'Clinically dead, braindead? Heart still beating sometimes?'

'Sometimes . . . correct.'

'Would you see that dead person?'

He shook his head. 'That wouldn't be my depart-ment. When a match is found a team goes into action and the organ is delivered to the waiting team.'

'So you have no idea where it came from?'

'You know where it came from because there is a nationally recognized transplant team in operation who match donor with recipient and they organize delivery.'

'Is it always them?'

'Yes ... unless it is being done illegally, which doesn't happen in the UK.'

'And you would know that? You would trust the people on your team to know that?'

'Yes.'

'Why? Because you work in countries where it does happen?'

'No, absolutely not.'

'Well, thanks for your time.' They went to leave. Carter stopped at the door. Justin had turned his attention back to the laptop on his desk.

'Just one more thing, Mr de Lange. Do you know Digger Cain – he's a nightclub owner who owns shares in your publicly listed company.'

'No, sorry. I don't.'

'It was a girl who worked at Digger's club who was found by the M25 the other day. She had also been harvested. Actually she was a lucky break for us because we have got the killer's DNA from her. It's just a matter of time now before we get the person responsible.'

'That's good news. I have a busy day ... excuse me.' De Lange stood and gestured towards the door.

'Of course ... but ... is your wife here?' Carter said. 'We went to say hello over at the flat where you live. Doesn't seem to be anyone living there?'

'Ah ... my wife and I are going through some personal and very private problems at the moment; we had intended to live there together but at present I am bedding down here and my wife stays with her father, I believe.'

Chapter 54

Tina sat in the departures lounge at Stanstead airport eating a panini with everything in it. She had no need to worry about the diet any more. A machine was going to suck out all her fat. She'd walk in a size sixteen and walk out a six. As she glanced at the newsstand outside the nearby WHSmith she saw the headline:

ORGAN HARVESTERS
Body snatchers continue to stalk London streets

For a few seconds she thought about phoning Ebony and asking her if she was alright. Asking her if she wanted any fat bringing back. Might actually give her some breasts . . . ha-ha . . . hard to know what was rib and what was breast with Ebony. Tina took out her phone and was about to press speed-dial when she thought twice: she knew that Ebony would be quietly stressed to hell; really feeling it. She knew it was her first murder investigation and it was a whopper. What if Ebony was in the middle of something? The last thing Tina wanted was to cause her more stress. Tina would tell her all about it when she was coming round from the operation. She'd ring from Poland.

Two and a half hours later she was collecting her bag and making her way through the 'nothing to declare' tunnel in Krakow John Paul II International Airport. On the other side of the doors, behind the barrier, a crowd of people looked her way hopefully.

She stopped wheeling her new case for a moment and looked for her name.

Stefan had been told exactly what to look out for.

He waved at her.

Tina wished she'd worn something smarter. He was not bad-looking, bit old, but worth a few hours of her holiday.

'Tina?'

'That's me.'

'Please follow me. I am your guide.'

He took the handle of her pull-along case and marched off towards the door. 'Follow, please. You have a coat? Very cold here in Poland. Minus twenty.'

'Jesus!' Tina caught the blast of arctic air as they neared the doors. It took her breath away.

'Here . . . please . . .' Stefan gave her a spare coat he was carrying for the purpose. He turned round to smile at her. 'Very lucky, huh?'

She smiled at him. She would have felt luckier if she had been about to walk out to heat and tropical paradise instead of minus twenty. Once they were in the car, it was not long before Stefan pulled up outside the hospital. He took her case out of the boot.

'Please . . .' He indicated the steps towards the hospital entrance and the reception just inside. Stefan went ahead and spoke to the receptionist.

Christ, what was it with these receptionists? Dark

lipstick, severe pulled-back hair. Great body. The kind that Tina wanted. Tina looked around. The smell of the hospital hit her. It looked smart, but she was expecting to be shown to a luxury hotel first. She was hoping for a couple of nights' fun before any cutting began.

'Am I going to a hotel first?' she asked Stefan.

The receptionist answered for him: 'Hello, Tina, welcome. There has been a small change of plan and we think it is better you are prepared for your procedures today. When it is over you will have a long time to rest.'

Chapter 55

Digger had retired upstairs to his apartment above the club for the evening. He was in a reflective mood. He sat in his old tapestry cloth armchair with his miniature dachshund on his lap. His apartment had not been decorated since the Seventies. Brown swirls went from the carpet to the walls. Above Digger's head hung a frosted-glass chandelier on spidery black fittings. At the other end of the phone he could hear the sound of breathing and in the background a woman was singing. Digger stroked the dog as he talked on the phone.

'It seems like just the other day when Maria died. Thirteen years go by in a flash.' He could feel the resentment coming down the phone but at least the line was still live. At least the person at the other end was still there.

'I have known you many years and I count you as a friend but you are a hard man to love. You kill everything that shows weakness. You demand submission and you kill those that kneel. You are a Praying Mantis. Ha-ha . . . You are a Black Widow spider. Ha-ha . . . you weave your web and you eat your prey and then you wonder why you're alone.' He listened in hope of an answer, but he got silence. He could no longer hear the woman singing.

'Listen to me, old friend, let bygones be bygones. You cannot help who you love. Maria was everything to me.' Digger listened. He heard an exhalation of breath. He heard the sound of someone's lips move as if to speak, but no words came.

'I know what you are going to say: she wasn't mine to love, but I could not help it. She was nothing to you. In the end we both lost her to madness.

'I know you didn't want me to see Nikki but I couldn't resist it, knowing that she is back in this country and she is the nearest thing I have to kin.' He heard a sharp intake of breath on the other end of the phone. 'But things are moving beyond my control. You must save Nikki. Get her away, take the boy, start a new life. The police are watching me and so is *he*. I am being squeezed. I will do my best to give you time to get away and I suggest you run far and fast. They will be watching all the airfields, all the hospitals now. They are on your tail, old friend. The police and the devil are coming for you.'

Martingale sat in the dark of his drawing room. He closed his eyes and tapped his fingers on the arm of the chair and turned the music back up. A child prodigy was singing *Nessun Dorma*. Her voice was so rich, so powerful, yet so delicate and beautiful. People marvelled at the little girl's lungs. Martingale didn't.

He looked up as she walked down the stairs.

'Please . . .' Martingale stood and beckoned her forward as he held out his arms to her. She turned her head from him but she didn't move away. 'Come, my little one . . .' She allowed him closer. 'That's it . . .' He took her in his arms and kissed her head and smoothed his hand down her back, over her hair that was like silk to his touch. He breathed her smell and closed his eyes as he hummed Brahms' lullaby. He didn't need to pull back to know that she had closed her eyes and was smiling. 'It won't be long now for you and then we'll be free of all this forever.' When he lifted his hand from her hair, whole strands of loose hair were stuck to it.

As she felt the warmth of her father, Nikki remembered the last time she had been this close to someone, felt the heartbeat of another. Hart was on her mind. He filled her every sense. He was inside her. She had never felt so close to another and never felt so vulnerable.

Chapter 56

Carmichael watched on the screen and saw the man approach the entrance to the Velvet Lagoon. He looked at the corner of the screen, where Micky was looking at the same screen image at the other end of the video link. The man looked up and into the webcam.

Carmichael logged into instant messenger and typed, *You got it?*

Yes, no problem. Identification beginning.

The camera zoomed into Justin's face as the PC searched for feature recognition. Just like the finger-print-identifying program, it was comparing images, taking reference points and aligning them with other images to find a match.

Justin de Lange. Age 46. Managing director of the Mansfield Group of private clinics ... head of the Mansfield research and development programme. On the board of the Chrissie Newton Foundation.

Carmichael typed in a question:

Was he in the UK thirteen years ago?

Yes he was.

Justin looked at the vacant lots either side. Carmichael knew what he'd be thinking ... *I'm screwed if this goes wrong.* He also knew that Justin must want to talk to him very badly. He hadn't checked Carmichael out thoroughly. He hadn't met first at a neutral place before coming to see the girls on Carmichael's home turf. He must want something very bad. Justin pressed the intercom to his left. He heard the door unlock. It opened just enough to let him through.

'Hey, Hart? You about? Digger gave me your address, said you had something for me. I don't have a lot of time. Hart?'

Carmichael was playing Green Day over the speakers. It boomed around the empty club; bounced off the walls. He was sitting in his usual place at the bar, his laptop open. He didn't answer.

Justin stepped further into the club, past the cashier's box on the left and the cloakrooms. The door swung shut and closed behind him. Inside was completely dark except for a light above the dance floor that circled and zapped randomly from space to space until it settled just in front of Justin's feet and stayed there. Carmichael closed his laptop and walked across to stand in the dark corner beyond the dance floor, in the DJ's box.

'Over here. Follow the light. I'm over here, come across the dance floor,' Carmichael shouted over the music.

Justin took a look around him. As his eyes got used to the dark he made out the bar, the booths, the blacked-out windows. He walked towards the beam of light now dancing in circles on the floor. He still couldn't see Carmichael.

'Yeah . . . you know what . . . not wanting to disturb your work but I'm a busy man. I need to see the girls now. Can we get on with it, Hart? Hart?'

'I'm here.' Carmichael stepped up in front of him and punched him in the throat. As he doubled up onto the dance floor Carmichael calmly walked around him and hogtied his hands and feet. He picked him up and hooked his feet onto the chain hanging from the ceiling. He hoisted him upside down high above the dance floor.

'You fucking maniac . . .' Justin rasped as he spun in the darkness, the lights dancing over him. 'What the fuck are you doing?'

'I'm seeking answers. I want to see how good your memory is. I want to see if you remember me.'

'I don't know you!' Justin screamed as the chain dropped six feet. 'Never heard of you.'

'Oh, I forgot to tell you the rules.' Carmichael tied off the rope and then sat down on the edge of the dance floor in darkness as Justin hung upside down. Carmichael picked up his rifle and aimed at Justin. The bullet grazed his arm as it passed.

'Fucking maniac . . .'

'Possibly. I'm going to ask you questions. How you answer me will dictate how close I get to killing you. Let's start. You killed the woman from Digger's club. You butchered her and sold her organs. You alone?'

'Yes. So what? What do you want from me? I'm a businessman. I set out to make money. If this is all about money, I will make you a deal. Fucking cut me down now and I'll pay up.'

'Wrong answer.'

Carmichael fired again and nicked Justin on the other arm; Justin swung screaming in the air.

Justin's voice went high. 'So what . . .? She was sold to me for that purpose. What do you care about her? Why does it matter how she died? I did it on my own, for profit. Okay?'

'The bodies at Blackdown Barn.' Carmichael could hear him listening, trying to think of what he was going to be asked next.

'What about them?'

'Who is Chichester?'

'Just a name.'

'Is it yours?'

'No.'

'How many people did you kill there?'

'I don't know.' Justin twisted on the rope.

Carmichael waited for him to calm down. Then he fired at him again. This time it just touched his thigh.

'Shit . . . stop fucking with me. The pregnant woman and the girl from the home. That's the truth.' He swung in the darkness. The soft patter of the first drop of blood landed on the dance floor. 'Let me see you.'

'In time. You forgot the baby. You killed the infant.'

'What? Yes. Okay. She was pregnant. What do you want from me?' Justin bellowed through the empty club. The chain creaked with his weight as he swung in the darkness. 'I don't even know you.'

'Maybe you do.'

Justin hung still. He listened.

'How?'

'Someone from Blackdown Barn knows me. Maybe that's Chichester and maybe that's you. Someone who was in Blackdown Barn knows me from thirteen years ago.'

'You're mixing me up with someone else.'

'No. I don't think so. You have a sideline going where you carve up people and sell them as spare parts. That's what you came here for now, to buy a girl and harvest her.'

'Yes. Okay. So what?'

'My wife was Louise Carmichael. She was killed along with my four-year-old daughter Sophie.'

'You're the policeman?'

'I was. Now I'm the man who will decide whether you live or die.'

Chapter 57

It was nearly six when Ebony knocked on the door. It was opened by a woman.

'Mrs Smyth?'

'Yes?'

Aaron's mum Julia Tompson-Smyth was talking on the phone. Ebony had heard her laughter in the hallway as she approached the front door.

She held the phone away from her ear and looked at Ebony.

'Yes?'

Ebony showed her warrant card.

'A word?'

'I'll have to call you back,' she said into the mouthpiece. Julia was an elegant-looking woman, expensive clothes, ex-model type: still immaculately turned out and pencil thin. She was about to go out: lipstick, cloud of perfume. She walked quickly away from the door and turned to talk to Ebony over her shoulder. The house immediately opened into a family room, with a full view onto lit up, manicured back gardens that looked like no child had ever played in them. 'How can I help?' She stood hand on hip, her keys resting on a work surface, her bag beside them.

'It's about the Alex Tapp case. Can I ask you if you've ever seen this woman?'

Julia Smyth took the picture from Ebony and studied it.

'No, sorry. God . . . poor family. Aaron still hasn't got over it. It's been four weeks now and still you haven't found him. He must be dead by now, lying in some frozen ditch somewhere. At first I thought that must be him the other day when they found that woman . . . be better if it was really. It's the not knowing, isn't it? A nightmare!'

'We are still hoping to find Alex alive.'

'Of course. Of course, well you have to say that, don't you?'

'Actually we have new leads and I wanted to clarify a couple of things with you.'

'Absolutely. Whatever I am doing can wait. I'm only going to meet my friends for drinks anyway. Please ask away.'

'Alex and Aaron? Are they best mates?'

'Not best mates, if I'm honest. Aaron was um-ing and ah-ing whether to go with him to the Arsenal match. I wish he'd said no now. In fact I had to insist he went, he said Alex was being weird. Or he said Alex had been going through a weird patch.'

'Weird?'

'He'd dropped out of the squash club; he was spending a lot of his time on his own, Aaron couldn't get hold of him, that kind of thing. He didn't answer Aaron's calls – moody, teenage stuff. Fourteen is a bad age for boys. I've got three. They start getting hormonal, throwing their weight about, flexing their muscles.'

'What kind of a child is Alex?'

'Sensitive. Like his mum. The dad, Michael ... different altogether; pushy dad, one of those that screams on the sideline at matches, always wanting Alex to do better. He's a bully to Helen. She always looks so harassed, never has time or money to enjoy life. Since my divorce my life has taken off. The kids are happier without the constant rowing; the house has a happier atmosphere. But I'm lucky – it was always my money, my house. Helen is not so lucky.'

'So you think there are problems in the marriage?'

'God, I feel for Helen. I hope you find Alex soon. As I said, I really wish I'd never allowed Aaron to go to the Arsenal match that day. I wouldn't have let him if I'd known that Michael had no intention of going with them.'

'You thought he was going to watch the game?'

'He said he was. He'd bought a ticket.'

Chapter 58

Robbo brought up the surveillance pictures from opposite Cain's. Ebony and Carter were looking over his shoulder.

'Here we see Tanya getting into the car. Here . . .' he blew up the image, 'is a man's arm. He's in the centre of the taxi. He has blocked out the window with his back but, there's more.' Robbo pulled his chair close and glanced across at Pam proudly. She beamed back.

'Pam and I have been looking through CCTV footage for hours.' Robbo moved the screen on to another image. 'This is taken from the corner of Brewer Street by the CCTV there.'

Carter leant in to get a better look.

'What's that?' Carter followed Tanya's eye line as she was talking to someone who sat across from her. Carter pointed to a light area in the frame.

'That's what I wanted to know. So I blew it up and here . . .' Robbo clicked on an enlarged grainy section of the photo.

'It's his blond hair,' said Ebony.

'It's Hakuna bloody Matata,' said Carter. 'Justin de Lange, got to be. Any more shots of him?'

Robbo shook his head. 'Still looking. The taxi cab disappears.'

'What about tracing it to the Mansfield?' asked Ebony.
'I tried. No sign of it.'

'We could ring the receptionist and ask her if she was working then? She's friendly.'

'I'll do it.' Carter picked up the phone and dialled the number Robbo handed to him.

After a ten minute chat with Ivy he looked very pleased with himself as an officer came into the Major Incident room to speak to him.

'Sergeant Carter? Chief Superintendent Davidson wants a word.'

'Who gave you permission to interview Mr James Martingale? Not content with visiting him at his work . . . you went to his house; invaded his privacy. I've just had him on the phone complaining.'

Carter stood in front of Davidson's desk.

'Part of the revisit into the Carmichael case, sir. With respect, sir, now we have the knowledge that the victims were all harvested we need to investigate every person capable and around when Chrissie Newton was murdered and when the victims were killed at Blackdown Barn.'

'He wasn't here. Martingale was in Poland.'

'We only have his word for that, sir. Both him and Justin de Lange could have been here. Martingale has a small airline company which transports medical supplies via Germany and onto the rest of Europe. He could have come here without being seen. I have a list of Martingale's financial concerns—'

'You asked him for details about his finances . . . his accounts?'

'Just an overview of which companies he's involved in, sir.'

'Don't waste your time in trying to unravel Martingale's financial dealings. It would take an army of lawyers to read all that small print. Don't get distracted, Carter. Focus on the victims.'

'I am, sir. We've just looked at the footage outside Cain's when Tanya left the night she was killed. We're still looking but there's a pretty good chance Justin de Lange was the man in the taxi with her.' Davidson looked away, annoyed.

'Doesn't sound like you have conclusive proof to me. If you're thinking of getting him in for questioning it has to be more than that.'

'We're working on it, sir. I just talked to the receptionist at the Mansfield. Doctor Harding put Tanya's death at six a.m. By seven-thirty a.m. on that morning one of the Mansfield's light aircraft had taken off. She says Justin de Lange booked it and he asked her to organize the transport of human organs to the plane.'

Carter waited for Davidson to speak. Davidson looked towards the window where the day was dark with icy rain and sleet hammered on the pane.

'And you're sure you have enough evidence against him to bring him in?'

'I want to force him to give us a DNA sample. We have Tanya in the morgue. She has enough DNA left on her to convict someone. Justin de Lange has links to Digger. He's got too much going for him now. We need to bring him in.'

'Okay. Bring him in for questioning. No squad cars.'

Chapter 59

Ebony was on the way to the canteen when Carmichael went into his office to call her.

'You know Exmouth Market?'

'Yes.'

'There's a small café on the corner of Duncan Crescent. I'll meet you there in forty minutes. Ebony . . . you on your own . . . no tricks now. I trust you.'

'Carmichael's set up a meet, Sarge.' She had found Carter back at his desk. 'Should we tell Davidson? He'll put out an alert.'

Carter thought about it. 'If he gets pulled in, we lose any help he could have given.'

'It's risky to ask for help from him.'

'Yeah . . . I know, Ebb . . . but Carmichael is the closest we have to an undercover officer at the moment. Let's give him a little longer and see if it works in our favour.'

'I want to talk to Davidson, Sarge. I don't feel like I can take the responsibility of it.'

'Then you do that, Ebony. I'll come with you.'

*   *   *

They stood in Davidson's office.

'How long have you known that he wasn't on his farm?'

'Not long, sir.'

'Did he have anything to do with Sonny's death?'

Ebony shook her head slowly. 'We're not sure, sir, but he could have, and now Justin de Lange isn't answering his phone and the hospital receptionist hasn't seen him. He's missed two appointments.'

Davidson's eyes went from Ebony to Carter.

'With respect, sir, Carmichael's got information we need. We have to work with him now. Alex Tapp is not going to be kept alive indefinitely. They must know we're on to them.'

'Okay.' Davidson said. 'So go and see Carmichael and tell him about this new development. This might make him see things differently. Tell him I will do my best to help him when this is all over. I want you to be extra careful, Ebony. You keep in contact throughout. We don't know what's in Carmichael's head. If we think he had something to do with killing Sonny then we have to accept this is a man who is on a vendetta that we can't control. The fact that we're using him doesn't make it any more palatable. You be careful.'

'Yes, sir. What do you want me to tell him? How much should he know?'

'You can tell him about the Bloodrunners. Tell him about our misgivings about Justin de Lange. Does he know where he is, Ebb? You think he has him?'

'I don't know what to think, sir.'

*　　*　　*

Ebony walked across to the café on the corner of the road. She bought her coffee and went over to a table where she could watch the approach.

The windows were steaming up. A small plastic Christmas tree in the corner flicked on and off.

She watched Carmichael as he crossed towards the café. He ordered a coffee and sat down opposite her. The hands that firmly held his coffee cup were still farmer's hands but he was a million miles removed from the farm.

Ebony was digging her fingernails into her face without realizing. She saw in Carmichael's face someone who bore little resemblance to the person she'd met at the farm. He looked frightening: his face was dark. She had a feeling of dread inside her. He was capable of anything. He was lost to reality now; more than he'd ever been, and he had that one trait that Ebony recognized in him: he didn't care whether he lived or died. He was hanging on till the ride was over. No one to leave behind. No one to mourn for him the way he mourned for Louise and Sophie. She wondered how many times he must have contemplated suicide in those lonely nights on the farm. But there was a look of purpose in his eyes now. He had left the farm for one reason – to hunt down the people who murdered his wife and child.

'Harding must be able to help with it,' he said. 'She must know who could have done this operation; who was around thirteen years ago. Who was corrupt enough or stupid enough or even ambitious enough to have done it and why.'

'Doctor Harding has been working on it, I know. Davidson is also committed to finding out who killed your family.'

'Why – because now it suits him? Because now he's worried for his pension? Or because he doesn't have any choice now? Don't bullshit me; you're worth more than that.'

She shook her head and held his eyes contact. 'He says to tell you he'll support you when this is over.'

Carmichael looked away for a few minutes; when he turned back he nodded.

'What does he want?'

'There is a kid missing, kidnapped.' She got out the photos of Alex and placed it on the table in front of them. His eyes scanned them. 'Alex Tapp, he's fourteen, been missing several weeks now, we found his DNA in Blackdown Barn. He was the lad wearing the Arsenal shirt.'

'How do you know the Bloodrunners still have him?'

'We don't, but they didn't kill him at Blackdown Barn. They must be saving him for someone special.'

'Yes. You're right. He's the perfect match for someone.'

'There is hope. They are still here. But I can't see them being here for much longer. They must know we're getting close. We've put Martingale under surveillance. We are going to bring Justin de Lange in for questioning. When we can find him.'

'What have you got on him?'

'We believe he killed Tanya, the dancer from Cain's, There is CCTV footage of a man with long blond hair in the back of the taxi with her. We don't have the proof we need.'

'What proof do you need?'

'She was raped – there's semen, and fingerprints in the flesh on her shoulders where she was held down. We don't have Justin's prints to compare them with.

He has all sorts of history. He was accused of rape in his younger years. Mother paid it off. We think he must be one of the Bloodrunners. He has shares in a company called Remed Ltd, which manufactures cosmetic surgery products from cadavers. We think Digger and Justin are working together to supply companies with bodies for research, organ transplants, cadaver products; it's big business.'

'Yeah ... I know. It's a perfect way to get rid of someone completely and make a few quid on the side. What can you tell me about the identity of the other Bloodrunners? Who are they? What about Justin de Lange's wife?'

'Nikki de Lange? We're not sure. She doesn't seem in control of things, not even of her own life. We think it's a sham marriage. We went round to their flat but no one's been living there. He says she moved back in with her dad. That would figure except surveillance say they've only seen her come and go and not actually stay the night there. But she seems to be the child from the attic. She never really existed on paper: she's an odd woman but I think her life has been odd. It looks like Martingale even did some work on her face. It's a strange set-up. It's not healthy.'

'How much did Martingale know of what Justin de

Lange was doing? How much is he involved?' asked Carmichael.

'We don't know. When we find Justin we'll ask him. He could well have been involved thirteen years ago. He was working for Martingale then and he was already in with Digger. The Bloodrunners may have changed their team slightly in the last thirteen years but the core remains the same: Chichester – maybe that's Justin, maybe not – Digger probably, and there is a woman . . . she lured Alex Tapp. Michael Tapp is having an affair. Maybe it's his girl-friend. We are watching him. Please, Carmichael, we need you to work with us . . . for the sake of Alex, don't kill the only hope we have of finding him. The Bloodrunners will know we're on to them. They will carry out what they came to do or they will just decide to cut their losses and run. Do you know where Justin de Lange is?'

Carmichael looked away, his eyes filled with reflec-tions from the lights on the Christmas tree. He turned back.

'I can't help you. You have to save the boy on your own. I came into this to get revenge; get justice for my wife and child, and that's what I intend to do.'

Chapter 60

'He bought three tickets.'

'Did you check it?'

Carter and Ebony parked up outside the Tapps' house.

'Yes, Sarge, ticket sales confirm it. It was tagged going into the grounds. I've sent you a text with the details. Aaron said the seat was empty next to them. Whoever used it didn't get as far as the seat but they did come into the grounds. They did go through the gates.'

'And it wasn't the father?'

'Unless he changed his mind, went in but didn't go up to the stand. He could have waited at the bar.'

'Except he wasn't going to meet them there. He waited for them at the Tube station.'

'We haven't found him on the CCTV footage yet.'

'Right, let's sort this out,' said Carter, getting out of the car.

'Mrs Tapp ... sorry to bother you again,' Ebony apologized as she smiled. Carter was looking down the street. He hadn't slept well. He'd drunk too much. Now it fought with his brain. The conversation with

Cabrina the other night still bothered him. He had analysed it so many times. He could see what he said wrong. What did he say it for? He had sounded like he was 'putting up with' the baby for the sake of having her home. Well, maybe it had been like that at the beginning but it wasn't intentional. It was alright for her – she had something growing inside her, changing her hormones, making her ready. He just had blind panic growing inside. But he would be alright. They would be alright, and the baby would fit in. He better think of some way to get her back before she became settled where she was. He better make it good.

They followed Mrs Tapp inside. 'We need a quick word . . . is your husband in?'

'Mike'll be home in a minute. What is it you need to see him about?'

They took a right into the lounge. The room held oversized tapestry sofas in a reasonably small space; there were stripped pine floors and white walls with arty posters.

Ebony and Helen left Carter looking at the book collection as Helen picked up Alfie, who was whinging half-heartedly, and they made their way towards the kitchen.

'How are things?' Ebony asked.

Helen Tapp obviously hadn't found the time to brush her hair that day. She looked like she was nursing a hangover. She put Alfie into a highchair, put a plastic pelican bib around his neck and went to fetch him a biscuit from the cupboard.

'It must be very difficult for you? Does Alfie go to nursery?' Helen shook her head. 'It must be hard

work being the one who stays at home for the kids.'
Helen didn't answer; she bent down to give Alfie his
biscuit.

'I chose it.' She kissed his head

'What did you do before you had kids?'

'Years ago, before Alex came along, I was in
publishing. After he went to school I went to work for
a literary agent, handled their foreign rights deals. It
was really interesting, going to the book fairs, talking
to authors.'

'Did you ever think of going back to it?'

'I haven't since Alfie was born ... Alfie wasn't
planned ... a miracle baby ...' She smiled and then
turned away and began cleaning the work surface.

'You've been married for a long time, haven't
you?'

'Eighteen years.' She didn't turn around as she
answered. She was searching for sugar to put in
Ebony's cup.

'You must have been very young when you married.'

'I was twenty.'

She turned around and leant her back against the
counter, staring out at the garden, the low winter sun
in her face, her eyes pools of sadness. Her face was
dry and grey. Through the bay window the day was
not getting any lighter and it was only just past eleven.
Freezing rain hammered against the windowpane. 'I
suppose I was young, but I was sure ... then ...' She
turned back from the window, close to tears.

They heard the sound of the front door opening,
the noise of traffic driving through the rain.

'Michael?'

They heard him throw his keys on the hall table. 'Who else would it be?' they heard him say.

Michael Tapp stopped at the lounge door. He wasn't expecting to see Carter. He looked embarrassed at first and then indignant.

'Any news?'

Carter shook his head. 'I'm sorry to disturb you. Do you have the afternoon off?' Michael Tapp was dressed in a suit.

'No.' He blinked a few times, gave a look that said: *what business is it of yours*? 'Excuse me . . .'

They heard his footsteps going up to the bedroom. Ebony watched Helen as she stopped what she was doing, frozen with one of Alfie's toys in her hands, listening to her husband. She knew every meaning of hard or soft feet on the stairs, quick or slow pace, whistling to himself or breathing through his nose. His disappointment in her had a language all of its own.

Ebony saw Carter looking at her from the hallway. He nodded, flicked his head towards the stairwell. 'Helen . . . can you just tell your husband that I need to ask him a couple of questions? I'll look after Alfie for you . . .' said Ebony.

Helen didn't need asking twice: she was itching to go to him, he had a magnetic pull for her, but it brought her nothing but pain.

Ebony listened to their words coming from upstairs. She heard the heated exchange that was squashed into a loud whisper.

Helen walked down the stairs, blowing her nose. She came back into the kitchen, bent down and picked up Alfie's dropped biscuit from the floor.

'He's coming.'

After five minutes Michael came downstairs. He had changed into T-shirt and tracksuit trousers.

'My wife says you want to talk to me?' He went into the lounge where Carter was looking at the bookshelves.

'Is she alright?' Carter turned back from the book-case and nodded in the direction of the kitchen.

'She is finding this a great strain, as we both are. It's not easy for any of us at the moment. What do you need to know?'

'I need a DNA test from you.' Carter took one out of his pocket, cleaned his hands with a wipe and tore off the top then handed it to Tapp. 'Swab it around the inside of your cheeks for a minute. Make sure it's good and coated, turn it as you press; we need the cheek cells not saliva.' Tapp handed it back when he had finished. 'You been a Gunner all your life?' Carter picked up the picture of Michael Tapp standing with David Seaman outside the old Arsenal stadium.

Michael nodded. 'Since I was a boy and used to live near the Arsenal. My dad had a season ticket.'

'I support Spurs.'

Michael Tapp grinned and groaned. 'Someone's got to.'

'Yeah, I know . . . wish I could go more often; I'm always working and you know how expensive tickets are these days, don't you?' Michael Tapp's face regis-tered that he knew when he was being led. His smile disappeared; he began tidying up Alfie's toys. 'You must have paid a lot for three tickets.' Carter got out his phone and checked a memo. 'Upper tier, block

102, Row 11. Three seats – 310, 311, 312 . . . very nice.' He looked up at Tapp. 'You bought yourself a ticket but you didn't go to the match with the boys?'

'That's right.' He stacked Alfie's toys into a corner.

'But you intended to?' Tapp started shaking his head. 'You bought three tickets.'

Tapp stopped what he was doing for a moment then renewed his tidying at double the speed. 'That's right. I bought three tickets but I changed my mind.'

'Why was that?'

He shrugged. 'I intended to go at one point, bought them way in advance, but things changed. Alex asked me not to go with them. I thought about it, and decided the boys were old enough to go on their own. I was going to suggest another friend have my ticket instead of me but Alex didn't want that.'

'Aaron's mother said she thought you would be going with them. She had no idea.'

'Really? I thought Alex and Aaron had agreed to it between them.' He made an unconvincing attempt to look surprised. His face turned red.

'What did you do while they were at the match?'

'I don't know . . . had a coffee somewhere, did a bit of window-shopping . . . what is this . . . do I need to account for my every move? Why don't you put the energy into finding Alex instead of harassing us . . . you can see the state my wife is in . . . she's very brittle at the moment.'

'Did you change your mind and go in after all?'

'No.'

Michael Tapp looked towards the door of the lounge. 'Where's your colleague?'

'I expect she's chatting with Mrs Tapp. How do you think she's coping with all this?'

'The same way we both are. We're devastated, what do you expect?' He looked at Carter accusingly. 'Someone's walked away with our son in broad daylight.'

'Not just someone . . .'

Tapp gave a small intake of breath but kept his eyes glued on Carter.

'What do you mean?'

'Well, she wasn't just someone, was she?'

'Sorry?'

'She was the person who had the spare ticket.'

Tapp tilted his head to one side, but his face became darker. His eyes narrowed onto Carter's face as if trying to read every expression.

'I don't know what you're talking about.'

'Can you show me the ticket?'

'I looked for it before; I must have thrown it away.'

'That's the only way she got near enough to Alex to take him. She gained access to the ground that way. She met him on the way to the toilet, but then he knew her, or he trusted her implicitly. She arranged to meet him at half-time. Why was that?'

Michael Tapp shook his head. 'I remember now.' He looked relieved. 'In the end I gave the ticket away to one of the people at Alex's school, one of the dads.'

'Did he pay you? It's what fifty pounds? It's a lot of money to right off."

'I don't remember. I owed him maybe. I just don't remember.'

*   *   *

In the kitchen Ebony was watching Helen with concern.

'Are you okay?' she asked, seeing her shoulders bow and begin to tremble. 'You and your husband . . . everything alright, Helen?'

Helen Tapp turned and looked at her: her face was flushed; she wiped her eyes with the heel of her hand.

'Bound to be difficult. He doesn't like showing his feelings. He's in denial.'

'Is he home a bit more to help you?'

'The last few days he hasn't been.'

'Helen, I'm sorry to ask you, but do you have a strong marriage? Have you been having problems?'

Helen Tapp nodded wearily. 'He has had affairs.'

'Has?'

She nodded again. 'I thought about leaving, but with Alfie so small – and I don't have a job. I don't have my own money. I wouldn't even know where to go or how to look after the kids on my own.' She clasped her hand over her mouth to suffocate the scream about to explode. Ebony went over to her and put her arms round her but she stopped, backed away, swung her head back and forth. 'No . . . please . . . he mustn't hear me cry.'

'We're going to do our utmost for Alex, Helen. I believe he is still alive. I believe we will find him. When we do . . . you and I will talk again and I will put you in touch with women who can help you in whatever you decide to do.'

Helen grabbed more tissues from the box on the side and buried her face in them and sobbed silently as she nodded. She looked up at Ebony, her eyes swimming with gratitude.

'Now stay strong, stay optimistic, because we have a team out there working twenty-four seven just to find Alex and we are going to do it. You have to do your side of things and be ready for him when he comes home.' She nodded. 'Any woman in your husband's life right now?'

Helen nodded. 'This one's special. I think it's been going on for a while.'

'Have you seen her?'

She shook her head. 'I've smelt her on him.'

Chapter 61

Carter and Ebony left the Tapps' house and walked back across to the detective's pool car. The smell of cold takeaway greeted her as Ebony opened the passenger door.

'Have you finished with that?' They'd picked up something for lunch from a drive-through on the way. A half-eaten burger was on the top of the dashboard.

'Be my guest . . .' Carter watched her, amused. He pressed another square of nicotine gum out of the packet and substituted it for the old one.

Ebony started on the cold chips.

'Nobody feed you at home?' Carter shook his head in disbelief as he watched Ebony foraging for lost chips at the bottom of the bag.

'Got to eat when you can, Sarge.' Ebony wiped the ketchup from her hands with the napkin provided and brushed the crumbs from her trousers. 'Tina feeds me sometimes. She likes experimenting. She likes doing Jamie's Thirty Minute Meals but we never have all the ingredients so it ends up as Tina's Two Minute Mash-ups.' She made a mental note to herself to find Tina when she got back to Fletcher House. She took out her pocket notebook and pen. 'So he didn't sleep there last night.' She talked and scribbled. 'He came in at half eleven in the morning the next day. He works all the way out in Hertfordshire. There's no way he's just popped back. Wherever he'd been he didn't want to talk about it . . . but it's not the first time he hasn't come home. You can tell when a woman has given up bothering to argue back or to stand up for herself. That's where Helen Tapp is. She's a bullied wife who is trapped. She said he's having an affair at the moment . . . with someone special, she said.'

'We'll get surveillance on him. He didn't have an answer about the third ticket. What if that was his girlfriend on the CCTV of Alex?'

They got back to Fletcher House and went up to their floor. Jeanie rolled her eyes sympathetically towards them and then towards Davidson's office as they walked into the ETO.

'Davidson wants to see you both.'

Davidson was fuming: pale and shaking with rage. 'He's complained. Michael Tapp's complained.'

'He's a slippery fuck, sir. We thought it was worth a shot.'

'What . . . to intimidate one of the parents of a missing child?'

Davidson drummed the top of his pen on his desktop.

'He's a liar, sir,' said Carter. 'He's hiding something, not least that he's having an affair.'

'Plus . . . the other mothers from Alex's school think he's a creep and screws around,' said Ebony.

'Being a serial shagger isn't illegal. Harassing someone for it is. You two stay away from them unless you clear it with me first. Leave it to the Family Liaison Officer. Leave it to Jeanie, for Christ's sake.'

'Yes, sir . . .' They turned to leave.

'Ebony . . . you went to see Carmichael – what did you find out from him? What were your impressions of the way he was?'

'I thought he looked quite rough, sir. He looks like he has gone beyond sleeping.'

'So he's working undercover?'

'Yes. And his name is Hart. He's been identified by the surveillance team looking at Digger's club.'

'That team is being shut down now. The objective was to find Sonny and it's been accomplished. What information could he give you?'

'He knew about Justin de Lange's past history. He says he doesn't know where de Lange is. I made it clear to him that we have a possible DNA link to Justin that we can't prove without finding him. I said that solving his wife and child's murder depends on solving this case and that there is the life of a fourteen-year-old boy at stake now.'

'How did he respond?'

'He seemed not to want to think about that, sir. He says he will do things on his own and his own way.'

'Then we'll bring him in . . . he can't be allowed to run around on a vendetta.'

'Sir,' said Ebony, 'he's working undercover. He could still prove a valuable link to Digger.'

'I agree,' said Carter. 'But I think we should put more men on to watch Digger and Martingale. We need to make them all nervous. Even if Martingale has nothing to do with it, he may be a target somehow. Carmichael may try and get to them. We should keep them under surveillance. Carmichael has to be contained until we find the killers and the boy, sir. We need to use him wisely but we can't afford not to watch him . . .'

Davidson pressed his hands against the edge of the desk.

'Ebony? You're the one closest to him . . . what's your opinion?'

'I think Carmichael is in the middle of something and if we pull him out now we may never find Alex Tapp.'

Chapter 62

Robbo had the details of Alex and Shannon's hospital visits in front of him. He called Ebony in to see him as she left Davidson's office.

'Staff lists for the two hospitals show a cross-over of some agency staff. Three nurses have worked in both hospitals around the time when Shannon and Alex were in having treatment. I suggest you head over to the King's College Hospital where Shannon was treated. The sister there on the ward remembers her and could be helpful.'

Ebony took the stairs up to Alice ward on the second floor in King's College Hospital. She showed her warrant card at the door and again at the desk. 'Sister Phillips?' Ebony read the name on her badge.

'Ah yes . . . Detective Willis. I have been looking out the information you wanted. Please come into my office. Please . . . sit yourself down now while I make sure I have what you need.' Ebony followed the sister behind the desk and into her office. 'The nurses who were working at the time Shannon Mannings came in to have her arm operation? November eighth 2009?'

'Yes. That's right.'

Sister Phillips handed Ebony the staff register open at that week.

Ebony studied the page then turned to see the rest of the staff rota for the preceding and following month. 'And . . . apart from the core staff there are an extra three staff who appear sometimes on this register? I'd like to ask you about: Josie Quirino, Mandy Spray and Linda Peters.'

'They'll be the agency staff.'

'Do you know these women personally?

'I have worked with all of them. There are some we will always choose to use if we can. Josie is a Filipina working here; she's married to one of the ambulance men. Mandy is an old friend who I have known all my working career and Staff Nurse Linda Peters is a very welcome new addition to the great agency staff we can call on. Now she is someone I would love to have working here full-time. She's very popular, and highly qualified. She loves the kids. She has a great rapport with the parents.'

Ebony took out the clearest of the photos taken of Alex with the woman as they prepared to get into the van.

'Do you recognise this woman?'

Nurse Phillips took it from Ebony and looked closely.

'It looks like Nurse Peters, Linda. But Linda's hair is blonde not dark.'

'Here Ebony showed her another photo of the woman's back view.'

'Yes. It could be her. It's definitely none of the other two.'

'Do you keep in touch with her? Have you got her home phone number? Address perhaps?' Sister Phillips shook her head. 'Not even from the checks that were run on her when she started working here?' asked Ebony.

'No sorry . . . I just ring the agency when we need someone. If she's free she comes.'

'How long have you had Nurse Peters work here?'

'I would say . . . about a year . . . on and off.'

'Which agency does she come from?'

'Here . . .' She pulled out a list from the front of the staff file. 'Top one . . . here's where I look when I need staff to cover. You can take that list; I have a spare one. I always start at the top.'

She handed it to Ebony.

'Do you have a better photo of her?'

'I'll ask the nurses that have worked with her. They may have one of her on their phone.'

'Thank you I'd appreciate it if you didn't tell anyone what my visit was about. We are in the middle of a murder investigation. If any of the agency staff who were working that week contact you again, would you please ring me straight away?'

'Absolutely.'

Chapter 63

Justin's head was swollen and throbbing as he dangled upside down. His feet had long since lost all feeling.

Carmichael watched him from the side of the dance floor.

'Let's go through things again.' Justin groaned. 'Why did you come back?'

'Business.'

'You can harvest bodies, sell organs, anywhere in the world.' Carmichael picked up his rifle and inserted a new magazine. 'Don't lie to me.'

'Okay. It wasn't just business. We came back for someone specifically. We needed a match.'

'For who? Martingale? You? Digger?'

'No.'

'The woman?'

It was the first time Carmichael had mentioned that he knew there was a woman in their team. Justin didn't answer. Carmichael repeated the question.

'The woman. Was it for her? Who is she?'

'She wasn't there when your wife was killed . . . leave her alone. She just does what she's told.'

'Who are the other Bloodrunners? Is Martingale involved?' Justin didn't answer. 'The woman?'

'I told you; she does what she is told. I won't tell you about her.'

'Do you think she would protect you?'

'No.'

'What then? Do you think she'll have time to get away? Has she got the organs she came for?'

'She will have.' Carmichael moved around him in the dark. 'I remember you at the graveside of your wife and daughter. You want to find out who killed your wife and kid . . . look to yourself, Carmichael . . . you fucking failed them both. They were never meant to be there.'

Carmichael aimed his gun, ready to fire. Justin laughed . . .

'Yeah . . . do it . . . you useless piece of shit . . . get on with it.' Justin laughed in the darkness. 'She begged me to save her daughter. All I could hear was *It's alright, Sophie, Mummy's alright*. She had no idea Digger had already killed your daughter. Digger made Louise suck his cock . . . should have seen it . . . her crying, gagging. Very funny. You know as well as I do that you had a hand in it all. If it wasn't for you she'd be alive today – you know I'm right.'

Carmichael steadied himself. He leant his weight against the wall and breathed deeply. He knew what Justin was doing. Justin knew he was going to die and he wanted Carmichael to get on with it . . . but it wasn't Justin's choice. It was Carmichael's. He picked up a pair of wire snippers.

Chapter 64

When the call came from her ex-husband Simon, Harding was busy examining the contents of Sonny's stomach. Seemed that Sonny liked to drink and snort coke but eating wasn't high on his list.

'Jo . . . how are you?'

Funny how the sound of someone's voice could evoke such a mix of feelings, thought Harding.

'I'm great, thanks. Over-worked, underpaid but people will keep dying on my shift.'

'Ha-ha . . . you were a bad girl in your last life; it's payback time.'

'You could be right. I saw James Martingale the other day. He said you were head boob man.'

'Hey . . . it's a dirty job but someone's got to do it. Not many men get to look at women's breasts all day.'

'And draw a line over them saying: "cut here".'

'Ha-ha . . . So . . . Miss "Acid Tongue", to what do I owe your recent communication?'

'Chrissie Newton's death. We were going through a divorce at the time.'

'I recall that . . . yes.'

'At that time you were a surgeon at St Bloom's?'

'Yes.'

'Did anyone ever ask you to perform an organ transplant in a private hospital and you thought to yourself, there's something not quite right about this?'

'Not sure I understand what you're saying. You know the procedure as well as I do. There's a lot goes on behind the scenes to free up an organ and match someone from the transplant lists. That part of it is someone else's responsibility. What's this about?'

'Have you seen the news about Bloodrunners?'

'I thought it was just the gutter press sensationalizing.'

'No. There's a lot more and it gets a lot worse than even they could imagine. People are being harvested to order. Bloodrunners offer a "made to measure" service. They hunt down a blood type, a body type, a lifestyle match – they offer anything the wealthiest require. Someone, somewhere pays big money for a bespoke service. We think they harvested Chrissie Newton thirteen years ago.'

'Does Martingale know?' Simon's voice was breaking. He coughed.

'He knows. The thing is, Simon, I need your help to make a list of all those surgeons who you worked with at the time, who you think have the expertise to carry out complicated transplants.'

'I told you, procedures are in place. It just wouldn't happen.'

'And you have to remember that it did and it still does. There are surgeons out there who are operating on living donors without knowing that they are perfectly healthy. They are taking life from one to give to another without ever realizing what they're part of.'

'Alright . . . okay . . . I get the point. I will help, of course.'

'I don't want Martingale informed.'

'No . . . I agree. Of course. Anyway, I value my job here. I'll email the names and what details I have over to you. But keep my name out of it.'

Chapter 65

Ebony looked at the postmark on the small padded envelope that had arrived at Fletcher house with no MIT number. It was simply addressed to DC Ebony Willis, Murder Squad and had been posted from a post box on the street outside. It had been franked at the main sorting office in London.

Ebony picked up the envelope and was about to tear the top open when Carter walked into the meeting room.

He was carrying a box-shaped exhibits bag in his arms, resting on a tray of files.

She tore off the top and slid out the plastic bag inside. Then she stood and walked down the corridor to Robbo's office.

'I've had a present in the post.'

He looked at her face first – she was pale; then he looked at what she had in her hands. The flesh was still soft and wet. The packet smeared with the blood: ten fingertips, severed at the knuckle joint.

'There's a note attached. It says: *Check for a match . . .*'

'Take it to Bishop.'

*   *   *

Bishop had just finished filling the bag around Tanya's shoulders with smoking Superglue. It had evaporated now and he took away the polythene and dusted her upper body with ink. The Superglue had stuck to the latent prints. He photographed the prints where someone had held her down. He was just feeding them into the PC when Ebony arrived.

'What have you got for me?' He waited until she pulled out the packet from a brown crime-scene envelope. 'Christ, is this how they teach you to take someone's fingerprints these days?' He grinned.

Harding emerged from the cold storage and came to look over his shoulder. 'Where did you get those?'

'They arrived in the post.' Ebony answered as Bishop went over to wash his hands and change his gloves and then he took the package from Ebony. He took them over to his lab table and filled a palette with saline. Then he took out the fingers from the paper they were wrapped in and dabbed each fingertip into the water until it was clean of the dried blood. 'Cut using wire clippers I would guess,' he said, examining the knuckle end of each digit as he dried them gently by dabbing the flesh. He rolled the washed and dried fingertips in ink and then onto the Cellophane. Then he fed the images into the computer.

Firstly he checked them with the crime scene at Blackdown Barn and with the print next to Sophie. Then he looked at the results both from Tanya and from the fingertips.

Harding and Ebony stood by and waited. He turned to them after several minutes.

'We have the person who murdered Sophie Carmichael and the person who murdered Tanya. Or rather, we have his fingers.'

'Not sure if we're going to get any more of him,' said Ebony.

'You better check the next post,' said Harding.

Carmichael was doing the rounds of clubs who offered partially or fully nude tabletop dancers. Club Persuasion was his fifth club of the night and he was waiting for the owner, Buster Mills, to come and talk business. He knew he had to do it as part of his cover, build his profile, but his head was in a dark place; he wasn't sure he could pull it off this evening.

Carmichael sat in the red leather booth and tried not to think about the news from Micky. He stared into space as the woman dressed as a cheeky schoolgirl swirled her gymslip round the pole in front of him.

She finished her dance and came up to sit next to him. 'Fuck off.' Carmichael was beginning to grow tired of the outfits, the smiles, the accents. He had enjoyed the first few dances but by this time he'd seen enough to make a living as a gynaecologist. The girl called him a pig and skulked off. Carmichael looked across at Buster making his way over. He was from Greece originally. His massive frame was a ball shape. Even his bald head had extra rolls of skin. He was an old player in gentlemen's clubs and had been bankrupt more than once. He was hedging his bets with Club Persuasion. It had something for everyone: DJ sets in the week, football on a massive screen in the day, and strippers by night. Carmichael stood and shook his hand. Buster looked him over. He had a smile he could switch on and off.

'Mr Hart. Nice of you to drop in. I hear you want to talk business?'

'Buster . . . nice to meet you.' He stood and shook Buster's hand. 'It's a great place you have here. I've come to see if I can interest you in getting the best dancers for your club.'

'Thank you. Come with me. Let's talk.'

Buster opened a door onto a private lounge with a couple of sofas, a long dining table, a pole and a picture of the Queen. An elaborate drinks trolley was next to the dining table.

'So come . . . sit down . . . I'll get you a drink.' Carmichael went round to sit at the far side of the table and Buster poured Carmichael a Scotch and handed it to him. He sat down opposite. 'You are new here in London? We normally deal with Sonny . . . I saw the news today about his drowning. It's a shame. Sonny's mother is a good friend of mine.' Buster kept his eye on Carmichael.

'It's very sad.' Carmichael gave nothing away with his expression. He sat back, kept eye contact. 'I'll do the best I can to fill his shoes. In fact, I can confidently say I can do better. I have already expanded the network of contacts and have new girls just arrived; being acclimatized as we speak.' Carmichael grinned. Buster smiled, tried to laugh; it came out high-pitched, strained. 'You interested?'

Buster nodded.

'Excuse me.' Buster took his phone out of his pocket and read a text message. He put his phone back and looked at Carmichael, trying to hide it, but Carmichael could see he'd read something that made him nervous.

'The thing is, Buster, I think Sonny made too many enemies. People felt ripped off by him. Take yourself, for instance. I understand that you felt loyalty but can you afford to waste hundreds of thousands a year? Sonny knew he'd captured the market with his father Dexter's old friends. He knew his mother was well-respected. He's been ripping off people like you for many years.'

Buster took a drink. He kept one eye on the door. Carmichael eased the revolver he'd stolen from Sonny out of his holster and held his hand steady, the silencer levelled against the underside of the table. He moved back slightly in his seat. Buster seemed not to be listening, to be thinking over what Carmichael had said, when the door opened and Deano walked in.

Carmichael concealed his gun as he turned to look over his shoulder at the man in the doorway. 'Hart?' Deano's voice hit a bass note that boomed through the room.

'Not here.'

Buster had started protesting but Deano was pre-programmed. Carmichael didn't wait to find out what Deano wanted. As Deano took a step into the room Carmichael turned towards him and fired from beneath the cover of the table straight into Deano's chest, three shots pop-pop-pop. He fell like a giant, just as Buster stood and reached for the gun he had concealed in his trouser belt. But it was like trying to get a monkey's hand out of a jar. Carmichael swung back around and steadied his hand towards Buster's chest and fired. He stepped over Deano and walked out.

He called Digger on his way back to the Velvet Lagoon:

'Buster's burst. Your mess . . . you clean it up. Don't fuck with me. No more games. Deal with me or deal with no one. I'm coming over.'

Chapter 66

Carmichael walked through Soho and into Cain's. Ray had been replaced by another barman he didn't recognize. 'Digger around?'

'Who shall I say is asking, sir?'

'Hart.'

The barman went away and returned a few moments later.

'Digger says to go up to his apartment. Jock will take you up there.'

Carmichael turned to see a big black guy walking his way. He smiled. 'Jock?'

'Follow me, sir.'

Through the club, past the podiums and behind the velvet curtain, Jock opened a door and led the way up a steep flight of stairs: the back entrance to the floor upstairs and Digger's apartment. Jock opened the apartment door for him and Carmichael heard the sound of laughter. He followed Jock around to the left and found Digger in a lounge that could have been used in a low-budget porn movie from the Seventies.

Digger greeted Carmichael from his armchair. He held up his glass as a salute. His eyes were watching Carmichael closely.

'Welcome, Mr Hart. We were just talking about you. You came just in time. These are the club owners I told you about. Meet Sim, Amir. We were discussing our futures.'

'Perfect timing then.'

Carmichael looked at the other men in the room: two young Turks and Tyrone with one of the girls. He recognized the young girl, Anna. She looked like she was barely conscious. Her head lolled back, her eyes half closed as she sat between the club owners. Tyrone was watching him nervously. He sat chopping up thick lines of coke on the tabletop, his nose dripping as he wiped it with his sleeve. Digger was watching Carmichael in between laughing at one of the Turks' jokes. He was stroking the dog on his lap. The jokes were all at Digger's expense. He knew they disliked him as much as he did them. They loved calling him *paramý*, which Carmichael knew was Turkish for cocksucker. The Turks followed Digger's gaze towards Carmichael.

'We were just discussing the loss of Sonny. These men own clubs in Leeds.'

Digger gave the faintest of knowing smiles, a tease, a secret shared that excluded them. He turned back to his guests and twitched his head in Carmichael's direction: 'Big man.'

Carmichael took his time as he removed his coat and hung it in the hallway; then he crossed the room towards them. As he got nearer he could see that Sim was too drunk to stop his eyes rolling round in his skull when he tried to focus. Amir sat back and tapped his finger slowly on the arm of his chair.

A new bottle of whisky arrived at the same time, via Jock. Carmichael spoke to Jock and the bottle was soon replaced by a fifty-year-old single malt.

'Can't have my homeland represented by a bottle of piss,' Carmichael said. He leant forward and poured Amir and Digger a generous shot, handed it to them, and saluted them.

'To Sonny.' The dog jumped down.

Amir watched Carmichael closely as he raised his glass.

Digger gestured his way. 'A little bird told me you took shipment, Hart . . .' Tyrone stopped chopping and looked up. Carmichael took his time to turn his attention back to Digger who said: 'Tyrone sings a tune for anyone who pays. Don't you, Tyrone?' The silence in the room was ended by a nervous snigger from Tyrone.

'Sure. I took shipment.'

'Where are they? Tyrone says they're not at his place.'

'Where I keep the girls is my business.' Carmichael smiled.

Sim staggered to his feet with what looked like a supreme effort; he lurched in the direction of the bathroom and didn't come back. Amir looked at Digger. Digger was smirking into his drink. His eyes twinkled in the gloom. Tyrone was trying to squirm his way out of the group. He went to stand up and move away from the table. Carmichael reached across a hand to push him back in the chair, all the while keeping his eyes on Digger. 'I've got plenty of girls. No one else is going to get them for you. No one takes my girls without my say-so. I make the rules now.'

'I didn't ask to come here, bro,' Tyrone whispered to Carmichael, half grimacing and half smiling as he did so.

Amir knocked back his drink. He stared at Carmichael.

'Of course . . .' Carmichael grinned as he poured out more drinks. 'The first five will be on me . . . as a show of good faith.'

Amir grinned and crashed his glass against Carmichael's. 'You make good business, my friend.'

Another bottle later and Amir got unsteadily to his feet, pulling Anna up with him. He swayed as he walked back towards the doorway and then they heard him crash along the corridor. Carmichael heard him open a door to one of the rooms.

Digger looked across at Carmichael.

'We have a lot to talk about, you and I?'

'Do you think so?'

Digger was watching Carmichael in the gloom of the lounge with the sound of squeaking as Tyrone scraped a credit card along the table top and gathered the dust into a pile and continued chopping; the coke was so fine now it was evaporating as he breathed. It blew across the glass table. On the mantelpiece an antique clock in a glass dome kept time in the room. Carmichael heard Anna crying from another room.

Tyrone had stopped chopping and was watching Carmichael.

Digger raised his voice to be heard over Anna's rhythmical cries that came with each thrust.

'I am sorry you had a spot of bother earlier. It was a misunderstanding. That's why I wanted you to come this evening to clear it up.'

'It didn't bother me. Buster was a bit upset though.'

Digger nodded, gently amused but still keeping his eyes on Carmichael.

'Deano's brains matched the size of head, I apologize.'

'So you didn't send him to kill me?'

'Of course not.'

'I would have.'

Tyrone's eyes went back and forth from one man to another as if he were watching ping-pong.

Digger tutted and shook his head. 'My new business partner? Of course not. I think we have a big future ahead of us.'

'Not a past?'

Digger gave a small flutter of his right eye: a nervous habit that had stopped him progressing in the game of poker. He frowned and shook his head pretending not to understand what Carmichael could mean.

'You recognize me, don't you? We know one another from a long time ago.'

Digger's eye stopped twitching, his body began to tense and his shoulders to raise a fraction. His hand went down to the space beside his left leg where he had a revolver hidden in the gap between the cushions.

'I don't know you.'

'I used to be a policeman?' Digger shook his head just one slow long movement. 'Yes I did. I came here once and talked to you about an incident across the street.' Digger feigned surprise. 'Yeah it was a career that was short-lived for me. I learnt a lot, some of it useful, but I was glad to get out.' Digger smiled, nodded his head wisely. 'I mean,' Carmichael continued, 'I still have a few contacts in the MET; it's always a useful thing to have.' He grinned. Digger laughed until his false laugh trailed into nothing. 'I need a piss.' Carmichael stood. 'Where is it?'

'The bathroom is round on the left.' Digger waved his hand towards the corridor that led from the lounge.

As he passed the corner in the hallway and out of view of Digger, Carmichael slipped his hand to his boot and took out his knife. He saw Sim passed out further down the corridor, slumped in a doorway. He walked past the bathroom towards the sounds of the girl. He turned the handle on the door and stepped into the darkness, shut the door fast. Amir had his back to the door, thrusting hard inside Anna, face down on the bed. He reached and pulled Amir back by his hair and slit his throat from left to right. He placed one hand over Anna's mouth to stop her screaming as the jet of blood hit her back.

Carmichael held out a flat hand in the air and then made a sign for her to be quiet. 'Stay here.' She nodded, fast, frantic little movements.

He pulled Amir's body off her and away from the door as he stepped back out in the hallway. Shutting the door quickly and silently, Carmichael crept further down, looked past him; the room was empty. The lounge had fallen silent. Carmichael slid down the wall and edged towards the corner, took his revolver from the inside of his jacket pocket and listened. No sound of Tyrone chopping or scraping, but he heard the noise of feet on the stairs leading to the flat.

Jock opened the door. 'Alright, Mr Cain?'

Carmichael was squatting against the wall on his right looking up at him; Digger was in the lounge straight ahead and to his left.

Carmichael motioned him forward with his gun. Jock stepped inside and closed the door behind him. Digger was silent. Carmichael flicked his gun in the direction of the lounge. Jock began moving forward, his arms in the air behind his head. Carmichael stepped in behind him. He felt the bullet as it passed through Jock and stopped when it hit the bullet-proof vest he kept as a souvenir from his days in the MET.

He dropped down to one knee just before Jock hit the floor and he fired at Digger. One shot. He didn't want to kill him. One shot in his stomach.

Tyrone scrabbled under the table.

He held his hand up to Carmichael.

'Let's talk.'

'You know who I am.'

'The policeman.'

'The father. The husband.'

Carmichael walked across and pulled Digger up to his feet.

'Thirteen years ago you were there at Rose Cottage.' Digger didn't answer. 'You raped my wife and murdered my child.'

Tyrone raised his head slightly from under the table. Digger looked up at Carmichael.

'No.'

'Yes.' Carmichael shot him once through each thigh and pushed him into the chair. 'And you don't have the guts to admit it. But you have time. There's a lot of pain between here and dying.'

'Fuck,' said Tyrone as he looked at the mess across the wall where Jock's brains were splattered. He looked back towards Digger, his eyes popping, as he fought for oxygen. 'We've got to get out. Shit man . . . we're dead.'

Carmichael went into the bathroom to wash the blood splatters from his hands and face. He opened the bedroom door and found Anna trying to hide. He pulled her up to the sink in the bathroom. 'Wash your face.' He turned her to the mirror. 'Wash.'

She ran to the tap and splashed water over her face. The basin turned red. Carmichael looked at her hair it was matted with Amir's blood. He reached across the bath and lifted up the hand held shower, turned it on, and dragged her across to the bath where he held her head under the flow of water until the water ran clear. He turned it off and threw a towel across to her and they went back into the lounge. Carmichael left her there whilst he checked out the other rooms in Digger's flat and then came back into the lounge.

'There's no other way out onto the street. We can get out through the club and through to the clip joint next door. There's a door that joins them. I estimate we have ten minutes before someone's going to miss Jock. Pick up everything that might have something of you on it.' He looked at the girl. She was shaking so violently that he knew she'd give them away.

'We have to leave her, bro,' Tyrone said. 'We might make it; she fucking won't. You can't shoot your way out of here.'

'I'm not leaving her. Here . . . put this on . . .' He threw Anna a coat from one of the pegs by the door and a Russian style fur hat that must have been Digger's. 'We have to cross over in front of the bar. Just before we get to the floor there's an exit on the left. We slip in there and through to the clip joint beyond. If we're lucky we won't find anyone in there.'

'We won't make it, bro.'

'Yes we will and when we do, I'll give you enough money to clean up and get out, after you deliver this girl where I tell you.' Tyrone nodded fast, nervous.

'Okay.'

'Let's go . . . no, wait a minute . . .' He went back to Digger, who was still breathing, staring straight ahead, his eyes wide. Carmichael took out his gun and forced it into Digger's mouth. 'This is for my wife and child.' He pulled the trigger. He picked up the towel that Anna had been using to dry her hair and wiped the gun. Then he walked across, got his own coat, opened the door to the flat and stopped to listen. The sound of the club drifted up from downstairs. Carmichael held Anna's arm as they crept downstairs.

'I'll take the girl first. Follow at least ten paces behind and don't look like you're going our way,' he whispered to Tyrone as they neared the club floor.

Carmichael opened the door just enough and drew back the velvet curtain. The music heralded a new batch of dancers coming out. It was prime time for punters arriving. Carmichael held onto the girl's arm as they slipped out and made their way towards the bar. He didn't turn to see if Tyrone was following.

They walked quickly through the club and through the door that linked to the Crystal Blue clip joint. Carmichael stopped as he heard the sound of arguments. Someone was being asked for two hundred pounds for drinks; the argument was getting heated. Tyrone came up behind them. Carmichael took out the revolver and tucked the girl between himself and Tyrone. He made a sign for Tyrone to follow him.

They walked around the corner into two of Digger's bouncers and a couple of lads on a stag do in Soho. They turned and looked at Carmichael's face and then at his gun.

'Move, lads . . . get out.' The stags scarpered up the stairs. Carmichael heard the Thai woman curse as they knocked past her. One of the bouncers lurched forward. Carmichael hit him with the butt of his gun and pushed them both back.

'Sit.' He motioned to them to sit down where the stags had been. 'You want to die?' Blood was pouring from where he'd hit the bald man on the head. 'No? Then stay where you are for ten minutes.' He reached inside his jacket and put money on the table. The men looked at him and at each other, then one man gathered the wad of cash quickly and slipped it inside his jacket pocket.

Outside, he pulled out a packet for Tyrone. 'Take her to Leeds railway station. Phone this number when you get there. I'll leave you instructions where you can find the rest of your money.' He handed it to him. 'Then fuck off for good.'

Chapter 67

It was six a.m. and nearly dawn.

Davidson called Carter, Ebony and Robbo for a meeting in his office. The atmosphere in the office was tired, sweaty. Davidson opened the window; a blast of cold air hit his face and filtered round the room.

'Have we found Justin de Lange yet?'

'No, sir.'

'The fingertips we received in the post?'

'We can't be sure who they belong to, only that whoever he was he raped and killed Tanya and that his fingerprints match the print at Blackdown Barn and the one next to Sophie Carmichael at Rose Cottage.'

Robbo handed Davidson a printout of an order from a company that customized ambulances.

'Justin de Lange ordered three ambulances and one of them was to be kept plain white. The small aircraft company that ferries medical supplies – it has booked airspace later on today. It's due to fly out from a small airport near Beacon Heath, just off the M25, at five this afternoon. Booked in for two passengers.'

'Do we know who?'

'No, sir,' said Ebony. 'But Martingale is due to operate today. I rang the hospital. He has an operation booked for early this afternoon. I think we need to get a warrant now, sir, if we're to stop the boy being operated on. I think Martingale must be involved.'

'Carter?' Carter had been checking his phone.

'When we went to his house, sir, he had plaques all over the wall for best orchids in this and that show. All the shows are in spring. I asked him if he was over at all around the time of his daughter's murder. He said he wasn't; he lied. He was awarded top prize just two weeks before she was killed. Here is the plaque to prove it. He just couldn't bear to keep it to himself.' He enlarged the image; it showed the date.

'Added to the fact he said he didn't know Digger . . .' He turned his phone around to show Davidson.

Davidson excused himself as he took a call from Harding. He looked up when it finished.

'Neither Helen or Michael Tapp is a match for their son Alex's DNA.'

Chapter 68

Ebony stood in Helen Tapp's kitchen.

'Helen ... it's important that everything is told now.'

She nodded that she understood.

'Is Alex your son?'

'Yes ... but I didn't give birth to him.'

'He's adopted?'

'Yes. We got him when he was eighteen months. We never thought we could have children; then years later ... Alfie.'

'Have you got all your adoption papers?'

'Yes ... of course ...'

'How did you come to adopt Alex?'

'He was called Adam when he came to us. His mother was murdered, we were told. She named someone else in her will in the event of anything happening. But that person died with her. It was her wish that he be put up for adoption, change his name, everything. He gets money put into an account for his needs. It's a generous amount from his grandfather but his mother left instructions that there was never to be any contact. We were delighted to take him on. We were having trouble conceiving, we'd been trying for years.'

'Do you think Alex might have been approached by any of his family?'

'I don't know. Looking back . . .'

'Before Alex disappeared did you notice anything strange? Did Alex ever ask you about his real mum?'

She nodded. 'Michael told me not to mention it before. He said it would make no difference to things.'

'We found no searches on his PC.'

'That wasn't one that Alex really used. He did his homework on it here in the kitchen where I could help him if he needed, but he used his iPad in his room. Michael bought it for him.'

'Where is the iPad now, Helen?'

'He took it with him that day.'

'To the Arsenal match?'

'Yes . . . I know . . . I don't know why he did that.'

'Because someone told him to bring it maybe . . . Did Alex know he was adopted?'

'We told him a couple of years ago.'

'How did he seem with it?'

'Not bothered in the beginning. In the last six months he's been asking a lot of questions about how his mother died.'

'Uncomfortable questions?'

'I found his questions really difficult to answer. How do you tell a boy his mother was murdered? I told him she went away. I told him she might still be alive but I doubted it.'

Ebony looked at Helen Tapp and she realized that Adam thought he'd found his real mum.

She got outside and called Carter. 'Adam never knew who he was until someone told him. What about the woman Tapp is seeing?'

'I had him followed,' said Carter. 'He's having an affair with Aaron's mum.'

Chapter 69

Ebony was sitting at her desk in the ETO. Across from her, Jeanie was on the phone trying to set up some help for Helen Tapp. Ebony listened to her making sure; Jeanie was persistent, dogged. Ebony knew that if she was in a tight corner she'd want Jeanie in there with her.

Ebony's phone vibrated on her desk top. A photo message was coming through. Ebony looked at the number of the person sending and didn't recognize it. She was about to ignore it when the photo flashed across the screen and she snatched it up from the desk as she watched the face form in front of her eyes.

Jeanie held her hand over the mouthpiece of the phone and mouthed: what is it?

Ebony turned the phone around to show her the screen. Jeanie shook her head in disbelief. Ebony went to find Carter.

The low winter sun was bright; too bright for Davidson's tired eyes as he swivelled the louver blind and turned back to look at the officers in the room. They were waiting for him. He turned and stood tall. On his desk was the print out from Ebony's phone. Davidson picked it up and looked at it.

'When was this taken?'

'Sister Phillips says it was when Shannon was being treated on the ward. It was one of the nurse's birthdays and Nurse Linda Peters was working that shift.'

'Nikki de Lange is the woman we've been looking for then? She was the woman who abducted Alex.'

'Abducted her own nephew, sir,' said Carter.

'Yes sir. She must have been involved whether she wanted to be or not,' replied Ebony.

'She's been seen going back to the Mansfield hospital regularly,' said Carter. 'I think that's where she'll be.'

'Okay,' said Davidson. 'Ebony and Jeanie go to the Mansfield hospital now. We can't risk Alex getting killed. If he's there, find him and make sure he's protected.'

Jeanie and Ebony left Davidson's office, leaving Carter and Harding.

'Sir? I would like to bring Mr Martingale in for questioning.'

Davidson's eyes flitted towards Harding and stayed there a second.

'Martingale is a megalomaniac.' Harding said. 'He thinks he's God.'

'But why allow the boy to live in the first place?' asked Davidson.

'Insurance . . . To harvest him when he's ready . . . for himself. Perfect tissue match . . . a whole new set of organs. He's a walking organ incubator.'

Davidson looked at her. 'And would he really be capable of harvesting his own daughter?'

Harding nodded. 'She meant nothing to him. He had no bond with her or her mother Maria. Maybe he didn't do it himself. I can't see him getting his hands dirty, but I can see him setting the seed and looking away whilst it's done and, most importantly, picking up the tab. I can see him making sure that there is nothing traceable to him. I think he tries to have a hold over everyone he meets. He makes sure of it. Martingale is a psychopath. He doesn't have the ability to establish meaningful personal relationships with anyone.'

'What about with his daughter, Nikki?'

'She is his property, his Frankenstein. He created her.'

'Could he kill her?'

'In a heartbeat.'

'Not just her,' said Carter. 'I also think he could have killed his ex-wife Maria easily. The sophisticated timers he has for his orchids could easily have been adapted to make a remotely detonated incendiary device.'

'He would have needed to get into her house to plant it,' said Davidson.

'She lives in the middle of nowhere, sir. He could have gone to see her in the weeks before she died. He could have rigged it up then set it off with a phone call. He lied about being here at around that time. We know he attended the orchid shows.'

Davidson was listening to Carter. He gave one sharp nod of the head as he pulled out his chair from behind his desk and sat down, his hands resting on the edge of the desk. 'Okay. I've heard enough. Carter, you go and arrest Martingale on suspicion of murder.'

Carter didn't wait around. He was out of Davidson's office before he could change his mind.

Harding smiled at Davidson once they were alone in the office. He returned it, relaxed, rubbed his tired face and shook his head.

'Getting too old for all this,' he said, looking at her and smiling.

'Ha . . . don't make me laugh. Anyway, when this is over you might just find it's worth staying on.'

'What you're trying to say is my retirement prospects will be non-existent.'

Harding shrugged, 'If Barbara has the sense to kick you out you can come and live with me; you're going to have to iron your own shirts though.'

He smiled and shook his head.

Harding took her phone out of her bag. 'I've narrowed it down to who, if I was Martingale, I would want to do an organ transplant. I've also been looking at whose career has sky-rocketed since that day.'

She dialled a number and set the phone to loud-speaker so Davidson could hear as well.

'Simon . . . it's Jo again; I got your list of possible transplant surgeons but the main one wasn't on it.'

'I don't know who you mean.'

'Thirteen years ago you started working for Martingale after the night his daughter was murdered, didn't you?'

'You know I did.'

'I was racking my brains to think of the one person I would have wanted to do a transplant at the time . . . and it's you.'

'I specialized in it at the time. You know that.'

'I looked at the list of surgeons operating the night Chrissie Newton was murdered. You were on the list. Since that time you've really risen up the ranks in the Mansfield Group.'

'What are you insinuating?'

'I want you to think back and see if it could possibly have been you that operated on Chrissie Newton that night.'

'I assisted Martingale that night. Afterwards I remember thinking that it was terrible to be working when your own daughter gets murdered. But then he claimed not to be in the country at the time . . . I was confused . . .'

'Where were you when Martingale contacted you?'

'I was working on the transplant ward at the Royal Free. I was a few months away from taking my final registrar exams.'

'What did you think when he contacted you?'

'I was flattered. He offered me a lot of money. He also said I could be sure of a new career in one of the hospitals he invested in and that I would be able to concentrate on the thing I was most interested in – cosmetic surgery.'

'So you were happy about it?'

'I was ecstatic. I was young, ambitious, things were going well for me at last. Martingale was already hugely respected. So when he asked me to assist I jumped at it.'

'You said he told you to take a few days off?'

'Yes . . . he wasn't sure when the organs would become available.'

'Where did he say they were coming from?'

'He said a woman on a life support machine, brain-dead; her family were intending to pull the plug over the weekend.'

'That's all you knew?'

'It wasn't my job to know more. I wasn't going to be the one doing the operation. I was assisting and being paid a lot of money for it. He got in touch in the evening on Saturday and said that the operation would definitely go ahead that night or the early hours of the morning. He told me to go into the hospital and prepare the theatre.'

'Go through it for me.'

'I arrived. The theatre was ready. The recipient was there. She was in pre-op. I was told I didn't need to do anything for her at that time.'

'Had Martingale shown up? What was going through your mind?'

'I was thinking . . . bit odd. Martingale seemed very erratic. We needed to have the patient ready. The new heart couldn't last more than an hour or so outside the body. We needed to put her on a bypass machine, get her old heart out and get going. But . . . I know things are tricky with this kind of procedure.'

'Did you go in and see the patient?'

'No. Martingale was being weird about it all.'

'What did you know about her?'

'She was a woman of about thirty, she was showing advance signs of heart failure. She was extremely breathless and so on.'

'You didn't recognize her?'

'I didn't see her face. We got a call; the heart was already on its way and we had to get a move on. I opened her up. The heart arrived.

'Martingale started to connect it but it just wasn't working. We took a good look at the donor heart and saw the scar tissue – the first signs of heart disease. He stopped the operation. It was a hell of a situation . . . there was no way we could put the diseased heart back in.'

Chapter 70

'Mrs Morell? Ivy? We need to have a look around. We have a search warrant.' Ebony held it up to show her.

'But we won't be ripping the place apart,' smiled Jeanie. 'We would just need to take a discreet look.' Ebony pushed the paper a little nearer to Ivy Morell so that she could read it through the bottom section of her vari-focals. She looked back up at the two detectives before her. 'I suppose so. What are you looking for? I've seen you before,' she said to Ebony. 'Normally with that good-looking Italian man.'

Ebony smiled. Jeanie laughed.

'Believe me, he's as much trouble as he looks, Ivy . . . Can we just take a look around?'

'And do you have a Nurse Linda Peters on your books? She helps out at other hospitals. She's an agency nurse,' asked Ebony.

Ivy checked out her staff lists.

'No . . . I'm sorry, we don't.'

'Ivy . . . is Mrs de Lange in today?'

'I am expecting her in the next hour. She telephoned me earlier to make sure everything is ready. There's a lot to organize with the donor organs being taken abroad from here. Mrs de Lange will take them herself this time. She asked me to make sure one of the ambulances was ready.'

'She makes the arrangements to get the organs to the hospitals that are waiting?'

'She or Mr de Lange. Actually . . .' Ivy lowered her voice. 'I'm not sure where Mr de Lange is at the moment. He hasn't been at work this past couple of days. I know the hospital in Poland have been trying to contact him urgently. They have a patient waiting for organs out there. I don't think all's well in their marriage. They don't seem a very together couple . . . if you know what I mean? I see them slipping round the back of the building sometimes. I don't know why. They just don't want to go past me here on reception.'

Jeanie could feel Ebony getting restless beside her.

'Does Mrs de Lange ever help on the wards? What about nursing? Is she qualified to help?' Jeanie asked.

'I've never seen her here on the wards. She spends a lot of time here, but not nursing. She has an office on the lower-ground floor where she does a lot of the charity work for the Chrissie Newton Foundation.'

'Where exactly is the office?'

'Down the end of the corridor, take the far service lift down to lower basement. But . . . you need to enter a code to get in.'

'Have you seen her in her office?'

'No. I never really had reason to go down there. I always just ring through if I want her. There are so many patients' files down there that they have a security system separate from the main hospital. You have to have access and I don't.'

'Would anyone here know the code for gaining access?'

'No. Sorry.'

'Is there just one way in?'

'There's a door to the back of the hospital and the car park there but that won't get you into her office. We take deliveries of cleaning materials for the hospital there.'

'We'll take a look. Thanks, Ivy.'

'You're welcome. Can't you tell me what this is about? I love all the crime things on the telly; especially the Scandinavian ones ... brilliant. Always work it out before the end though. Always think I could have a crack at writing a crime novel. You must have some stories.'

Jeanie smiled. 'Tell you what, Ivy, you keep in touch and if ever you get going with a crime novel I'll be your inside source. How's that?'

'Brilliant ... thanks so much ... I'll hold you to that.'

They walked along to the service lift, and went down two floors to the lower basement. They stepped out into blinking fluorescent orange light, which was activated by their arrival.

Jeanie took a scout to her right. 'Cupboards, storage. Cleaners' equipment. Nothing this way, Ebb. Not exactly a nice place to have an office.' The rest of the floor was in darkness. To the left, at the far end, was a set of doors.

'Ivy on reception was right,' Ebony said as she walked over to take a look at the entry pad on the doors. 'We'll never get in without an invite.' She phoned Robbo. 'Can we get past this system?'

'Yes . . . probably. Text me the make and model, serial number. Take a photo of it for me. Then give me five. I'll ring you back,' Robbo said.

Ebony took the picture with her phone and sent it to him. She turned to Jeanie. 'Five minutes, he says.'

'Okay . . . I'll go and check out the back of the building. See what the other exits look like. Phone me when you get in.'

Jeanie went back up to reception. 'Back in a min . . .' She smiled as she passed Ivy.

She walked down the front steps, turned right and walked around to the back of the building. Three ambulances, one unmarked, were waiting on a tar-macked area, under cover. Not far from them was a broad section of tarmac leading to the back entrance.

Robbo phoned Ebony back. 'Here's the sequence. It's one used for the emergency services.'

'Okay.' Ebony tapped in the code and the lock released. 'Thanks, Robbo. I'll be in touch. I'll ring you and tell you what I find. Where's Carter?'

'He's gone to arrest Martingale.'

She texted Jeanie . . . *I'm in.*

Jeanie replied: *Found the ambulance.*

Chapter 71

Martingale's fingers played piano on the mouse pad, humming away to *Nessun Dorma*. He felt the beads of sweat gather at his brow and begin the descent down the side of his face. He could still see her in his mind. The bittersweet pain of love remembered from summer days and summer nights brought a smile to his lips and a sting to his eyes, brought him pleasure in the pain; but only for a few seconds; his eyes snapped open. He wiped them irritably. Nobody understood what he was trying to do. Nobody ever would, but it was him that history would remember, not the small insignificant people. Nicola was the only other human being he had ever loved. She had become part of him, like his right arm, like his beating heart. All those years he watched her grow, only to find that she had a fault in her. A fault that he had given her. It was unbearable . . . but luckily for Nicola he could even mend that. He could make everything right for her. He gave her life. He made her into his angel.

He stood and went to the window. He had seen the car parked down the street. As if he wouldn't know he was being watched! As he shielded his eyes from the low sun he saw another car pass and park and he recognised it as another detective's pool car. The number plate not fixed, the colour blue, an insignificant little car. He saw it pull in front of the surveillance car.

Chapter 72

Ebony stood looking down the corridor, listening to the hum of the pipes overhead. There was a sickly heat in the corridor from the pipes that ran overhead and served the hospital central heating system. She walked on to the next room: a treatment room. Shelves packed with dressings and tubes, syringes in packs. Ebony looked at the floor; it was the same linoleum as in the room upstairs in Blackdown Barn.

The last door at the end of the corridor opened up into someone's world. This was a place where someone lived and slept, dreamed of being somewhere else, thought Ebony. She stepped into a world with posters on the world of faraway places – Greek Islands and Asian cities. A small kitchen area and microwave was in the far right corner. There was a bed at the other end of the room, a bathroom off to the right. There was a woman's pair of pink fluffy slippers at the end of the bed. There were photos of puppies and kittens and, on top of the television in the corner, there was a framed photograph of a man; Ebony recognized that it was Martingale in his youth and in his arms was Nikki. Her face was almost the same as it was now. Ebony walked across to the bed and knelt to smell the pillow. It was stuffed with lavender flowers. Next to the bed was an orchid.

Chapter 73

Martingale turned back from the window and looked at the clock. He took a deep breath and switched up the volume on the music. He closed his eyes and listened to the girl's beautiful voice that filled his senses. This was ultimate perfection. Martingale looked at the clock again . . . he texted Nikki.

I can't go with you, I'm sorry, my darling. Go straight to the plane. Run, my darling. I will be with you. Always. Run . . .

He took a few deep breaths; he was calm now; his heart was racing but all around him he had gained a clarity; his life in high definition, 3D. The orchids filled his senses with memories of perfection.

He walked out through the kitchen and trailed his fingertips along the flowers that hung down from the ceiling or grew up from the floor. They bent a little to his touch and then sprang back, resilient . . . survivors . . . Martingale reached into the cupboard where he stored his gardening tools and took out the fuel he used to start up the bonfires. He took the bottle and the box of matches back to the living room and poured a third of the contents over the armchair before sitting in it and pouring the rest over his head, then he switched the music up as loud as it would go and he lit the match.

Chapter 74

Nikki didn't check her phone; it was on silent. She parked up in the hospital car park and stopped briefly at reception.

'All ready for the operation at one, Mrs Morell?' Ivy jumped at the sound of her voice. Ivy nodded. 'Everything alright?' She nodded again. She opened her mouth to say: 'There are police officers here with a search warrant and they're probably in your office right now' but nothing came out and then it was too late because Nicola had passed her and was gone. Something told Ivy she'd done the right thing.

In the basement below them, Ebony left the room and doubled back along the corridor; she opened the first door on her left and heard the sound of a ventilator. She saw a young lad amidst a sea of tubes and machines that flickered and beeped. She crept nearer to look at his face. It was hard to tell whether it was Alex: his face was so bloated. She looked around the room and saw the Arsenal shirt on a chair. She backed out of the room and sent a text: *Have found Alex.*

Nikki walked down the corridor to the service lift at the end. She checked her phone on the way and saw a message from her father:

. . . *run, my darling, run* . . .

Chapter 75

Carmichael packed up his belongings from the office in the Velvet Lagoon. He took his rifle from behind the bar.

'Alex Tapp? Is he still alive?'

'Yes.'

'Where is he?' Carmichael let a minute pass then he aimed his rifle. A bullet burned past Justin's earlobe.

'Fuck you, Carmichael. Fuck you . . .' He screamed as the pain pumped into the ends of his finger stumps.

Carmichael watched Justin hanging; he saw his shape sway in the darkness.

'Who else? Tell me everyone who was involved that night thirteen years ago.'

Justin's breathing grew coarse, laboured. His voice rasped through the air:

'We didn't go there that night to kill your wife. We went to harvest Martingale's daughter. It's your fault your wife and child are dead and you know it is.'

Carmichael lowered the chain until Justin hung a foot from the ground. He was bleeding badly from his gunshot wounds and his hands. He could see the floor now. He struggled against the chain as the rats watched him and crept forward in the darkness.

Chapter 76

Ebony was walking back along the corridor towards Alex's room when she heard the click of the lock releasing on the door. She stepped into the treatment room and hid behind the door as she heard what sounded like a very agitated woman running along the corridor and straight past her. Someone was crying, hysterical. The door to the far room opened and Ebony listened. There was a frantic pulling-out of drawers. Ebony stepped out into the corridor and walked towards the open door. Nicola stopped and turned as she saw her in the doorway.

'You are under arrest, Nicola de Lange. You have the right to remain silent. You—' Ebony didn't get the chance to finish her caution as Nicola picked up a knife from beside the microwave and took a step towards her. Ebony fought the urge to run. She looked at the knife in Nikki's hand and saw her mum turning on her too as Ebony had walked into the kitchen and seen the blood. 'Nikki de Lange, you are under arrest—'

'You move or I'll kill you. I'm leaving now. I have to go . . . please . . . I don't want to hurt you . . .'

Ebony could see how her hand was shaking. With her other hand Nikki picked up her passport and a small bag she'd hastily stuffed with a few possessions and she walked towards Ebony.

Ebony instinctively looked away from the knife . . . 'Nicola de Lange, I am arresting you . . .'

'I haven't done anything wrong. I've been looking after him. I've kept him alive down here.'

'You helped to kidnap him and you've kept him hostage down here with the intention of murdering him and stealing his organs. You have to give up now. You're not going to get any further than this hospital, Nikki. Believe me . . . it's the only way. Alex is alive. That's the main thing.'

'No. The main thing is he was my only hope of life. Let me go; I'm dying. You need to look after him. He needs constant care. Bring him back slowly.'

Nikki de Lange was edging closer to Ebony as they spoke. She knew she had one purpose and that was to escape.

'Put the knife down . . .' Ebony hadn't faced this fear since the day she faced her mother in the kitchen. She couldn't stop her mother then. She couldn't stop Nikki de Lange now. But she knew she had to. She stood in the middle of the doorway.

'I'm not going to let you pass, Nikki. Put the knife down.' Nikki just stared. Ebony steeled herself ready for Nikki's attempt at passing her but when it came she looked away for a second and was knocked backwards as the knife sliced across her jacket. She fell against the doorframe as Nikki de Lange got away.

Nikki ran down the corridor, through the doors, and turned right into the delivery area towards the doors to the ambulance bay at the back.

Outside, Jeanie called Ebony on her phone and got no reply. She began walking back around the side of the building and stopped as she heard the back doors being unlocked. She came back to see Nikki de Lange running towards the ambulance bay.

Ebony rolled over onto her knees and traced the slash across her chest. It had gone right through the first layer of her stab vest and nicked the inside of her arm. She was angry with herself. 'Shit.' She looked at her phone and saw that Jeanie had tried to ring her. Ebony felt a new rush of panic now. She'd left Jeanie vulnerable. She'd failed in her job. She got to her feet and raced down towards the doors.

'Don't come near me . . .' Nicola was fifteen feet away from Jeanie.

Jeanie stayed where she was. 'I'm sorry for you, Nicola. You are just as much a victim here as all the others your father has killed. He's used you all these years. He's used you to help him murder just to make sure he created the perfect world. Just to make sure he went down in history as a genius.' Jeanie took a step towards her.

Nikki shook her head. 'Please . . . don't come near me . . . I don't want to hurt you.'

'I only want to help you, Nicola. I can't let you get in the ambulance. Trust me . . . I can help you.'

'Let me go. You don't understand.'

Jeanie walked quicker, her feet crunching over the gravel. She wasn't as fit as she used to be. She needed to get back to the gym. She was still a stone overweight from having Christa. She broke into a jog. She had to get there. She began running. Nicola's hands were shaking so much she dropped the keys to the ambulance. Jeanie reached her as she bent down to pick them from the gravel.

Jeanie felt the pain as she looked down and saw the knife sticking out of her groin before Nikki pulled it back out and ran. Jeanie remembered that as a child she'd been running with a bottle of red lemonade in her hand and had dropped it. It had hit the pavement and smashed and sent a jet of red liquid out into the air just like now; but this time it was her blood. Every beat of her heat sent another spurt out from the wound. She fell slowly to the ground ... slow motion ... such a long way ... she stayed where Nicola had stabbed her, sandwiched between two ambulances, and watched Nicola drive away. She heard the sound of the helicopter above whoosh-whoosh, as it glinted in the sky. She shivered and she looked down: the blue of her trousers was turning red.

Chapter 77

With his rifle on his back, Carmichael kicked his bike off its stand and into life. He was near to the Mansfield hospital now; he looked into the sky and saw the helicopter hovering over. He spun his bike around and kept the helicopter in his sights as he headed past the roundabouts and joined the M25; caught up with the ambulance speeding along the outside lane.

Ebony ran around to the back of the hospital towards the ambulances. She found Jeanie on the ground. 'It's alright, Jeanie . . .'

She grabbed Ebony's arm. 'Don't let me die here . . . I want to hold my baby . . . please, Ebb, don't let me die here.' Ebony looked up at the sound of a helicopter in the sky above. She looked around; there was no one about.

'I'll go and get help, Jeanie.'

'No, Ebb. Don't leave me alone here. I don't want to die alone.'

Ebony took out her phone and phoned Robbo:

'Ring the reception here. Tell them to get a paramedic out to the back of the hospital fast. Jeanie's been stabbed.'

*   *   *

Carmichael followed the ambulance as it swerved erratically and turned off at an exit. The police helicopter was circling. He knew they would have spotted him. He knew he only had to see this through. He followed from the end of the lane as the ambulance drove up towards an intersection and took a left turn as it continued to climb up over the brow of the hill. Carmichael could see a few small planes to his left, a flattened field, a landing strip. He watched the ambulance park haphazardly and saw Nicola get out and run towards a small six-seater aircraft whose pilot was waiting. Carmichael drove his bike onto the runway and stopped between Nicola and the plane. For a few seconds his heart stopped.

'Linda?'

Nikki de Lange stood watching him walk towards her. His rifle in his hands.

Chapter 78

Davidson and Harding stood alone in his office. Harding was still on the phone to her ex-husband. On the other end of the phone Simon was feeling a growing nausea in his stomach. She had it on loudspeaker for Davidson to hear.

'I thought it was a miraculous thing, but you have to understand: I was the surgeon standing there with a woman with her chest open, waiting for a donor heart. I wanted to have a happy ending for this scenario. When Martingale said he had another heart I was relieved, I didn't really give a shit where it came from. I wanted my patient to survive. We waited another hour and the heart arrived. It was healthy. The blood supply to the new heart was good. We performed the transplant and I left.'

Carmichael walked towards Nikki. She didn't move. She stood waiting for him. When he reached her she took his hand and placed it on her chest.

'You knew when we met . . . when we made love . . . our hearts recognized one another.' She smiled sadly. 'You can't kill me; the heart that beats for you inside this breast is your wife's. I'm dying. She's coming home to you. Let me go.'

Chapter 79

Carter saw the smoke billowing out of the ground floor of Martingale's house way before he reached it.

Carter ran back to his car and pulled out the fire extinguisher from under the back seat. 'Call the fire brigade,' he shouted to the officer in the surveillance car as he passed him and ran towards Martingale's front door. He kicked it open as he opened the valve on the fire extinguisher and aimed the jet of foam into the hallway. Flames ripped along the ceiling as he made his way into the living room on the left. He looked towards the middle of the room where there was a solid ball of flame with a human being sitting in the middle of it.

Chapter 80

'Hold on, Jeanie.'

Jeanie let go of Ebony's hand as the trolley pushed through the operating theatre doors and Ebony stood and watched them swing. Noel came running in, recognized Ebony and handed her Christa, who was making her mind up whether to cry as she stared at Ebony in confusion ... Ebony smiled nervously at Christa and took out her phone to call Carter.

'How's Jeanie?'

'She's gone in to be operated on now. Nicola got away from here. I don't know whether she made it.'

'She got away. Carmichael could have shot her, apparently, but he didn't. He chose to let her go. I don't know why. She's unlikely to get far. They'll arrest her when the plane touches down in Berlin, hopefully.'

'Is Martingale in custody?'

'Killed himself ... couldn't face it. He set fire to himself.'

'Jesus.'

'Why do you sound like you're running?'

'I'm bouncing a baby and trying to keep Christa from realizing she doesn't know me and bursting into tears. Noel's just run in to be with Jeanie.'

'Ebb . . . left holding the baby.'

'Don't think it suits me, Sarge.'

'Yeah, can't see me having a big family either. I'll be a Saturday dad, I suppose. See you back here when you can.'

'Noel shouldn't be long, Sarge.'

Christa started to wail.

'What did you do?'

'I made the mistake of looking at her.'

Carter laughed. He sat in the police car outside Martingale's house, watching the fire crews finish damping it down. He switched on the engine and drove to a home improvement store on the way back from Hampstead.

He rang the doorbell and waited for Cabrina's father to come to the door.

'Hello, Theo. Okay?'

Theo nodded. He looked at Dan like he had come to ask his daughter out on a first date.

'I want Cabrina to come home.'

Theo nodded. 'And for Christ's sake take that damn buggy blocking up my hallway.'

'Will she come . . . do you think?'

'Maybe . . . *Cabrina*?' He turned and called down the hallway. 'You have a visitor.'

She didn't hurry towards him; she took her time; she wasn't smiling. Oh God . . . it had all been for nothing. He should feel a fool but he was beyond that now. In fact Carter felt like a teenager again when he saw her. He had a terrible urge to cry. When she reached him she put her hands either side of his face and looked really hard into his eyes: he'd forgotten how hers made him melt. *Any minute she's going to say it, 'Just go . . . Sorry,'* thought Carter.

'What took you so long?'

'Pink or blue?' He held up the paint pots.

'Purple.'

Chapter 81

Bridget heard the bike coming as she finished chopping wood. She watched Carmichael park it in the barn and go inside the house. He found the young girl Anna feeding one of the lambs with a bottle of milk in the kitchen. Rusty got out of his basket to come over and say hello. Carmichael bent down to pet him.

'You made it then? Good boy.'

'And you made it then?' Bridget came into the house. 'Are you staying?' He nodded. 'Then Anna can sleep with me in the spare room. No problem,' Bridget said and smiled. He nodded again. 'You need a rest,' she said and left him in the lounge.

Carmichael unzipped his bag, took out the photo of Louise and Sophie and phoned Ebony.

Ebony was waiting in arrivals at the airport. Tina had phoned her and asked her to pick her up. She saw her walking towards her.

'Where have you been, Teen? The canteen said you were sick and then asked for holiday leave? What's happening?'

'I went to Poland. I was supposed to be having some work done but you know, when it came to it, I thought, *fuck it*. Men either like me as I am or fuck them. Besides, I was frightened I wouldn't make it back in time to buy stuff in for Christmas and I knew if I left it to you we'd be eating beans on toast.'

Ebony stepped aside to take Carmichael's call.

'Hello, Carmichael. You back at the farm?'

'Yes. Did you have an officer injured?'

'Yes, Jeanie. She's alright; she'll make it.' Ebony listened to Carmichael. He sounded distant: calm, spent. She spoke: 'I don't know how things will go but I want to say thank you to you.'

'Yeah?'

'You cleared your name.'

'The kid okay?'

'Yes . . . being brought back to consciousness. Thank you for what you did . . . what you didn't do.'

'I couldn't kill her.'

'Yeah . . . I heard. I couldn't have either. Her life expectancy is not good. A sample of her hair shows that she's on a large dose of anti-rejection drugs. Martingale had a heart condition. He was a carrier for it. It doesn't always get passed on. Nikki must have had it. He must have sought out the perfect match. As it happened, Chrissie had inherited the heart condition too. And as her other organs began to fail, they came for Adam . . .' She heard him breathing. She knew where he would be standing. By the side of the fire, looking at the photo of Louise and Sophie. 'They found Justin de Lange: following the trail of Mr Hart. His fingerprints matched the set on Tanya and the print left by Sophie's bed.'

'Hope you didn't get there too soon. Was he still alive?'

'He had a pulse. I don't know how. He was covered in rats. They cut him down but he was dead before he got to hospital. You know that I need you to hand yourself in.'

'I know. I'll be there in the next day or so. Just have to tidy things up here.'

'I understand.'

Carmichael put the phone down and took out Louise's journal from his bag. It was still stained with blood. He had recovered the journal from the floor of the bedroom she had shared with Sophie at Rose Cottage. He had read most of it. He had read to the point where she said she knew he had had an affair. He had never been able to read beyond that. Today he stood at the window overlooking the yard and opened the next page.

Callum, if ever you come to read this journal I want you to know that I love you more than life itself. I love you for all your faults, your weaknesses and I was born to love you. I forgive you for being unfaithful to me. I know you did it because you have so many demons in your soul that need to be defeated, but I tell you, Callum . . . I will be by your side all along the way. For every demon that appears I will be your angel. Me and Sophie . . . we were sent to save you, Callum . . . all my love, your wife Louise.

Carmichael went outside and knelt to examine the latest in the fox's kills: a newborn lamb dragged from its mother's teat.

Bridget stood next to it.

'Another dead one . . .'

'It must be the vixen; since I killed her mate, she has to be the provider. I'll see to it.'

Carmichael picked up the rifle and walked through the yard. Tor snorted into the air as he passed. He nuzzled into Anna's hand as she brushed his coat and slipped him a Polo mint. He took it so gently it made Carmichael smile and shake his head; the number of times that horse had bitten him.

He climbed over the gate and turned back to see Bridget watching him. She was standing in the first rays of sunshine. She had buckets of feed in her hand, steaming in the morning air. She had taken off her hat. He paused as he climbed the gate and she stopped where she was. He had never realized how beautiful she was until that moment. She blushed and turned away smiling.

He jumped down the other side of the gate and walked upwards across the field, the grass yellow beneath the melted snow. It would return before long, this was just a little promise of spring but it was still a long way off. Everything would happen in due course.

He tracked his familiar route, keeping to the outside of the field and heading up towards his favourite place. He knew the fox would favour the far side, sheltered from the blasting wind. There the vixen would have made her home.

Silently he kept downwind of the place where he knew the fox had made a den. He steadied the gun and stood and listened. The first birdsong in weeks made him want to cry. The sun dazzled him for a moment. The breeze, still cold, brought the sound of something else. Carmichael crouched low and inched forward. Ten feet away he saw the cubs playing in the sunshine; beside them their mother lay on her side, resting from her feed and feeling her bones warm with the sun. Carmichael looked back down towards the farm. He heard Anna's laughter ringing up to his ears and he smiled to himself. He didn't realize he was crying. He closed his eyes for a second as he steadied his aim and placed the end of the barrel into his mouth.

Bridget put her hand on Tor's neck to calm him as the sound of gunshot rang through the air. Anna stopped laughing. Bridget buried her face in Tor's neck.

Carmichael opened his eyes and looked towards the fallen tree trunk on the mount; blinded temporarily by the low winter sun he saw the figures running towards him and heard the laughter as clear as church bells. He got to his knees and opened his arms as he looked up into Louise's face and scooped Sophie into his arms.

Acknowledgments

My thanks and gratitude go to all the people who have helped me in writing this book: Ian Hemmings; Detective Sergeant Nick Moore; Neil Rickard; Pauline Selley; Crime Analyst Catherine Ash; the staff at Visage; Frank Pearman; Clare and Peter Selley; Graham and Sue Burton; David and Charlotte Laquiere; Viv Steer; Detective Inspector Dave Willis (retired); the officers in Murder Investigation Team 11 (MIT11); the real Callum Carmichael and Ebony Willis for allowing me to use their names; my agent Darley Anderson and the team; my new publishing team at Simon & Schuster; finally my friends, family and 'the boys'!